Praise for *Open M...*

'I knew nothing about open relatio...
wondering how anyone had the time)...
fun and completely engrossing read...
and Fliss for a long time after I was done. Truly spectacular.'
Rebecca Ryan, author of *My Extraordinary Life*

'The most insightful book about love I've read in
a long time. A hilarious and sharp take on not just romantic
relationships but friendships too with incredibly relatable
characters and dating experiences. I LOVED IT.'
Kate Weston, author of *You May Now Kill the Bride*

'*Open Minded* offers a fresh new perspective that hasn't been
done before! Funny, charming and unique, I'll be thinking
about Fliss and Holly's friendship for a long time.'
Lauren Forsythe, author of *Dealbreakers*

'Funny, joyous and wise, this is a story which reminds
us it's OK not to have the answers, to be working things
out, and to be living life on our own terms.'
Simon James Green, author of *Noah Can't Even*

'A clever, funny and totally gripping look at modern
relationships. I absolutely loved it!'
Tom Ellen, author of *The Lifeline*

'A joyful, chaotic exploration of love and monogamy. I absolutely
fell for Fliss and Holly, and their relationship adventures in
this gorgeous, funny novel. Laughs out loud guaranteed.'
Lizzie Huxley-Jones, author of *Make You Mine This Christmas*

'Refreshingly candid, whip-smart and painfully funny.
A perfect exploration of what it's like to navigate the never-
ending challenges of love, dating and adulthood.'
Hannah Tovey, author of *The Education of Ivy Edwards*

'A warm-hearted romcom for all kinds of curious daters. . .Whether
the reader is committed to monogamy, polyamory, or something
in between, *Open Minded* gives a chance to see in broad
as well as more nuanced strokes how relatable characters
might go about stepping outside of their comfort zones.'
Lily Lindon, author of *Double Booked*

Chloe Seager is Director of Children's and YA at Madeleine Milburn Agency. Chloe lives in London and in her spare time she likes listening to noughties emo music, watching reality TV and shouting at Spurs games.

Open Minded is her debut adult novel and centres on relationships in all their diverse and messy glory. You can find her on Twitter @chloeseager and Instagram @chloenseager.

open minded

CHLOE SEAGER

ONE PLACE. MANY STORIES

HQ
An imprint of HarperCollins*Publishers* Ltd
1 London Bridge Street
London SE1 9GF

www.harpercollins.co.uk

HarperCollins*Publishers*
Macken House, 39/40 Mayor Street Upper,
Dublin 1, D01 C9W8, Ireland

This edition 2024

1
First published in Great Britain by
HQ, an imprint of HarperCollins*Publishers* Ltd 2024

ISBN: 9780008591960

For anyone who ever talked me off a ledge in a ladies' loo

CHAPTER ONE:
SCUBA DIVE BEFORE IT'S TOO LATE

HOLLY

I'm getting engaged tonight.

Oh God. There I go again. I remind myself, for the billionth time, that it's not *definite*. So Will booked a fancy restaurant – I looked it up. It's got a roof terrace and floor-to-ceiling windows with a three-sixty view of London and serves a lot of things I can't identify on the menu. Therefore it's not any old run-of-the-mill restaurant. It's very obviously a place where one might propose. And so he's been shifty all week, like he has something to hide. Also, I noticed, he's wearing his best jumper – the one he bought from Shetland that's not dyed and is unique in colour to the sheep from which it was shorn – even though it's not near either of our birthdays (mine's in May and his is September) and we've just had Christmas and neither of us has recently had a promotion that I know of and it's biologically impossible for him to be pregnant.

I

So, what? Maybe Will is just doing something nice because he feels like it. January is a gloomy month . . . maybe he's sick of only ever doing nice things in December? Maybe he read an article in a men's magazine about spontaneity and making more of an effort and 'spicing up' one's day-to-day life.

Except . . . Will *never* books a surprise. Never in all the years that we've been together, unless it's one of the aforementioned special occasions. We're both turning thirty this year, so we're the right age. We've been together nearly a decade. We had Mason and Leah's wedding in October – beautiful, but a shame about her aunt who nearly died choking on an olive during the speeches – and Laurence and Philippa just got engaged. It's happening all around us. It makes sense. It's *time*.

I coat my left eyelashes in mascara. My hand is shaking so it doesn't go on neatly and then I blink, smudging it down my face anyway. I've never been naturally skilled at putting on make-up and being nervous doesn't help.

As I'm trying to undo the damage, Will appears behind me in the mirror. I quickly stop pulling 'mascara face' and try to apply it in a casually attractive way instead. He roots around in a cupboard and pulls out a hardly used bottle of aftershave.

'You look nice.' He observes me, spraying some product on his neck.

'Thank you.' I flush. I'm wearing a square-collar gingham dress that I chose because I remembered Will likes it. I savour the feeling of his eyes on me.

I correct my mascara mishap and put the finishing touches to my lipstick, then stand back and look at myself in the mirror. I *do* look nice. I had my hair cut yesterday in preparation for this evening so I have no straggly split ends. I've even painted my nails. Despite the fact that I can never get my eyeliner quite symmetrical and my hair never stays in place no matter how long I spend on it, there is nothing I love more than getting dressed up. This feeling is why I started working in fashion.

As Will passes behind me on the way out he squeezes my bum. Ten minutes later, I'm watching him lock our front door. I look up at our little grey brick terrace flat with the blue front door that's been our home for four years and wonder how long we will stay here once we're engaged. Will's always talked about wanting to move to the countryside one day. I'd like to as well; if it wasn't for my job I'd have gone by now. I've never been as enamoured with London as everyone else seems to be. Mostly, I find it intensely stressful.

We walk hand in hand down to the train station. It's an unusually mild, bright evening for this time of year and I savour the crisp air in my lungs. Everyone we know had so much angst about turning thirty but, I muse to myself as I picture walking down the aisle towards Will, I think I'm going to like it.

We're both quiet on the train. Will's quite a Serious Man – it's intensely sexy – and when he's nervous about something he retreats far into himself until that thing is over. An interview, an important meeting, lunch with his parents. Not that he's *necessarily* got anything to be nervous about tonight, I remind myself, because he's not definitely proposing.

On the walk to the restaurant I observe everything around me closely, trying to take a mental snapshot and remember the little details of this – possibly, but not definitely – momentous evening in our lives. Obviously, if he doesn't end up proposing, then it's no harm done. I'll just forget how many street lamps we passed and that little dog's yappy bark and the middle-aged woman complaining to her friend about how she just doesn't 'trust' the food in Asda. But if he *is* proposing, I'll be able to tell our children everything exactly as it happened.

We arrive and step into a clear glass elevator that takes us to the fifth floor. It's beautiful in an obvious, chic-modern sort of way. It crosses my mind how bizarre it is that people live their entire lives together like normal people and when it comes to proposals suddenly hire a giant sparkling orb that hangs off a mountain or ride in on a giant, bejewelled throne on horseback. But I quickly check myself. Will's clearly gone to a huge effort to organise this evening and it's not as if this is *totally* unlike us. Unless the other diners and staff are actually paid actors ready to jump up and start singing.

I eye the woman on the front desk suspiciously. God, I hope not. How would I arrange my face to look relaxed as she performed?

'We've got a booking at 7 p.m. for Will Mayhew.' Will clears his throat. I always find it adorable that he's uncomfortable saying his own name out loud.

We're shown to our table right by the window. The view is pretty. I look across the city and think it doesn't seem so daunting when you're up here in the sky, above all the noise and people who will watch you sit on a tube seat they know is wet and say nothing. The waiter asks if we want a drink to start.

'What do you want?' Will peers at the wine list. 'Shall we go for champagne?'

Will doesn't usually want to buy champagne because it's too expensive, but I nod. It seems like the sort of thing you should order when you get engaged.

Not that we're definitely getting engaged.

Will puts the menu down. He coughs and takes a sip of water. Then his eyes scan the room. 'It's all right, isn't it?' he says. 'It's supposed to have excellent lamb.'

I copy him, glancing all around me. 'Yes, it's stunning.' It's not got very welcoming vibes, but it's objectively appealing.

'You don't like it,' Will observes.

'Oh no! I love it!' I panic, worried about offending him on our special evening. I've never been treated so thoughtfully before. This is every girl's dream.

The waiter brings our bottle of champagne. He pops the cork to start the celebrations. In that moment, looking at Will and across London, I soften to the idea of people doing something out of the ordinary to mark the agreement of binding their lives together forever.

When the waiter leaves, Will raises his glass. 'Cheers,' he says, and we clink.

'What are you going to order?' I ask, trying to decode the menu. There are a lot of things on here I don't understand and I couldn't even study up because they seem to change the menu every day. What is poussin?

'The cocotte of morels to start,' he says, 'and then the crisp lamb belly.'

I nod. 'I was thinking I'd start with the pea soup . . .' Mostly because I know what it is.

Will shakes his head. 'Oh no, it's a waste to come here and get the pea soup. Get the sardine rillette, you'll like that.'

'OK, sounds lovely.' I shut my menu. I like how much Will knows about food and how he thoughtfully recommends things he knows I'll like.

Will takes a big gulp and then cracks his knuckles. 'Holly,' he says. 'I actually brought you here because there's something I want to talk to you about.'

My heart flutters. We're diving straight in, then. Oh my God. *This is actually happening.*

Except . . . no. He wants to *talk* to me about marriage? That doesn't sound right. I don't have time to process because he keeps speaking.

'You know how we've always said we might want to explore the world? Maybe learn French? Or how you wanted to teach scuba diving?'

I frown. 'Erm . . .'

I might have said those things, in passing, once upon a time. Way back in our early twenties when I would still attempt to pull off a beret. But I can't remember having any distinct yearning to teach scuba diving. I've never even *been* scuba diving. What is he talking about?

'I don't think—' I start, but Will cuts me off. He's rocking back and forth in his seat.

'Do you ever think about those things you *really* want to do and think, I don't know, that you're running out of time?' He's talking quickly and there's a rehearsed cheer to his tone, like he's giving a sales pitch. 'If I don't teach scuba diving now, then . . . when? I mean, we are turning thirty this year.'

Again, I'm horribly confused. I'm running out of time to

6

teach scuba diving? Is he suggesting we quit our jobs and move to Hawaii?

'Do you want to move?' I ask. 'Are you bored of the UK?'

'Well, I . . .' He sighs, looking deeply uncomfortable.

'I'm not sure now would be the best time to take a sabbatical,' I reason. 'We've both worked so hard to get to where we are. You only just got this job. I know it's been stressful but it will be worth it. It's your dream company . . . I think if you left now you'd regret it.'

Will looks sheepish. He takes another gulp of champagne. 'Yeah, no. I don't want to leave the country.'

'Oh.' Then what on earth is he going on about?

'You know how . . .' He falters. I can see him reaching around inside his mind for the right words. 'You know how we've both always wondered what it would be like to see other people?'

I feel like I've just been hit in the back of the head with a really fast, hard ball. I was just sitting in the park basking in the sunshine and it came out of nowhere and now my ears are ringing and my eyes sting.

'We have?' My voice is small. I'm dazed. I get the sense the ball isn't all that's coming for me. I'm about to step into a road and get hit by an oncoming bus.

'Yeah, our little chats. Like at Mason's wedding. I *love* that we can talk about anything, Holly, and I know you'll understand.'

I rack my brains for what we spoke about at Mason's wedding. I think Will might have made a comment like, 'It's wild that they'll only ever be with each other now' and I'd said, 'Yeah.' But I thought he meant it was wild like planes are wild or . . . owning a pet is wild. Yes, it's objectively mind-blowing that human beings sit in little airborne containers that take them from one country to another or keep small animals in their houses that were once feral and have been domesticated through generations of selective breeding, but also completely regular. I hadn't realised he meant that it was *wild* wild or that by agreeing with him I was complicit in some understanding about wanting to 'see other people'.

Is *that* what he's angling at? Surely not?!

'Is this still about scuba diving?' I ask, desperately hoping that it is. I would take a move to Hawaii over where I sense this conversation is going.

Will drains his glass and tops up. 'I don't know, now that we're turning thirty I just think . . . Now is the time, you know? If we were ever going to do it, it would be now.'

My head is spinning. 'So . . . just to clarify.' I can barely get the words out. 'You want to . . . date other people?'

'I just think, if not now, when?'

Uh . . . *never*? He's making it sound like it's something I've thought about too. Like we've been knowingly building up to this together. Have I really given off the impression that I was interested in other people? I'm categorically not. I can't remember the last time I properly thought about another man like that. I did have a sex dream about our letting agent Stefan after seeing him at the supermarket buying a mini milk. But I felt guilty about that for a week afterwards. And how would Will know about that?

'*Will.*' I sound out of breath but I'm desperate to clarify this. 'I think there's been a miscommunication. I don't want to see other people.'

Will looks pained, as if I've said the wrong thing. And then I realise he *wants* me to want this. I've failed a test I didn't know I was taking.

'Oh,' he says.

He sounds disappointed. I *hate* disappointing Will. I only ever want to make him happy and it appears I've not been tuned into how he's been feeling at all. A hot ball of shame and fear starts coiling in my belly. Oh God. I'm utterly humiliated by how far off I was. How have I misread the situation so spectacularly? Why wasn't I on the same page as him? We're supposed to be a team and he's trying to throw a ball to me but I'm on the other side of the pitch.

How long has he been thinking about this? I wonder. How many times, throughout our relationship, has he wanted it? It's not like I want to live in a world where all his exes are dead, but the thought of him dreaming this up – and now, acting on it – makes me feel a bit sick.

I can't believe I thought he was coming here to propose. That-Holly and now-Holly are now two wholly separate people existing in completely different worlds. Within five minutes I've been yanked out of my old life and handed a brand-new reality. One where my boyfriend wants to 'see other people' and, apparently, I'm supposed to as well.

'So, you've never thought about it?' Will goes on.

'Well.' I think of Stefan carefully unwrapping the mini milk. 'I suppose . . . I mean . . . I notice that other people are attractive?'

It's the best I can do to soften my inadequacy. A measly offering, but I feel like I'm going to cry. Oh, no, I *am* going to cry. My eyes become hot and my vision blurs. I think about two-hours-ago-Holly putting all that effort into her mascara because she thought she was getting engaged and want to cry more.

'Holly, please don't cry,' Will mutters, looking furtively at the table next to us, terrified someone's going to notice. He reaches for my hand. I grip onto it like a life boat and try to pull myself together. I blink furiously and manage to stem the tears.

'I just think it would be a brilliant idea for us, in the long run,' Will explains soothingly, rubbing his thumb over my palm. 'When we're sixty, we don't want to look back and think we missed out on any experiences and resent each other for that. I read this article about how temporarily opening up a relationship can be helpful for couples who met when they were very young. Once they get to a certain age, they're glad they did it.'

I swallow. The twisting, nauseous ball in my stomach loosens slightly. Will's thinking about this for *us*, and what will be best for our future, even if I can't quite wrap my head around it right now. He's thinking about what will be best for us in the long term.

'So . . . what do you want, exactly?' I ask.

'Well.' Will takes a breath. 'I'd like to try an open relationship.'

'An . . . open relationship,' I repeat.

The sentence sounds ridiculous coming out of my mouth. It sits awkwardly on my tongue. Open relationships are something that happen in Louis Theroux documentaries or . . . Jilly Cooper novels (probably). They're not something that real people do. They're not something that *we* do.

When I don't say anything else Will goes to top up my champagne, but I've barely touched my first glass.

'What do you think?' Will goes on. 'Would you be willing to try it, at least? See if it might be good for us? I don't want us to have any regrets getting in the way of being happy together, forever.'

Forever. He's not proposing, but he still wants to be with me forever. My gut is screaming no, but part of me can see the logic in his words. If we are going to stay together forever I don't want Will to have any regrets. I don't want him to end up resenting me.

'I . . . Maybe?' I acquiesce. 'Do we have to decide right now?'

'No, of course not. Take your time. Think about it.'

Will smiles at me and reaches for my other hand, so he's holding both across the table. He squeezes reassuringly.

'Excuse me,' I mutter, sliding my hands out of his and standing up. I have a sudden urge to be as far away from him as possible, even though I know that's not fair and he genuinely thinks this will be good for us. I grab my handbag. 'I need the bathroom.'

Will nods. I can't quite look him in the eye. I walk quickly to the other side of the restaurant, looking for the ladies', but I can't find it. My brain isn't working properly and my feet are moving on autopilot.

I end up leaning against a wall, around a corner, in between some empty tables. I'm compelled to reach out to someone. Someone who can help me process this, who will make it better. Someone who might corroborate what Will's saying about how this would ultimately strengthen our relationship and be a positive in the years ahead. I reach into my bag for my phone. But as I circle through my friends – *our* friends – I know instinctively that none of them would understand where Will's coming from. Most of them are engaged or married now and have never been in an open relationship. They'd be cynical at best and horrified at worst.

I think about messaging Tomi. I don't think he'd be judgemental in the same way my other friends would, but I can't hide my feelings from him. He'd know instantly how upset I am and tell me in no uncertain terms that I shouldn't do anything that makes me feel uncomfortable, which isn't what I want to hear right now because what if this is something Will really needs me to do?

I look around me at the fancy bar, the dimmed lighting, the twinkling city outside the window. It doesn't feel beautiful anymore, just alien and unfamiliar. This whole evening has turned from a dream to a nightmare and we haven't even had our starters.

I can't believe I thought I was getting engaged tonight.

CHAPTER TWO:
ALWAYS PEE AFTER SEX

FLISS

God is punishing me for having too much sex. That's the only reason I can think of that I would get cystitis twice in three months.

'Jennyyy,' I cry desperately, clutching my cranberry juice to my chest.

I took all the precautions. I peed and showered *straight* afterwards. To the point where I was quite rude, to be honest. *Thanks for the D, gotta jump in the shower this instant.* And still cystitis rears its ugly, bladder-searing head.

'JENNY,' I cry again, banging on the front door. I can hear her speaking through the open window so she's definitely in and pretending not to hear me. I get that she'd rather not engage with my salacious lifestyle – her word, not mine – and my coming home mid-morning having clearly stayed out all night on a date is really rubbing it in her face. But it's not like I make a habit of it – I usually creep softly in at 1 a.m. instead and am there in the morning – only, when I realised

I'd lost my keys yesterday, I could hardly wake her up in the middle of the night.

'JENNNYYYYYYY,' I howl.

Finally, I hear movement. She makes her way downstairs at a leisurely pace and takes ages fumbling for her keys. She places them in the lock and slowly turns . . .

The minute the door opens I dash past her, spilling cranberry juice everywhere. I leg it past Jenny and her fluffy pink dressing-gown, to the toilet where I sit down and wait for sweet relief to arrive. It doesn't, obviously, because that is cystitis's cruel trick.

Jenny knocks on the bathroom door. 'Sorry,' she calls. She doesn't sound sorry. 'I was on a Zoom meeting and my phone was on the other side of the room. I didn't hear you.'

Like hell she didn't. She loves me really, but in the way you love a younger sibling whom you also enjoy torturing.

'No problem,' I lie as sweetly as possible.

'Bad day to lock yourself out.' She chuckles.

'Yes,' I reply through gritted teeth. I hear her giant slippers shuffle back down the hallway and upstairs.

My phone beeps. It's Ash.

How's your morning?

Painful. Full of regret and proanthocyanidins.

Fine, I type. Jenny's being a bit of a cow, but what's new?

No point mentioning the cystitis. We haven't had sex in over a week, so he'll know it's not from him. Even though I'm allowed to have sex with other people, I find it's best not to allude to it all the time. For us, a successful open relationship involves the right amount of honesty and the right amount of tiptoeing around the giant, unholy elephant in the room. We used to talk about our dates constantly, until eventually we worked out what information was serving us and what wasn't.

My phone buzzes again. This time it's not Ash.

Still thinking about last night

URGH. So am I, Finn with the Shiny Hair, and wishing it NEVER HAPPENED. There's one thing getting cystitis when the sex was actually good, but when it was questionable at best it's a fucking travesty. He kept looking at himself in the mirror rather than me – rude – and flicking his lustrous hair back and forth like he was in a Pantene advert. It wasn't worth setting my urinary tract on fire.

You give good head ;)

You don't.

One of many things I still don't understand about men – even after dating a great number of them – is why some of them text you dirty things at, like, nine in the morning. I'm all for sexting but maybe wait until midday? Please let my Rice Krispies be pure.

Finally, I get up from the toilet and move to the kitchen, where I keep swigging my ineffective cranberry juice. The doctor is calling me at 2 p.m. and I am dreading it. I can already hear his judgemental tones. 'Cystitis, again? I can see that we prescribed you antibiotics for this same problem twelve weeks ago.'

At least I don't have to call the office to explain why I'm not coming in to work. Thank the Lord for flexible hours. The fact that there's always space if I want to go in, but that no one cares if I work from home, is one of the main reasons I like working at a freelance translation agency like Traduire.

Ash texts again.

Haha, what's Jenny done now? Tell me all about it later. See you at 6.30? I'll bring stuff for fajitas

Bless him. I let his sweetness wash over me and wonder again why he wants to come over on a Thursday. Ash and I have a reliable weekly schedule. Wednesdays, Fridays and Sundays we spend with each other. Any other days we don't ask too many questions about what the other person is doing. Vague honesty is the solid foundation our relationship is built upon. It's not that I don't *know* he sleeps with other people, but I don't want to know *exactly* when it's happening. If we see each other only on certain days then we never have to do the awkward, revealing 'Errr, no I'm busy that evening.'

It also avoids having too many clashes with each other. It's a carefully managed, highly serviceable system that's been working for years now, so I was taken aback by his request. Thankfully I didn't have a date planned, but I easily could have.

My scorching bladder briefly distracted me from this puzzling turn of events, but now I can't help thinking over it. Does he have a concussion from when he fell off his bike the other day? Has he got the days of the week mixed up? Or does he have some terrible news to deliver? But he's not acting like anything is wrong. Maybe it's good news?

I spend the rest of the day buried in some legal papers I'm translating into German, trying to keep my mind off the burning pain. Nothing too unusual about the document, nothing I haven't worked with a million times, so somehow I manage to do some work before 2 p.m. when the doctor calls. I practically sprint to the pharmacy to pick up my sweet, *sweet* drugs.

***

As soon as it hits 5 p.m. I check Jenny isn't in the kitchen and pour myself a gin. One time, when she caught me drinking this early, she hid my big fishbowl cocktail glass for a month. Jenny does not approve of alcohol before dinner. Jenny doesn't approve of much of anything that I do, for that matter, but at least her quiet tutting in the style of my mother makes me feel at home.

At 6.30, Ash rings the bell. I'm curious about this unexpected Thursday appearance, but I'm excited to see him. I open the door and drink in the sight of him. Long, dark hair frames his light brown skin and delicate cheekbones. He's wearing jeans and a T-shirt so he must not have been in court today. He looks shattered. I bet he was in Brixton with the family who just adopted triplets.

'Triplets?' I ask.

He nods and I note the dark circles under his eyes. Our jobs are worlds apart in this respect – freelance translator and social worker – as Ash thrives on the personal nature of his job, whereas I've always needed something I can separate myself from. The documents don't have feelings or come to me about their problems and once it hits five I don't have to think about them. Ash is helping people by being involved in the most intimate parts of their lives, so he can't exactly leave it at the door. Sometimes he'll be up all night worrying about a case.

It used to concern me that this struggle to compartmentalise would affect our relationship. I like meeting new people and spending time with them, but strong emotions don't get involved and my other relationships are very brief. We used to have a two-week time limit on seeing other people, but we ended up extending it as that was too short for Ash; he's such a people person, so he wants to be with other people for slightly longer than I do. But I can appreciate that we both have our own reasons for being in an open relationship and his feelings for other people don't change his feelings for me.

'It was a tough day,' he says, walking past me into the kitchen. I follow him.

He puts the shopping bag down on the kitchen counter and collapses into me. I put my arm around his shoulders and breathe him in. Hugging Ash always makes everything else seem less stressful. He's an ice pack on a flaming hot forehead. A dock leaf in a field of stinging nettles. Antibiotics on an inflamed urinary tract.

'Are you OK?' Ash sits up and looks down at my legs. I've been shifting from foot to foot. My bladder is starting to itch again. Definitely shouldn't have had that gin.

'Fine.' I grin, but it probably comes off more like a grimace. 'Are you?'

'Yeah.' He smiles. 'Yeah, I'm good.'

It can't be bad news then, I realise, relieved it's not going to be one of *those* conversations. I look into his eyes and all I find there is warmth. The gross, needy part of me that no one else ever touches wakes up and I lean in to kiss him.

There's always the possibility in the back of my mind, no matter how faint and faraway I keep it, that Ash might meet someone else. Someone better, someone less prickly, less of a know-it-all, more caring, funnier, brighter. Or maybe none of those things; just someone that, for some inexplicable reason, he has a stronger connection with.

But then I remind myself, that happens to people in exclusive relationships, too; it's not like not dating other people actually eliminates that risk. Ash and I are just choosing to trust our bond is strong enough that acknowledging feelings for other people won't affect it. And we have a rule that if our feelings for someone else do become confusing, we will tell the other immediately.

I also like to think if Ash *did* meet someone else he wanted to be with more than me, I'd be happy for him. Ash is the kindest, smartest and all-around best person I've ever met. If there's someone out there that would genuinely make him happier than I would then I'd want that for him. And I'd want it for me, too. I don't want to be with each other out of habit or because we didn't get the chance to meet that other person. I want to always be choosing each other and I struggle to see how we could fully be choosing each other if we were shutting ourselves away from other people. If there was someone else he preferred, I'd rather he knew about it and went for it.

Doesn't mean it wouldn't hurt like a bitch, though.

'So . . . ?' I continue, less nervous about what he has to say. Maybe it really was a mistake? 'You do know it's, er . . .' I'm about to point out that it's Thursday but I falter. It's unusual for us to speak about our schedule. We did when we set the ground rules, but for the three years we've been together since, our routine is just understood.

Ash takes a breath to speak when Jenny's black, glossy curtain of hair and round, smiling cheeks appear in the doorway. She's still in her fluffy robe. Ash is here so often that she doesn't bother getting changed when he's here anymore. 'Ash!'

'All right, Chenny?' Ash turns to her. Jenny's last name is Chen. She giggles. Story of my life . . . Everyone likes Ash more than they like me. He's my disguise. My beard. My ticket into normal society. I can't blame them; he's undeniably likeable. I'm probably at least twenty per cent nicer since I met him.

Thankfully, Ash's last name is Ogawa-Taylor and there's no immediately obvious pally nickname Jenny can give him in return. That might push me over the edge.

'I didn't realise you were coming. It's Thursday?' She looks between us suspiciously.

'You hungry?' He tactfully avoids the question. 'Want in on fajitas?'

'Ooh.' Jenny's eyes widen. 'Yes. *Gossip Girl*?' She gestures behind her towards the living room. Ash fulfils all of Jenny's TV-bingeing needs in a way that I can't. I'll watch it with her, but she's perpetually disappointed by my reactions. I never seem to gasp at the right moments.

'Yeah sure, in a bit. We'll be down in a sec.' Ash smiles

and takes my hand, squeezing past Jenny and leading me into the hallway.

As we make our way upstairs, my heart starts beating faster. If he wants to talk to me right now – privately – something *must* be wrong. My nerves return and I don't like it. I feel like I do when I'm about to interpret in front of lots of people in court or go home to see Mum and Dad.

We reach my bedroom. I sit down on the bed while Ash closes the door behind us.

'What's up?' I try to sound calm.

He sits down next to me and takes my hand. 'I've been thinking a lot about this, and I want to go exclusive,' he says simply.

One of the things I always like about Ash is the way he comes out with things. It might take him a while to work up the courage to confront me about an issue – like when I kept talking to him when he was trying to read *A Little Life* – but once he decides to speak up I never have to try to decode what he's saying. I'm notoriously terrible at working out subtext. On this occasion, though, I can't help but wish he hadn't laid it out so plainly, because I don't know what to say.

I stop feeling nervous. I stop feeling anything.

I stare at the wall with my mouth slightly open and Ash waves his hand in front of my face. 'Fliss?'

Is this what shock feels like? Like you're just living blancmange?

'Fliss?' Ash repeats.

'Sorry, I just . . . wasn't expecting that,' I say.

'Really?' Ash raises an eyebrow. 'So all the hints about

having nothing to do on Tuesdays, Thursdays and Saturdays went over your head?'

He has been staying in to do jigsaws an awful lot, recently.

'I thought you'd just . . . got really into puzzles?' I answer lamely.

Wow, I'm *so* dense. He's right. This is the first time he's outright asked me to hang out on a Forbidden Day, but there were signs. He bemoaned not getting us tickets to a gig because it was on a Saturday. He was irrationally irritated about having to wait extra days to finish our *Godfather* marathon, even though we've both seen those movies a million times. Last week he phoned me, right in the middle of a date, 'just to say hi'. This has been coming for a while and a combination of being bad at reading undertones and sheer denial has meant that I've just not picked up on it. I'm happy and I wanted to keep believing that he was, too.

A million things start racing through my mind. How much I love my freedom. How much I can miss Ash during the week. How sometimes the sex with other people is shit. How sometimes it's great. How great the sex is with Ash every time. How much I love meeting new people. How much I love Ash.

'What are you thinking?' asks Ash.

'Lots of things,' I answer honestly.

Ash nods and smiles. The muscles in his face twitch and I can tell he must have been nervous to ask me, which is heartbreakingly adorable.

'I love you so much.' I squeeze his hand.

'I love you too.' He squeezes back. 'Look.' He gets up off the bed. 'You don't have to say anything now. Let's go make some fajitas and watch TV with Jenny. We can talk about it more another time, OK? No pressure.'

'Sure, yeah.' I nod, soothing myself that nothing has to change *right now*.

With effort, I stand up too. Have I always been this heavy? My legs feel like they might give way under the weight of my body.

Ash leaves the room and I follow him out, trying to walk normally. As we go downstairs I think how nice it is to have him here on a Thursday, and what a huge step it is that he basically just asked for all my Thursdays.

CHAPTER THREE:
DON'T CRY BEFORE STARTERS

HOLLY

I've just been told my eyebrows are 'retro'. I sit at my desk, combing through pictures of glamorous people with their eyebrows brushed upwards. Now I'm panicking that everyone thinks I don't belong in fashion because I don't subscribe to current eyebrow trends.

Tomi comes up behind me and leans protectively over my chair. 'Are you OK? I could spot your creased, sweaty forehead from way over there.'

'My eyebrows are antiquated,' I despair.

'Says who?'

'Alice from accounts.'

'Alice ditched Claire's bao bun night to have sex with Gael from the mailroom.' He shrugs.

Aghast, I swivel in my chair to face him. 'How do you know that?!' I gasp.

'I know everything.' Tomi taps the side of his nose.

He really does. He also has this way of soothing me within five seconds. A lot of people make the mistake of going one of two ways with anxious people; they either dismiss you, which makes you feel ridiculous, or engage the problem *too* much, which feeds the spiral. Tomi never makes me feel like my worries aren't valid but he knows how to swiftly shut my panic down.

'So, do you really want to take life advice from Alice?' he concludes.

I shake my head. I guess not. Gael isn't a bad guy, but he does spend a lot of time smelling stationery.

'I thought you'd be grimacing about Amber.' He leans in conspiratorially and whispers Amber's name.

'Haven't seen her this morning.' And for that I am grateful.

'Oh my God. You haven't heard.' Tomi bites his lip.

'What?!'

'OK, there's no easy way to tell you this. Amber is taking over while Julie's on maternity leave.' He looks at me like I'm a poor fluffy animal he just hit with his car.

Julie is senior designer and Amber is a junior designer. On the womenswear team I assist Julie and Amber and one other junior designer, Lucia, although while Amber and Lucia are above me – the lowly design assistant – Amber wasn't technically my boss. Given how much she passes to me anyway, with this promotion it's inevitably going to get even worse. Especially as we're only just over a month away from our seasonal trade showcase. I was hoping Lucia might take over or they'd get someone else in.

'Really? Why not Lucia?!' I say under my breath, careful that no one hears me.

Tomi shakes his head and rolls his eyes. 'Honestly, this is your fault. You shouldn't do her job for her and then everyone would see how little she actually does.'

I shrug. 'It's my job to do what she asks.'

'It's not your job to design her entire contribution to the spring line.'

I shrug again. It's true that a lot of the ideas that go through, via Amber, are mine. But that's just the nature of being an assistant.

We have to stop talking because Amber appears on the other side of the office in a flurry of auburn hair. Her eyes scan the room and land on me. I feel Tomi tense up. He's on the menswear team so he doesn't work directly with Amber, but he can't stand her. Mostly because of how much work she gives me that isn't technically in my job description, which is justified, but partly because one time she said she couldn't get into Taylor Swift's *Red* album, which is less so because everyone's entitled to their opinion. But in Tomi's eyes 'All Too Well' is the best break-up song of all time and anyone who doesn't agree is a 'pretentious try-hard without a heart'.

'Hi, Amber,' I say as she strides towards me. 'Congratulations on your promotion.'

'Thank you! That's so sweet,' she answers, looking down at the big file she's carrying. The thing I find confusing with Amber is that her words never match her tone. She says 'thank you' like she's just opened a disappointing birthday present and the elongated 'e' in her 'that's so sweet' tails off as though she's got bored of speaking to me in the middle of her sentence.

'I've got some CADs for you to do.' She sighs. 'I wanted to get to them myself but it wasn't possible what with everything else I've had on.' I input most of the team's hand-drawn sketches digitally, but Amber and Lucia are supposed to do some. Lucia always does hers but often Amber runs out of time and passes hers back to me.

'OK.' I smile even though my heart is sinking at the thought of fitting more laborious, time-consuming CADs into my already busy week. 'No problem.'

'*Amazing*, thank you.' She sighs again. 'They need to be done by Friday.' She passes me the folder containing the sketches.

'Sure.' I take it from her. There are quite a few in here, so I'm guessing she didn't get a chance to do many of them.

'*Wonderful*, thank you.' She turns on her heel and exits the room as quickly as she entered. Amber is always power-walking, even if she's only going to the kitchen to fill a glass of water. I'm never entirely sure what she's actually doing, given how much I do for her, but she walks around the office at warp speed and types frantically so everyone assumes she's slammed.

'THE SIGHING.' Tomi sighs dramatically, mimicking her. 'As if *she's* the one being given extra work!'

'I know, I know,' I admit. 'But she's not all bad, remember?'

This year Amber said she'd make sure I get full credit for one of my designs at the showcase. Amber might ask a lot from me, but the other designers mostly keep their heads down and don't really notice me. At least Amber is giving me a chance, so I've got to put my gripes to one side and take it.

'But you deserve that,' Tomi says. 'You don't need to be grateful for being credited for your *own work*.'

I shrug. Tomi doesn't understand. He's a senior menswear designer now and has understandably forgotten how much grafting it takes to get a foot in the door.

'You look nice today.' Tomi suddenly looks at me as if he's seeing me for the first time.

'Oh, do I?' I pull at my light-blue check shirt dress that brings out my eyes.

'You're wearing eyeliner.' He swivels my chair around to face him and leans in close to me.

'Oh . . . am I?' Crap. I took feigning innocence too far. As if I wouldn't remember putting liquid eyeliner on when I hardly ever wear it to work.

'Another hot date?' Tomi continues.

My blood freezes.

Does he *know*?!

He does know everything. *No* . . . He couldn't possibly.

It's been nearly two weeks since The Night We Didn't Get Engaged. For about a week afterwards we didn't mention the open relationship idea again and I hoped Will had forgotten about it. But then he asked me if I'd had a chance to consider it and I realised it wasn't going away. It's something that's important to him. I agreed and we settled on a date night. Just a date to start with, which didn't seem like *too* much to ask. I can do a date. A singular date.

So, tonight is date night. Just not with each other.

'Will's spoiling you a lot recently . . .' Tomi goes on.

'Um, I guess . . .'

Oh God. *Keep face neutral. Keep face neutral. Keep face neutral.* Tomi can instantly sniff out the smallest shift in my emotions, which is really quite inconvenient when you're trying to pretend everything is OK. He started out as a 'work friend' but one time he found me by the bins frantically burying shards of Claire's special mug that I broke and we've been in 'real friend' territory ever since.

Claire had missing posters up for weeks. Every time she sent another 'all staff' email about it Tomi and I would share a furtive look.

'Look, all I'm saying is, if anything should happen, you'd better message me straight away. No staring dreamily into each other's eyes, yeah, you've got an important phone call to make?' Tomi nudges me.

I give a small, weak smile, which is the most I can manage.

Tomi frowns. Crap. He senses something is wrong. 'Are you OK?'

'I'm fine,' I lie.

Thankfully, it's time for his 3 p.m. design meeting that I'm not allowed in to, and Amber starts tapping her wrist at him from the other side of the room.

He gives her a thumbs-up. 'All right, well, wherever you're going, have a nice evening, yeah?'

I nod.

Tomi gives me one last concerned look before walking away. I turn my chair back around to my computer, relieved that he's gone. I don't like lying to Tomi. I don't like lying . . . *full stop*. One time in year seven Mathilda Farr, a notorious pen thief, asked me if I had a spare pen and I said I didn't even though I did, because I'd already lost several pens to her. It's eighteen years later and I still feel bad.

I can't tell Tomi about this, though. I know what he'd say. *Whose idea was that?*

This doesn't seem very you, Holly?

Are you sure you want to do this?

And the answer would be . . . no, I'm not, but . . . I won't be totally sure about every decision I make, will I? And relationships are about *compromise,* aren't they? To make long-term relationships work, you sometimes have to do things you don't want to, for the other person, right?

Well . . . this is me compromising.

For the first time in nine years, I'm going on a first date. And so is my boyfriend. The fact we're actually doing it still seems completely bizarre. I keep expecting Will to text me, saying, *Holly, what are we doing? This is madness! Come home and we'll watch* House of the Dragon.

But he hasn't.

I think about Will. He'll be in the office right now, too. Maybe thinking about his own date later. A million questions race through my mind. Who has he chosen to go out with? What's her name? What does she do? What's he wearing? How's he feeling right now? Is he excited, nervous, full of regrets . . . thinking about cancelling? Wondering about me? Or has he not thought about it much at all? Maybe it doesn't require this level of analysis. As Will often points out, I have a tendency to make a big deal out of things.

For the twentieth time today, I look though 'Andrew's' profile. Andrew, who will be taking me out to dinner this evening. Instead of my boyfriend.

Crap. There I go again . . . Making a big deal out of things! What's going out to dinner, really? It's just two people mutually consuming edible goods in order that their digestive systems might break them down and provide them with the energy they need to survive. And what's a date, I mean, when you really think about it? Just two human beings meeting at an agreed time and place and exchanging words in a common language.

No big deal.

Except, if it's no big deal like Will is suggesting, why is he so desperate to do it? What is he looking to get out of this one date? What should I be looking to get out of it? I know there must be something important I'm missing here but I didn't want to *keep* asking questions because I felt stupid. It all seems obvious to Will and he seemed so pleased that I'd agreed and that I 'got it'.

I definitely don't 'get it'. I feel like someone in their sixties who lives in Kent and is a fan of Piers Morgan trying to understand the concept of being non-binary.

I'm so out of the game, I actually had to google what dating apps people are using these days. I think I spent all of ten minutes on my profile; uploaded some not-revolting pictures of myself. Said some basic things about my job and liking holidays. I couldn't bear to put any effort into it, because hopefully I'll be deleting it in a couple of weeks anyway.

'Andrew' is well dressed. In the first picture he's standing in a café with a reusable coffee flask, wearing a white wool crew-neck sweater with cord trousers. He has round, tortoiseshell glasses. In the next picture he's windswept next to a grey beach, wearing a red hat and a quilted green coat, with his friends. In the next, he's wearing a grey cable-knit jumper and holding a puppy. I appreciate the thought that's gone into selecting both his outfits and his profile images. They say, 'I care about my appearance *and* ethical consumption' and 'animals don't hate me' and 'look, I have other well-dressed friends and we go on bike rides together, so I must be normal'.

He's a graphic designer, like Will, so we have similar interests given that I work in design. On paper, there's potential.

Except . . . do I *want* there to be potential? I've already found the person I want to spend the rest of my life with, so what's the point of having potential with someone else if it can't go anywhere? But then, equally, why would I go on a date with someone if there *wasn't* any potential? Isn't this whole situation just lose-lose?! Crap. I'm overthinking it again.

I try to work for the rest of the afternoon but I keep reading the same lines of emails over and over. In one I accidentally write 'angora' instead of 'alpaca' and send the entire shipping team into a confused spiral. I'm unbelievably anxious. It's been *nine years* since I went on a first date. In fact, I've never really been on a first date. Will and I met when I was nineteen at university, at a party. We lived in the same building. By the time we went on an actual 'date' we'd already been sleeping together for weeks.

Breathe, Holly. Breathe. Remember, it's just one person meeting another.

No big deal.

As soon as it hits five o'clock I grab my coat and hurry out of the building with my head down. We're not meeting until seven, but I have no desire to spend the next two hours hanging around in the office, in danger of Alice referring to any of my other body parts as 'retro' and making me even more nervous.

I head to my favourite coffee shop around the corner, where I order a latte and barely touch it. I check for lipstick on my teeth every time I so much as twitch my mouth. I pee twelve times. I apply more deodorant because I've already sweated my way through half a can. I'm a *mess*. I think about cancelling but I've left it too late now. That would be unbelievably rude. He might already be on his way. Plus, what would I tell Will?

At half past six I start making my way – incredibly slowly – to the restaurant.

When I get there, I'm relieved that the place is cosy and atmospheric, without being *too* obviously date-like. I had a fear I was going to turn up and be fumbling around in the dark, surrounded by candles and sexual tension and people roguishly touching each other's knees under the table. This is OK. For all anyone else knows we could just be two friends out for dinner. Two old colleagues . . . two *buddies*, if you will.

I'm the first one to arrive. Good. That gives me time to settle and take off my coat and check my teeth for lipstick again. Except . . . Oh my God. What if he's not coming?! That would be the ultimate humiliation. Stood up for a date I didn't even want to go on.

I wonder if Will is also out there waiting for his date, thinking about me.

The waitress leads me to my table and offers me water. She has kind eyes. If I *do* get stood up, she doesn't seem like the type to laugh about it in the kitchen, at least. Maybe she'd even give me a free dessert. I scan the menu, just in case. Crème brûlée seems like a good thing to order in that situation. It would make the memory of this evening slightly more elegant. Going home alone with crème brûlée is less depressing than going home with, say, a sponge pudding.

As I compare the relative poetic value of each item on the dessert menu, a well-dressed man in a dark blue sweater I recognise from one of his pictures steps inside. My heart starts pounding. Oh my God. He's here. He's an actual man. An actual man I'm about to *date*.

I'm a little disappointed about the loss of potentially free crème brûlée.

The waitress points at my table and he looks over here. We make eye contact. Crap. I should have pretended not to notice him enter. Now we have to endure the awkward process of moving towards each other and not knowing where to look. He observes fellow diners. I scan my phone for imaginary messages.

'Hi!' he calls as he approaches the table. I stand up and he leans in for a hug. 'How are you doing?'

'Hi,' I say. 'Nice to meet you.'

Words! Precious words are coming out of my mouth and making actual sense. Thank God!

I'm so busy congratulating myself that I managed to say 'nice to meet you' without messing it up, that I miss whatever he says next entirely. I realise that he's staring at me expectantly.

'Come again?' I say.

He smiles. 'I just asked if you were waiting long?'

'Oh, *no*,' I reassure him. 'No, no. I only just got here.'

Is there some kind of etiquette about this that I've missed, I wonder? Was I supposed to get here last? That is just the sort of nonsense I would hear Alice from Accounts blathering about. Someone has to be the one to arrive first. If we were all hanging around waiting to be the last one to arrive no one would ever go anywhere.

Andrew takes off his jacket and hangs it on the stand beside the table. We both sit down. At least, I think with some relief, he does actually look like his pictures; he's not a catfish. Oh God. What if *I'm* the catfish? What if he's disappointed? I should've uploaded less flattering pictures.

'So do you . . . work around here?' I ask, realising no one has spoken in about five seconds.

Look at me go! Asking questions on a *date*. Maybe it won't be so bad.

'Yeah not too far, what about you?'

'About a ten-minute walk,' I answer.

My mind blanks. Crap. I've run out of questions already. How can that be?! There is an entire person sitting across from me, a whole lifetime's worth of thoughts and feelings and memories and stories, and my limit is 'do you work around here?' I wonder if the conversation is flowing easily on Will's date. Suddenly the dinner stretches out ahead of me and I wish I'd organised something more casual, like a coffee. A blissfully short, easily escapable coffee.

'Shall we get some drinks?' Andrew says.

Oh God. Thirty seconds with me and he's already reaching for the bottle.

'Sure,' I say, and he begins scanning the wine menu. It gives me an opportunity to assess his face properly. Do I find this man attractive? Objectively, yes, he is obviously attractive. He has a nice jawline. I wonder if he's going to have a similar, sneaky inspection of my face when I'm eating my food. I hope not. What if I accidentally take an unusually large bite and have trouble chewing it?

I wonder if Will is finding his date attractive. Was she

better on the app or in person? Oh God. What if she's better in person? Is he out there right now being *pleasantly surprised* by another woman?

'What kind of wine do you like?' Andrew asks.

'Um.' I rack my brains for *any* knowledge of wine and find none. Will always chooses the wine. 'I don't mind, you choose.'

'White? Red?'

'Uhh . . . white?' I guess.

'Not a big drinker?' He smiles.

'I, well . . .' I do drink; it's more that I usually have no concept of what it is that I'm drinking.

'Ah!' He snaps the wine list shut. 'No worries. I'll just get a lager, then.'

'Oh, we can definitely get a bottle,' I oblige.

'No, no, it's cool.' He waves dismissively. 'So, busy day?'

'Not too bad, you?' I manage to respond, worrying that he's dismayed by my lack of interest in wine.

'Oh, you know,' he says. 'It was all right until four-thirty, then someone comes along and does the old, *Oh, Andrew, can I just ask you something really quickly . . . ?*'

I nod. Will complains about this constantly. People are always asking him to make 'quick' adjustments to designs with no concept of how long it would actually take him.

'Something really quick that's actually an hour-long task, which they wouldn't know, because they're not a designer?' I joke.

'*Exactly!*' Andrew laughs and claps his hands together. 'Is it the same for you in fashion?'

I come dangerously close to explaining that no, actually,

36

my boyfriend is a graphic designer, and stop myself. Of course, Andrew doesn't know I have a boyfriend.

Should I have told him that I have a boyfriend?!

I mumble something about just being an assistant and Andrew continues complaining affectionately about his colleagues and people 'asking for multiple versions' and being sure they'll 'know what they want when they see it' and it's like I'm listening to Will talk about his day, sitting across from him in our kitchen, holding his hand, nodding along in all the right places.

Except I'm not. I'm with a man named Andrew. Will is God knows where with God knows who. But everything that Andrew is speaking about is just reminding me of him.

Suddenly, I'm aware of being horrendously out of my depth. With Will I'm safe, and without him I'm someone who can't swim and has been dropped into the middle of the ocean without so much as a float. My breaths get shorter and shallower and I can't focus on what Andrew is saying.

I stand up abruptly. 'Excuse me,' I say. 'I just need the bathroom.'

'Sure, yeah.'

In need of a moment to compose myself, I find my way to the ladies' toilets and hurry into a stall. I close the door behind me, my eyes blurry with tears.

CHAPTER FOUR:
AVOID THE DANGER ZONE

FLISS

I sit across from a man named Eric, watching him examine the wine menu and order the most expensive option. Eric always picks the most expensive option. He works in private equity investment, which, from what I've gleaned, I *think* means he essentially gets paid huge amounts of money for gambling with other people's money.

Eric is attractive. Eric is smart. Eric is loaded. I could spend hours talking to him about global economic emergencies and making my way through bottles of his fancy booze. But I can feel that we're approaching 'the danger zone'.

I told Eric that I had a boyfriend after date one, about five weeks ago. Unless I meet someone on an app specifically for people in similar situations to me, I don't like telling people about Ash before I meet them because it changes the entire tone of the first date. Some men ask a lot of questions about how it works, which entirely ruins the mood. I can't tell whether I have chemistry with someone if all they're doing is asking me questions about my boyfriend. Some guys show up assuming you're *definitely* going to have sex with them, because if you're in an open relationship, why wouldn't you? (Just because I'm *allowed* to sleep with them, doesn't necessarily mean I'll *want* to sleep with them.)

So often I go on a first date and never a second, in which case it's irrelevant. If I don't want to go out with them again anyway then I can disappear into the ether and I've saved myself an arduous conversation. I prefer to meet them once and then, if we like each other, I explain. Then it's their choice whether they want to go out again. I don't owe anything to someone that I've never met, but as soon as we have met it's only fair to be up front, just in case they're not OK with it.

Most men are. Or at least, they pretend to be.

Eric, I'm realising, is a *classic* case of pretending. I think he suspected at the beginning that he might win me over, but as time goes on and it's become apparent that's not going to be the case, I'm noticing little cracks beginning to show. He doesn't want his masculinity to be threatened by seeming like he might actually care whether I'm emotionally invested, but he does. If I'm being kind to Eric, maybe he genuinely likes me and it's starting to take its toll, but I don't get that vibe. More likely, his ego can't stand the fact I'm not vying to marry him by now.

Either way, entering 'the danger zone' – when I can feel a man trying to cross the boundaries I have fastidiously laid down – is the signal that I need to get out.

'So,' he says, once the waitress has gone to get his Flaccianello della something. 'My friend Simon is having a dinner party on Saturday. He wants to show off his new kitchen. Do you fancy it?'

He hinted about an event with his friends last time we met and I swiftly changed the subject. This is the first time he's directly asked me. I try to keep my expression neutral.

'I can't,' I answer. 'Make sure you get pictures of the new kitchen, though. I want to see this floor-to-ceiling wine rack.'

Eric looks down at the table. I can see him carefully considering what to say next. 'If you want to see it, you'll have to come along.' He looks up at me and smirks in a way that, if I was in a better mood, I might have found charming and playful.

But I'm not in a good mood. My conversation with Ash has been playing on my mind since Thursday and there's a definite atmosphere between us. After Ash went home he'd texted me to say, *Really, take as long as you need*, but every time we've spoken since, our chat is stilted and full of gaps where we're obviously both thinking about it. Once an ultimatum is out there, it's out there. I know Ash said no pressure and meant it, but we can't just keep going along as normal now. The timer doesn't have a set countdown yet but I can hear it ticking.

'I really can't,' I lie instead. 'I've actually got a friend's birthday that night.' As a rule, I don't make up excuses. I'm candid about what I have to offer and people can take it or leave it. But after the last few days with Ash I'm feeling too weak for an awkward confrontation.

'Oh yeah?' Eric mocks. 'Didn't know you had friends.' He winks.

I smile sarcastically. I have friends, although most of them are in different countries.

'What friend is this, then?' he continues.

'Sarah.' I say the first name that comes into my head.

'How do you know Sarah, then?'

'School.'

'Thought you didn't keep in touch with anyone from school.'

'Except Sarah.' I grin and he grins back. We both know he's not buying it for a second.

Then he takes a different tack. 'Look, just come with me,' he says, reaching across the table for my hand.

Suddenly I realise how tired I am. It feels *late*. Is it really only seven-thirty? Did we really only just get here?

'No.' I shake my head. It comes out more weary than I intended. Eric withdraws his hand and actually pouts. He folds his arms like a cross child.

He opens his mouth to say something else when the waitress brings our wine, so he ends up exhaling loudly instead. The waitress obviously notices the change in mood as she approaches the table. She shifts her gaze between us, not wanting to hold eye contact for too long.

'Flaccianello della Pieve?' she asks timidly.

Eric nods. Then the poor girl has to open it. She can't get the cork out and we sit watching her struggle just for something to do.

She pours a little into a glass for us.

Dear Lord.

Eric gives the glass a cursory sniff and nods. She darts back to the kitchen at the speed of light.

'Look.' Eric breaks the silence that's settled over the table. 'I think you need to clarify your thoughts on me and the other man.'

Oh. Eric is going to be one of *those*. I take a big, long gulp of wine.

'Clarify my thoughts?' I repeat. Feeling irked momentarily boosts my energy. 'Would you mind explaining what it is you'd like me to clarify? I feel like I've been pretty transparent.'

Eric shakes his head. 'Well, you say you don't want me to be your boyfriend, and yet sometimes you act like I am. It's very *mixed messages*.'

Men like Eric love accusing me of giving them mixed messages. Christ. We're well past the 'danger zone' now. My hand is on the electric fence. I'm caught in the weir.

Rather than attempting a response, I take another gulp of wine. There's no point getting sucked too far into this conversation. Eric obviously hasn't been listening to me for the last five weeks anyway. No matter what I say he will hear what he wants to hear.

'For instance,' he continues, 'the other day, you texted to ask how my meeting went. And you left a hairbrush at my house.'

Wow. I give a non-committal nod and drain the rest of my glass. I was interested in how his meeting went; it was important to him and I'm not a robot. I forgot my hairbrush; I wasn't leaving it there as some dastardly ploy to get a drawer in his room. What is in the water this week? Why are all the men being so *needy*?

It's not like I haven't had conversations like this before. Eric is not the first man to feel like I've led him up the garden path, even though I've been clear from the start. Usually it bounces right off me. I'm brilliant at engaging them just the right amount – friendly but aloof – and getting swiftly out. But tonight I don't feel equipped to cope.

'I'm sorry if you feel I've misled you. I didn't mean to,' I say. 'I have a boyfriend and I'm not looking for another one. Maybe we'd better leave things here.' The words are the right ones but, with my mind still half on Ash and wanting things to be OK between us, I can't keep my voice light. I sound hassled.

Eric splutters and turns a little red. 'Right, well, we'll just get the cheque, then,' he finally comments.

He leans back in his chair, trying to catch the waitress's attention, but she's assiduously ignoring our table. We sit in silence until he finally just grabs his coat, gets up and pays the bill on the other side of the room. He exits the restaurant without looking at me.

Wow. I guess that's goodbye to Eric. At least he paid for his ridiculously expensive wine and left it.

I take a swig straight from the bottle.

I guess I'll go home and watch *Sex Education* with Jenny, then, seeing as I'm not getting any tonight. I'm relieved that interaction is over – obviously, he wants more than I can give him and it needs to end – but I allow myself a moment to mourn Eric's firm opinions and beautiful roof terrace.

I put on my coat and, clutching my £150 bottle of wine, head to the bathroom. I look in the mirror. *Damn*, I look fine tonight. All that time getting ready . . . Wasted!! I briefly consider reaching out to one of the numbers stored in my phone but I feel apathetic even as I imagine doing it. I'm really off my game. To be honest, all I want to do right now is go home and cuddle with Ash. Normally tonight would be off limits and, for a second,

I allow myself to imagine a world where I could be at his right now. In this moment, it's tempting to have that option.

I've been going back and forth for the last week. He explained a little more about why he wants to go exclusive and why now, which made me even more confused. He said that he increasingly misses me when we're apart – which is adorable, and I understand, because I often end up missing him, too – but he also said some things about us being 'nearly thirty' and how 'it's time' and that he 'never thought we'd carry on like this forever', which threw me.

The Ash I know doesn't do things because it's what people are expected to do around a certain age. He does things because he's thought them through carefully and decided they will make him happy. I remember when Ash and I first admitted that we still had feelings for other people, even though we were falling deeply in love, and agreed to never make our love feel like an obligation. I was so elated that I could admit how I really felt and that he felt the same. We loved and trusted each other enough to know that we both were sure nothing else would beat what we had, but that we could keep having all the new experiences that we wanted.

And now he wants to change all that.

If I'm being honest, I hadn't thought about what was going to happen in the 'forever'. I only really think as far ahead as my next holiday. But knowing that Ash had thought this was only a temporary state until we inevitably became a 'regular' couple makes me question everything we've built together so far. Has everything so far just been a warm-up, waiting for our 'real' relationship to start?

We can't carry on like this forever.

It's time.

I sit down on the toilet when I hear a sniffling in the cubicle beside me. It's an intimate restaurant so there are only two tiny stalls crammed right next to each other and you can hear everything. As I pee I think about how odd it is that I can hear some woman sobbing and she's listening to me urinating, within three feet of one another, without knowing anything about the other person at all.

Fuck. There's no loo roll.

'Erm, excuse me,' I call out gently. 'Sorry to bother you but there's no paper. Would you mind passing some under?'

The noise stops. 'Sure,' a small voice mutters. A dainty, pale hand with neat, natural nails my mother would admire appears near the floor. I glance at my own chipped purple nail polish as our hands meet to make the exchange.

'Thank you,' I say.

Double fuck. As I use the paper I see that my period has come early. I search my handbag and . . . Nope. Of course. Ten condoms and zero sanitary products. Classic.

'Erm, hello. Me again.' I knock gently on the wall dividing us. 'I don't suppose you have a tampon?'

The hand appears once more, holding a pad.

'Bless you!' I exclaim. 'You're an angel.'

At least I've distracted her from crying, I think. But when I come out and start washing my hands the sobs resume.

I don't know if it's that I'm feeling at a loose end with my date abandoning me in a huff, or fragile because of everything with Ash, or if it's simply that this woman gave me a sanitary towel so there's an unspoken bond between us, but as I go to leave I find myself hesitating at the door.

'Are you all right?' I call out.

There's a pause. 'Oh, fine thank you,' she says through tears.

Convincing.

'Are you sure?' I ask again. 'Is there anything I can do? Can I get you an Uber?'

'Ugh,' comes a little wail. 'I can't go home. I'm on a *date*.'

I laugh out loud. 'It's going well, then?' I quip and move closer to her stall. I lean against the door. 'Are you safe? Do you need me to call someone?'

'He didn't do anything. He's nice,' she burbles. 'It's *me*. I'm the problem. It's me.'

I'm stuck for something to say. I'm not usually one for deep, meaningful conversations in girls' bathrooms. I was imagining I'd just check she was OK getting home and leave.

Then the stall door swings open. A tallish pale woman with pixie-cut, dark brown hair emerges. She's wearing a long, blue check shirt dress that matches her eyes. She'd look good if her face wasn't all red and blotchy and make-up wasn't smeared down it.

'I'm going to have to go back out there,' she says, rubbing her cheeks. 'Is it obvious I've been crying?'

CHAPTER FIVE:
DON'T DATE CLONES

HOLLY

I can tell from the look on the woman's face, it is *very* obvious I've been crying.

'Erm.' She doesn't even attempt to lie to me.

She's short and tanned and has long blonde hair almost down to her stomach. She's wearing tartan trousers with black boots, a black crop top and a black leather jacket, and she looks stunning, which does not make me feel better when I look in the mirror.

I am *hideous*. I grab some loo paper, wet it and start dabbing at my face in an effort to reduce the swelling.

'I think that trick's an urban legend.' She appears behind me in the mirror. 'I have a make-up wipe, though.'

I stop dabbing in defeat. 'Yes, please,' I whimper.

'OK.' She reaches into her handbag and passes me the wipe. 'Don't start crying again, though, or it's back to square one.'

'Thank you,' I say. 'I'm so sorry.'

'A make-up wipe for a sanitary towel. Seems like a fair

trade.' She smiles awkwardly and watches me clean my smudged face for a moment. She clearly feels like she has to stay and make sure I'm all right, which is *beyond* mortifying. But I don't want to tell her she can go in case it seems like I'm ungrateful for her help. Oh my God, what must this woman think of me?

'OK, well, I'd best be going. Good luck!' She gives me an awkward thumbs-up. I cringe.

'Of course! Go! Please, enjoy your evening. I'm so sorry. You know, I'm not normally like this,' I garble. 'I mean, I don't usually cry in toilets. On dates. I mean, I don't usually have dates full stop.'

Stop talking, Holly. This woman doesn't want to hear your life story.

She shrugs. 'We all have those days.'

She seems very assured of herself. I wish I could be that confident.

As she turns to go, I realise with utmost horror that I'm running out of time that anyone could credibly have been in the loo. I'm going to have to walk out the door and return to the table and sit down and smile like nothing's wrong and make conversation with a man named Andrew for at least the next hour and a half, which, if I remember correctly from listening to colleagues in the office, is the absolute minimum that polite society dictates that I remain. It feels like an unmanageable task.

My chest heaves. I try to hold it in and fail miserably. My head starts to feel light and I find it hard to breathe in. With a crushing feeling, I realise I'm having a panic attack. Of course. I grip the sink to steady myself.

'Woah, woah.' I hear the woman's voice behind me. I thought she'd left and I find myself grateful that she's still here, even though I barely know her. 'Deep breaths. Bend down. Put your head between your legs.'

I obey her. She gingerly pats me on the back. 'Look, let me get rid of your date. Which one is he?'

'Wait, no . . .' Trying to speak is difficult when you're working just to get oxygen to your lungs. 'Don't. I'm fine.'

She snorts. 'Which one?'

I don't have the energy to fight her. 'He's . . . Glasses . . . Dark blue jumper.'

'Glasses. Dark blue jumper. Got it. Just keep breathing, all right?'

I nod, still staring at the bathroom floor between my knees. Someone's dropped a twenty-pence coin and I focus on it, trying to clear my mind. I hear the door swing open and footsteps. A minute later she comes back.

'He's gone.' She crouches down next to me. 'How's the breathing?'

'What did he say?' I ask. I'm managing to take air in and out more freely, but I can feel my stress levels creeping back up thinking about Andrew. Is he OK? I hope he doesn't feel too rejected. It was nothing to do with him. But of course, your date disappearing into the loo after ten minutes and never re-emerging cannot feel good. I feel terrible.

'Don't worry about him. Worry about you. Are you OK?' the woman asks.

I almost laugh. That's a big question right now, and I don't even know where to start. I take my head out from between my legs and sit back against the bathroom wall. I don't say anything for a while and just focus on returning my breathing to normal. I feel completely drained.

The woman sits against the wall beside me. For a moment, we both stare ahead at the cubicles. I bet this isn't how she was expecting her evening to go.

'I'm Holly,' I offer lamely.

'I'm Fliss,' she returns.

The door opens and another woman enters the bathroom. She frowns at us. God, we must look so weird.

'Are you waiting?' she asks.

'No, go ahead.' Fliss waves her hand towards the toilets.

'Oookay,' she says.

We sit in silence, listening to her pee. We share a look that feels almost conspiratorial. I want to ask Fliss about Andrew, but I'm conscious the woman in the cubicle can hear us. When she comes out she widens her eyes at her own reflection, as if to say to herself, *They're still out here? What the hell are these women on?*

'I'm sorry, I know this looks a little odd,' I explain. 'I had a mild panic attack.'

'Oookay,' she says and washes her hands. She leaves.

Fliss bursts out laughing. 'You don't have to explain yourself to random women in bathrooms, you know.'

'I'm not,' I defend myself quickly. 'I'm not normally like this, I promise. This is my first date in nearly a decade. And it was just . . . a little overwhelming. My partner and I are . . .' I gulp. What is this woman going to think? She will probably be shocked. But I'll never see her again in my life and I feel compelled to give some sort of context for my behaviour. 'Well, we're trying an *open relationship*. So it's all a little bit new and scary.' I whisper the words 'open relationship' for some reason.

Fliss turns to look at me, like I've said something that's struck a chord. She looks faintly amused. 'Again, you really don't have to explain yourself to random women in bathrooms.'

I smile. She's aloof yet strangely warm at the same time. 'So, really, what did you say to Andrew? How did he take it?' I ask.

Fliss brings her knees into her chest and pushes herself up. She dusts herself down and offers me her hand.

'He's fine. I told him you were throwing up from some kind of bug and he was out like a shot. Shall we eat?' she asks.

At her suggestion I realise how faint I am from the panic attack and from being too nervous to eat today. I could definitely use some sustenance.

'Weren't you about to go home?' I ask, taking her hand and hauling myself from the floor. Having dinner with a stranger I just met seems a little odd, and after the panic attack I feel like a battery on one per cent, but the thought of returning to an empty flat knowing that Will is still out on a date makes me feel so hollow that I'd rather be anywhere except home. Plus, this woman has an oddly calming presence. Nothing I've said or done seems to have fazed her in the slightest. Actually, she reminds me of Tomi; helping to sweep the worries to one side without making me feel like they're irrational.

'Come on.' She opens the door and I follow her back into the restaurant.

Andrew's and my table is still available. A bemused waitress reseats us and hands us menus.

51

'Should I message him?' I ask.

'Who?' Fliss scans the starters.

'Andrew, obviously.' I keep thinking about him on his way home, wondering if there's something wrong with him. He probably feels awful. 'If someone did that to me, I'd go home and cry.'

Fliss peers at me over the menu. 'I usually find that men's inflated egos and internalised bias confirmation help them to bounce back quickly,' she says. 'But sure, it might be polite to send a message.'

I get out my phone and start drafting something. By the time the waitress comes back I haven't had a chance to decide what I want. I don't want to keep Fliss waiting so I just point at something and then continue writing.

'Christ!' Fliss thumps her hand on the table. 'Are you retelling *The Odyssey*?'

'Oh.' I suddenly realise I've been ignoring her. 'I'm sorry. I'm so rude! I'll write it later.'

Fliss smiles and shakes her head. 'No, it's fine, carry on.'

I quickly finish my heartfelt apology to Andrew and press send. Then I put my phone away. I look at Fliss across the table, studying her chipped nail polish. It's *completely* bizarre that half an hour ago I was on a date and now some random blonde woman in a crop top is sitting in his seat. I guess it's a good story at least.

Not that I'll be telling *anyone* about this.

'So what do you do, Holly?' she asks. 'I mean, when you're not weeping in public toilets on a Thursday night.' She grins.

'Oh God. I'm not normally like this, I swear,' I protest again. 'I'm actually very regular. Average. Reasonably well adjusted. I can't remember the last time I cried in public. Well, OK, actually . . .'

Fliss laughs. 'Holly, I was *joking*. What do you do for a living?'

I feel myself relax. I genuinely don't think she's judging me at all. It makes *me* stop judging me, just a little.

'I work in fashion,' I explain. 'I want to be a designer.'

'Oh that's cool!' She wouldn't think it was so cool if she could see me making all of Amber's tech packs and chasing up lost fabric orders, but I smile anyway. 'Is it anything like *Devil Wears Prada*? Do you get to go to Fashion Week?'

'No,' I say honestly. 'I'm at a high-street brand, not high fashion, although maybe one day. What about you?'

'I'm a translator.' She reaches for a bread roll and tears off a chunk.

'Oh wow, what language?'

'Well, I studied French with Spanish. And I taught myself to speak German.'

That is so impressive. 'Oh my God. I can barely speak English,' I say.

She laughs and I can't help but feel a bit pleased.

'It's not easy. But if you can find the time I'd really recommend downloading Duolingo or something. There is nothing like being able to communicate in another language. That moment where it all clicks into place when you're becoming fluent is like opening a door to another world. And I love learning about all the little quirks of another place and words that don't even have an equivalent in English.'

'You must have a knack for it,' I add.

'I used to. But I'm actually trying to learn Japanese at the moment – my boyfriend's mum is Japanese, and he has family out there – and it's taking a lot longer.'

'Isn't that a whole different alphabet? I wouldn't be too hard on yourself.'

'Yeah, well, it's actually more complicated than that. It's like . . . three different writing systems . . . Still, it's not coming as quickly as it used to. I'm worried my brain is too haggard to learn anything new. I can hear it protesting like, *stop trying to learn new things, prepare for the urn.*'

'I'm sure you'll get there,' I encourage, cringing at how I sound like some sort of motivational meme.

'Eventually. So.' She pours out some oil and dips her bread into it. 'I mean, you don't have to talk about it but, what happened on your date?'

Oh God. I'd forgotten about it momentarily and the horror comes crashing back. 'Nothing really,' I say. 'I guess I'm just getting used to . . .' I'm still not comfortable talking about it, but I've already told her, and she didn't seem to react like it was a huge deal.

She looks up at me. 'The open relationship?'

I nod. 'I know it's a bit . . . I mean . . . I wouldn't have ever thought that *I'd* . . . But . . . I mean . . . we're nearly thirty and . . .' I tail off. I try to remember all of Will's reasons for wanting to do this, so I can echo them, but I'm still a little fuzzy on them. Something about not wanting to have any regrets and eliminating those regrets somehow solidifying our future. That's the key thing I hold on to.

'You don't have to defend yourself to me.' Fliss smirks. 'I've been in an open relationship for nearly three years.'

My jaw drops. '*Three years?*' I repeat. I'm elated to

meet someone else doing this. I knew logically other people did, but they seemed sort of like aliens. I assume there must be other life in the universe somewhere out there but I'm probably never going to come face to face with it. And she seems so . . . normal. Although, now that I think about it, I'm not quite sure what I pictured people in open relationships to be like.

I can't quite wrap my head around the fact that anyone could sustain an open relationship for three years. It seems like something you'd do for a couple of months, tops. Or in my case, ideally, one night and never again.

'Yup.' Fliss pops the oily bread in her mouth.

'How does it *work*?' I ask. I want to know it all. I'm hungry for every little detail. This woman can *help* me. And the best part of it is . . . she doesn't know me. She has no connection to any part of my life whatsoever! Everything I've been thinking about for the past fortnight, since Will suggested doing this, spills out of me.

'Do you live together? Do you know when you're out with other people? Do you talk about it? How long do you see other people for? Is it just about sex or do you have relationships with other people? What if you meet someone else you really like? Do you feel guilty? Do you get jealous?'

Fliss's eyes dart from side to side as if she's looking at all my questions tumbled out in a big pile in front of her and wondering how to sort through them.

'I'm sorry.' I don't want to overwhelm her. 'I just haven't felt able to talk about this to any of my friends.'

She makes an understanding *mm* noise. 'I can talk about how ENM works for me,' she answers diplomatically. 'But obviously, that might not work for you. I mean, only you know why you're doing it.'

Because Will wants to and if I don't he might leave me, I think, but I know that's not the right thing to say, so I just nod.

'But what happened tonight? What triggered you getting so upset?' She looks straight into my eyes.

'Uh, well, I guess he said something that reminded me of my boyfriend,' I admit.

'What was it?' Now done with the bread, Fliss goes in for the olives.

'Uh, well, he was moaning about work and he was saying all the same stuff that Will says. They're both graphic design-ers.'

Fliss reaches her hand out and beckons for my phone. 'Let's see.'

'My date?' I ask.

'Yeah. And your boyfriend.'

I get out my phone and hand it to her. 'Will is my back-ground. And that's Andrew's profile.'

She stares at them for a moment and then barks with laughter. 'This is the *same man*,' she says, through laughs. 'What?! Are you kidding? Are these men actually different?'

I feel indignant but her laughter is infectious. I smile too as I snatch my phone back. 'What are you talking about?' I squeal. 'Apart from their jobs they're completely . . .' I look at the photos and suddenly see what she sees. Two skinny, white, brunette men in muted cable-knit jumpers, identical tortoiseshell glasses and the same haircut.

'. . . Different,' I finish.

We both continue laughing.

'Oh my God.' Fliss nearly chokes and reaches for her water. 'OK, so, personally . . . my first bit of advice would be to step outside your comfort zone. What's the point of dating clones of your boyfriend?'

I'm still staring at the pictures of Andrew and Will. I can't believe I didn't see it. It's literally like trying to figure out who is who among the *Bridgerton* brothers.

'How long have you been with . . . Will, is it?' Fliss continues.

'Nine years,' I answer. 'We met when we were twenty.'

Fliss nods. 'Yeah, well, your first date in nearly a decade was always going to be a bit weird. Don't worry about it. Just . . . maybe pick someone a bit different next time. Try a graphic communicator instead.' Fliss laughs at her own joke.

Our starters arrive and we carry on eating and chatting. She's so confident, and she makes it all sound so easy and natural that, for a second, I almost start believing I can do it and it will be totally fine. It's *so* nice to have someone to talk to about this. Someone who knows nothing about me and doesn't judge me. Despite how disastrous this evening has been on paper, for the first time in weeks I feel a weight start to lift.

CHAPTER SIX:
DON'T TELL YOUR MUM

FLISS

I smile as I step off the bus. I guess tonight turned out to be a successful date after all . . . I mean, I got a number out of it.

I've thought about Holly – and her situation – most of the way home. Ah, two lovebirds embarking on their first experimentation . . . I'm not usually that interested in the intimate details of the personal lives of others. Normally, I'd really rather people kept their off-putting feelings to themselves. Please, bottle it all inside, then well up at the donkey sanctuary advert and pretend it's really about donkeys like everyone else. But it makes me happy to help someone else looking to free themselves from the oppressive unspoken rules of a society that blindly prizes monogamy above all other kinds of relationships.

It makes sense that she feels she can't talk to anyone about this – I choose to be up front with everyone in my life, but it's challenging. When I first started telling people, their reactions made me want to keep it secret, but I hate lying more than I hate uncomfortable conversations, so I made the call to just plough on through. A lot of people are overtly judgemental about it. Or some people pretend to be cool about it, but make awkward jokes like calling Ash my 'part-time' boyfriend. Sometimes, I genuinely think someone understands until they say something that implies Ash and I aren't in a serious, committed relationship. I am serious about Ash, and we are committed, just not in exactly the same way they are. Or people make assumptions, like we don't want to get married or have children, when I've never considered those doors closed to us. We could have an open marriage, we could have kids.

One time a colleague said to me, 'When you meet someone you want to settle down with . . .' Which basically implied that Ash and I are just each other's stop gaps until we find someone we like enough to be monogamous with. I replied that I like Ash so much that our bond is strong enough not to be broken by allowing ourselves to explore attraction to other people.

I don't think people are trying to be unkind; they just genuinely can't wrap their heads around it. To them, monogamy and commitment are synonymous. It blows my mind how many people are unhappy in their monogamous relationships and wouldn't even think to try another way.

Then I wonder . . . am I that person now? Am I the one being narrow-minded? Maybe monogamy could work for us . . . How will I know if I don't try it?

I'm so lost in thought when I open the front door that I barely manage to greet Jenny, who's watching *New Girl* and chuckling to herself. I grunt.

'Ahem, you have a visitor,' she calls out.

'Oh, is Ash here?' Another surprise visit? I'm partly delighted – it's been a *long* day and I'm desperate for the solace of climbing into bed with him – and partly flustered. Has he come back to ask for more? Coordinated outfits? A shared pet? Commitment to burning myself on a pyre should anything happen to him?!

Jenny points behind me. I notice a familiar green suitcase that, deep in my own self-involved rumination, I must have walked straight past.

My brother is here.

'Henry?' I call up the stairs, taking them two at a time. 'Hen?'

I rush into my room, where Henry is lounged across my bed, littering my duvet with Fruit-tella wrappers. Henry eats ridiculous amounts of chewy sweets like he's still five, but in every other respect he's a proper grown-up. Henry's been working for the same company since he graduated at twenty-one – something to do with financial something or other, I'm not entirely sure but he wears a suit – and at age twenty-six, he married Laura, whom he met at university. Two years later Laura was pregnant with Sam, who's now three. They have a dog, a cat and two guinea pigs called Mish and Mash.

I love my brother, but we are not similar.

'Fliss, sis.' Henry gets off the bed and gives me a long hug. 'Sorry, I'm making a mess up here. Jenny was watching *New Girl*.'

Hen has an unfair aversion to Zooey Deschanel because she looks like his first girlfriend.

'I understand,' I mumble into his shoulder, pleasantly surprised and comforted to see him. 'So, it got too late to go home?'

As soon as I ask, I realise that can't be true, because he came prepared with a suitcase. On a *very* rare occasion, when Henry has got drunk after work in the city and missed the last train back to Tunbridge Wells, he's stayed at mine.

Henry doesn't answer. He just sweeps up his Fruit-tella wrappers and puts them in the bin.

'Hen? Is everything OK?' I nudge.

He sighs. 'Laura and I are getting a divorce,' he says quietly.

I laugh, then realise how inappropriate that is when I see that he's not joking. He looks aghast at me.

'Oh God.' I clap my hand over my mouth. 'I'm sorry. I didn't mean to laugh I just . . . Fuck. *What?*'

Hen lowers himself back down onto the bed. I sit next to him. We both stare at the wall in front of us so we don't have to look at each other. Emotional conversations have never been our strong point as siblings and we both sense one coming on.

'You're not getting a divorce,' I state.

'We are.'

'You're not.'

'Fliss, this isn't helping.'

'You can't be. You're having problems. You're taking some space. You're not getting a *divorce*.'

'We've been having problems. We've taken space. We are getting a divorce,' he reaffirms.

'You can't have had space!' I fling my arms out, but still don't look at him. 'You live together!'

'I've been sleeping in the spare room. We've been going out more with our friends and taking turns to look after Sam. To be honest, at this point, we're living totally separate lives.'

Everything I thought I knew about Henry and Laura combusts. I've never even seen them have an argument. One time Henry forgot one of Laura's friends was vegan at a dinner party and bought all regular cheese and I saw her give him *a look*, but that's it. That's *all* the conflict I can think of in ten years.

'But . . . But . . .'

Hen turns to me, then, and puts his hand on my shoulder. 'Fliss, we haven't had sex in nearly two years.'

'Oh.' I turn back to him, his words finally starting to land. I guess they really are getting a divorce.

Fuck.

'I'm sorry I didn't tell you anything before. I feel bad dumping it all on you at once. But . . . I don't know. I kept putting it off. And by the time I accepted that it was time for me to move out, it had already been so long and well . . . now, here I am.'

I nod. It's not surprising. Our family have never been great at communicating. I'm only better now because Ash and I have such an understanding relationship and he's good at drawing things out of me.

'It's OK,' I say. 'But I'm still annoyed about the poem.'

Hen laughs. When we were at primary school he won a poetry competition and the headteacher read his poem in front of the whole school. It was about our pet rabbit – which I still believed had been adopted by some nice people in

Somerset – being crushed to death by our weird neighbour's pet snake.

'Ah,' he says. 'The peak of my creative writing career.'

He takes his hand from my shoulder and we sit in silence staring at the wall for a bit longer.

'Do Mum and Dad know?' I ask.

'No.'

Didn't think so. I don't question him further on that. He must be dreading telling them. I'd be petrified, although at least I'm used to disappointing them. I made the mistake of being honest about the setup of Ash's and my relationship when we first started dating. I was over the moon to have found something that seemed to be working so well for me and naively thought they would be pleased that I was happy.

They were not pleased.

Mum and Dad have taken against Ash ever since. They don't directly invite him to family occasions or ask about him. If he does come up in conversation they won't refer to him by name and Mum's left eyebrow slides all the way up her forehead. That arched eyebrow of disapproval is exactly why I stopped telling them anything about my life ever since.

But Henry is their darling eldest son who did everything they wanted at exactly the age they wanted him to. Henry has *never* disappointed them before. He won't be emotionally prepared for the eyebrow.

Fuck.

I have so many questions.

'What will happen with Sam?'

'He'll split time fifty-fifty between us. I'm going to get a house nearby.'

'How's Laura?' I say. 'Or, sorry, am I allowed to ask that? Do we hate Laura now?'

Hen smiles. 'We don't hate Laura. Laura is lovely. It's me.'

I wait for him to expand. He takes a breath and for a moment I think he's going to. But then he starts unwrapping another Fruit-tella and I decide maybe I've asked enough questions for one evening. He'll tell me more when he's ready.

'. . . Tea?' I manage.

Classic. When you can't think of anything helpful to say, hide behind a caffeinated beverage.

Hen nods. I get up and go downstairs, still trying to piece together this new, wild world where Laura and Henry don't sleep in the same bed and don't make each other happy. They won't be married anymore. Their futures had a colour and a shape and now they're blank and mouldable again. The places they're going to live are waiting to be found. The people they're going to meet next are out there, living their lives, waiting to be met.

First Ash wants to be exclusive, then I have dinner with a sobbing stranger I meet in the toilets and now Henry and Laura are getting a divorce. This week just keeps getting weirder and weirder.

I put the kettle on and close my eyes, leaning against the kitchen cupboards. I feel like everything's shifting around me in a massive vomit-inducing teacup-ride nightmare and I need it to stop.

'I'll have a lemon and ginger,' Jenny breathes right into my ear.

I open my eyes and leap back. How does she always walk

around the flat so silently? And why does she have such a poor concept of personal space?!

'Sure,' I say, leaning away from her and reaching for the cupboard behind me.

'Is *everything okay*?' Jenny whispers and points at the ceiling. She tries to sound concerned but can barely mask her low-level glee at the unexpected drama. Jenny loves a gossip.

'Not exactly,' I answer.

'How long do you think he'll be staying?' she continues when she realises I'm not going to share any further details.

'Um, good question. I'm not sure.'

I'm always cagey with Jenny. Still, she never gives up trying to squeeze me for information or pin down what nights I'm going to be home late so she can put her earplugs in.

I finish making Jenny and Henry their teas and head back upstairs. As I re-enter my bedroom, my phone buzzes.

It's Mum.

'Mum's calling me.' I wave my phone in front of Henry's face and go to answer it.

'Don't!' Henry yells. 'I've been dodging her calls.'

'She must know you're here, then?'

'Maybe. She might have spoken to Laura.'

'Well, if I don't answer I'll get the blame somehow.'

The phone stops buzzing. I put it down on the table. Five seconds later it starts ringing again.

'She definitely knows.' I grab for the phone, my palms sweating. Something about Mum calling always makes me afraid to answer, like some sort of naughty schoolchild hiding from a scolding. 'Hello?'

'Hello, darling? I've been trying to track Henry down. Is he there?'

Henry frantically swipes his finger across his neck in a knife motion.

'Uh, he is.'

Henry stops jumping around and glares.

'Why hasn't he been picking up his phone?' Mum demands. 'I don't . . .'

'Have you been distracting him?'

Ah, I love picking up the tab for other people's wrongdoings.

'He's just popped to the shops, Mum,' I say.

Henry presses his hands together as if in prayer and mouths 'thank you'. Then he dives face forwards onto the bed like a salmon and sticks his head under the pillow.

'*Oh*. Well, tell him to call me back. How are you, anyway? What have you been up to?'

'Uh, I was out for dinner.'

'With who?' Mum presses.

I always try vague honesty with Mum, but it never works. She always manages to back me into a corner so I'm forced to tell out-and-out lies, which I hate. 'With Ash,' I say. She doesn't love hearing about Ash, but she'd like hearing about my dates even less.

Henry pops his head out and widens his mouth in mock surprise.

'Ah,' Mum says. There's the little 'ah' every time Ash's name comes up, like she's disappointed he's still on the scene. 'What did you have?'

'Uh, a prawn risotto . . .'

My heart tugs with guilt, both at fibbing to Mum and because I haven't spoken to Ash at all today. Henry sits up and shakes his head at me. I take the pillow that he's displaced and hit him over the head with it.

'What's going on? Is that housemate of yours causing trouble?'

One time Jenny dropped a plate when Mum was in the house and she's never forgotten it.

'Errr, yes, she is actually. You know Jenny. I'd better go sort it out. I'll tell Hen you called.'

'OK, well, tell him I need to speak with him!'

'Bye, Mum.' I hang up.

'Liar, liar, pants on fire,' Henry sings.

'Says *you*,' I reply. 'You're going to have to tell her.'

'Why? You don't tell her anything anymore.'

'She'll figure out you're not living with your wife eventually.'

Henry's been putting on a brave face, but for the first time I see a hint of everything he must have been going through cross his face. When I look closer, I notice how exhausted he looks and how much older he seems than the last time I saw him.

'Distract me, please. What hot date were you on tonight?' Hen reaches for the pillow, places it behind his head and settles back. 'And how is Ash?'

'Date was a flop.' I sit opposite him on the bed and cross my legs. 'And Ash is . . . Well . . .'

Henry scrutinises my face. 'Oh God. Don't tell me you and Ash are breaking up as well?'

The irony. 'No, er . . . Well. Ash wants to . . .' I think about how to phrase this. 'Ash wants to be exclusive.'

Henry doesn't say anything, continuing to eyeball me as if to check I'm being serious. Then he hoots with laughter. 'Oh my God. Your *face*. You are endlessly entertaining, Fliss. You look like you're being dragged to the gallows.'

'I do *not!*' I sound about six. Why is it that no matter how old you get, you spend five minutes with your sibling and you're an actual child again?

'So you're considering it?' Henry goes on. It's unusual for him to ask me so many questions but I suppose we've opened the floodgates tonight.

'Yes.' My voice is still all petulant because he made fun of me.

'Nah.' Henry blows air through his lips. 'It's not you.'

'It could be!' I sulk.

'Nah,' Henry repeats.

'Oh, what do you know,' I mutter.

'True.' Henry laughs. 'Don't take advice from your divorcé big brother.'

It's a joke, but there's pain in it.

'Sorry,' I say. 'I didn't mean it like that.'

Henry reaches over and pats my knee. 'I know. Right, I'm going to get ready for bed.'

Hen brushes his teeth and I set up the camp bed for him on my floor, all the while thinking how strange it is that he's here and wondering how Laura is doing over in Tunbridge Wells. This memory pops into my head, of sitting at our local Chinese – I'm about fourteen and Hen is sixteen – and our dad opening a fortune cookie and reading out, 'The older

I get, the less I know,' then yelling, 'Don't I know it!' and guffawing and slapping his thigh.

Twenty minutes later Henry is fast asleep but I'm still wide awake. I listen to him snoring gently in the dark and am gripped with how fragile everything seems in light of this news. I try to imagine how I'd feel without Ash and feel sick. I have the overwhelming urge to speak to him. He's a night owl, so he won't be asleep yet.

I creep out into the hallway and dial his number.

'Fliss?' The sound of his voice puts me instantly at ease.

'Hi.' I lean back against the wall, beaming.

'You OK?' he asks, and I tell him about Henry arriving, and the bombshell he just dropped. Telling Ash makes it feel more manageable.

Somehow it feels like an age since I've seen him, and I miss him. Maybe he's right, maybe we do need more of each other. In this moment, processing the news of Henry and Laura's break-up, being exclusive with Ash doesn't feel so scary. Thinking of losing each other, like Henry and Laura somehow have, is what seems terrifying. If I like the idea of spending more time with him and I can't stand the thought of him not being around, then this seems like the obvious choice.

'Ash, I've been thinking about what you said,' I whisper, trying not to wake Jenny. 'And . . . OK. Let's do it.'

CHAPTER SEVEN:
COMMUNICATE

HOLLY

I open my front door cautiously, like I'm a burglar. I pause and listen, but it doesn't sound like Will is back yet. I'm not sure if I'm relieved or not. I'm apprehensive to see him, but his not being here must mean his date went better than mine, which hurts.

I tiptoe through the hallway and take off my shoes and perch on the sofa in the darkness. It feels like I'm in someone else's home, somehow. I shake myself. *You're being ridiculous, Holly. This is your home. You picked out that paint. You ordered those table and chairs. You bought those flowers.*

I lean back on the sofa where Will and I have sat most evenings for the last four years. It's an L-shaped sofa and Will usually sits to my left, on the corner bit, and I curl into his right side. I try to get comfortable but no position feels right. How do I normally sit on this sofa when Will isn't here? I wouldn't usually think about it but it suddenly feels unnatural. Like when you notice your breathing and inhaling becomes an effort.

I get out my phone and start texting Will.

When do you think you'll be back?

I hesitate before pressing send. Am I allowed to ask that? I would if he were out with his friends . . . But am I still allowed to have questions about his whereabouts when he's out on a date? My heart plummets. Oh my God . . . What if he doesn't come home at all?! I'd assumed that we'd both go out for dinner and then return home to be together, but I now realise that we didn't actually agree on that. We didn't agree on anything except that tonight was 'date night'.

Fliss and her partner seem to have everything worked out. They have lines, parameters, rules. They know where their boundaries are and how much they want to share with each other. Will and I don't know any of that! I feel myself getting stressed and then I remind myself that of *course* Will and I don't know any of that . . . Fliss and Ash have been doing this for three years. This is only day one.

God. Day one. How is it only day one? I feel about fifty years older than I did yesterday. How long do I have to keep this up until Will and I can just get married and be with each other? I dismiss the thought and pick up a fashion magazine. Will makes fun of me for being one of the only people who still buys them, but I love them. I love the chunky feel of them and the glossy sheen and the outrageous outfits, which just don't look the same online.

I always spent all my pocket money on them when I was growing up. I would flick through the pages, imagining the amount of detail and care that went into making them and how the models must feel putting them on.

I open up the pages of *Vogue* and breathe easier looking at the perfect details on a black dress with a corset top and floating tulle skirt, my brain spiralling with ideas for my own designs.

My phone goes off. I jump on it, hoping it's Will. It's Fliss.

Remember, communication! You need to know how each other are feeling!

Communicate. Communicate. Communicate. I repeat it to myself. After 'don't date clones of your boyfriend', 'communicate openly' was Fliss's next piece of advice. She said it's the only way that Will and I will figure this out, especially at the beginning. She suggested lots of good questions to ask that I hadn't even thought of, like how long we'd be doing this for and how long we'd be seeing other people. I am lost at sea and clinging to this random woman's instructions like Kate Winslet to her piece of door.

The key turns in the lock and my heart flutters. Thank God . . . he came home. And also . . . urgh, I don't want to hear about his date. But I think I have to?

Will's head appears round the living room door. 'Hello? Holly?'

'Hi, I'm here,' I say meekly. I have the overwhelming urge to jump up and hug him but I stop myself. I'm being silly.

I hesitate, hoping he will rush over and hug me instead.

Declare that this was a huge mistake. How could he have possibly had such an idea?! Thinking he could have any interest in anyone else was utter madness, even if it *was* for the greater good of our relationship . . .

'Why are you sitting in the dark?' Will switches on the main light. I suddenly feel ridiculously dramatic, sitting here ruminating in my dingy gloom cave.

I assess Will's outfit, which is nearly interchangeable with Andrew's, and stifle a giggle. But then I picture him dressing up to go on a date and my smile fades. One part of me is dying to know how his evening has been, but the idea of it makes me feel nauseous.

Will sits next to me on the sofa and puts his arm around me, but it feels stiff.

'Have you been waiting long?' he asks.

'Oh, no,' I answer. 'I just got in.'

He takes his arm away and starts undoing his laces. I can't tell if that's the answer he wanted or not. We sit in silence as he takes off his shoes.

I shift back into the corner of the sofa and he follows me, and we sit like we always do, with me tucked under his right arm. Except both our bodies are rigid. Neither of us seems to know how to act around the other. Why is he so tense? Is it – like for me – an adjustment to return home to me after being on a date, or has he met someone he's already fallen head over heels for and he feels guilty?

'And how was your evening?' He sweeps his free arm out, speaking in a grandiose voice, like he's a TV presenter. Sometimes when Will is uncomfortable he talks like that. It's endearing.

Well, within ten minutes I started crying and had a panic attack. My date left and I had dinner with a woman I met in the ladies' loos.

How honest is too honest?

'Fun . . .' I say. That's not exactly a lie. Surprisingly, I did have fun meeting Fliss, although it wasn't the evening I expected.

'Fun? Yeah?' A hint of hurt crosses Will's face.

'I mean . . . I . . . Not that much fun. Obviously, I would have had more fun with you,' I rectify. Oh God. This is a minefield. I thought he *wanted* me to go out and have fun?

'It's all right, Holly. You had *fun*.' It doesn't seem all right, though, from the venom he puts behind the word. His arm around me slackens, like he wants to pull it away. I've upset him. My heart melts.

'No, I didn't,' I garble. 'I lied. I actually left the date pretty quickly and had dinner with a . . . friend . . . instead.'

I realise I've been holding my breath and remember to breathe out. I can't stand upsetting Will, especially not when I didn't have fun at all.

'Aww.' Will's grip tightens around me. He rubs my shoulder. 'That's OK. First dates are shit. And it was your first date in years.'

For the first time this evening I begin to relax into him. Relief starts spreading through my limbs. 'First dates *are* shit,' I affirm. By the sounds of it, he didn't have fun either? Maybe we can put this behind us now. 'Oh well, at least we can say we tried it, right?'

And I did try. I tried really hard. I just couldn't make myself want to be there.

Will doesn't say anything. He gets up and pours himself a glass of whisky from the decanter he keeps by the window. I sense that I've said something wrong again. 'Well . . . I didn't mean giving up that easily,' he says to the wall.

Oh. My relief is short-lived. It's not over yet.

I wait for him to sit back down. 'Holly, this is important to me.' Will puts his drink down on the coffee table and clasps his hands together.

'I know,' I say. 'I know and I want to do it.' Not strictly true. I want to want to do it. 'I just . . .'

'I think this is important for *us*,' Will carries on. 'I want to have a future with you. I think this is something that I need to do first in order to make that happen.'

'I know,' I say. 'I know.' We've been over this. It's something that Will feels he needs to do and I want to be able to do it.

'But if you're feeling uncomfortable, then obviously I don't want you to be upset . . .'

'No. It was just the first date,' I insist. 'I can do this. I'll be fine.'

I'm aware of tears welling up but I'm determined not to let them spill over. In disagreements Will always seems to be able to keep his cool and I'm always the one who ends up letting my feelings get in the way of being rational.

Will nods. He takes both my hands and kisses them. I lean forward into his chest.

'What about you?' I mumble quietly into his shirt. 'Did you have a good evening? When are you thinking you want to do it again? Should we set a trial time period on this? And, are you . . .'

'Oh, we don't need to talk about that now. I just want you to feel better. Maybe when you're less fragile.' He puts both arms around me and gives me a squeeze.

I'm filled with warmth. Will can sense that I'm exhausted and he's protecting me.

'Shall we watch something?' Will asks.

I would love nothing more to watch something and forget all about this, yet I still feel like this is unresolved. Fliss said that talking about the ground rules was imperative, especially in the beginning.

'I don't know, can we keep talking about this first?'

'OK, what about?' Will holds my hand.

I get the impression that for him our chat is over, and in the pressure of leading the discussion my mind blanks. I know I want to keep going but I'm not sure what else I have left to say, so I just shake my head. I'm being silly. We can hardly keep talking about it if I don't know what it is I want to talk about.

'Never mind,' I say. 'Let's put the TV on.'

Will puts on *Squid Game* and I try to concentrate on it. I don't love it – too violent – but Will is enthralled. We lie back in our familiar position. Eventually, in the embrace of the man I've loved for nearly ten years, I start to re-anchor myself. My phone vibrates. It's Fliss again.

How did it go?

I think about how to reply. Well, we certainly didn't figure everything out tonight, but I said all that I could think to say and Will and I are lying entwined together as he strokes my hair. It's late. Will and I can talk again in the morning. Now that I have Fliss's advice, I know I can work this out eventually. I start typing.

Good. Thank you for all your help. xx

CHAPTER EIGHT:
DON'T FOCUS ON WHAT YOU'RE GIVING UP

FLISS

By the weekend, Henry is still sleeping on our sofa. Every day Jenny has asked me how long he's staying and every day I have mumbled some avoidant apology. Asking him means asking more about the situation with Laura and, although Henry has given the bare basics of their split, he hasn't gone into any more detail. I did ask why he couldn't go on sleeping in the spare room anymore, as he apparently has been doing for months, but I got a grunt in response.

Henry is at the shops and Jenny is watching TV in the living room. I've skilfully avoided her all day and I try to tiptoe behind her on my way out, but fail. She hears like a bat.

'Are you off to Ash's, then?' she asks without turning around.

'Er, yes,' I reply.

'On a Saturday?' She swivels round, her eyes narrowed in suspicion. 'What about your . . .' She pauses. 'Special friends?'

I try not to laugh. 'It's just going to be me and Ash from now on.'

Jenny's face lights up. 'Oh yay! That's such great news!' she exclaims. 'I love Ash!'

'Me too.' I beam back at her.

Wow. For once in my life I actually pleased Jenny. I hate to say it, but it feels nice.

'Well, have fun.' Jenny turns back to the TV. I wait for the inevitable question about how long Henry's staying, but then she says, 'Do you know when Henry's back?'

'Er, I don't. I'm really sorry. I've been meaning to talk to you about . . .'

'No, it's cool. Just trying to work out whether I should carry on watching *Vampire Diaries* without him.'

Vampire Diaries? Yet another person has found their way further into Jenny's heart, through mutual binge-watching, than I ever could. But at least she won't mind how long he stays now.

'Oh right, great, well, have fun. Back tomorrow,' I call as I slip out the door.

I get on the Northern line towards Ash's house, still cackling at Jenny's use of the term 'special friends'. I'm also picturing her joyous expression as she celebrated more Ash.

More Ash. I have to admit the thought makes me happy.

I'm holding onto the rail, somehow squished in the middle of a group of lads bizarrely listening to Yazoo, 'Only You', on repeat. I flick onto my messages where I see that Eric's icon has turned blank. Ah, of course . . . he's blocked me. Classic. I wonder how his party with his friends is going. I feel bad that we left it on such a sour note. I stand by that I did nothing wrong, but I could have handled the confrontation better. There's no point texting him now, though; I doubt it would lead to the closure that I'm looking for. I'd probably get accused of sending him mixed signals again.

With a lurch, I realise that may well have been my last date *ever*. And it lasted all of twenty minutes. We didn't even have sex.

I check myself. It's not my 'last date'. That's a stupid thing to think. I'll get to have more dates with Ash. And I love dating Ash. It was my last date with someone new, though, which is a totally different thing to someone you've been with for years.

One part of me feels lucky and excited, but I can't deny that the reality of giving up date nights with other people suddenly hits me in full force. I try to brush it aside and focus on how much I love Ash and how much extra time I'm going to get with him, but dear God I really wish those boys would stop playing 'Only You' over and over. It is *not* helping.

When I finally get to Ash's and he opens the door, all of that drains away. He's wearing his Totoro onesie, firstly, but also he smiles at me like he can see every last one of my unappealing personality traits and somehow the sight of me still pleases him. Like he'd go to the supermarket with me a hundred thousand times and still find me interesting. Love is a funny thing, isn't it. Sometimes I'll be sitting around the house eating a yoghurt and Ash will stop, fascinated, like, *oh my God you're mesmerising* and I'll be like, *pal, I'm just eating a yoghurt.*

Ash brings me in for a hug and the smell of his aftershave

and the feel of his chest on my face make everything else stop mattering.

'Hi,' he mumbles into my hair as he holds me.

'Hi.' I clutch his onesie.

Ash lives alone and his flat is always serene and noise-free, unlike mine at the moment. We go to his living room and I settle down on the sofa amongst Ash's millions of plants as he goes to get snacks. It's a bit of a crime that Ash lives in a city when he has such a yearning to garden. Unlike me, who bought a plant once and – to quote Jenny – 'killed it off at impressive speed'. He's been on the wait list for an allotment since forever but they're a rarity in London.

I stare into his goldfish tank at all the little fish swimming around. Ash also really wants a dog but he's not allowed one because of his landlord.

Ash comes back with a bowl of Doritos and we sit opposite each other with our legs entangled, and dive straight into dissecting his week. He finished two books; Ash reads at an alarming rate. He's been having an uphill battle with the triplets in Brixton and their father, who won't cooperate. His friend Kai adopted a kitten and didn't realise the person they're dating is allergic to cats. His friend Emily cooked him a new recipe from *Saturday Kitchen*. His sister Sara is stressing that 'nothing has been done' for her wedding but it's still eighteen months away. I soak up all the gorgeous, mundane details of the last few days that I've missed.

'Sara's problem has always been that she wants to do everything herself until she realises she can't do everything herself and then suddenly "no one is helping".' Ash laughs, crunching into a tortilla chip.

I laugh but I don't want to agree *too* emphatically, because mocking your own family is never permission for someone else to join in. It's true, though. At her and Ava's engagement party she told me to 'sit down and relax' then demanded to know why I hadn't refilled the nuts.

'How's Ava coping?' I ask.

Ash thinks for a second. 'She looks a bit like Kai did when they tried to go hiking.'

Kai wore thigh-high, heeled boots to climb a mountain, got separated from their group and returned seven hours later with one boot and a lot of twigs in their hair.

'Poor Ava . . .'

'Yup. But she knew what Sara was like when she proposed, so.'

'True.'

'What about you?' Ash asks, submerging another chip in dip. 'What did you do today?'

'Well, I carried on with my Japanese course.' I've been letting it slide because it's so difficult, but it would be unbelievably nice to be able to have a proper conversation with Ash's grandmother when she calls. She is very sweet and always wants to speak to both of us but I usually end up just sitting there like a lemon. When I get to a certain level the plan is that Ash and I will continue learning together, as he'd like to get better at speaking it, too. His mum did teach him some as a kid but, being a human-rights barrister, she's pretty busy so his primary carer was his white dad.

'Oh cool!'

'Eh, I shouldn't have left it so long. I'm a bit rusty now.'

'You'll pick it up again. You have a knack for languages. It's incredibly annoying.'

Ash tried to learn Spanish when we went to Spain last year – bless him – but he never got past stumbling over stilted phrases from the guide book.

'It was hard to concentrate with Henry around to be honest . . .'

Even though he's not messy, there just isn't enough space in my bedroom for the camp bed and all his stuff. And he's not loud, but when I'm learning I need total silence and every so often I hear him chewing on a Fruit-tella and I remember all those years of trying to do homework with the same distracting sound and wanting him to choke on one.

'Oh my God, yes. Henry.' Ash gives up reaching for the Doritos and just brings the bowl over to his lap. 'Did you find anything else out?'

I fill him in on everything that's been happening and spend the next half an hour speculating about Henry and Laura, in that totally useless way where you have no new information but it feels good to analyse what you do know over and over until you've completely bored the other person to tears.

'I just . . . What happened?' I'm still ranting when it gets to midnight. 'Surely it can't be that terrible? Henry's not a cheater.'

'Did he get them into debt?' Ash suggests.

'It can't be to do with money . . . Henry's good with money. He works in finance! Unless he has a secret gambling problem? But . . . Hen's always been so sensible.'

'Do you think he's gay?'

'I don't think so.'

'Laura?'

'Maybe? But Hen definitely made it sound like it was more to do with him.'

Ash frowns and presses his lips together. Theorising has got us nowhere, obviously, but I'm ten times lighter having talked everything through with Ash. Ash who cares about my problems as much as I do.

I suddenly realise how shattered I am. We've been talking for hours.

'It's late,' I say. 'Shall we go to bed?'

Ash's head is drooping in his Totoro onesie. 'Yep. Come on, you.'

We brush our teeth next to each other and I stare at him in the mirror, marvelling at how sexy he is. The first time I saw Ash I couldn't stop staring at him like a creep and, three years later, that hasn't changed.

After getting changed, we climb into bed and lie facing one another in the darkness. It's freezing cold and I warm up my feet on his legs. He takes both of my hands under the covers and rubs them together to heat them up.

'Hey, so what you doing this Thursday?' he mumbles.

'Thursday is . . . *Oh*.' I keep forgetting. But it's only day three. I'll get used to it. 'Nothing. Seeing you?'

'Hope so. There's this film I think you'll like on at the Picturehouse.' His lips find mine and he kisses me softly, and a little thrill runs through me imagining how much more we're going to get to do this now.

Ash rolls over to fall asleep. I'm just thinking what a lovely Saturday night this has been, when a notification from one of my dating apps pops up, lighting up the dark room. Some guy

I was chatting to last week – a journalist called Karl – wants to know if I'm free next Thursday. I write back that I'm not, then I curve myself around Ash's back, but as I try to sleep I can't help but feel a flicker of disappointment.

CHAPTER NINE:
STEP OUTSIDE YOUR COMFORT ZONE

HOLLY

When I emerge into the kitchen on Sunday morning, Will is making breakfast and listening to BBC Radio 6. He looks solemn as he scrambles the eggs and adds various herbs, as if he's doing something momentously important. Will looks like this doing most things. It's highly endearing.

I don't make half as much effort with breakfast as Will does. I usually come down late after Will – he's an early riser and I prefer to sleep in – and just grab cereal. I sit down at the kitchen table and pour myself some Shreddies.

'Morning,' I say.

'Hello.' Will puts a piece of bread in the toaster. I watch him for a while, mustering courage to restart Thursday night's conversation. I'm itching to find out more and I'm desperate to know what to do next. Is Will seeing the person he saw on Thursday again? Is he going to meet someone new? Do we organise another 'date night', like last time? Or was that just to get us started and now it's a free-for-all and I'm supposed to go out with other people at any time I want?!

'So, I realised . . . I didn't get to hear much about your evening,' I venture. 'How was it?'

Will is silent as he takes the pan off the heat and butters his toast. For a second I think he hasn't heard me, but then he says, 'I still think it's best if we don't talk about it. I don't want to upset you.'

I'm disappointed, especially as he knows how *my* evening went. But I suppose that makes sense . . . He's only trying to save my feelings. Fliss did say to communicate but also that knowing *what* to communicate was important. Do I really want to hear about whether Will had a good time on his date with another woman? I mean, yes – it's all I've been thinking about for days – but possibly only for self-destructive reasons. Maybe he's right . . . I would only get upset, and why would I want to make myself sad?

'OK, you're probably right,' I admit. 'OK, well . . . And . . . Should we agree on another date night, then?'

I don't *want* to go another date. But I want to know what I'm supposed to be doing.

Will finishes serving his lavish breakfast. He sits down opposite me at the kitchen table and starts eating. It smells incredible. 'Yeah,' he says through a mouthful. 'I wrote it on the calendar, sorry, I thought you'd see. How's Tuesday?' he asks.

I glance at the calendar, where under Tuesday's date he's written *Will: Out?* I was expecting another conversation, like last time, but I guess it's stupid to expect a whole discussion every time we go out with someone else.

It occurs to me that if he's organised another date this quickly, he must be seeing the same woman again, surely. Twice in one week. The revelation is like a little stab in my gut, but I'm determined not to show that I'm upset, and appear up for it.

'Tuesday?' I repeat. 'Yes. OK.'

'Cool.' He chews another forkful of eggs.

As he continues eating, I look for signs he's falling for this other woman who he felt compelled to meet twice within one week. His focus on his plate means he's avoiding eye contact because he feels guilty. His looking out the window means he's thinking about her. His sigh means that he'd rather be with her. When he gets up and kisses me before going to take a shower, it's half-hearted because he'd rather be kissing her.

Ugh. I'm definitely overanalysing. We don't usually stare at each other while we eat breakfast. Will always sighs a lot . . . He's a sigher. Couples who have been together nearly a decade can't kiss like they mean it every single time. We're the same as we have been for years. We're solid. We're *good*. This is just something Will needs to get out of his system and once it's done it will be just us forever.

I sit nibbling at my Shreddies but my appetite has dwindled and they've turned to mush. Ten minutes later Will reappears in the hallway. 'Ready?' He points at the front door.

Will and I have a dependable Sunday routine. Normally we go for a long walk around Brockwell Park. Will makes his own coffee using his AeroPress Go and takes it in his carry cup. I usually buy a latte or a mocha at the local café and Will lovingly pokes fun at me for not drinking real coffee. Then if I'm meeting Tomi for brunch, like today – we have a monthly brunch date for a proper catch-up outside work – Will walks me to the café where I'm meeting him, then heads back to get started on making a lengthy Sunday roast.

Today, as I observe Will feeding the ducks and lick froth from the side of my cup, I can almost trick myself into feeling like everything's the same. I love our muddy morning walks, our wholesome Sunday roasts. I'd never questioned our life together before. Except, watching Will hurl chunks of bread into the water, I'm overcome with the painful worry that this isn't enough for him after all.

Of course it is, Holly. He's not breaking up with you. He's doing this for us. I shake myself, and nestle into Will's side.

Ten minutes later, I'm being pulled into a hug by Tomi.

'You two are cute as ever on your little morning coffee runs. We love to see it.' Tomi nods at Will's retreating back as he begins walking home.

I don't reply and pretend to concentrate on hanging my coat on a hook.

'First things first.' Tomi identifies a table. 'Priya just messaged that she doesn't want to come in on Monday, after all the Slack drama. She thinks she's not going to pass her probation.'

'Slack drama?' I repeat.

'Oh, I can't *believe* you haven't heard this story already.' Tomi pulls out a chair and takes off his scarf, sitting down. 'What are you doing when you're in the office? Like, actually working?'

'Pretty much,' I say.

'Tragic. Thank God you have me. *Well,*' Tomi continues as I sit down opposite him, 'apparently Gina from marketing and Mel and Eloise from sales have a private thread . . . You know, as you do . . . But because Priya – you know, the new girl on fourth?' I nod, even though no, I do not know Priya. I am not nearly as sociable as Tomi, who somehow manages to talk to everyone in the building and remember the names of their partners and children and first pets. 'Anyway, because her Slack account is new, there was some malfunction where she could see all these private chats and she didn't even realise they were private, because she's never had Slack before.'

'Oh God.' I'm getting second-hand embarrassment already.

'*Yeah.*' Tomi puts his hand up as if to say, *wait for it*.

The waitress comes over and once we've ordered food and mimosas, Tomi carries on.

'So basically, Trish was training Priya and running through all the Slack threads and what they're used for, and Priya – God bless her heart – pointed at this extra one and was like, what's *this* one for? And then Trish opened it and . . . Oh. My. God. Holly, you don't even want to *know* what was in there.'

'I do, obviously,' I say.

'Well, obviously.'

Tomi tells me the whole story. It sounds like Gina, Mel and Eloise are basically the three witches of sales and marketing and had all sorts of scandalous stories about people all across the department. Secrets you would not want Trish – head of sales and marketing – to be reading.

'Anyway, she called them each in individually and their Slack privileges have been revoked and it's a whole Thing,' Tomi finishes.

I shudder. 'Can you *imagine* if someone read ours?' I say.

'Right?' Tomi agrees. 'There's a lesson to be learnt here. Keep it to WhatsApp. Except I wouldn't mind if Lara Pearse saw that you basically do Amber's entire job.'

'I wouldn't say I do her *entire* job . . .' I say in defence.

'You absolutely do. OH. By the way. I decided where I'm going to have my thirtieth birthday . . .'

'Oh yay! Where?'

He gets out his phone. 'I'm going to book the restaurant in Mayfair, and then go on dancing at the place Jay was talking about the other day, you know, the one with the roof garden . . .'

I nod again. It looked pretty. He starts showing me pictures of a very fancy place that looks like it could be on *Made in Chelsea*. Tomi doesn't usually make a big effort for his birthday but I have a feeling that his thirtieth is going to be memorable. He even invited Alice from Accounts.

'It's Saturday, the fifth February, OK?'

'Why not your actual birthday?' Tomi's birthday is the twelfth.

'I'll be in Nigeria,' he answers.

'Oh yay!' I clap. Tomi's mum and dad moved to the UK before Tomi was born but he has extended family over there and he's not visited in years.

'Yeah, I'm excited.'

I open up my calendar on my phone. 'OK, got it. *Tomi's birthday dinner and dancing.* So, is Jay coming?! How's it going with you two?'

Tomi has been seeing Jay for two months. They met when both reached for the last avocado in Tesco. I think this is cute, but Tomi is forever disappointed that it makes them such a millennial cliché. He sometimes tries changing the story to broccoli.

'Oh it's good,' he says. 'But I'm a bit nervous about him meeting all my friends at once. I don't know if we're quite *there* yet, you know, and normally I'd want to do it gradually. One at a time or at least one group or something. But I can't really not invite him to my thirtieth birthday, can I?'

I ponder this. 'No,' I say honestly. 'Probably not.'

'At least Mum and Dad aren't coming. They relented because of our trip. There'll be big celebrations.' Tomi puts his hand on his heart in relief. 'But you know who *is* coming?'

'Who?'

'Isabella,' he says in a low tone.

'OH.' I make a face. 'Really?'

Tomi dated Isabella before Jay. They went out for about six months and it didn't end very well. But they're in the same group of mates from Tomi's French class – Tomi really does make friends everywhere he goes – so he found it too awkward not to extend the invite.

'I wasn't expecting her to say yes,' I remark. 'Given how she moved tables and refuses to make eye contact.'

'Yeah,' Tomi concedes. 'Me neither.'

'Maybe she wants to bury the hatchet.'

'Maybe she wants to show up looking phenomenal and make out with one of my friends right in front of me,' Tomi grunts. 'Also, am I supposed to introduce her to Jay?'

I shake my head in ignorance. I'm notoriously terrible for dating advice because I've never really dated. Well, until now, I suppose. But I'm not sure running to the loos crying after meeting the identical twin of my current boyfriend qualifies me yet.

'I'm nervous,' Tomi says. 'I can't watch them all night and I feel like Isabella is exactly the kind of person to go up to Jay and make a below-the-belt comment. But you'll be there, right? You can run over and intervene if you see her on the prowl?!'

I nod. 'Oh, absolutely. Consider me Jay's bodyguard.'

'Thank you.' Tomi grips my arm in relief. 'I can always count on you. Anyway, enough about me . . . Do you have something you want to tell me?' He puts his palms on the table and leans forward conspiratorially.

I feel like a giant spotlight is shining on me. I'm exposed, naked on stage. *How does he know?!*

'I . . . er . . . what?! What do you mean?' I try to sound casual.

'You've been acting weird for weeks,' Tomi comments. 'My first guess was that you were pregnant but you just ordered that mimosa, so.'

I exhale. My pulse rate starts to return to normal. *He doesn't know.*

'No, definitely not pregnant.' I laugh and it comes out like Tommy Wiseau's.

'So what's up?' Tomi leans his head to one side. 'You and Will seem to have been going out loads recently. I love it. Super romantic. I kind of thought . . . Maaybe . . .' He raises his eyebrows and points to his ring finger.

I force my mouth into a smile. My cheeks feel heavy. 'No!' I inject energy into my voice, even though I feel like a walrus just sat on my vocal cords. 'Oh my God, no! We're not even *thinking* about that.'

Ugh, I overplayed that. I should have denied it with less vigour. I suppose it's not technically a lie. I was thinking about it until Will dropped his bombshell, but I'm not thinking about it *now*. I mean, it's still the ultimate goal, but a demonstrably more distant, fuzzy one.

'Right.' Tomi doesn't appear convinced. Probably all those bridal websites he caught me looking at earlier this year. 'Well, forgive me. I'm just too keen to dance to Robbie. I feel like that's only acceptable at weddings. I mean, when he tours *no one* wants to go with me, because that would mean admitting they like him, but stick it on at a wedding and suddenly everyone's his number one fan.' He points two fingers at his eyes, then at mine. 'I see you.'

I'm grateful to him for going along with my pretence and making this about Robbie Williams. But I'm not out of the woods yet.

'How are you and Will, though?' Tomi asks. 'I mean, weddings aside?'

I flounder. How am I supposed to answer this question? I can't convincingly tell him that we're great.

I'm nearly saved by the arrival of our mimosas. The waitress puts them on the table in front of us and Tomi gets distracted by the gaudy little umbrella floating in his drink. But thirty seconds later he's asking me about Will again.

I deflect, badly, but I can feel myself starting to get hot. He knows me well, he knows something is up and he's not going to let it go.

My phone buzzes and I see I have a notification from some guy called Ian saying 'hey.' I don't want to be mean – we're all trying our best, aren't we? – but can he really not think of anything else to open with?

'Will?' Tomi points to my phone.

I think about answering him honestly. *No, it's not Will, it's some guy called Ian who wants to exchange mundane pleasantries in the hope I might be that one person out of eight billion others who can fill his own specific kind of lonely void. Or maybe he just wants to bang. Who knows.*

Ugh. Pressure is building in my chest. Sneaking around, feeling perpetually confused, actively lying to my friends. This is all too much.

'Are you OK?' Tomi asks.

I have a strong urge to tell Tomi the truth. But then I imagine the look on his face, the questions, the secret judgement. And I don't mean judgement-judgement, like with our other engaged and married friends; I don't think Tomi's going to be cutting behind my back. But friends *always* judge, no matter how well meaning they are. They can't not. They know you. They know your history and your dreams and desires and all your little expressions that give you away. Tomi will realise I don't *really* want to do this within five seconds flat and try to talk me out of it. But the thing is, I do want to do it, because I want my relationship with Will to work. So really, that *is* wanting to do it. But I know Tomi won't see it like that.

Plus, I've barely got my own head around it yet. Where would I even begin explaining it to someone else?

'Yeah, I'm fine.' I make my voice sound light. 'Show me the pictures of the place with the roof terrace again?'

Thankfully, he drops it, and we spend the rest of lunch planning his birthday party.

When I get home, the smell of roast chicken stuffed and rubbed with fancy herbs fills the air. Normally I would take delight in these habitual, homely smells, but all I can think about is how I need to find myself a date for Tuesday.

I take myself to the living room and open up the dreaded app on my phone. I remember what Fliss said about straying outside of my comfort zone. OK . . . someone unlike Will.

I have a look through who's 'liked' me this week. I haven't 'liked' someone first yet. I'm terrified of being rejected, especially when I didn't even want to be on here in the first place. Ian – the guy who said 'hey' – has a Will vibe so he's an instant no.

I go to the second guy. His name is Pete. He's got a regular haircut that's in no way trying to be fashionable, so already different to Will. He looks quite sporty; lots of pictures of him playing tennis and football . . . Not my usual type at all. I mean, like all cis-gendered heterosexual white men in their early thirties, Will occasionally goes climbing but to call him 'sporty' would be a stretch.

I look at the message Pete has sent me. 'Fancy crazy golf next week? Loser buys first round.'

Well, that seems fair.

'Tuesday?' I write back.

He sends a thumbs-up emoji, which I take as confirmation. Done. He's a) a man who looks nothing like Will and b) wants to meet in person quickly without making any initial small talk. I had to chat to Andrew for *three days* before he asked me out. This way, it means I don't have to keep looking through any more profiles and can avoid thinking about the date entirely until I actually have to go.

Having still not told Tomi anything, I feel like I need to tell *someone*, so I text Fliss.

I have another date on Tuesday.

As soon as I send it I cringe. Will she care? Or will she think, why is this oddball still oversharing with me? But then I remind myself that our meal together was her idea and she did message me later that night.

She replies quickly.

Ooh, that was fast! Not another Will clone?

No. He appears to like golf.

Haha. A great start.

Talking to her is such a solace that I find myself asking if she'll meet me afterwards. I won't dread the date as much if I know I can debrief with Fliss as soon as it's over. I feel a little silly, especially when she doesn't reply for ten minutes or so and I think I'll never hear from her again, but then she says:

Sure. Let me know where to meet you!

I breathe. Tuesday will be fine. Whatever happens, my evening will be salvageable.

For the next couple of days, I successfully put the date out of my mind. I notice that I'm much less nervous about meeting Pete than I was about meeting Andrew. With Andrew I put so much thought into the selection of and preparation for the date. I analysed every detail of his profile, I obsessed over every message I sent and what to wear and how to act.

I've barely looked at Pete and therefore cannot imagine him well enough to wonder what he'll think about me, which is quite freeing. Who knows what Pete is like? This man that I shall be hitting balls into tiny holes with, using giant sticks, mere days from now. I'm trying it Fliss's way – rolling the dice with zero expectations – and it feels so freeing. Look at me go. I'm *experimenting*.

CHAPTER TEN:
ACTUALLY READ
THE PROFILE

FLISS

I approach the café where I'm supposed to be meeting Holly. When she texted me saying she had another date lined up and would I mind meeting her afterwards for a debrief, I found myself welcoming the invitation, despite having enough of my own problems to focus on right now. Maybe it's searching for a blissful escape from Henry's incessant Fruit-tella chewing. Maybe it's because giving her advice is making me feel in control, when recently I feel anything but. Or maybe it's because I'm saying goodbye to the thing she's leaping into, but for some reason I'm irrationally invested in this woman's love life. I really want it to go well for her.

I think as well . . . Ugh, and I *hate* admitting this, but I'm also curious about whether she might have some advice for me. Every time someone pops up on my phone I have to resist the urge to answer and it's not getting easier. If anything it's getting harder.

I thought about reaching out to some of my friends but a lot of them I've not seen in a while, because they live so far away, and it feels like a lot to dump on them via text. Henry's marriage has just broken down so I feel terrible going to him for relationship advice. Plus, I know he's sceptical about my ability to be in a monogamous relationship, and I don't want to prove him right. Holly's got no preconceptions about me or Ash. She's been so open with me about her life; when I met her she was literally having a panic attack. And she did this for nine years, so she must have *some* answers. I feel like if I can come to anyone, it's her.

She's already inside; I recognise her pixie haircut and clogs from the window. She's staring into space with a haunted look in her eye.

I guess her date didn't go well.

'Hey,' I say, coming up behind her. She jumps and spills tea over a big glossy magazine. I didn't know anybody still bought those.

'Hi!' She leaps up. 'Thanks so much for meeting me. I know it's a bit . . . Well.' She reaches forward and hugs me like she's squeezing a long-lost relative. It makes me feel bad about the awkward shoulder pat she gets in return. I didn't come from a family of huggers. The only person I'm truly comfortable hugging is Ash.

'I wanted to come,' I say truthfully.

She smiles warmly and we sit down opposite each other in cosy red-and-brown armchairs. It's a quirky, vintage-style café with old-lady lampshades that appears to double up as a bar in the evening and serves cocktails out of teapots. Even though I don't know her well, it feels very Holly.

'So, bad date?' I ask.

'*Yes*.' Holly sinks back into the chair like she wants it to swallow her. 'The worst. How did you know?'

'You're early,' I say. We were supposed to meet at eight. It's quarter to. She can only have met the guy at six.

'Ugh,' Holly moans. 'It felt like it went on for *years*.'

I wrinkle my nose in sympathy. 'The bad ones always do. What happened?' I shift around to get comfortable, eagerly awaiting her to tell me about her evening.

'OK, so when I got there I was actually feeling pretty good. I was riding high on confidence. Or at least, I hadn't done any nervous wees. I was thinking, this has *got* to be better than the last date, at least.'

I cringe. 'Worse than having a panic attack in a public toilet? It must have been really bad.'

She cringes back. 'So I saw him – Pete – leaning up against a wall in the waiting area, scrolling through his phone. His hair was *completely* different to Will's!'

I resist the urge to laugh because she seems so genuinely pleased with herself.

'We went to collect our golf clubs and balls and went to the bar. He was talking about his tube journey here and how there was a "massive dog" in his carriage that looked like a wolf. All perfectly polite, pleasant conversation. I was thinking, *we're off to a good start . . .*'

'And then?'

'And then I offered to buy him a drink and he wouldn't let me. At first I thought he was just being really polite but then he got kind of defensive . . . Eventually he said, you're not a feminist, are you? And laughed.'

'Noooo.'

'And it didn't get any better from there. I just don't understand.' Holly massages her temples. 'How can someone go on a date and ask . . . *no* questions about the other person?'

I laugh. I can tell from her bafflement that she hasn't been on a lot of dates. I'm so used to feeling like the naive little sister to know-it-all big brother Henry that I'm quite enjoying this switch-up of dynamic. I barely know her, but something about her presence is uniquely comforting. I don't know if it's that she seems to be as much in limbo as me – even though I've made the commitment to Ash, my feelings about the decision are still vacillating – or that her innocent questions make me feel wise, or that she's just so genuine, but I am feeling more drawn to her company than anyone else's right now.

'So this was your experimental guy?' I go on. 'Your wild card?'

'Yes.' Holly nods. 'I guess it doesn't work for me. Maybe I have a type and that's that. Maybe Will is the only . . .'

'Woah, woah, woah.' I beckon for her phone. 'Back up. Show me the profile.'

She reluctantly hands it over. I scroll through pictures of an average-looking white brunette bloke eating steak, playing golf, tennis . . .

'What? What do you think?' Holly moves her head from side to side, trying to peer at her phone upside down.

'Yeah, I don't know, he looks . . .'

Then I get to the gold.

'I'll like you if . . . *you're good with balls*,' I read out loud. 'Holly, Holly, Holly.' I shake my head.

'What?! Does it say that?' Holly snatches the phone back, eyes wide in horror. 'Oh my God. Oh my God!!!'

I honk with laughter. 'Holly!! When I said go outside your comfort zone I meant . . . I don't know . . . date an intense musician or a . . . hippie surfer . . . Not a LAD.'

Holly is still staring at her phone like she can't believe what she's seeing. I keep snorting.

'Did you even *read* this man's profile?!' I ask once I've recovered.

'Errrrr.' Her cheeks turn a little rosy. 'Not really. I just . . . kind of . . . said yes to the next man who asked?' She slaps her forehead. 'Oh my God! I'm such an idiot!'

'No.' I wave my hand dismissively, eager to make her feel better. 'Well, I mean, yes. But to be honest apps do feel completely random anyway, sometimes. I've had some of the best dates of my life with people I could barely muster the enthusiasm to meet and some of my worst letdowns have been people I thought I had a spark with from messaging. One man I texted for nearly a month had a surprisingly squeaky voice. It's hard to tell.'

Holly smiles gratefully.

'Maybe just do a basic red-flag check next time, though,' I add, and we both start laughing again.

'Ughhhh. If you're *good with balls*.' Holly leans forward and puts her head in her hands. 'It's not even original. I could have saved myself an hour and fifteen minutes of pure pain.'

'You added an extra fifteen minutes to the obligatory hour,' I comment. 'Classy.'

'I thought an hour and a half was minimum?' Holly mumbles through her fingers.

'Nah.' I shrug. 'If I'm not attracted to them they aren't getting a second over sixty minutes.'

'Ugh,' Holly mutters, propping her head up on her elbows. 'Dating is *awful*.'

I assess her moping in front of me, slumped forward, cupping her cheeks in her hands. When I met her the other night, I assumed her reaction to her bad first date was just anxiety. I imagine it's hard to launch yourself back into dating after that many years exclusively with someone, even if you want to. Especially if you're a shy person. No, she's not shy exactly . . . Maybe gentle is more the right word. But something in her last comment makes me wonder why this woman actually *is* doing this.

'Can I ask, Holly . . .' I lean towards her and clasp my hands together. 'What it is that you're looking to get out of this?'

She looks like a deer caught in headlights and her eyes dart from side to side. Then she catches herself and neutralises her expression.

'I mean . . . What do you mean?' she stumbles.

'Well . . . Is it just flirting? Sex? An emotional connection?'

Holly looks blank. Her bottom lip quivers. 'I . . . What is it for you?' she deflects.

'For me it's all of the above, I guess. Except I don't love other people – I'm not exactly polyamorous – but it's not just about sex either. I like to get to know people. But I get all different things from different people,' I say.

She still looks impassive, so I add, 'Liiike . . . living in different cities. I can't imagine staying in one place forever, no matter how much I love it.'

'How long have you been in London?' Holly asks.

'A few years now. Before that I was in Paris. Before that Barcelona. Before that New York . . .'

'New York! Wow. I've always wanted to go. That must have been amazing?!' Holly's eyes shine. She's cleverly changed the subject, but she's not getting away that easily.

'Yeah, yeah, it's magical.' I remain monotone. 'But what about *you*?'

Holly crosses her legs, then uncrosses them again. Her eyes shift around the room and she pouts a little as she concentrates, like she's sifting through her brain for something to say.

'If you haven't worked it all out yet, that's also—'

'*Sex*,' she interjects decisively.

OK. Not the answer I was expecting.

'Sex?' I repeat.

She nods firmly, but her face looks a bit like my childhood Barbie doll when I stepped on its head. I'm not convinced. Still, appearances are deceptive. Her being timid means nothing. We know so little about other people, really. Plenty of people are probably interested to sexually experiment but too anxious to ever do it. Good for her.

'OK.' I tilt my head to one side as I consider this new information. 'Well . . . that's . . . good. Maybe just date with that in mind? I think knowing what you want out of the experience is important for open relationships to work. If you go in confused, you'll come out confused.'

Holly nods again. 'I'm not confused,' she asserts.

'Right, well, good.' Good for her, I think, because

I definitely am. 'You know, if it's just about sex, there are different apps you can . . .'

'No,' Holly says quickly. 'I mean, er . . . Maybe further down the line. I don't think I'm confident enough yet for . . . those kinds of apps.'

I'm not convinced Holly's ever been on 'those' kinds of apps to know whether she'd feel comfortable on them, but obviously that's a no-go for her, so I don't push it. 'So is it just men?' I continue. 'Or are you exploring your sexuality?' I know *so* many women who have been in long-term straight relationships who discovered they're bi around this age. Trained to think they just 'admire' other women for years until they realise it's more than that. It wouldn't surprise me.

Holly looks like I've handed her an explosive device. 'It's just men,' she asserts, but it's almost like she's speaking on autopilot. I suspect no one's ever asked her that before, including herself. 'Is it for you?!' Again, she flips it back to me.

'Painfully straight,' I answer. I've given myself enough freedom and introspection to know that about myself. But something tells me Holly's not even thought about it. I'm not sure that she's thought about much.

Holly chews her lip, lost in thought.

I sense she's had enough grilling for one evening, so I start seeking my own advice. 'Holly?' I venture. 'How did you do a closed relationship for nine years? I mean, you've decided to open it now, so I'm guessing it wasn't working, right? I mean, it must've been hard?'

On some level, I'm half-hoping she will tell me it was

too difficult and that Ash and I shouldn't do it, because we'll only want to open it up again, but her eyes shine. 'Oh no, it was easy.'

That is *so* not the answer I was looking for.

'So you didn't find it difficult to shut off your attraction to other people?' I ask.

'No.' She shakes her head. 'They just never really entered my head. I loved Will so much, I didn't want anyone else . . .' Her voice goes all dreamy before she coughs and steadies it. 'Obviously I'm excited to see other people. But it's temporary. Ultimately, Will and I both want to be exclusive again.'

Again, not exactly the response I was hoping for. I hadn't seen it as temporary, but everyone else – including Ash – seems to.

'Ash and I have gone exclusive,' I tell her.

'Oh!' Holly claps her hands together. 'That's lovely! What amazing news!' Her voice is all full of romance and swoon. 'Well . . . Cheers to that, Fliss. Congratulations!'

She raises her glass. Her assumption is that I'm over the moon, as if she couldn't fathom anyone potentially *not* wanting that in the long run. She and the rest of the world, I guess. I almost don't have the heart to tell her that I'm having doubts.

'Yeah.' I play with my ponytail, moving it from one side of my head to the other and fiddling with the ends. 'I just . . . I'm not sure.'

'You're not sure?'

'I mean, I'm totally sure about *Ash*,' I explain hurriedly. 'I love Ash and I know he means more to me than anybody else does. I just . . . Holly. I don't think I know what I'm doing.'

'Don't know what you're doing, how?'

'Monogamy.' I shove my phone across the table towards her. There are a few messages from various apps. 'I'm finding it difficult saying no to meeting people and shutting down conversations.'

'Right.' She picks up the phone and looks at the messages.

'The thing is, I . . . Well. I haven't done this before. Well, I did have an exclusive boyfriend once, but I was twenty. That was nearly a decade ago. And it ended badly.'

'Sure.' She puts the phone back on the table.

'I . . . Well. You did this for nine years. So, I figured if I was going to come to anyone for advice . . .' I continue.

'Oh. OH. Of course!' She seems to suddenly clock that I'm asking for *her* help, and looks gleefully flattered. 'OK, well.' She sits back. 'So you're finding it difficult stopping talking to other people?'

'Yes.' I pour myself another cocktail out of the teapot. 'I am enjoying spending more time with Ash, but then every time I have to say no to some fit guy, I can't lie, I'm a bit devo.'

'OK, well . . .' She bites her lip. 'That's normal. You're used to seeing lots of people so don't beat yourself up about finding the transition period tough.'

'Really?'

'Yeah. And it seems to me like you're making life harder for yourself than it has to be. It would be like trying to quit cheese and then . . . going to a cheese bar.'

'Why would anyone quit cheese?' I ask.

'What I mean is.' She glances meaningfully at my phone. 'You might find it easier without the constant temptation.'

At first I don't understand what she's saying. 'Delete your dating apps,' she clarifies.

I stop drinking. 'Delete them?' I repeat. 'Like . . . entirely?'

'Yeah, I mean . . . You're not using them. They're only reminding you of what you can't have.'

I put my mug back on the table. I know it's serious when I lose my thirst for booze. 'Yeah, no, you're right. Of course you're right. Duh.'

She picks up my phone and hands it to me. I take it slowly.

'What like . . . right now?' I sound like a strangled ostrich. I clear my throat.

'Why not?' she asks.

I don't say anything. It feels too soon. But she's right; what's the point in having them now?

'OK, help me pick my next date and I'll delete your apps. Deal?' She brings out her phone and offers it to me.

I take a breath and hand her back my phone. We complete the swap.

'OK.' She swipes and presses. 'Gone. Gone. Gone. Gone and . . . OH. Fliss, what is this one?! Never mind, I don't want to know. GONE.' She puts the phone back on the table and we both stare at it.

Neither of us says anything for a while, like we're having a minute of silence. I feel like I should be wearing black.

'Well, that's that,' I say.

'Are you OK?' Holly asks.

I feel quite emotional, but also ridiculous for feeling that way. So I stifle it like a middle-aged businessman from the fifties and nod.

I open Holly's phone and find the familiar logo of a dating

app I've been using since my early twenties. It's weird knowing that it's not on my phone anymore.

'OK, come round.' I pat the seat next to me.

Holly gets up and settles herself beside me and we start flipping through various profiles. I sense Holly is delighted to have someone else taking over for her, and using the apps on her phone is sort of like a nicotine patch for me.

We spend the rest of the evening sipping cocktails out of our china mugs and laughing at half the stupid shit cishet men write on their profiles supposedly to advertise themselves. When the bar closes and it's time to go home, I feel much better than I did when I got here.

CHAPTER ELEVEN:
BE UP FRONT

HOLLY

Sex. Sex. Sex. Why did I say sex?! Out of all the answers, that is what I am *least* interested in. A week later I'm running over my last conversation with Fliss, which is still haunting me.

Probably because I just got a text from my disastrous date Pete saying:

> Sorry this is a bit late but I wasn't feeling it the other night, nice to meet you

I'm sorry but, was that really necessary? I hadn't tried to contact him. I hadn't even thought about him again until he popped up unceremoniously in my phone. Did he think I was waiting around for him to message me? It seemed perfectly clear to me that neither one of us was 'feeling it'. Talk about rubbing salt in the wound. Still, of course, I replied like the polite young woman I am.

Nothing to be sorry about! We're on the same page. Nice
to meet you too.

Then, of course, I worried about whether the 'we're on the
same page' was too passive aggressive. Why must women
be forever cursed to care about the feelings and opinions of
others? Pete certainly doesn't.

At least it's reassuring to know Fliss has her own problems.
Obviously I'm not happy that she's got problems, but it's
satisfying to discover that everything isn't completely breezy
for her either. She may be struggling with the exact opposite
of what I'm struggling with – I can't help but feel a pang of
jealousy that her issue is that her boyfriend *doesn't* want to
see other people – but she's feeling just as lost as I am.

Going through the profiles with Fliss the other night, it
didn't seem so daunting, it actually was kind of fun. On my
own I become quickly overwhelmed; there are just So. Many.
People. And I have so many questions. Why do so many men
reference their love of pizza? Is that a euphemism? How are
they all over six foot? But thinking about what she said about
shaking things up without being totally random about it has
helped a bit.

Tonight I'm meeting a man called Liam, from Dublin, who
is someone that Fliss initially pointed out. Liam has a good
sense of humour, from what I can tell by the three comments
he's written about himself. He has nice hair (different styles
ranging from Afro to shaved, so I deduce that he's not afraid
to try new things) and Fliss said he has 'beguiling' eyes.
He works for a consultancy that's trying to make energy
companies greener so he's unlikely to be a sociopath – and

on the slim chance that he is, at least he's a sociopath who cares about the planet – and there was no mention of balls anywhere on his profile.

The one thing that gave me pause was . . . He does have a questionable tattoo. On his left wrist it says, 'It's a beautiful new day, hey hey.' Now, I like 'Mr Blue Sky' as much as the next person, but having the lyrics emblazoned on one's body seems *very* enthusiastic. So my assessment is that there's a distinct possibility he's the sort of toxic positive person who thinks it's appropriate to tell people to smile away their mental health problems and owns a mug that says 'Live Your Best Life' on it. But we'll see.

Anyway, this is what Fliss said was the optimum way to step outside my comfort zone, i.e. don't pick people *completely* at random, but if you like a lot of what you see about the person, don't dismiss them on the basis of one detail that's not exactly to your taste. His tattoo is exactly the sort of thing that would make Will shudder and I would normally nod along in agreement as he deemed the person 'basic', so tonight I am meeting Liam and his bad tattoo with an open mind.

Sort of open, anyway. Obviously I still love Will. Oh God. Fliss would say, 'Of course you still love Will, that's not the point.' I'm not sure, despite Fliss's best efforts, I'm *quite* getting the hang of this.

I'm meeting Liam at three at a cosy pub by the river in Hackney, which suits me as Will and I never spend time in that area, so I don't have any lingering memories of Will to distract me. Will thinks Hackney has become so hip it's essentially now a parody of hip so it's gone full circle back to being somewhere people from *TOWIE* might go, or something. In all honesty, even though I work in fashion, I couldn't really care less about the rules of what's hip and what isn't. I just like nice clothes. Is hip even a term that people use anymore?

Hip or not, when I arrive I'm struck by how pretty the place is. It has outdoor lights on a terrace overlooking the water and people are huddling around heaters in their coats and scarves. I spot Liam in the far corner. He appears to be wearing some sort of anorak Will would never be caught dead in but at least he'll be warm. He's also got us a whole heater to ourselves, which I'm glad about, because can you imagine being on a first date and having other people listening to your awkward introductions? The other day the girls in the office were laughing because they overheard a man on a first date ask, 'Do you . . . like plants?' My own uncomfortable first-date small talk would surely be prime water-cooler banter.

He's absorbed in looking out over the water and, when I sit down opposite him, he startles and nearly falls off the bench. I panic that I've already ruined the date but he laughs and his smile puts me at ease instantly.

'Oh my God.' He puts his hand over his chest. 'You scared me. Hi.'

'Liam, I hope?' I confirm.

'Yes, hi, Holly. It's lovely to meet you.'

Oh my God. The Irish accent. Its charms are not a myth. Am I allowed to be swooning over another man's accent?

Yes. I am. That's the whole reason I'm here, I remind myself.

He pulls the hood of his anorak down, revealing a full Afro – I wondered which of the various hairstyles on his profile he'd have gone with – as he stands up and goes straight in for the hug. A proper hug, not a shoulder pat. I hug him back, noting how strange it feels to put my arms around someone taller than Will. Will is about my height so I'm not used to having to reach up.

'Don't look now.' He lowers his voice as we sit down. 'But there's a couple over there who haven't said a word to each other in nearly ten minutes. I've been trying to work out whether it's a comfortable silence or they're having an argument.'

'Oh, I want to see now,' I say.

'Wait, I'll turn this way, you turn to your right.' He looks out over the water again.

I subtly crane my neck sideways to get a glance. Two older women are, indeed, sitting across from each other not saying anything and avoiding eye contact.

'Definitely an argument,' I whisper as I turn back. 'That's frosty.'

'How can you tell?'

'Look at the body language! The one with the blue scarf is livid.'

Liam watches them again as I pretend to look at my gloves. 'I don't know. They look like my aunt and uncle do most of the time. They're never having an argument, they just hate each other.'

'Well, debatably, that is an argument,' I say. 'Just a slow, drawn-out, silent one that's been going on for many years.' Suddenly I realise how far over the line I am. 'Sorry, that was rude of me, I don't know anything about your family.'

Liam looks back at me and smiles.

'No, no, pretty much hit the nail on the head. Child of divorce?' He grins.

I'm surprised by the question. Even Will and I don't talk much about our childhoods and I've known this man for less than ten minutes. But the way he's asking me about it seems like he doesn't think it's a big deal.

'Uh. Sort of,' I say lamely.

'What happened?' he continues.

I'm not sure how to approach this subject in a socially acceptable way. Is he really asking me about this? Whatever happened to small talk?! Isn't he supposed to be asking me about the adequacy of my tube journey? 'I, er . . . Well. My parents were never married, but my dad left before I was born.'

'Ah,' Liam comments. 'Why?'

Again, I'm taken aback by the directness of the question and the honest answer is, I have no idea. I've never asked Mum. She doesn't talk about a lot and she doesn't invite questions. She just sort of . . . gets on with things.

'I don't know,' I answer.

I've never given it much thought because I never felt like it was my business to know, but Liam's surprised face makes me wonder otherwise. Do other people talk to their parents about things like this? The idea feels impossible. I cannot conceive of sitting down and asking Mum what happened between her and my dad, whom she avoids mentioning at all costs.

'So you've never met him?' he asks.

'Nope,' I say.

'That must have been hard on you,' Liam remarks. He looks straight at me like he really means it. He's talking about my past and my emotions about the past like it's a completely normal topic of conversation, so he's obviously very kind, but there is no way he really wants to hear about this, surely. Plus I'd have *no* idea how to answer, even if I wanted to.

'So you're from Dublin?' I dodge his comment. 'What's it like? I've always wanted to go.'

'Ohhh, brisk change of subject.' Liam raises his hands. 'All right, I get it.' He fixes me with a laser-like stare, like he sees me hiding and he'd rather I didn't but he's letting me off the hook. It's quite disconcerting. Will would be welcoming a change of subject right about now, but this man seems almost disappointed. 'Well, it's busy but laidback, if that makes sense. It's much friendlier than London.'

'Not hard,' I say, thankful to be back on more comfortable ground.

Liam laughs. 'No, you've got me there. It's not perfect, but it's home. Are you a Londoner born and bred?'

'Ha, no. I'm from a little village outside Norwich.'

'Oooh, a country lass. Do you miss it?'

We keep chatting and learning about each other. I discover that his parents met when his dad was on holiday in Barbados, where his mum grew up, and fell head over heels in love. His dad didn't leave for months after all his friends flew home, until he had to come back for work, so they decided to move back to Ireland together and get married. They had three children, all boys – Liam is the youngest – and they're still intensely romantic.

I also learn that his dad is a therapist, which potentially explains a lot about Liam's disarming conversational style. Not only does he ask a *lot* of questions but he interrogates how I feel about everything. He will ask a simple question like, 'What was your first pet?' And then follow up with something intense like, 'Did it destroy you when it died?'

Most people, when they learn that I work in fashion, want to know the ins and outs of London Fashion Week and gossip about models or how things get designed and made. Liam seems less interested in the details and more interested in whether I love what I'm doing.

'So did you always want to work in fashion?' he asks.

'Yes.' I nod emphatically. I'm not assured of most decisions, but working in fashion was always an easy choice for me.

'Why?' He leans across the table towards me. 'What drew you to it?'

'Erm,' I start. 'Well, no two days are ever the same. It challenges me and keeps me on my toes . . .'

'Nah. Come on.' Liam waves his hand. 'Those are interview answers. Why do you do it? Is it just a job or do you love it?'

'I love it,' I affirm. 'I really love it.'

Liam's face lights up. 'What do you love about it?'

My mind goes blank. Oh my God. Why *do* I like fashion? And why is this such a difficult question? Surely I should know why I love the thing that I love?! It occurs to me that Will has never asked me this. Clearly, I've never asked myself, either.

'I . . .' I run through my day-to-day job in my mind. Most of it I don't like . . . Emails. CADs. Making sure different departments are communicating with each other. Which they never are. Reviews of sales and returns numbers. Getting stuck with jersey year after year and designing the same pair of sweatpants over and over. But there are parts I feel invigorated by. 'I love seeing all the different elements of a piece come together. Seeing a look take shape. Making people feel special and good about themselves. The bits that I love I don't *really* get to do yet,' I add. 'But hopefully, soon.' I think of Amber's promise about the autumn showcase.

Liam looks all exhilarated, like he's genuinely riding high on my excitement for my work. I am exhausted – I've expended a lot of energy this evening, I'm not used to speaking so much beyond surface level – but I feel alive, too. I am highly uncomfortable about the spotlight he's put me under, and weary at the amount of introspection and honesty he seems to expect, but I can't lie . . . I'm bizarrely enjoying it.

I notice it's dark and look at my phone. Somehow, three hours have passed. *Crap.* I was only planning to stay for two at most and then go home and start making dinner. It was only supposed to be an afternoon pint. A cursory hello and goodbye. I wanted to be back by eight so I could have food ready for when Will got in. I bought ingredients for a pie. I'm just thinking I should leave when suddenly, Liam gets up and comes to sit beside me. He puts his arm around me and rubs my shoulders to warm me up.

I can't lie, his proximity is intoxicating. I feel like I'm getting drunk on the smell of his aftershave and I'm all snug under his arm. I was *not* expecting this.

'Holly,' he says. My name sounds much better with the accent. 'Can I kiss you?'

So many thoughts start flying across my mind at once. *This is a huge betrayal to Will. But Will wants me to, so is not throwing myself into this the real betrayal to Will? I've not kissed anyone except Will in almost ten years. What would kissing another man be like? What about the pie?*

I realise that Liam is still waiting for an answer.

I try to imagine what Fliss would say. And I think she would say, *Holly, there is only one important question here. Do you* want *to kiss this man?*

I can hardly believe it but I think the answer is *yes, I do.*

I nod. Liam leans in. And then we're kissing.

I'm kissing a man who isn't Will.

I didn't realise just how familiar Will's lips must be to me now. Kissing each other is as normal as brushing our teeth or putting the kettle on. I don't have to think about it. I know exactly how he does it and how it's going to feel. I know how he'll kiss me when he's in a rush; a businesslike peck. I know how he does it when he's in a loving mood; he'll press his face firmly and insistently against mine. And I know how he kisses me when he wants to have sex; gently probing my mouth open with his tongue.

This isn't anything like Will's kisses. It's slow and soft and inquisitive. His lips are asking more questions without speaking. My lips silently answer, finding a rhythm with his. My body begins sinking into him, before my brain gets in the way. This is *not* Will's face. An unfamiliar face is attached to my face. An alien face.

Liam leans back. 'Call me crazy,' he says. 'But I feel like your head is elsewhere.'

Crap. How did he know?! This man is a mind-reader. Before I can respond, he keeps talking.

'What are you thinking about?'

I must look dumbfounded, because he continues, 'There's no right answer here, I'm not trying to trick you, I'm just curious.'

Oh God. He says there's no wrong answer but . . . *I'm thinking about how I was only looking for dates to kill a few hours with each week because my boyfriend thinks it's important we see other people before moving forward with our relationship? And I wasn't expecting to have a nice time or want to kiss anyone?* I definitely can't say that. But I have to say something. He's staring at me with large brown eyes that ask questions directly of my soul.

What are bold, confident women – like Fliss – thinking about on first dates?

'Sex,' I blurt.

Oh my GOD. Did I really just say that?

Again?

To a man who just kissed me?!

'I mean, er, sorry. I didn't mean I'm thinking about it right now. I just mean, er, I'm just on the apps for sex. I thought it was better to be up front.'

Liam leans his head back in mock astonishment. He looks from my left eye to my right and back again. He leans from side to side to inspect my face. I can feel my cheeks burning. Then he bursts out laughing. His laughter is so infectious and this situation is so ridiculous that I end up laughing, too.

Thank the Lord, he doesn't interrogate me on that point any further.

'All right, you're a dark horse, aren't you.' He winks. 'One more drink?'

I nod. Then I look at my watch. It's seven-thirty. I can have one more. The pie can wait.

Fortunately, he doesn't ask me any more intense questions and neither of us brings up the 'sex' comment again. We keep chatting until I absolutely have to go if I'm going to make it back in time to see Will. With surprise, I realise I'm not as eager to get home as I was four hours ago.

I get up to leave and Liam walks me along the canal to the station. It's freezing and our breath makes little clouds in front of us as we talk.

'So, Holly, look, I'm not usually one to have sex on the first date, sorry, but . . .' He grins. I can tell that, despite my earlier comment, he knows that I'm not either. 'Can I see you again?' Liam's eyes fix on mine.

A vague alarm bell rings in my mind. This is the moment when Fliss said she usually explains her situation. After one meeting, before arranging the next. It made a lot of sense when she said it but now that I'm here, it feels daunting. I open my mouth to explain but no words are forthcoming. Oh my God. I should have asked Fliss for more specifics. How does she even *begin* to have this conversation?

Yes, I would like to see you again, but actually I have a boyfriend?

Without a shadow of a doubt, I know those words are not coming out of my mouth.

I nod. Liam leans down and kisses me again. This time I'm not thinking about Will.

CHAPTER TWELVE:
DON'T BRING RELATIVES ON DATES

FLISS

I've never liked asking for help. I've never needed much help. I've always preferred doing things on my own. Even in school I hated asking teachers to explain things a second time and would sit for hours painstakingly trying to work out something I didn't understand before I'd put my hand up, and usually I'd manage to figure it out for myself. I taught myself an entire language, for fuck's sake. So going to Holly the other night was mildly soul-crushing. But I have to admit I already feel less out of my depth after having spoken to her.

Do I believe her about genuinely not wanting to sleep with other people for nine years? No, not really. Because why would she be trying an open relationship now, if she didn't? If anything it only confirmed my long-held suspicion that a lot of monogamous people are low-key lying to themselves. But she *was* right; deleting the apps was such an obvious thing to do. I mean, I can't help but reflexively check my phone for messages and feel a bit flat when it's just Jenny saying we need more loo roll. But now I don't have men messaging me, it *is* a lot easier to forget about them.

I am noticing a rather large void appearing, though. Dating was such a big part of my life. It's nice that I've got more time to learn Japanese, and obviously I've got more time for friends now, but it's like there's this huge hole that I'm now trying to fill with things that don't fit.

For years, people have asked me, Why do you need to be in an open relationship to go out of your comfort zone? Why can't you just try new things and meet new people in a non-romantic way? I always find these questions frustrating to answer because they're so reductive.

Of course I can try new things. Of course I can meet new people non-romantically. And I enjoy both of those things. I do both of those things all the time. But they're completely different and noncomparable. Yes, I love going to a random Tuesday night salsa class, but is it comparable to having sex with someone new? No. Yes, I love meeting new friends – like Holly – but is meeting someone platonically in any way the same as meeting someone romantically? No.

Much like different friends bringing out different nonsexual sides of me, different romantic partners bring out different romantic sides of me. That part of my life is being limited now, and Ash is the only one who can fulfil it.

I'm contemplating all this, cross-legged on my bed, Henry snoring softly on the floor, when my phone buzzes with a message from Ash.

What are you up to tonight? X

It's our second Saturday since we agreed to be just us and I'm unsure how to respond. I love hanging out with Ash, but we did see each other the last two nights in a row. I'm not sure whether it's a good idea for us to go from such a rigid schedule to spending so much of our time together. Or am I being overly cautious? Should I just throw myself in at the deep end with this?

I wait until Henry's up and in the shower before phoning Holly. She picks up after a few rings.

'Holly, I need your advice again,' I say.

'Of course. What do you want to know?'

A little voice in my head starts firing big questions. Why does my love mean more if it comes with ownership, instead of less? Why is it socially acceptable to have multiple friends but not multiple partners? I bat them away.

'Well, Ash wants to spend tonight together. We saw each other last night, and the night before, and we're going to the cinema tomorrow. I'm not sure it's such a good idea to start spending *so* much time together?'

'Hmm.' I hear her sipping from a cup of tea. 'But tonight is a date night, right? As in one of the nights you'd normally be spending with other people?'

'Yup.' I think wistfully of the fit chef who was supposed to be teaching me to make sushi.

'So it sounds like it would mean a lot to Ash if you spent it with him. You're in a transitional period; he probably needs some reassurance.'

'OK, yes.' I see what she's saying. 'Good! A gesture, yes. I can do that. Maybe a romantic meal. Just not sushi.'

'Huh?' Holly says.

'Nothing.' I untangle my legs and stand up. 'I'm on it. Thanks, Holly.'

'You're welcome, Fliss. Have fun tonight.'

I text Ash saying I'm free tonight. He replies within about 1.5 seconds.

Yes! <3 What do you want to do?

Dinner? I've been wanting to try Austin's for ages

Sure. Meet you there at 7?

Austin's is a Texan-themed barbecue place with line dancing. It's supposed to be appalling food but good fun and they mix the cocktails with an 80/20 liquor-to-mixer ratio, probably to get awkward British people on the dancefloor. I'd actually meant to try it with Eric, because he had a soft spot for country dancing.

I arrive just before seven. It's delightfully tacky and the staff are wearing cowboy hats. I wait for Ash at our table and start drinking one of the lethal cocktails.

Ash is beaming when he arrives. Any nagging doubts dissolve. I've never loved anyone else like I love Ash. I want Ash to be happy. I'm making Ash happy.

We kiss and I feel that delicious sense of calm soak through me, quietening any lurking reservations.

'Good day?' I ask as he sits opposite me.

'Sorry?' He holds his hand to his ear.

'I said did you have a good day?'

'Oh, yeah,' he shouts. 'I finished *Wolf Hall*.' I swear he only started that the other day. Ash is always reading huge tomes that take other people months to get through in under a week. 'Went for a walk. Oh, I think my maidenhair fern is coming back to life!'

'Yay, well done.' I clap. Ash and I went to Bruges in December and he asked his neighbour to look after his plants. Most of them were OK but the fern suffered.

The waitress comes over and we order Ash a cocktail.

'What about you?' Ash asks when she leaves. 'What did you do today?'

'Well, I watched *The Ultimatum* with Jenny, because Henry . . .'

'Can't hear you, hang on.' He gets up and comes to sit beside me in the booth. 'That's better. Go on.'

'I said I watched *The Ultimatum* with Jenny, because Henry was out.'

'That's sweet.' He leans in. I search again for the solace I find in his kisses, that I had just moments before, but it's gone this time. I think it's his proximity to me in the booth. There isn't really enough space for both of us over here.

The waitress brings Ash his cocktail. He takes a sip and coughs. '*Fuck.* That's strong. How much is in this?!' He pushes it to one side. Then he looks at the menu. 'Is there anything vegan on here?'

'Shit, isn't there?' I grab it. I knew this was a meat place but I could've sworn they had some options he could eat.

I feel like a hideous monster for bringing my classy, vegan boyfriend here instead of Eric. Eric liked loud music, tacky decor and meat. He drank alcohol like kids drank Sunny Delight in the nineties. This place is so not Ash's vibe.

I guess now that I'm only seeing Ash, I'll have to stop going to places like this on dates? But I like having a man pressed against me when we dance to terrible music and getting rowdy in a drunk debate over some topic or other, shouting over the noise to be heard and feeling like what you have to say is *the most original and mind-blowing thing anyone has ever said* because you're so wasted. I guess I could come here with friends and flirt with some random guy instead . . . even though it's not going to lead anywhere? That's what some monogamous couples do, right? But knowing nothing could happen makes it totally different. Mostly, that just sounds frustrating and pointless.

This is only week two. There are going to be so many other things I'm giving up on. I can feel myself panicking as the huge life shift I've agreed to starts to dawn on me.

'You're not going to drink that?' I drain my cocktail and pick up Ash's discarded one. Ash shakes his head.

'Do you want to dance?' I ask.

'Oh, I probably won't dance.' Ash smiles.

I nod. I already suspected that would be the answer. I'm catastrophising but in that moment, Ash not wanting to dance feels like I've signed the death warrant of a huge part of my life . . . of *me*.

Stop it. You're being ridiculous. I sip the disgusting cocktail through a straw and run through all the things I love about Ash in my head. He's kind, generous, sociable, caring, funny, loving, gorgeous, intelligent. So he doesn't want to dance like a tit in public. I can live without doing that in a romantic context. But I can't live without Ash.

My phone buzzes in my pocket. It's Henry.

> What you up to? Had a bad day. Hoping you feel like
> taking pity on your big bro and coming out for a beer

Oh, poor Henry. He was seeing Sam and Laura today. I hope it wasn't too awkward with Laura.

'Ash.' I put my hand on his arm. 'Is it OK if Henry joins? He was seeing Sam and Laura today. I think he's sad.'

'Of course,' Ash says, although I can tell he's a little disappointed not to have me to himself tonight.

> Of course. I'm with Ash, I reply. Come meet us.

He starts typing and deleting, then sends:

> Jenny asked if she can come too?

'And Jenny?' I ask Ash.

'Oh, fun,' Ash says.

> Sure!

'Sorry,' I say. 'I feel like I have to be there for Henry right now.'

'Of course. I understand.' He takes my hand again and rubs his thumb across my fingers.

I feel bad about their crashing one of our first Saturday nights together in years, but it's hard to say no to Henry when he's going through this.

About twenty minutes later, Henry and Jenny arrive. We order food and Henry talks about his colleague who accidentally forwarded a catty email to the person it was about and

Jenny shares her suspicion that the neighbours are stealing our Wi-Fi. Apparently it is 'very slow' as soon as the man at number twelve comes home. I don't ask how she keeps track of his movements.

I bask in their glorious, inane chatter and realise, with a little blow to my conscience, that I'm relieved that they're here.

I don't think inviting my big brother and my roommate on our big date would have been Holly's advice for how to kick-start my new relationship, but secretly I'm partly glad this has happened, given that I was on my way to a freak-out. I know part of Ash's reason for wanting to close our relationship was to spend more time together, which part of me has been loving, but I wonder if maybe we are doing too much too soon. Maybe I need some space to adjust. How do I tell him that?

For now, I brush those thoughts aside. We eat, we drink, we lose our minds laughing at the serious look on Jenny's face as she pretends to wave a lasso around her head with concentrated precision.

At the end of the night we all head back to mine and Jenny's together. Jenny and Henry walk on ahead of Ash and me, laughing and whooping. They're giddy because Henry stole one of the waiter's cowboy hats.

As we trail behind them and it's just me and Ash again, I steal a glance at him, illuminated in the streetlamps, contemplative and still in contrast to the city's noise. He's magnificent, but can he be everything I need? Can anyone? Again, I squash those thoughts down.

My phone buzzes in my pocket. At first I think it's probably Holly checking in to see how our 'romantic' evening went, and I wonder how I'm going to tell her it ended up with Henry and Jenny singing 'Jolene' on the street. But the name that pops up is not Holly's. The shape of it is unfamiliar; an alien invader on my phone screen.

Hey, how's it going?

Why is Rowan messaging me? I've not seen him since I was last in New York for my previous job, about two years ago. Before I can reply he sends:

I have a surprise

'Who you texting?' asks Ash.

'Oh, er, my friend Holly.' The lie falls out of my mouth.

I have no idea why I hide it. Two weeks in a monogamous relationship and I'm lying about an innocent text from an ex. Well, OK, it's not *completely* innocent, because my heart rate has sped way up, but it's not like it was a naked picture. I want to take the lie back, but it's out there now. I wonder if this is what monogamy does to people . . . Drives them nutty, jumping at any contact with the opposite sex.

I reply:

. . .?!

You'll find out soon! Rowan replies.

Ugh. So cryptic. I hate that he's got under my skin so easily, but I can't help wondering what this 'surprise' could be.

I swear to God, how do all exes have some sort of radar for when you're feeling restless? Usually I'd only speak to Rowan when I'm in New York and I'd be the one to reach out. He never messages first. And as soon as I'm going through a thing with Ash he pops up? *The winds of the Atlantic Ocean have carried the scent of Fliss's discontent halfway across the world, like an invisible carrier pigeon for horny distress signals, now is obviously my time to send that text?*

I'm quiet for the rest of the journey home and, when Ash and I finally crawl into bed and turn off the light, I can't sleep.

CHAPTER THIRTEEN:
NOT EVERYONE IS READY FOR ASS-LESS CHAPS

HOLLY

I'm taking off Liam's shirt.

Oh my God. Am I really taking off Liam's shirt? I barely know this man.

And now he's taking off mine.

And now I'm undoing his belt. Or . . . trying to. Oh God, it's stuck. Why are belts so difficult to undo with one hand?! But my left hand is in his hair. Using it now would be like admitting defeat. I'll call attention to the fact I need both hands and he'll realise how inexperienced I am at belt removal and how I've only ever slept with Will, my high school boyfriend Kelvin and a couple of other guys I can barely remember, including one who couldn't get the condom on so humped my leg instead. Does he even count?

'Holly,' a voice sighs.

Except it's not Liam sighing with pleasure. It's Amber sighing at the sheer injustice of being expected to do her job.

I snap out of my imaginary world. If anything can throw an ice-cold bucket of water over a lewd daydream, it's Amber's voice. I'm almost grateful to her. It is not OK that I'm thinking about failing to take off Liam's belt!

Why, even in my own daydreams, am I so awkward?

'Yes, hi.' I smooth out the imaginary kink in my hair from where Liam pushed me up against a wall. At least the daydreams are preferable to running through all the ways I might have already made a fool of myself before 10 a.m. I didn't even obsess over it when Alice from Accounts said, 'Oh my God, I *love* your side-parting, it's so nostalgic.'

'Do you have the research?' Amber asks.

She was supposed to be doing that but, at midday, she declared that she 'wouldn't have time' and asked me to do it instead. Her meeting is at three-thirty. I worked all the way through lunch. It's been getting worse since she took over from Julie. Every time I hear her voice my heart sinks because I know what's coming. I might as well not have a lunch break anymore.

I wouldn't mind as much about Amber lumping me with most of her job if she at least did it punctually. What tends to happen is that she starts out under the illusion that she'll finish everything herself, doesn't get *anything* done, then asks me at the last minute, which is ten times worse than if she'd asked me in the first place.

'Yes, just pressed send on the email to you.' I mock-push a button on my keyboard.

'You're a star, thank you,' she says as she turns and runs back to her computer.

Tomi appears behind my desk. '*The run.*' He bursts out laughing. We play Amber Bingo throughout the day. Every time she runs, sighs, types furiously or utters the phrase 'I would but I'm absolutely swamped' we send each other a witch emoji on Slack.

'What did you do for her this time?' Tomi asks.

'Target market research for the new line,' I answer.

Tomi shakes his head. 'You can't keep dropping everything to take on her shit.'

'Technically my job now Julie's gone,' I say.

'No.' Tomi shakes his head more emphatically. 'You're here to support, not carry. When did she ask?'

'Four hours ago.'

'You should tell her that you need proper notice because, unlike some people, you plan out your time effectively.'

'I'm sure she starts out with the best of intentions,' I comment.

Tomi snorts. 'No, wrong. If she asks you in advance it means she has to admit you're doing her job for her. If she imagines it's just the odd thing here and there that got away from her then she can keep pretending.'

I shake my head. Amber is disorganised and thoughtless, but she's not scheming. 'Remember, she said I could take full credit for my design at the showcase,' I say. 'It will all be worth it. Amber's not all bad. I'm finally going to get my foot in the door because of her. It's not like all this work will be without a payoff.'

Tomi tuts. 'Bribery.'

'Definitely,' I agree, but I can't help my heart lifting at the thought of being acknowledged for something I created in front of hundreds of industry people.

'Oh! Guess who managed to get two extra spots on the guest list!' Tomi waves his arms victoriously. No one except industry is allowed into the showcase, but friends and family are allowed to come to our huge after-party. We're celebrating ten years of the brand. Tomi had several family members fighting over the coveted spaces. 'Is Will coming?'

'Oh, er, no.' I try not to let the disappointment show on my face, but a blush starts creeping up my neck. 'He can't. He's got a friend's stag do. It's one of his best friends, so he really can't miss it.'

I emphasise the word 'best' and cringe. I hear what I sound like. It's coming across like I'm making excuses for a crap boyfriend who's not supportive of my career. But Will's not like that. He's always looking at my work and helping me, which means so much more than being able to attend some flashy party where my name will get read out. I may have exaggerated that this is Will's 'best' friend, but he is a friend and stag dos are important once-in-a-lifetime things.

'Oh, I'm sorry, Hols.' Tomi rubs my shoulder. 'That's a shame for you.'

'No no, it's fine, really,' I assert. It *is* fine. I completely understand. I wouldn't want to let a friend down on their hen do either.

'Right, I should do some work. Just don't leave too late tonight, OK?' Tomi puts his hands on my shoulders. 'Go home. Do a jigsaw. Knit something for Will.'

'What is it you think I do at home?' I wrinkle my nose.

'Whatever, as long as you're not here until ten while Amber swans off on some hot date.'

Admittedly, I was here until ten yesterday. It's on the tip of my tongue to tell him that I'll definitely leave on time because *I'm* the one with a hot date tonight, but I stop myself.

'I won't,' I say instead.

'Thank the Lord.' Tomi pats me on the back one more time and returns to his own desk.

He's right that Amber has been heaping a lot of extra work on me. But what he doesn't know is that I've actually wanted to stay in the office this week. I can't face Will. I don't know how to act around him. Even though Will wanted me to do this, I feel like I'm hiding a terrible secret. I'm sure he'll be able to sense that another man's lips have been on my face if he looks at it long enough.

Ugh. And I liked it. All week I've been fluctuating between queasy guilt and lurid daydreams. Why are human beings so full of conflicts? And why are we so desperately pathetic? This man is only exciting to me because he's new, surely? I feel validated because someone I don't know has deemed me acceptably sexually attractive and I feel a rush of adrenaline because I'm not used to an unfamiliar hand on my knee. It's all so shallow!

I'm appalled with myself.

I want to correctly undo his belt.

My phone buzzes. It's Liam.

So seven at Tottenham Court Road, yeah?

I wish you'd tell me where we were going

It's a mystery location

A 'mystery location'. A butterfly of exhilaration flutters in my stomach, more about the mystery of Liam than where he's taking me. But mystery is always thrilling, until you see what's behind the curtain. No one on planet Earth is *actually* mysterious. By its very definition, mysterious means difficult to understand or explain, but with human beings there's always an answer. Someone lives here, eats those, likes that. Someone behaves this way because of this reason in their upbringing, their experience, their genetics. A person appearing mysterious to another person depends entirely on one person not knowing the other well enough, so it's all an illusion.

I've got Will all worked out. He can be defensive because he grew up with two older, louder brothers who always shouted their opinions and mocked his. When he can take the opportunity to assert his own opinion as if it's Gospel, he'll take it, but if he views someone as more dominant than he is, he'll become quiet and oversensitive. He has specific tastes in clothes, music and food and hates anything he perceives to be basic or mainstream, and his whole family is that way too. He enjoys discovering new places, but only if he found them first. He hates being told what to do. He drinks fresh orange juice every day because it reminds him of childhood family holidays to Spain. He doesn't like books unless they're a challenge. He thinks cats are pointless pets when you could have a dog. He disagrees with the meat industry but still thinks vegetarians are unnatural. And about another Olympic-sized swimming pool's worth of knowledge you pick up in nearly a decade with somebody.

What do I know about Liam?

Liam is Irish. Liam changes his hair a lot. Liam wears bright colours. Liam jumps easily and would probably be a nightmare to watch a horror film with. Liam has an aunt and uncle who hate each other but remain married. Liam likes people-watching. Liam talks about feelings. A lot.

That's it. That's the sum total of what I know about him so far. Of course I'm intrigued. He's *new*. As soon as he became not-new and we had an actual relationship, I'd stop feeling this way and we'd be just another mundane couple. Right? Which leads me back to square one . . . what's the point of this? I already found someone I want to spend my life with, which is the end goal of dating, surely? At first I was annoyed at myself for not being able to get into this. Now I'm annoyed at myself for enjoying it.

The fact that this was technically Will's idea does nothing to assuage how wrong it feels to think about undressing Liam. I feel bad about Liam, too, because he still doesn't know I'm unavailable. I typed out several messages this morning which are still sitting in my drafts.

> Hey, before we meet up again, I should probably make you aware I'm actually in a relationship, so I'm not looking for anything serious. If that's ok with you it would be lovely to see you but I understand if not!

Then I realised that sounds as if I've assumed he's looking for something serious with me, which is presumptuous. I added:

> Obviously I have no idea what you're looking for, but I wanted to let you know in case.

But that turns it into a ramble. No one wants to receive a heartfelt essay before they've even been on a second date. Then I tried to be 'chill'.

> By the way I'm in an open relationship, forgot to mention. Hope that's cool.

But that completely fails to sound genuinely easy-going. I tried a few other variations but none of them were any better. I have a long way to go before mastering the art of casual dating. I bet Fliss would know what to say but asking her to literally write my texts for me would be sinking to a new low.

Plus, we're meeting in a few hours so it's too late to send it now. He'd probably wonder why I didn't say this before? And if he *did* want to cancel, he might feel like he couldn't because it was such late notice, and then I'd spend the whole date thinking he was only there out of polite obligation.

It's OK. I'll tell him after tonight, in person. It's only one date more than when Fliss said was an ideal time to tell someone. It's hardly like he's going to get down on one knee after the second date, is it?

When it hits five-thirty I hide in the loos before Amber can give me something that 'has to be done by tomorrow morning'. I do my make-up, read my book in a cubicle, then creep back through the office to exit the building.

As I walk towards the tube station I feel light and jubilant with the pure, simple energy of a person on their way to meet someone they fancy. Then I remember my situation is a hundred times more complicated than that and start stressing again.

Liam is hard to miss as I come up the escalators at Tottenham Court Road. He's wearing a loud, pink-and-blue zig-zag-patterned shirt and skinny jeans. I make a mental note not to accidentally mention that skinny jeans haven't been in fashion in a while. They'll probably come back soon and he'll have ridden out the trend. Despite his interesting clothing choices, he is undeniably fit. He's shaved the sides of his head so his Afro has a different shape today – neater and taller – and it suits him. Warmth spreads across his face when he sees me and my mouth goes dry.

'Holly!' he calls and waves loudly. A couple of people turn their heads and my knee-jerk reaction is embarrassment, because Will is always conscious of being too loud or people overhearing our conversations. But Liam doesn't seem to care. He hugs me with easy familiarity and kisses me. It makes me realise how reserved Will is. I can't imagine him kissing me in public. I thought I didn't like PDAs either, but maybe I do? This is . . . nice? Then I feel bad for thinking that.

We start criss-crossing through the narrow Soho streets full of vibrant, thronging crowds. 'Are you going to tell me where we're going yet?' I ask.

'You're bad with surprises, aren't you?' Liam glances at me, amused. 'Why is that?'

'Uhhh.' I reflect on that statement. I suppose he's right. 'I like having a plan.'

'That's not what I asked.' He winks.

'Why?' I repeat, dodging a man looking at his phone who nearly walks into me. I've never thought about it. 'I don't know. I suppose it's because my mum, er, well, my mum wasn't always in a great place when we were growing up, so

I had to look after her a bit. I mean, not *had* to, that makes it sound bad. I didn't mind. Of course. She's my family. But yes, maybe that's why I'm organised.'

Liam smiles knowingly, as if something about me makes sense to him now. He got the answer he was looking for. I've never thought so much about the *why* of things in my entire life as I have in one and a bit dates with Liam. At least, not about myself. And I've never spoken so openly about my mum, but Liam makes it feel like no topic is off the table.

It makes me realise how many subjects are off limits with Will, even though we've been together nearly a decade. Then I shake myself. Of course topics aren't 'off limits' with him. I'm sure there's nothing I couldn't speak with him about if I really wanted to.

'Only a few moments of torture left. We're nearly there.'

We come to a little wooden door on a quiet side-street. Liam knocks. Nothing happens.

'Are you sure this is . . .' I start. But then the door opens a fraction.

'Password?' says a voice.

Oh my God. Where is he taking me? Am I going to die?

'Zenith,' says Liam.

Is he a member of a cult? If that's what this is, then I'm done for. I always suspected I'd be too weak-minded to resist the allure if I ever came across one. I might as well get some scary symbol tattooed on a random body part immediately.

The door opens to reveal a man with a long fringe in one eye, wearing a black T-shirt and jeans. No visible tattoos that instantly point to cult status but I'm not ruling it out. We're given some form about 'respecting people's boundaries' – of course, I always respect people's boundaries? – and not using my camera, which I sign after looking for any small print about animal sacrifices. The man nods and Liam grabs my hand, pulling me down the hall. I hesitate.

'Umm,' I say. 'Where are we?'

'You'll see.'

And then, more out of politeness than any real confidence that I'm not about to be murdered, I follow him.

We walk down what feels like a lot of stairs and enter into a dark, cavernous space with low-hanging ceilings. Iron tables are dotted around, topped with candles and roses. A couple of people are here but it's pretty quiet.

'This is so . . .' I start. I'm about to say 'romantic', when I notice a man in ass-less chaps.

I nearly choke on thin air. I turn abruptly to Liam, who looks unfazed.

'Hi.' A waiter approaches us. He's topless, apart from leather braces. 'Sit anywhere you like.'

I search Liam's face for any sign that he is unsettled, any at all, and find none. The waiter turns and beckons us to follow him to a bunch of tables in the corner. His butt is glinting in the flickering orange glow.

When we're seated, I notice little rooms off the edge of the main bar, hidden away with curtains.

'What's through there?' I ask.

'People having sex,' Liam answers matter-of-factly. 'That's kind of the rule of entry.'

My eyes widen. So far I've managed to keep my panic at bay, but I feel like I'm about to have a heart attack. Oh my God. What if I see something and am scarred for life? I shield my eyes from the horror of an imaginary nude person I've never met. Who is this man? Does he think I'm going to have sex with him in this sex dungeon?! Why, oh why, did I tell him I was only looking for sex the other day? I'm about to mutter a breathless apology and bolt out the door, when Liam bursts out laughing.

'Priceless!' he screams, banging the table with his fist.

'What?' I demand, heart still hammering.

'Your face!' He cackles. 'Oh, Lord, that was worth it. Don't worry, Holly, I'm *joking*.'

I feel myself start to breathe. 'Thank God. So there aren't people . . . having sex?' For some reason I whisper the word 'sex'. '. . . In there?' I look over at the curtain.

'Oh, there will be later. But it's early. And you're under no obligation to join them, don't worry.'

'But . . . but . . . it's a Tuesday!' I choke out.

This prompts Liam to have another laughing fit. 'People are allowed to have sex on Tuesdays.'

'So do you . . . come here?' I ask cautiously.

Liam keeps spluttering. 'No. My mate does, though. He gave me the password for a laugh.'

My shoulders finally unclench.

'It's not always here. It's more of a moving party, from what I gather,' Liam adds.

Now that I realise I'm under no pressure to partake, I can see the funny side of Liam bringing me here. I start laughing, which sets off Liam again, and we're both snorting.

'How do you think I'd look in a pair of those?' Liam nods towards the ass-less chaps.

'I'm not sure,' I answer. 'I've never seen your . . .' I pause. 'Bottom.'

That sets Liam off again. I can't believe I just said the word 'bottom'. Should I have said 'ass' or 'bum'? There is no elegant word for it. I'm glad the lighting is too dim in here for Liam to see me blushing.

When Liam manages to stop laughing, we order drinks and Liam dives right back in with intense questions about my day.

'So, you must be close with your mum?' he asks once he's finished analysing my relationships with Tomi, Amber, our head of department Lara Pearse and the entire HR department. 'If it's just the two of you?'

Only Liam could bring me to a sex club and then start quizzing me about my relationship with my mother. 'Yeah. In a way. I mean . . . Yes, we are,' I correct myself. But Liam's already caught onto my slip.

'In a way?' he asks.

When I hesitate, he says, 'I'm sorry, you don't have to talk about anything you don't want to.'

But surprisingly, I find that I *do* want to talk about it. I never talk about my mum to anybody. Not in this way. 'Well, we're close in the way that we only have each other,' I explain. 'So she's basically my only family. And in that way that all families are, where you're just intimately familiar. You know, no matter how long you're away from your family, it's always exactly the same when you come home, isn't it?'

Liam nods.

'But there's a lot that's unspoken between us,' I finish. 'There were some years where she wasn't herself.'

'Like how?' Liam asks.

'I guess she used to be quite . . .' I search for the right word. 'Reactive. She was upset a lot. I helped loads around the house. When I was a bit older she pulled herself together, but it was like in order to do that, she shut down. I think she's ashamed. We never talk about it.'

'I'm sorry. I can't imagine being a child caring for a parent with mental health problems.' Liam takes my hand and squeezes it.

His casual use of the phrase 'mental health problems' jars me. I'd never really thought of myself as 'caring' for my mum or her having 'mental health problems'. I just looked after her because she was sad. I don't reply as I absorb this perspective of my situation.

'That must have been lonely,' he adds. It *was* lonely. I knew that, obviously, but it's like I've never really allowed myself to acknowledge that properly.

'Yeah, it was,' I reply.

Suddenly, I have a lump in my throat. Crap. I can't believe I'm banging on about my difficult relationship with my mother and coming close to tears on a date. That is classic temperamental me. Will would hate it. I quickly compose myself.

Except . . . Liam did bring it up, so he must not mind hearing about it. He's not looking away embarrassed or changing the subject. He's just looking right at me and waiting patiently in case there's more that I want to say. It's . . . *nice*.

Not that Will is *not* nice. Will just doesn't want me to be sad. There's nothing wrong with that.

'I'll get us another drink,' Liam says when I don't expand further.

He goes to get us a round. I look around me, taking it all in. Wow. I wasn't aware parties like this happened. At least,

I never thought I'd be at one. Incredibly, in chatting with Liam I'd almost forgotten where we were.

If someone had told me, even a month ago, that tonight I'd be sitting in a sex bar (Is it even called that?) with a fit Irish man I'd kissed the week before, I would have scoffed. I feel like I'm in a movie. In another life. This is wild.

When Liam sits back down, he sets two cocktails on the table and leans towards me.

'So, Holly, in all seriousness, why *did* you say you just wanted sex when that so obviously isn't the case?' He maintains eye contact.

Here it is. *The moment.* The perfect segue into explaining my situation.

'Well, I . . .'

I'm about to do it. Once again, I try to find the words. But it's hard working out how to explain something I'm still not sure how I feel about. It's hard to tell him what I want when I don't really *know* what I want. Will and I still haven't talked about how this should work. Liam's the kind of person who will interrogate that and then I'll have to admit I didn't really want to do it in the first place. Then he might think I don't want to be here and that's not strictly true, anymore. I was actually looking forward to tonight.

Plus, we're having such a good time. I don't want the night to end. I feel so light and free after talking about things – like my mum – that I never even realised I wanted to talk about. I'm loving learning more about Liam's own family. If I say something now, won't that ruin the atmosphere entirely? I don't even want to think about Will right now, let alone speak about him with another man. The thought makes me nauseous.

'I should have said . . . I'm not looking for anything serious,' I say instead.

That's basically the same, right? What's the difference between that and being in an open relationship, really? They both amount to the same thing; me being unavailable for a relationship. He might not know about me and Will but he knows what I've got to offer.

'OK, sure, I hear you.' Liam doesn't look entirely convinced but he's not going to press me further. He nods and smiles. 'Anyway, cheers.'

'Cheers,' I say, relieved to have cleared that up in my own way. Fliss said it was different for everybody, didn't she? I raise my glass to clink against his.

CHAPTER FOURTEEN:
EX-BOYFRIENDS ARE OFF LIMITS

FLISS

'Morning.' Ash puts a coffee down on the bedside table as I open my eyes.

'Morning.' I sit up, moving a pillow behind me and reaching for the mug. 'Thanks. Aren't you going to be late?' I notice he's not dressed.

'Oh no, my home visit got moved so I'm working from home today.' Ash puts his own coffee down and gets back into bed. 'I thought we could work together? We could stay here or go to a café?'

I feel awful, but I don't want to be together today. We've now spent nearly an entire fortnight in each other's company. It's so sweet that he's excited there are no boundaries limiting how much we can be together anymore, but I'm beginning to seriously need some space. Every time I try to bring myself to tell him that, I can't do it. I don't want to hurt his feelings.

Historically, Ash and I were always on the same page. I never *had* to hurt his feelings because we always wanted the same things. This unbalance is new territory and going into the office will provide a much-needed escape.

'Oh, sorry, I can't today,' I fib. 'The managers want us in.'

'Oh cool, no worries. We still on for tomorrow night?'

I nod and kiss him, feeling terrible for having lied, but better for not upsetting him.

I get dressed and head into Traduire. We don't have assigned desks, but some people who come in every day have their habitual places. I wave to Marian and Monty – two regular office-dwellers in their usual seats by the door – as I wander through the open-plan space and set up in the far left corner of the room.

I settle down with my laptop, draining the last of my Pret coffee. I check the deadlines I have for the week and look through the documents I have to translate. Today is mainly marketing copy for products being sold in various different countries . . . An easy, but not particularly interesting, day ahead.

Suddenly, someone spins my chair around. For a millisecond, I can't compute what's happening or what I'm seeing. It takes me a moment to recognise the person in front of me because he's so out of context. I cast my eyes over his trademark mid-fade buzz cut and scruffy beard and the sight of him finally clicks. I'm face to face with Rowan.

'Surprise!' His familiar voice reverberates around the room. Everyone at the four rows of desks lining the room stops what they're doing and looks over at us.

'Um, hi,' I say, trying not to betray my shock and acting

as if it's totally normal that he's here. In the country. In my workplace. Rowan has always enjoyed wrong-footing people and I always enjoyed remaining steady in the face of his attempts. But he wins this one, because I am obviously stunned to see him here.

'Hello, new colleague.' He takes his hands off the side of my chair and stands back, offering me one to shake. I take it.

'You're working here?' I'm trying not to sound too curious. I don't want to give him the satisfaction of knowing he's rattled me.

'I am.' He pulls up the chair beside me. 'I think I'll sit here.'

You've got to be kidding.

He rolls up the sleeves of his jacket and turns on his laptop, saying nothing, waiting for me to probe him with questions. A small smile plays at the corner of his mouth. He is *loving* this. The role reversal – usually I'd be the one dropping in on him – but mainly just winding me up.

Rowan and I met just after graduating, working at a travel company in New York. He was a modern-languages student as well and it was a good job for people just out of university wondering what to do with their degree in Spanish. Adventure Travel organised trips for solo travellers who wanted a group to visit South America with.

Rowan didn't stick around at AT for very long. He did a language degree more out of not knowing what to study than being passionate about speaking Spanish or wanting to use it in his career. He ended up getting a job at a big New York marketing firm because it paid more for less work. I ended up moving to Barcelona when the company opened up an office there, and then to Paris when they opened an office there.

We dated *very* loosely – we spent a lot of time together but we were more like friends who had sex than boyfriend and girlfriend – for about eighteen months in New York before going our separate ways when I moved. The company would send me back to New York every so often – maybe once a year – and for the fortnight or so that I was there, it would always kind of feel like I never left. But I've not been there in a while.

'What happened to New York?' I ask, giving in. Another point to him, but I refuse to be so childish that I'm not going to ask normal questions.

'Europe has a more varied selection of cheese.' He shrugs. Typical Rowan response, not giving anything away. He gets his notebook out of his bag and lays it on the desk, making sure the bottom of it aligns with the keyboard. He places two pens alongside it, parallel to the notebook. I always found Rowan's fastidious neatness an interesting contradiction. He's walking chaos but God forbid his pens are askew.

Fine. Two can play at this game. If he's not going to talk to me properly then I'll stop asking.

I turn back to my computer and start translating the copy for a new fertility app. I'm unsettled by his sudden, unexplained arrival, irritated by his manner and vexed by my body's alertness to his proximity, so concentrating isn't easy, but I'm determined to not get distracted. *He will not win.*

But God, I forgot how attractive he is. His dark, smooth

skin looks really good in contrast with the dusty pink T-shirt he's wearing. He smells good, too. *Stop it.* How am I getting horny while reading about womb linings?

Just as I reach the word 'uterus' and try to remember what the hell that is in German, I find Rowan peering over my shoulder.

'What you working on?' he asks.

Ugh. It all comes crashing back to me how annoying it was to work with Rowan, who can't concentrate on anything for more than two minutes.

'Oh, now you want to talk to me?' I retort.

Rowan mock-rolls his eyes, and relents.

'OK, OK. You win, Flissy. I've got everything I could out of that job, that city. It's time for a change. I remember when you left AT you said this place was pretty flexible, easy money, which is appealing to me right now while I figure out my next steps. I haven't been to London in years and the Brits dig my wholesome American accent. Plus, hadn't seen you in a while.' He grins. 'Did you forget about me?'

I can't help but smile. I could never *forget* Rowan, but it's true that since I stopped working for AT I haven't had a reason to visit New York. I went about two years ago to see Rowan and our friends out there, but it's expensive when your flights aren't being paid for.

'You know I didn't,' I admit, and he smirks.

'So, fill me in on the office dynamics,' he says. 'Who fancies who? Who got too drunk at the Christmas party? Who has long-standing resentments about stolen Tupperware that have escalated to deranged levels?'

'Um.' I give up any pretence of working and look around

the room. The agency has a lot of employees coming in and out on various days, many in their early twenties who don't stay longer than six months, so I don't know everyone in the room that well. I point to a pale, grey-haired woman in the corner. 'That's Marian,' I whisper. 'She sits by the door and waits until you go to the shop, then asks if you can pick her up an apple. She never pays you back. Two years. Hundreds of apples.'

'Iconic.' Rowan rubs his hands together. I catch the scent of his aftershave. He smells exactly the same and I am transported back in time to eating dollar pizza in his tiny Brooklyn apartment, sleeping on hostel floors when we got to sample the newly devised AT trips, drinking all night in Buenos Aires, having sex in the office after everyone else left.

I lean away slightly.

'What about him? What's his story?' Rowan points at Monty, a middle-aged, balding guy who sits by Marian.

'He walks up and down behind the computers and coughs if you're on YouTube,' I say.

'But he's not in charge or anything?'

'No, just teacher vibes.'

'Perfect. I'm going to line up something distracting.' He leans back to his computer and starts googling 'fursuit parade'.

I can't help but snort. Despite remembering how much Rowan annoys me, it is good to see him. It's unreal that he's here, sitting next to me, and yet it feels completely normal. He's one of those people where no matter how much time passes in between seeing each other, things never fail to be exactly the same when you do.

We spend the rest of the day *somewhat* working, but I can't imagine that the owners of Traduire would feel they got their money's worth out of me today. Mostly, we spend the day reminiscing about old times and trying to freak out Monty. The furries don't so much as raise an eyebrow, nor does the man punching a kangaroo in the face, but 'big-headed baby dance' gets him. He's so transfixed he forgets to cough in disapproval, then when he remembers he shakes his head and tuts. We wait until he's gone and then almost fall to the ground shaking with laughter.

As soon as it hits 5 p.m., Rowan looks at me and says, 'Quick drink?'

I hesitate. A 'quick' pint with Rowan is never just one drink. I know what Holly would think about this . . . That getting plastered with an ex-boyfriend mid-week isn't the most serious start to my newly monogamous relationship. I can picture her eyebrows flying off the top of her head.

But despite Holly's imaginary foreboding warnings, going out with Rowan for a few drinks isn't seriously against any laws of monogamy, so far as I know.

I look at my watch and then back at Rowan. 'Yeah, guess I've got time for one,' I say.

Four hours later, we're still in the pub and Rowan is teaching me how to play the harmonica. Every time I see Rowan he's got some new, bizarre hobby. The last time I was in New York he'd accumulated a coin collection and mastered the art of whittling.

I've just learnt how to hold the instrument correctly, but I can't seem to play a single note at a time.

'You're not getting your lips far enough around it.' Rowan puckers in demonstration. I can't help but stare at his lips a bit too long.

I readjust and blow again. Multiple notes come out.

'Come on, don't be shy. Like you're trying to kiss someone. This should be easy for you.' He nudges me.

'Oh, ha-ha.' I take the harmonica out of my mouth and put it back on the table. 'I think I'm done with lessons for today.'

'OH.' Rowan wipes the harmonica and puts it back in his pocket. 'Of course, I forgot.'

'Forgot what?'

'How much you hate being told how to do things.'

'I don't . . .' I tail off, because it's true. I like learning on my own – I *love* learning on my own – but God how I loathe it in a group setting. Other people *instructing* you and witnessing you *fail* . . . Eugh. I make a mental note to buy a harmonica and start playing it in private.

This simple comment reminds me how well he knows me. It's partly why the timing of his arrival is so unnerving; almost like he knew.

'So, Rowan.' I'm speaking loudly because I'm pretty drunk by now. We're on about round one hundred. 'How long are you staying? I mean, Traduire is fine, but it's hardly a big New York marketing firm. You must be taking somewhat of a pay cut.'

'Not sure. Depends.'

'On what?'

He doesn't answer and picks up his pint. 'What about you? Still enjoying it?'

I nod. 'Yeah, I like that I can mix it up with other stuff. I've done some teaching. Sometimes they need an interpreter in court. Obviously I can leave without much notice.'

'But you've been there two years?' Rowan asks.

'Yeah . . . Nearly three, actually.'

'Time to move on soon? Where will you go next?' Rowan peers at me over the top of his glass.

How did this become about asking *me* questions? He's still deflecting. But he's right. Now is normally about the time I'd leave a place. I haven't stayed anywhere longer than three years before.

'I don't know,' I answer. 'I'm not getting the bug to go anywhere.'

'God, don't tell me you're settling down in the UK of all places?'

'I'm hardly settling down.' I say it a little too quickly. My defensiveness grants him a small, smug smile. He chose that phrase on purpose. Damn, one–nil to him.

'Your parents must be thrilled.' He smirks. He knows that my parents are a sore point. How they would have loved for me to be like Henry and be married with children and living within a ten-minute walk of them by now.

'Well, they're pleased that I'm here, but . . .'

'But they don't like the guy?' Rowan fills in.

How does he know about Ash? We haven't spoken in a couple of years and I don't have social media. Rowan grins at my puzzled expression.

'Intuition.' He nudges me playfully. 'I *knew* you'd fallen for a Brit, to be lured back here . . .'

'I didn't move back for a guy,' I say. 'Henry had Sam.'

I came back here initially because I didn't want to miss out on my nephew being born. I'd wanted to be around more for that . . . And, yes, then I'd met Ash.

'Ah, of course. I saw the little man can unbutton his coat

now.' Rowan puts a hand to his chest. 'And draw spoons? He is very cute.'

I turn to him. 'You've seen the spoons?'

Rowan brings up a photo of Sam's cutlery-inspired artwork on his phone. 'I'm a big fan of Mama Henderson's Instagram.' My mother would not shut up about this masterpiece for at least three weeks; makes total sense she posted it.

Rowan grins and brings up another photo; one of me from a few months ago, with Sam on my knee. We're both beaming. Sam is very happy with a small penguin toy that I bought him. At least he was for five minutes before he became more interested in my shoe. 'I have to say, this one is especially lovely.'

It's a nice photo but I can't help but think it is not my angle. I'm cringing thinking of what other unflattering pictures my mum might be sharing on the internet behind my back. I wonder what else he's seen. I knew they kept in touch a little on Instagram – Mum will sometimes say things like, 'oh, Rowan's been promoted' or 'Rowan's in Hawaii' as if he's her friend, not mine – but it didn't occur to me that pictures of me would be making their way to Rowan through her profile.

My parents met Rowan a couple of times when they came to visit me in New York, and one year he spent Christmas with us in Kent, mainly because Rowan had really wanted to visit London. They *loved* him. Dad will sometimes comment how 'it's a shame your nomadic lifestyle ruined things with that Rowan boy'.

'OK, so, there's no guy.' Rowan turns it back to my love life and raises his arms in surrender.

'Well, I didn't say that,' I admit.

Rowan slaps the table. 'I knew it! Also, I did actually know, because I saw a picture.'

'So why did you ask?!'

'Well, I wanted *you* to tell me. Go on. Looking *incredibly* cute together here, I have to say.' He brings up another picture from Sam's last birthday. I'm guessing that Mum doesn't post a lot about Ash – seeing how she'd rather pretend he doesn't exist – but this is a group shot. Ash and I are holding Sam as he tries to blow out his candles. 'Very *domestic*,' Rowan adds.

Another well-chosen word that he knows will spook me. 'His name is Ash,' I say, ignoring his comment.

'So this is the same guy you'd just started seeing the last time you came to New York, right?'

I'm surprised he remembers. I'd met Ash about six months before that last trip.

'Yes.'

'Tell me about him. Is he as good-looking as that skinny model with the cheekbones? Smarter than the astrophysicist?'

Huh. I forgot about the astrophysicist. I wonder what he's up to.

'He's . . . lovely.'

'Lovely' is such a meagre description of Ash. He's warm and affectionate. He remembers little details about people he's met once. He doesn't waste words so when he speaks it's always with care and consideration. Thinking of him makes it feel like the sun is rising in my stomach.

'Must be getting serious,' Rowan says. Emphasis on 'serious'.

OK, it's game set match. I'm officially freaked out. A few weeks ago Rowan's strategically placed taunts wouldn't have got to me. Ash and I are serious. We have been serious for a while and it's been years since I've been sure that I want him in my life forever. It's not the seriousness of our relationship that I'm freaked out about, it's the sudden shift to monogamy, and up until now – in my mind – seriousness and monogamy were not one and the same for us. But now, apparently, they are for Ash.

I nod. Rowan takes a long gulp of beer and makes a satisfied noise. 'Well, good for you, Flissy. Another drink?'

We stay until closing time and later, when Rowan walks me to the station, there's an awkward pause. I realise that nine times out of ten, this is when we'd go home together. But that can't happen tonight. The reality that I'm not allowed to do as I please anymore, that I have to go home now, that I'm not *free*, hits me and I'm breathless with how stifled I feel.

Or maybe that's the six pints I drank. Either way, it's the first time since my and Ash's new agreement that I've felt properly restricted, and I don't like it. I don't like feeling that my desires are wrong, like I'm some sort of criminal for having them, and having to bury them down and lock them away to feel like a good person.

I can't believe Rowan is here *now*. Of course he is. The timing is terrible. The timing is perfect.

Rowan leans in towards me. I can feel my body reacting. He's familiar and dangerous at the same time. My skin tingles and my lips soften and I'm very aware of my breasts. What bra did I put on today?

No, stop it. Bad Fliss! Bad Fliss! It doesn't matter what bra you're wearing because he's not going to see it. This is NOT allowed anymore.

'I've got an early start,' I mumble lamely.

Rowan raises an eyebrow in amusement. He keeps his face near mine and looks from my right eye to my left. 'Yeah, me too.'

He's expectant. He's going to lean in. I want him to and he knows it. Oh God. I can't avoid it anymore. I'm going to have to say something. 'And I . . . Well. Ash and I are in an exclusive relationship.'

The words hang in the air. Christ, that was difficult.

Rowan's reaction is *infuriating*.

'Oh, cool?' he says with a questioning tone, as if to say, *whatever, why are you telling me that?*

Ugh. We both know why I'm telling him that. Rowan and I have never made it through an entire evening in the same city without having sex before. Except once when I got a vomiting bug in Peru.

'Night, Flissy,' he adds. We stare at each other silently for a moment longer. How is this going to work? How are we going to keep working together when I'm this tempted after a few hours? I can't see it playing out well if he stays. But I don't want him to go back to New York either.

'See you in the morning,' I say.

He gives an almost imperceptible wink and turns and walks in the opposite direction, into the night. I watch him go. Christ. I am so drunk and turned on I should get a medal for that. Monogamy is going to be so much harder than I thought.

CHAPTER FIFTEEN:
COMPARTMENTALISE

HOLLY

I wake up on Saturday morning to a text from Fliss.

> How much contact with exes do you think is an appropriate amount of contact in a monogamous relationship?

Zero contact, I reply. And then I wonder why she's asking me this.

> Why?!?!

> My ex turned up as a surprise. We've not seen each other in years. He's kind of working with me. But before you say anything, we're friends!

> He's working with you?!

This sounds dodgy to me. My friends don't show up unannounced after years as a 'surprise'.

> Personally, I think this man sounds like a murky grey area and if you really want to just be with Ash, it's easier to keep things black and white.

> Yeah, OK, thanks, she replies, after starting and stopping typing several times.

I'm not convinced she's taking my advice on board at all. I get out of bed and brush my hair, making a mental note to ask her more about this person the next time I see her.

In the kitchen, I find Will reading the paper and waiting for me in front of two empty plates. I genuinely do a double-take. Will's an early riser so normally on weekends he'd get up before me and make himself breakfast. When he sees me he springs up and seats me at the table, pulling out the chair for me and gesturing.

'Good morning,' he says. 'One slice of toast? Or two?'

'Um. One please.'

This is so . . . lovely. I feel fluttery and light as he tucks my chair underneath me and dashes to the fridge. It's probably because we've not seen much of each other recently. I watch him bustling around the kitchen, winter sunlight streaming through the windows and the sound of clattering pots and pans filling the room, and think how we're the picture of domestic bliss.

Except, not really. Because we both have dates with other people tonight.

The way Fliss talks about it, it's like she can keep her other relationships completely separate from her relationship with Ash. Like they don't touch it. I've been trying to think like that, I really have, but I'm still struggling to compartmentalise in that way. It feels like all I do when I see Will now is try not to think about how strange it is that I've started dating someone else who I actually like, or I obsess over what might be going on for Will. Has he met someone else he likes, too? I suppose I'd be a huge hypocrite now if I was upset that he had, but it doesn't stop me dwelling on it. Somehow I can know that the fact I like Liam doesn't stop me loving Will, but Will liking someone else would still wound me.

And all that is when I get to see Will at all, in between all the extra hours at work and making time for a second boyfriend.

Ugh. *Second boyfriend*. Liam is not my second boyfriend! *Will is still my only boyfriend*.

'What tea do you want?' Will asks.

'Oh.' I'm brought out of my brain ramblings. 'Earl grey?'

Look at us, exchanging words about mundane household things as if nothing has changed. *Ugh*. There I go again . . . it's not supposed to change anything between us! And it hasn't, really. Logically, I can see that it hasn't. It shouldn't. I *can* master this. I can.

Will grabs my plate, brings it over to the counter and serves. He sits back down and puts the eggs in front of me; presented beautifully with garnish on top and sun-dried tomatoes on the side. Everything Will makes looks like it belongs on an Instagram account for artisan food lovers.

'Thank you so much.' I reach for my cutlery. 'Wow. What a treat.'

'I mean, I make this for us sometimes,' Will counters.

'Nope,' I state gently. 'Not since uni.' I don't mean it as an affront, but as soon as I say it, I realise it sounds like it. I've been getting so used to direct communication with Liam that for a second I forget Will won't react well to that statement, even though it's the truth.

Will's eyebrows knit together as he sifts through years of hazy memories.

'You know I like to get up early,' he says defensively.

I nearly don't say anything else. I normally wouldn't. Usually I wouldn't take any risks that might spoil the mood. My pulse is already quickening at this minor confrontation, but . . . I'm only stating the facts.

'Yeah.' I nod. 'I was just saying . . . It's nice to eat together.'

'Well, we are. How's work going?' Will asks.

I notice that he's deciding not to pursue a vaguely uncomfortable conversation and changing the subject instead. I don't know if I'd even have picked up on it before meeting Liam. It wouldn't have occurred to me as something to be bothered about. Today it does bother me, but I let it go anyway to keep the peace. He is doing something nice and making an effort, after all.

'Have you finished what you want to put forward for the new collection yet?' Will continues.

My heart does a little dance at the thought of the showcase. Once the autumn collection is shown and I'm credited for the first time ever, I want to have some other designs up my sleeve. I want to be ready for if I'm finally given a category that isn't jersey. 'No,' I say. 'I keep going back and forth.'

'Want to show me?'

I reach for my phone and share some of the inspirations I've been circling through with Will. Different styles, different materials.

'Oh, yeah.' Will peers at my screen. 'I like that material. But not with that cut. And I like that, but not with that colour.'

'Yeah, that's what I was thinking.' I pull out my sketch book to show him what I've mocked up. 'I thought maybe that material, this colour scheme, this shape.'

Will nods. 'I really like that.'

I flush with pride. After sharing my designs with Will, I always feel less afraid – excited even – about sharing them with the world. Even though Will and I design different things, he's always interested and useful when it comes to my job. Not just in the way that most people will say, 'Oh, that's nice.' He helps me think through what's working and what's not and dissects them with me at length, and they always end up getting to a better place with his input. And he wants my opinions on his stuff, too. Our mutual interest in each other's work is one of my favourite things about us. Things have been strained lately, but in this moment I remember exactly why we're so well suited.

'Thank you. I'm nervous, though,' I say. 'What if no one likes my design in the showcase? Or what if it's received well but I can't follow through with more good designs?'

He shrugs. 'You'll be fine,' he murmurs through another mouthful of eggs.

I can't help but be a little disappointed in his answer. Liam would have acknowledged my concerns and talked them through with me. I banish that thought. Will just supports me in a different way, by not entertaining my negativity.

'Do you want to watch a movie tonight?' He puts down his knife and fork.

I'm confused. Tonight? But . . . tonight is a date night. Isn't it?

'Erm,' is all I can think to say. I take another bite. Were we not supposed to be going out with other people this evening?

Generally, at the start of the week Will marks *out* on the calendar on certain days, and I assume those are the evenings he's going out on dates, so I make plans around him. Crap. I must have got the wrong day. I feel awful.

'I was thinking a takeaway?' Will continues when I don't answer.

'Oh, I thought you were busy tonight?' I question.

'No, I'm not.' Will reaches a hand out to me across the table. 'I feel like I've barely seen you, it would be good to spend an evening together.'

'That sounds so lovely,' I say. 'But . . . I have plans. I'm sorry. I must have marked the wrong day.'

'Oh.' Will withdraws his hand and fixes his gaze on his food. 'Right.'

There's an instant atmosphere. The eggs are officially soured.

'I'm really sorry,' I repeat. I can't swallow the bite that I've taken, so I put down my fork. 'I didn't know you wanted to do something.'

Will makes brief eye contact before looking down at his plate again. He gives a terse nod and clears his throat. For a moment, I think he's not going to say anything else and that will be the end of it.

Then he says, 'I didn't realise I had to book you so far in advance. My mistake.'

My heart starts racing. I don't deal well with confrontation and we've never had this level of conflict before. Usually, I would always be available. I have a few university and school friends but they don't live in London so any time I spend with them is planned well in advance. Will and I have friends as a couple but then we'd be going out with them together. Sometimes I go out with Tomi, but there are no huge demands on my time. I suppose things have rapidly become quite different. But then, I thought this was what he wanted?

'I'm sorry,' I apologise again. I'm not sure what else to say.

'So, you're not going to cancel your plans, then?' he continues.

I feel hot and flustered. He's completely blindsided me. Cancelling on people this late makes me uneasy. 'It's a bit last minute.'

'OK.'

He gets up and leaves the table. He looks so upset. Guilt courses through me. Should I cancel on Liam?

When I think about not seeing Liam this evening I feel disappointed. That makes me feel even guiltier.

I finish my breakfast alone, even though I've lost my appetite. I sit for five more minutes, taking deep breaths and trying to remain calm. Upsetting Will and cancelling on Liam are both options that make me highly anxious and I have no idea what to do. I've just reached the conclusion that I'll cancel, if Will's going to be upset, when Will comes back into the kitchen.

'Will, I'll cancel,' I say, standing up.

'Holly, it's fine. Go out. I thought you didn't want to go. I was only thinking of you. I've made plans now, so.'

He's pretending everything's fine, but his voice has that defensive quality it gets when he's talking to his brothers about politics.

'It's obviously not,' I say. 'I don't mind. It was my mistake. I thought . . .'

I point at the calendar, which is when I notice that today's date clearly says *Will: Out* underneath it. I *didn't* make a mistake.

'Oh,' I say.

Will follows my eyes to the calendar.

'It *does* say out,' I assert. 'So . . . I'm sorry, I'm so confused.' Why is Will getting so upset? 'Will,' I continue. 'Maybe we need to talk again about the ground rules, here? I thought that when you wrote "out" on the calendar, that was when we would both . . . you know. Be . . . out.' I point to where it clearly says that. 'Is that not how you wanted this to work?'

Will folds his arms. 'Yeah, no, it is. But I cancelled because I wanted to spend time with you.'

I can't help but feel pleased that he decided he wanted to keep Friday night free for me after all. But . . . was he expecting me to suddenly be available without even checking with me?

'But why did you think *I'd* be free?' I ask, genuinely puzzled.

'I thought you'd be pleased. I thought you'd rather spend the evening with me.'

Oh. It hits me. He *did* think that I had plans. And he just assumed I'd cancel them instantly to be with him?

'It's not that I don't want to spend the evening with you, but Will, I can't just—'

'I miss you, Holly.'

My heart softens. I miss him, too. I think about what Fliss said about setting clear parameters. We can sort this out if we decide on a better system going forward.

'Me too,' I say. 'OK, well . . . what do you want the system to be from now on? Should we clear more nights for each other?'

Will strides across the room, takes my head between his hands and kisses me. It's not a habitual, routine kiss. It's firm and slightly aggressive. It's almost like he's trying to tell me something, which should be sexy, but I can't help wishing he'd just answered my question instead.

He keeps kissing me and it doesn't feel romantic or seductive. It's too hard and rushed. His lips are smushing against mine and my neck is being pushed backward and I don't know what it is that he's trying to say. I can feel him trying to close this growing distance between us and I want to close it too, so badly, but this isn't doing it.

Ugh. I shake myself. This is Will. *My* Will. Kissing him should be natural and normal, but this feels anything but. I don't want to kiss right now. I want us to use actual *words*.

He picks me up and sits me on the kitchen counter. Does

he want to have sex? Here? Right now?! Straight after this horrible fight that we haven't even resolved?

We haven't had sex in weeks. Not since we started having an open relationship. Before that we would normally have sex about once a week, in bed, right before going to sleep. Never in the kitchen at 9.30 a.m.

It should be exciting, I guess. I should feel alive and aroused. But in reality the counter is cold on my bare thighs. It's an uncomfortable angle to be kissing. I'm in my giant, stained pyjamas. And it feels forced and not at all like us.

Has Will been doing this with someone else? Some sexual, alluring woman who is always horny even when she's eating her morning eggs?

Maybe Will wishes we were a couple that threw down in the kitchen at nine-thirty, but we're not. Maybe Will is that person with somebody else. Maybe *I* could be that person with somebody else. But it's not what we are. I don't know what we are, anymore, and I want to figure it out together but not like this. We're physically as close as two people can be right now, but I feel alone. I'm hit with the overwhelming feeling that this is all wrong.

Will is still kissing me and I can't breathe. My chest is tight. I have to stop before another panic attack comes on.

'Will,' I say as he kisses down my neck. 'Will. Not now.'

He stops and looks at me. 'What's wrong?'

I hop down from the counter. 'I'm just not in the mood.'

He nods, but he can't help but look dejected. 'OK.'

'Can we talk instead?'

He shrugs. 'Nothing to say,' he answers. 'It's fine, Holly,

171

go out tonight. Have a good time.' He leaves the room and I hear him shut the bedroom door.

I stand for a moment, trying to take deep breaths and hoping he'll come back again to sort things out, but he doesn't reappear.

CHAPTER SIXTEEN:
PRESENTS DON'T SOLVE PROBLEMS

FLISS

I sit at my desk, staring at the message from Holly.

> I feel like I have no time for Will anymore! Help! How do you do this? xx

I reply.

> Very careful time management. Plan when you're going to be seeing each other and stick to it.

> We did. Or, at least I thought we did? But then Will seemed to think I'd be free to be with him the other night. And I wasn't.

> Well, that's Will's problem.

But I felt so bad! We've barely seen each other at all. xx

I wish I had that problem, I think. I feel like my entire life has become The Ash Show. I wake up in the morning and he's eating his cereal. I get home from work and he's in my shower. I close my eyes and the vision of his face is imprinted on the back of my eyelids like a beautiful, monotonous mosaic. Is this what monogamous relationships are like? Surely not? Obviously I thought we'd see each other more, but I didn't think he'd want this level of contact.

I've stayed in the office all week. Jenny and Henry asked me why I haven't been working from home and I told them it's a new policy, but really I just need the space. Ash seems to want to come over to mine, or for me to go over to his, most evenings and I still haven't had the heart to tell him I'm feeling suffocated.

I was hoping he'd catch on but it seems like the more I try to withdraw, the more he wants us to be around each other. He's trying so hard to transport our relationship to this new place and I'm constantly guilty for feeling like the train is moving too fast.

On cue, my phone beeps. It's Ash.

How's your morning? x

I JUST SAW HIM. WHY IS HE ASKING ME THIS? What exciting news could I possibly have to share between my leaving the house and arriving at work? We'll have nothing to talk about when we next see each other because I'll already have told him everything. Christ, does he want to set up a camera at my desk? Follow me into the toilet?!

I saw some cats having a fight, I reply.

Cool.

Aghhhhh.

I, on the other hand, am seeing way too much of Ash, I text Holly. How do you do this?!

Do what?

See someone every day and talk to them all the bloody live long day?!

What do you mean? You feel like you need space?

YES.

Just ask for it. I'm sure he'll understand. You're going through a transitional phase. And just because you're monogamous doesn't mean you have to spend all your time together xx

She makes it sound so easy and I know she's right. It's the advice I'd give someone in my position, so why is it so difficult for me to follow? But it's much harder to take advice than it is to dish it out. It's challenging to say this to Ash because we've never had to outright ask each other for more or less time before. That was so in-built into the structure of our relationship and, until now, it felt like we were both totally satisfied with how much of each other we were allotted. Our relationship was set up so perfectly. Or at least, I thought it was.

Throughout my twenties I'd become pretty direct about asking for what I wanted from partners, but becoming monogamous has completely changed that for me. With anyone else I was seeing, I didn't fear hurting their feelings because everything was laid out so clearly from the start and we weren't having especially deep relationships. With Ash, we were always on the same page about what we wanted, so I never had to fear hurting his feelings either. What I wanted and what he wanted were one and the same. But now that it's not anymore, asking Ash directly to give me some breathing room feels like an impossible thing to do. He's a sensitive person; I can't bear the thought of upsetting him.

Rowan arrives and sits next to me. He's only been here a week but, by now, it's an unspoken rule that this is his seat. It's still utterly wild having him here, in my city. In my workplace. I think at any other time I might have found it even stranger. But given Ash upending our entire relationship, as well as Henry moving into my flat, I'm finding myself genuinely appreciative of his presence. It's not comforting, exactly. But . . . it's an escape.

I think of Holly's horror when I said I was hanging out with Rowan. I gather that Holly is not the sort of person who stays in touch with exes.

I told her we were friends, but I knew Holly wouldn't see it that way. We're not friends like Holly and I are friends. We don't see each other often, communicate regularly or share huge amounts of information about our personal lives. We would meet up when I was in New York for work and talk about stupid shit, books or politics or ideas and get really drunk, with a side of casual flirtation, and usually end up sleeping together.

It's a sort of friendship. There are lots of different kinds of friends. We're more like family, in a strange way. We might not talk all the time but no matter where we are on the planet we're always connected . . . A bit like distant cousins . . . except, distant cousins who bang.

'All right, Flissy. Got any nice plans for the weekend?' he asks as he turns on his computer. He sets down a mug, then adjusts its position so it's in the centre of the coaster. 'What are you up to with the overbearing boyfriend? Matching tattoos?'

I flex my fingers with irritation. He's always known exactly how to push my buttons. I hate that Ash has already been characterised by Rowan in this way. I should never have tried to explain our situation to him. But we've been drunk together twice already in the week that he's been here – I *may* have been using him to hide from Ash – and it was all bound to come out at some point. Especially when he keeps asking so many questions about my life to deflect from talking about his own. I still only have a vague idea of why he left his high-paid job in New York to be here.

'He's not overbearing,' I snap. 'Like I said, we're going through a . . .' What was the term Holly just used? I glance down at our message thread. '*Transitional phase.*'

'Right.' Rowan nods, pleased to have irritated me.

Like I said, comforting would be the wrong word.

'I got a message from Mama Henderson today.' He waves

his phone in my face. 'She saw that I'm in London and she's thrilled.'

'Of course she is.' I roll my eyes.

'She said we must go out to dinner.'

Typical. She never invites Ash and me for dinner.

'Don't worry, I'll get you out of it.'

'What?! No! Don't you dare!' Rowan points in my face.

'You want to hang out with my parents?' I raise a sceptical eyebrow.

'I'm dying to see your parents again!'

'Well . . . all right. Maybe.' I'm hesitant to organise this when Ash never sees them. I feel a stab of loyal protectiveness over him, when they dislike him for such unfair reasons.

A man wearing a blue shirt and cap, who's been conferring with someone on the other side of the room, walks over to us. 'Felicity Henderson?'

'Uh, yes?' I ask.

'Sign here.' He passes me a clipboard and a pen.

'What is this?' I glance suspiciously at Rowan.

He shrugs. 'Don't look at me.'

I sign and the man retreats into the corridor, returning a moment later with a bouquet of flowers. *What the hell?*

He sets the flowers down in front of me.

'Have a good day!' he calls as he retreats.

I stare at the bright coral roses and fresh eucalyptus. There's a note tucked into the leaves. It reads: *Just wanted to brighten up your day. Ax*

Oh . . . that's so lovely. This is every girl's dream, right? Is this the part where I swoon? It's so sweet. It's so . . . *much.*

'You were saying?' Rowan leans around the flowers with wide, angelic eyes.

Ugh. He's the *worst*.

I start work on a French book I'm translating into English for an independent publisher. It's a task that will take me much longer than most of the jobs we're given and requires a lot more concentration. It's the perfect excuse to ignore Rowan, which I do, pointedly, for a whole hour.

'What you doing?' He eventually breaks the silence.

'A book.' My answer is short.

He whistles. 'Oh no, what did I do?'

'Nothing,' I hiss. 'I'm just trying to work.'

Ugh. I hate this. I hate how much he's got to me. I hate how obvious it is.

'Is it because of what I said about your boyfriend? I'm only teasing, Flissy. He seems like a sweet guy.'

Ugh. Rowan calling Ash 'sweet' is even more infuriating. When Rowan and I were together, we'd make fun of sentimental, mawkish gifts. The flowers sit between us like a glaring symbol of everything we would usually mock each other for.

'I mean, I never had to work so hard for your attention, but respect to him for making the effort.'

URGH. I don't respond to Rowan's loaded comment, but any pretence of focusing on work is long out of the window. I look into his eyes as if in a challenge and he stares right back, unfazed and gloating. He is maddening. He is *highly attractive*.

Fuck.

'Shall we get out of here?' he says.

Typical. One week on the job and he's already ditching. He never takes anything seriously.

'No,' I reply. 'I have work to do.'

'Come on,' he wheedles. 'You can do it tomorrow, no? Who's going to care?'

He's right in a sense. At the agency we're more like a bunch of freelancers who take on the work we want and they take commission, rather than employees. I don't have a 'manager' as such. I don't even *have* to come into the office. If we left, Monty might raise an eyebrow, but nobody would say anything. The thought of just strolling out of work in the middle of the day to do whatever we like is quite liberating.

It's one of the things I always liked about Rowan. He reminds me that most of the time rules are self-imposed. That everything in life is a choice and that I can choose anything I want. It's like you move through the world with these invisible bars surrounding you . . . *No, I can't eat that, I can't wear that, I can't live there, I could never do that . . .* And Rowan's always there to inform me that I'm my own jailer.

But today he's incredibly annoying. Because he's right. Ash is trying too hard and things are becoming forced between us.

'I care,' I reply, even though I'm not sure that's true.

I continue translating, but I've only done another sentence before I'm distracted by another text from Ash.

Did you get the flowers?

Yes, so pretty, thank you!

Do you want to go for lunch? I have a meeting not far from your office.

A sense of pressure that's been building in my temples takes hold. I feel a full-blown headache coming on. We just saw each other this morning and will see each other tomorrow. I'm hit with the overwhelming sensation that if this is really how much Ash wants from me, I can't do this. I know I'm going to have to bite the bullet and talk to him about it at some point, but for now, I choose avoidance.

'Let's go,' I say to Rowan, turning off my computer. He grins and starts shutting down his own. I quickly type out a reply to Ash.

Sorry, I already have lunch plans. See you tomorrow X

CHAPTER SEVENTEEN:
DON'T COMPARE

HOLLY

'Holly.' Will bangs on the bedroom door, startling me. 'What are you doing in there? Why is the door locked?'

Crap.

'Er, I'm just having a lie-down,' I call.

'I bought you a latte.'

He . . . bought me a latte? Will detests lattes. He ridicules me for buying them. And he went and got me one voluntarily? I'm floored.

'Thank you. That's so sweet. But errr . . . I can't move at the moment,' I lie. 'I'm not feeling very well. Cramps.' Any mention of periods usually gets rid of him. Liam asked me about my period outright the other day and I nearly fell over in shock.

'Oh,' he says. 'OK, don't worry.' I hear him shuffling away and my heart rate returns to normal. Will *cannot* see what I'm doing.

I look back down at the wax strips in front of me. I've been willing myself to use them for at least ten minutes.

'OK, all right, come on,' I encourage myself, opening the box. 'You can do this.'

Before I can change my mind, I peel one apart and lay its waxy interior against my inner thigh. Then another, and another, and another.

There is no going back now.

I rip one off.

'*MOTHER OF CRAPPING HELL*,' I whisper as quietly as possible.

I forgot how painful this was. This is actual torture. Oh God. And there are six strips left. I don't usually wax but I'm self-conscious about someone new seeing me undressed.

Not that Liam will definitely be seeing me in my underwear tonight. Just because I'm going to his flat tonight doesn't mean anything. I'm just waxing as insurance. Just in case *the mood* should so take us.

Twenty minutes later, Will knocks on the door again. 'Holly, I've got paracetamol, let me in?'

'Uh, thanks!' My voice sounds strangled. I leap up and scramble to hide the wax strips in my cupboard, along with the new underwear that I bought when I realised that nearly all my pants are threadbare or stained. If Will sees any of this, he'll know immediately that it's not for his benefit.

I throw on a pair of pyjama shorts to cover up my half newly naked bikini line, with the other half covered in strips, and open the door. Will passes me some drugs and a glass of water, and then the latte.

'Here you go,' he says.

'Wow. Thank you.' I take it from him, still hardly believing it.

'Are you still leaving at three?' he asks.

I'm going to meet Fliss before seeing Liam. Since the abortive attempt to have sex in the kitchen right before my date, resulting in me showing up to see Liam disturbed and agitated, I've decided it's best if I don't go to dates from the house. I've started going from work or going out somewhere first.

I wrote *out* on the calendar myself, so there's no confusion about whether I might be free. Before our big miscommunication I hadn't even questioned the system. But the more I thought about it, the more I thought . . . of course Will figured that I'd come running. Everything so far has been on his terms. Why wouldn't he assume I'd drop everything for him at a moment's notice?

We need a new system and much as I'd love to have spoken about it first, given that Will wouldn't, I just started doing it differently. Why shouldn't I be the one to write *out* on the calendar first? When Will first saw it I could tell he was bothered because he went a bit red and spluttered, and he was a bit off with me for the rest of the day, but he never asked me about it. I guess he realised that would be hypocritical.

'Yes, I should feel better in a bit,' I say.

'OK,' he says, and heads back to the living room.

I shut the door, re-lock it, take a sip of my latte and remove the remaining wax strips without screaming. Then I put on my new underwear. The bra is a balconette, navy blue with a lace edge. I wanted something nice but not *too* nice. Something alluring but not something that says, *I've been plotting to have sex with you tonight.*

I look at myself in the mirror. I feel *sexy*. Owning nice clothes that make me feel good is one of my favourite things to do. I buy new outfits regularly. When and why did I stop doing this with my underwear?

It crosses my mind that my boyfriend is in the next room and I'm standing here half-naked in new lingerie. I think about walking next door, standing in front of Will and climbing on top of him, but something stops me. Since the incident, neither of us has tried initiating sex again. I'm sure we'll be back to normal soon, we just need a bit of space from what happened. Instead, I get dressed and give him a goodbye kiss on the cheek.

'How's the latte?' he asks as I put my coat on.

'Oh, delicious, thank you,' I answer.

'All right, well, bye then.' For a moment I think he looks a little lost, but he's written *out* underneath my *out*, so he must have his own date later, too. Bemused, I kiss him again and hurry out of the house, still taking sips of my beverage.

An hour later, I'm sitting across from Fliss in what has become our usual spot, in our customary armchairs. She's sipping in a childlike manner on a strawberry milkshake and I can tell something is on her mind. She seems distracted and cagey. Whereas a few weeks ago she was coming to me for advice about Ash, today she's skilfully avoided my questions about him.

'So, what have you been up to?' I try a new tack.

She shrugs. 'Oh, same old, same old.' She turns her head and looks out the window into the bright Saturday afternoon sunlight. 'Oh, I went to Roller Nation last night,' she adds, like she's only just remembered. This is something I truly admire about Fliss. She does things like . . . go roller skating . . . without a second thought. I mean, I'd *go*, but I'd be trying to assuage my anxiety about it for a week beforehand and then probably talk to Tomi about it for a week non-stop afterwards.

'Oh cool!' I say. 'How was it? Did you fall over? Did Ash have fun?'

'Errr, I wasn't with Ash,' she says. 'But yes, I did fall over. About five million times before I just gave up and drank. Look at this bruise, Christ.' She starts showing me a nasty purple mark under her sleeve.

'Who were you with?' I ask after giving due diligence to her injury.

'Rowan.' She says his name after a moment's pause. Her eyes dart away from mine and fixate on her milkshake. She knows I'm going to have something to say about this.

'Rowan?' I try not to sound like a school teacher. 'Have you seen much of him this week? He works with you now, right?' Again, I try to keep the judgement out of my voice. But Fliss's ex-boyfriend showing up without any warning and joining her workplace is serious red-flag behaviour. And now they seem to be spending all their time together. Maybe it's just a coincidence but I feel like every time I've spoken to her over the last fortnight, she's been with this man.

She shrugs again. 'Yeah, I guess. And yes. It's been really nice having a pal at work, actually.'

A *pal*. I haven't had sex with any of my 'pals'.

'Is Ash OK with that?' I ask. If Will's ex-girlfriend had started working with him and he was suddenly with her all the time, I'd definitely have something to say. Or at least . . . I *would* have . . . before we started open dating. Now I don't know what I'm allowed to have a problem with and what I'm not. But Fliss and Ash are in an exclusive relationship. He wanted her to stop seeing other people, so presumably he'd have some feelings about her hanging around so much with her ex.

'Why wouldn't he be? We're not doing anything.' Fliss sounds a little defensive.

'Yeah . . .' I bite my lip. She's technically right, but when it comes to exclusive relationships, in my opinion, she's all wrong. I'm not sure whether to keep talking, but a few weeks ago she did ask me to help her make things work with Ash, and I can see this *Rowan* guy quickly derailing all her efforts. 'Except . . . I don't know. Is this guy really just a friend?'

Fliss takes a long slurp of milkshake. 'No,' she admits. 'No, I suppose not. I guess he's hard to classify.'

I knew it.

'Mm,' I say. 'I just think . . . For me, anyway, in a long-term closed relationship, it can feel like even though you have all these more obvious lines, following the unspoken ones is equally important. Like . . . not spending all your time with hard-to-classify people, even if you're not technically doing anything wrong.'

Fliss frowns. 'But we're not sleeping together.'

'I mean, you *want* to sleep with him though, right?'

Fliss sucks the last of her milkshake from the bottom of the glass. The air coming up through the straw makes a loud sound.

'No,' she says eventually. 'I don't want to sleep with Rowan.'

I relax back into my seat. 'OK, well, if that's true then I guess you're right.' I'm still not totally convinced – Rowan seems shady to me – but I feel better knowing that's not what Fliss is thinking. I've never met Ash, but I'm rooting for him and Fliss. He just sounds like a good egg. And this Rowan person sounds like an ass, quite frankly. Showing up out of the blue and, by the sounds of it, trying to undermine her committed relationship? I don't like it at all.

'But what about *you*?' Fliss sets her empty glass down on the table. 'Come on. I want to hear all about Liam.'

I can't help but smile at the mention of Liam's name.

'Oh, the smile says it all,' Fliss asserts. 'What's the sex like? Let me live vicariously.'

I'm about to say we haven't had sex yet, then I remember I told Fliss I was in this for sex. So I change the subject instead. 'Can I ask a question? Did the fact you were having sex with other people ever affect your sex life with Ash?'

I keep thinking about that painfully contrived attempt at sex with Will.

'In what way?' Fliss asks.

'Well . . . I don't know. Will and I tried to do it the other day and it's almost like we were . . . pretending to be another couple. I think . . . I think maybe he's been doing stuff with other women that he now wants to do with me?' The thought makes me feel hollow. 'Whereas, I don't know, I thought the point was to be with different people, not try to make each other into someone else.'

'What kind of stuff? Like . . . bondage?'

'*No,*' I exclaim. Then I try to sound cool. 'I mean, no, not that. I was about to go out on my date, and then he tried . . . well . . . he tried to . . . *do it with me in the kitchen.*'

Fliss blinks. 'He tried to . . . do it with you in the kitchen? That's it? Christ, Holly, you really *do* need to sexually experiment.' She nudges me jokingly.

Heat rises in my cheeks. 'It sounds stupid when I say it like that. But . . . I don't know . . . it just felt kind of desperate and fake.'

Fliss nods. 'Hmm. Yeah, I get you. Doesn't sound to me like he's been passionately throwing other women across kitchen counters, to be honest. Sounds to me like he's jealous.'

Jealous?

'What?' I splutter. I can't help but feel a little thrill at the thought of Will being jealous, even though it's obviously not true. What an absurd thought. He's the one who asked for this!

'I think someone wanted to make sure you were thinking of him on your date,' Fliss continues.

'That's ludicrous. This was all his idea,' I assert.

'People are complicated.' Fliss sighs. Then she looks at me with her head tilted to one side. 'I didn't know this was Will's idea?'

'Oh, yeah,' I stumble. 'I mean, initially. But . . .' I reach for Will's words in my mind, back from when he first brought this up. Back when I thought he was going to ask me to marry him. God, that feels like a long time ago. 'We've always been on the same page about wanting to try it.'

I feel bad for continually lying to Fliss about this, but I know she wouldn't be supportive if she knew the truth that

I only went along with this for Will. The more I do this, the more I don't know what I'd do without her help.

'Do you think it's going well for him?' Fliss asks. 'Is he enjoying it?'

'Uh . . .' I think over the last few weeks. My instant answer is yes, of course. But now that Fliss mentions it, I'm not totally sure. All I can find evidence of is him suddenly making me breakfast and bringing me lattes and asking questions about when I'm going to be out.

I dismiss the thought. Of course Will's enjoying it. This is what Will wanted. And now I need to focus on enjoying it, too.

'Anyway, enough about Will. What about *Liam*?' Fliss asks. 'How's he?!'

'He's . . .' I search for the right word. '. . . *Accessible*. He wants to let himself be entirely known, and to know others, and you can't help but feel like anything you had to say to him would be OK as long as it was the truth.' I feel a little stab, then, because I haven't been entirely honest with him. But then, I remind myself, that what I told him versus telling him I'm in an open relationship amounts to the same thing. 'It's the opposite of Will. Often I don't know what Will's thinking. I mean,' I add hurriedly, 'I sort of don't need to. We've been together so long we just *get* each other, you know?'

Fliss nods slowly. She looks at me thoughtfully, then says, 'Holly, I'd try not to compare Will and Liam so much. Enjoy the different things they have to offer, obviously, but if you only look at Liam in how he's different to Will, you're not really going to get to know him in his own right. And it could become like you're weighing up who you like better, which isn't the point of this, right?'

'Right,' I bluster. 'God, no, obviously. I'm with Will. I love Will. No comparing necessary.'

We keep chatting until it's time for me to go and meet Liam. When we say goodbye, I walk away with that little boost of reassurance that I've started to become used to; the one that keeps me going through the week. Someone else has done this. Someone else understands. There is someone who can help me get through this and get back on track with Will.

Except, as I walk to meet Liam, I realise I'm actually looking forward to seeing him. Obviously doing this for Will is how it started, but a niggling feeling is starting to appear. Now I'm not sure I *am* doing this just for Will or that being with him is my end goal here. I'm not sure I know exactly what my end goal is anymore.

Is marrying Will still what I want?

I shake myself. Of course it is. I'm being silly. This is something Will needs and we're doing it, so I may as well enjoy myself, right? It doesn't mean I don't still want to be with Will ultimately.

I'm meeting Liam at his flat in Dalston. I've avoided thinking too much about it until now but . . . I'm going round a *boy's house*. I feel giddy. The last time I 'went round a boy's house' I was a teenager. His name was Ethan Baxter and we were going to lose our virginities because his mum was out, but she ended up staying in and we all watched *Eastenders* together. Ethan Baxter lost his virginity with Victoria Atcherley in the second-floor girls' bathrooms the following Monday instead.

When Will and I met, it was different because we were in halls together. After uni we moved in together pretty quickly. It occurs to me how strange it is that most of my adult life I've been with Will. Until now, I didn't know what adult Holly was like on a first date. I think of all the experiences I've missed out on by being with Will. Except, I never looked at it that way, because we were happy and you can't ask for more than that. At least, I thought we were happy.

What am I thinking?! We *are* happy.

I'm nervous by the time I get to Liam's street. Chatting with Fliss was a distraction, but now all I can think about is whether my deodorant is holding strong or whether I should have gone for sexier underwear after all.

Not that Liam is *necessarily* going to be seeing my underwear.

I identify the right house in the row of Victorian terraces but pretend to miss it and continue to walk up and down the street for a few minutes, just to give myself space to mentally prepare. Did I definitely tweeze the hair on my big toe? I breathe in, and out.

Except, no amount of deep breathing outside some random person's front garden is going to help me calm down about the fact that *potential* sex with the first new person in a decade is *possibly but not certainly* happening in the next few hours. I just need to ring the doorbell.

For a second nothing stirs. I think maybe he's forgotten and almost feel relieved. I'm just thinking I can go home and make hot chocolate and watch *Drag Race* instead – because Will's out, he'd moan otherwise – but then I hear movement stirring and footsteps coming towards the door. By the time Liam opens it, my heart is thudding.

'Hello,' he says. 'Come in, come in.'

I try to smile and reply but my face and voice both appear to have frozen. I move past him into the hallway.

'Can I take your coat?' he asks.

I nod and hand it to him. He hangs it on a peg and I observe his back. It's a really nice back. Leading into a beautiful neck. Oh my God. I'm such a creep. I haven't even said a word yet and here I am staring intently at the back of his head.

'How was your day?' I manage. *Words!* Thank you!

'Yeah, good. We're done consulting with this one company and we've managed to make them at least forty per cent more energy efficient, so, job done. Let's go up.'

'Oh that's cool,' I comment. 'Sure.'

I take off my shoes (big toe hair *definitely* gone). We leave the communal hallway and walk up the stairs to Liam's flat on the first floor. I'm greeted by an open kitchen/living room with wooden flooring, beige rugs and a big, blue sofa running parallel to the kitchen cabinets. Some vegetables are already lying chopped on the surface. There's a big TV in one corner and a darts board on the other.

'Welcome!' Liam throws an arm out.

I'm in a boy's house.

'Are you into darts?' I manage to ask.

'Not really. That's Elijah's. My housemate's. Although it's good fun when we have parties.'

'Oh cool. Is he here?'

'Nah, he's on a stag.'

His housemate is *away*. Classic sign that he thinks we

might have sex tonight. Right?! Ugh. Holly, you're twenty-nine years old, on a fourth date at someone's house. Of course he thinks there might be sex. But if you don't want to, you don't have to. *Relax.*

Except, I do want to, even though I'm scared. Is it OK that I want to? Kissing and talking is one thing. Actually sleeping with someone else is . . . a new level of weird.

'Make yourself at home.' Liam picks up a knife and resumes chopping.

'What are we having?' I sit down on the sofa.

'Penne à la Liam,' he says. 'Sorry, that was a dad joke. Spaghetti bolognaise.' He grins. 'Not a chef, I'm afraid.'

I think of Will and what he'd make someone on a first date. Definitely not a spag bol. He can't even make scrambled eggs without making them extra. I wonder if he's at some woman's flat right now, making her creamy spinach-stuffed salmon or macadamia-crusted lamb. Everything he makes for dinner takes hours to prep. I do enjoy the food but sometimes it's exasperatingly long. Three hours to make and three minutes to eat. We don't have time for anything else during the rest of the evening and Will is concentrating so he doesn't talk much, so even though he's made me dinner I don't feel like we've properly spent time together.

I think of what Fliss said. *Stop comparing him to Will.*

'How's work been this week?' Liam asks. 'Stressful? Busy? Tiring? Fun? Creative? Fulfilling?'

I laugh. 'All of the above.'

'Is that Amber person still giving you grief?'

'Always.' I smile. I've noticed that Liam remembers details about the people in my life, whereas Will asks more about my designs but is less interested in office dynamics. He knows Tomi, obviously, but aside from that I'm not sure he could name anyone I work with.

Stop comparing him to Will.

'I don't know how you put up with it. Or do such long hours. But I suppose you're really passionate about what you do. I care about the planet but I don't love what I'm *actually* doing when I sit down at my desk, if that makes sense. I like that I'm working for a good cause, though, and I can leave it behind at 5 p.m. and go down the pub, so it suits me. But I think it's great that you care so much and actually get paid to be creative. So many people would kill for that.'

'I guess, yeah.' I feel myself reddening and try not to sound big-headed. Compliments are so awkward. 'There's a lot to the job that's *not* creative.' I think of all the admin I did for Amber this week that I needed hourly biscuit incentives from Tomi to make it through.

Liam waves his hand dismissively. 'I mean, you can't escape that. If you're doing something you love at least ten per cent of the time, it's better than most.'

I swell with pride. I love the way Liam makes me feel about myself. Will is positive about my work but in a totally different way. He'll compliment what I've done in a way that Liam doesn't – Liam's not really got a design eye – but he doesn't make me feel so good about how I'm choosing to spend my life.

Stop. Comparing. Him. To. Will.

We eat the spag bol, which is delicious, and I try very hard not to compare it to Will's cooking. Then we sit on the sofa and Liam puts on some music I don't know that he can't believe I've never heard. We open a bottle of red wine, and then another.

This is SO much better than watching *Eastenders* with Ethan Baxter's mum.

At about ten-thirty, Liam starts to yawn. 'Ah, it's getting late.' He looks at me and holds eye contact. The question of what's going to happen next hangs in the air. The nerves I felt earlier, which dissolved in Liam's company and copious amounts of wine, flicker in my stomach.

I can go home, or I can have sex with this gorgeous man. I notice that, since we ate, I've not wondered what Will is doing. Obviously I'm wondering it now, but I'm wondering about wondering it, which is not the same. When we first started doing this, I would constantly burn with curiosity about what was happening for him. Thinking of him even looking at another woman made me feel nauseous. It's not that I'm not curious, but tonight I've used more brain space on Liam than I have thinking about what Will might be up to.

Liam puts his wine down on the table and kisses me. I put my own glass down.

I'm used to the way he kisses now. But I'm not used to the way his hand is sliding up my shirt and towards my bra. Or how his other hand is unbuttoning my jeans, a thumb dipping beneath my underwear and brushing across my hip. My whole body shivers at his touch. It's unfamiliar. It's terrifying. It's thrilling.

I feel like you do right before the roller-coaster goes upside down. Am I really going to have sex with someone else?! Really? Am I doing this?

Then Liam takes his top off and, casting my eyes over his bare chest and defined stomach muscles, I realise I already knew the answer to that question when I came here.

CHAPTER EIGHTEEN:

MENTAL CHEATING ISN'T BETTER THAN ACTUAL CHEATING

FLISS

I don't want to sleep with Rowan.

The words that I said to Holly yesterday afternoon ring around in my head.

Big. Fat. Lie.

I'm not normally a liar. If there's one thing I can say about myself, at least since I hit my mid-twenties, it's that I'm unreservedly honest. I want what I want, I do what I want and I don't hide it or apologise for it. But for the past few weeks, I'm going around fibbing all over the place. Pretending I don't think things that I do.

It's OK that I want to sleep with Rowan! It's normal and natural and ridiculous to pretend that I wouldn't. We've been having sex on and off since I was twenty-two. There's a chemistry there that's probably never going to go away. For years, Ash and I have lived under the mutual agreement that it's fine to be attracted to other people. Now we're not supposed to sleep with anyone else, so I feel like I can't admit that I *want* to anymore. But it's not like my feelings can just disappear. Or can they? Is that the idea of monogamy? Eventually, because you're not allowed to have sex with anyone else, you stop wanting to?

I don't believe that for a *second*.

I can't help but feel all I've done is signed myself up for a life of dishonesty and sexual frustration.

I had one monogamous relationship before Ash. His name was James and he was charming and kind and a total sweetheart; actually, he was quite a lot like Ash. I met him during my last year of university. I was drawn to him from the start, but about six months into our relationship I knew I was still attracted to other people. Not just in a *I notice they're attractive* way, but in a *I am using every ounce of willpower not to have sex with this person* way.

I ended up moving to New York after uni and we agreed to do long distance. I missed him and it was hard and I ended up getting drunk at a costume party and calling to tell him how I felt. I think there was some particularly fit guy there, dressed as a sautéed potato.

I thought he'd understand, but he couldn't seem to wrap his head around it. It was like he thought that I couldn't love him like I said I did, if I still felt that way about other people, and no matter how much I told him that wasn't true, we couldn't see eye to eye.

The next morning, James broke up with me. He was so

upset with me and I felt like I was going to die of guilt. I tore myself up over it for weeks. I took freezing-cold showers and stopped eating because I deserved to be punished. I felt sick every time I saw a potato. It absolutely crushed me that I'd crushed him.

That was around the time I met Rowan. I told him what had happened and waited for the inevitable judgement to follow. But Rowan just shrugged and said, 'Hey, Flissy, don't beat yourself up about it. It's OK.'

'It is?' I asked.

'Yeah. Some of us just aren't built for relationships.'

I remember feeling deflated at the suggestion that maybe I just wasn't built to find love, but I was relieved that at least he didn't think there was something wrong with me. I was destroyed by what had happened with James. All the songs about all-encompassing, obsessive, consuming romance and TV shows and films where people fall in love and never look at another person again were starting to make me feel like an aberration, and Rowan was the first person who made me feel normal.

Rowan and I were never in a relationship, exactly; we were more like mates who spent all their time together and had a lot of sex. He was fun and interesting and we ran about New York in between travelling for AT blowing all our money and making fun of people in their 'boring' relationships. We did this for over a year before it ended because we went our separate ways geographically. It was always more of a 'see you later' than a 'goodbye'.

Over the years, we stayed friends and both continued to dodge serious relationships. I was too traumatised by what had happened with James and I thought my only option was avoiding relationships altogether. So I had a lot of things that lasted a few months and then phased out. I focused on my job and travelling and seeing the world. I preferred keeping it casual, even when I liked someone.

When I met Ash, it was different. I didn't want to keep it casual, because I fell in love with him. But I didn't want to stop seeing other people, either. We agreed about love being free and never wanting it to feel possessive or habitual and that was part of the reason I fell for him in the first place. That was when I first discovered there *was* a relationship that existed in a way that I wanted to do it. That I could create any kind of relationship I wanted. I know now people have all kinds of different relationships – it's not like Ash and I are doing anything new – but you don't see it normalised anywhere, and my own family are so traditional that the discovery was like opening my eyes to an entirely new planet.

Was it all just some youthful bullshit he was pretending to think? Kind of like how when you're a teenager you swear you're never going to be interested in game shows even though you secretly feel that rush of adrenaline when you get a question right on *The Chase*? Did he ever really believe it? Because I did. For me, it didn't have an expiry date.

I sit in Ash's bed, looking around my familiar surroundings. The blue bedspread, the tidy desk, the pretty fireplace. A month ago, I felt like I belonged here. Recently I've felt like an old piece of furniture you want to find a place for because you love it so much, but it just doesn't go with anything.

The bedroom door opens and the sound of Classic FM that Ash listens to in the mornings floats in. He comes in with a breakfast tray.

'Morning. You're so pretty,' he says as he looks at me, cowering from the morning light underneath a nest of unwashed hair. Love really does make fools of us all.

'I made you pancakes.' He sets it down beside me. 'With maple syrup and bacon.' He makes a vomit face. Ash and I have serious disagreements about what constitutes a good pancake. I like the little fat ones that make me feel like I'm back in America. Usually he refuses to make them thicker than a centimetre. Obviously today he's decided to put his pancake morals to one side.

He's so sweet, but every attempt to show me affection is just strengthening the walls I'm putting up. I can feel them closing in around me, creating a barrier between us. But I don't know what to do to stop it. I know Holly said to be honest with him about it, but what can I say? Please stop making me pancakes, you asshole?

'Thank you, that's so kind,' I say instead.

I eat the pancakes while Ash reads his chunky book about the history of humankind. When I'm done, he puts it down on the bedside table and leans in towards me. He starts kissing my neck in a way that says *I want to have sex*.

On paper, our sex life has been the same since we agreed to be exclusive. Irregular and always a surprise in one way or another. Every time we have sex is totally different; it could be quick and satisfying or long and intense, but it's never routine.

Ostensibly nothing has changed, but the connection we usually have – the one that feels like it's just me and Ash and our bed and that is where the world ends – has gone a little wobbly. I can't keep my head in it. I feel so detached from Ash. Which is ironic, given that we've just agreed to attach ourselves to one another for the rest of time, if all goes according to the big, heteronormative, monogamous step-by-step life plan.

Ash starts lifting my pyjama top. I try to relax into it. I kiss his cheekbones and around his eyes. This is Ash. *My Ash.* He's the same person as he was a month ago. I'm the same person as I was. Everything is going to be OK. I just need to give it time to settle into the new order of things. We love each other. We'll get there, somehow. I don't want to lose him.

I kiss his chest and he runs his hands through my hair. Then he pulls my head up and looks me deep in the eyes. It's so earnest. I think about how Rowan looks me in the eyes with a mischievous glint. As if he sees every little thing that I'm thinking and he's giving me an internal wink.

Rowan?! Why am I thinking about Rowan right now?!

Get out, get out, get out!

Ash keeps kissing me but now Rowan's entered my mind, it's all I can think about. The more I try not to picture him, there he is. Sitting at his desk not doing any work. Playing card games with Monty and Marian. Ordering four pints at once and then lining them up neatly on the table. Rollerblading into a wall and almost taking down a little child with him by clinging on for support. Doing me from behind in a public bathroom that one time.

No. No. NO. What is this bizarre montage of Rowan-based memories when I am trying to have sex with Ash?! Something has gone very, very wrong. I have never *once*, in all the years Ash and I have been together, had anyone else enter my mind when we're about to have sex. I can't carry on like this. Absolutely fucking NOT.

I break away. Ash pierces me with a questioning stare. 'Are you OK?' he asks.

'I'm fine,' I lie. 'I just need the bathroom.'

I grab my phone and hurry to the bathroom, where I climb into the empty bathtub and write out an emergency text.

> Holly. I lied. I do want to have sex with Rowan and now I'm thinking about it in the middle of making out with Ash

I stare at my screen. Please, please say she's got her phone on her. The little 'typing' dots appear instantly and I feel a sweep of relief sail through my limbs.

> Ha! I called it

> All right, all right. Stop being smug and help me

I hate how much I'm having to lean on Holly like some sort of co-dependent teenager. I'm an independent, self-sufficient woman, for Christ's sake, and I've been reduced to a fretful mess who can't have sex with her boyfriend and hides from him next door in an empty bathtub, desperately texting her friend. If there's one thing that's always come easily to me, it's sex. Who am I? Who is this person I have become?!

Holly hasn't replied.

Holly! He's waiting for me and he wants to have sex! I'm hiding in the bathroom

She starts typing again and I stare intently at my screen.

Oh Fliss <3 If you're really serious about making this work with Ash and you keep thinking about Rowan, I say you need to cut back on the amount you're seeing him. You're spending all your time with him . . . Of course he's on your mind! I think mental cheating isn't necessarily better than actual cheating and you probably have to draw some new boundaries with Rowan in order to move forward with Ash

I sit back in the bath and take a few deep breaths. Cut back on Rowan? Even if I'm technically following all the rules? Rowan's been in my life since forever. I'm already having to give so much up . . . Is the way to stop yourself mentally cheating really to stop spending time with people you fancy?! And apparently, for monogamous people, this is preferable than just having sex with them and getting it out of your system? Running around hiding from all the world's temptations and pretending you're not really tempted?!

Monogamy SUCKS.

Fliss? Are you ok?

I'm fine. Maybe you're right. I definitely can't carry on like this

Just tell Ash you're not in the mood today, get Rowan off your mind, and next time will be better

Yeah. Thanks

You're welcome <3 xx

There's a knock.

'Fliss?' Ash sounds concerned. 'Are you all right?'

I heave myself out of the tub and open the door. Ash gives me a searchlight stare.

'I'm OK,' I say. 'Do you mind if we don't have sex today?'

'Of course.' Ash puts his arms around me and leans his forehead against mine. 'What's up?'

'I just . . .' Can't stop thinking about another man? '. . . Came on my period.'

I've been telling so many lies, what's one more?

'Oh,' Ash says. 'Poor you.'

Almost as if on cue, my phone starts ringing. It's Rowan. Instinctively I don't want to pick it up in front of Ash, but Ash has seen the caller ID. Would it look weirder if I *didn't* answer it? Ash knows Rowan is an old friend who's working with me, but that's about it. Since we agreed to be exclusive I haven't known how much I should share about him.

I decide it's weirder to ignore it. I pick it up. 'Hey?' I say.

'Hey Flissy, what are you doing on Friday? Want to go laser tag?'

I do. I really do. But Holly's advice is still ringing around my head. Maybe I *have* been spending too much time with Rowan. I'm going to need to say no to some of his invites and work from home for a little while. Maybe not sitting next to him in the office every day will help.

'I can't,' I force out.

'Why not?' he mocks. 'Cosy night in with the boyfriend?'

'No,' I retort. 'My friend . . . Holly . . . is coming over.'

Ugh. Why did I say that?!

'Oh, well, if *Holly* is coming over. OK, Fliss, see you Monday.' I can basically hear him winking down the phone.

'Holly? OH, this is your new friend from the restaurant, right?' I told Ash about how we'd met and how I've been giving her advice. I did not tell him how much advice she's been giving me. 'Can I meet her?!' He's all excited.

'Sure,' I say.

We go back to bed, where I finish my pancakes and think resentfully about how much better they'd taste if I was eating them after sex.

CHAPTER NINETEEN:
BE CAREFUL WITH YOUR TIME

HOLLY

After talking Fliss down from her ledge, I think about messaging her saying, *I HAD SEX WITH ANOTHER MAN.* But it seems like she has enough on her plate this morning. Without Fliss, I would have literally no one else to talk to. Even though it's been a whole month now, no one else in my life – except Will – knows what's going on yet. I know Fliss said to communicate openly but there's no way I'd tell Will I had sex with another man. He won't even talk to me about his dates.

I look around Liam's bedroom which, in my wine-fuelled state last night, I wasn't paying much attention to. It's pretty tidy, but not in a too-tidy way. His walls are grey and he has a bright blue feature wall that Will would call tacky. There's a computer, desk and an office chair on one side of the room for work-from-home days. There are a couple of plants dotted around that he's managed to keep alive. A couple of endearing Post-its reminding him to remember his lunch.

I don't know why, but the Post-its give me a strange, lucid flash of reality. I am really waking up in another man's room after sleeping together. An actual, real-life man who needs written prompts in order to avoid forgetting the food he's prepared before going to his real-life job and generally walking around in a well-fed state in his real-life existence.

I didn't sleep much last night. I'd doze for a while but then wake up again and stare at the ceiling, listening to the sound of Liam breathing or tossing and turning in his sleep. At one point around 4 a.m., I got up to get a glass of water and caught sight of myself, in Liam's T-shirt, in the hallway mirror. I had a long stare at my reflection, thinking how this was not where I thought I'd be in my life, even a few months ago, but here I am. Then I got paranoid Liam was going to wake up and find me lurking in the darkness staring intently at my own face and wonder what sort of weirdo he'd invited to stay the night, so I went back to bed.

I lie back, thinking about the sex. I can't lie . . . It was *good*.

At first I kept thinking about Will. Comparing every little touch. Thinking how strange it was that these weren't Will's hands on me. Liam even paused and asked if I wanted to continue because he sensed my hesitation. But I didn't want to stop.

After a while, I got more used to it, and thoughts of Will faded into the background.

I don't think it was *better* than sex with Will. Even entertaining that as a possibility feels like a betrayal. Of course I could never have sex that was better than with Will!! I mean . . . it was just . . . different.

It felt like we were riding a tandem bike and if I lost concentration we'd both fall off, whereas sometimes with Will I feel like I'm more of a . . . passenger. He's doing his thing and driving along and I'm there for the ride. Will's more dominant. I always thought I liked dominant but, I don't know, this wasn't bad. It wasn't bad at all. I suppose there was more . . . communication. He asked questions. He was reactive to me and my body and seemed to notice every little thing that was happening for me. There was nowhere to hide.

I think that's normal, though, isn't it? Will and I don't need to be attentive to every microscopic detail in our sexual relationship, because we know each other so well it's basically instinct by now. We're not learning each other anymore. It was a long time ago but I'm absolutely sure, back in those dorm rooms at uni, there was a huge process of getting to know each other's bodies that went on. We have a routine down to a T now. It's all negotiated, worked out, settled. There's a way that we have sex with each other. And it's good. The best. Yes. The best.

I don't orgasm *every* time, but that's not realistic, is it? Of course I'm going to have an orgasm – or two – with someone new. Their touch is unfamiliar and exciting. You're both paying lots of attention because it's the first time. If I was nine years down the line with Liam it wouldn't feel so heightened. And I'm sure eventually it would become more of a disconnected activity . . . Except, I know as soon as I think it, that isn't true. Knowing Liam, even from four dates, I'm not at all surprised by the way he has sex and I can't see him ever not being that way.

As I said, not that I *preferred* it to the way Will does it, though. I'm definitely not saying that at all.

God. Stop comparing him to Will.

Liam comes in with a cup of tea and a bacon sandwich. 'Morning,' he says, putting it down beside me.

'Aw, this is nice, thanks.' I take a bite. It's been a long time since I've eaten something as simple as a bacon sandwich. It's so good. I try to picture Will eating this. I don't think he would. He'd have to put it on sourdough bread. He also doesn't approve of breakfast in bed because crumbs get everywhere.

Stop comparing him to Will!!!

'You look good in my T-shirt,' Liam says.

I blush. I try to say thank you, but I've got a mouthful of bacon so I just make a *mm-hm* sound.

'What are you up to today?' Liam sits on the edge of the bed and puts his hand on my foot, over the duvet.

'Ummm.' I swallow. Nothing, really, but I realise that I've got to get back to Will.

'Do you want to go for a pub lunch or something?' Liam continues. 'There's a nice place that just opened down the road, that I've been meaning to try.'

I would *love* to be able to go for a pub lunch with Liam, and hang around here in his T-shirt, but with a sinking feeling I remember that I can't. I'm hit with a huge, engulfing wave of guilt. I'm not free in the way that Liam wants me to be free. Sitting half-clothed in his bed, my 'I'm not looking for anything serious' loophole doesn't feel so clever and I wish

I'd been more up front about my situation. Should I tell him now? It feels a bit shady to tell him just after having sex. Oh God. I'm a trickster. A swindler. A user.

No, I'm not, I remind myself. I have said I don't want anything serious. I haven't committed to spending Sunday with Liam. I could very well have plans and that's fine. But even though I tell myself that, I can't help feeling like I'm not actually convincing myself anymore.

'I can't,' I answer with a stab of remorse. 'That sounds lovely, though.'

'No problem.' Liam smiles. 'Another time.'

'Yes, please.'

'Oh, what's this?!' Liam reaches down and pulls a glinting, golden card out of my bag. It's an invite to the ten-year anniversary party of our label.

'Oh, er . . .'

'Looks fancy,' he says. 'I sometimes forget you work in *fashion*.' He says 'fashion' with a camp, playful tone.

'Yeah, that's our anniversary party, we're having it after the showcase for the new line.' I try to make myself sound nonchalant, even though it's a huge deal to me, because I can sense imminent danger ahead in this conversation.

'OH! Is this your big work event?! Where Amber's finally going to let you have some of the glory?' He starts shaking the invite around. His energy is contagious. He has unreserved joy for others. I'm touched and surprised that he's remembered the situation and Amber by name.

'That's the one.' I make my voice sound flat. 'So, er . . .' *Quick, Holly, change the subject.* Why can't I think of anything to change the subject to? 'Nice weather to—'

'Can you bring people?' he interjects.

Yep. There it is. The danger that I was trying to avoid. Even though part of me is floating that he wants to come so badly, just to cheer me on, I seize up with dread. Liam meeting my work colleagues . . . Liam meeting Tomi . . . Introducing himself as my 'date' . . . Everyone's pure confusion as they ask what happened to Will. Liam wanting to know who the hell Will is.

Liam's adorable reaction makes it harder to pretend to myself I wasn't heartbroken that Will couldn't make it. Even though I told myself that I wasn't, and reminded myself how supportive Will has been of my career in other ways, I was gutted that he chose a stag do – with someone who is only a casual friend – over a night that's really important to me. I was even more disappointed that it wasn't even a question that he would choose me.

In that moment, I long to have Liam come. His enthusiasm is so enticing. It's exactly what I wanted from Will. But bringing Liam into my life with my friends and colleagues would be way too complicated.

'I . . . Er . . .'

Why am I so terrible at lying? Just say no!

'It would be amazing to come and see you in action.' He's so keen to come. Saying no would be like poking a bunny in the eye.

How can I get out of this? Do I want to get out of this? A big, big part of me *wants* him to come.

'Yeah, OK,' I agree. 'I can put you on the guest list.'

Maybe it will be fine. Somehow. I'm not thinking about that now. I'm just thinking about the warm, luscious feeling of having someone desperate to turn up for me.

'Oh *sweet*.' His eyes swim with childlike wonder. 'I'm so there!'

I give a weak smile and get dressed quickly, suddenly ready to be out of Liam's building. Last night was incredible and the fact that he wants to come to my work event is heartwarming. But also *terrible*. I feel addled and agitated by the guilt of it all and now I just want to get home. Liam walks me out and kisses me at the door and I feel like a slug.

When I get home the guilty feeling I have about Liam transfers over to Will. He's sitting there in his cute glasses and his big, grandad cardigan, reading *The Power* by Naomi Alderman because someone at work accused him of never reading books written by women. I feel awful because I love Will and . . . How can I love Will and be forming genuine affection for someone else? Someone I had sex with? And *enjoyed having sex with*? It goes against everything I've ever believed.

In that moment, I hate Will for putting me in this position. I hate myself even more. For playing it down and for letting myself get carried along with this. I was so desperate to keep him that I'd do anything and now I'm so confused and I can't help but feel like nothing will ever be the same again.

Will looks up from hunching over his book as I enter the living room. 'Hi,' he says. It's frosty. I sense that he's angry with me for not coming home last night and for once I don't do anything to try to smooth it over. We never agreed that I was coming home and I texted him to let him know that I was fine. Presumably, one of the end goals of this brilliant scheme of his – not that we've really spoken about it still – was that we *would* sleep with other people, so how would he expect me to achieve that without staying out overnight?

'Hi.' I match his glacial tone.

Will looks taken aback. He was expecting me to be apologetic, but I realise that I'm tired. I'm so tired of never knowing what it is that I have to be sorry for.

'What's wrong?' he asks with a weary tone. It's so unfair to characterise me this way, as if I'm a drag. I've thrown myself headlong into this huge, discombobulating mess at his request, which has uprooted my entire life, and I've barely complained about it at all.

'Same question to you,' I say.

'Nothing,' Will says incredulously. Of course. Will never actually admits to being upset because that would be weak. I'm the only one out of the two of us who has any human emotions. And I have enough for the both of us. Poor little Holly, who's always irrational, always hysterical.

Incredibly, he doesn't say anything else. He's so surprised by me fighting back that he's backed down immediately. And it feels *good*.

'Did you have fun at Tomi's?' Will asks, clearly not wanting to bother with a fight.

Tomi's?

Alarm bells start ringing.

'What do you mean?'

'I saw the pictures,' Will continues. 'Did he like the tickets?'

Oh my God . . . I open up my phone calendar. Was that last night?!

It's in my calendar for the nineteenth. Oh my God. I thought it was the week after his birthday and it must have been the week before. Oh my God. I cannot *believe* I put it in on the wrong date. He did ask me if I knew what I was wearing a few days ago and I thought it was a bit overkill given the event was still weeks away. That makes *so* much more sense. Aghhh! I've completely spaced with everything going on at the minute! Tomi's so understated that he would never think to remind me about it twice. Oh my *God*.

I flick frantically onto Tomi's profile. He's posted a couple of shots. Ugh. Isabella and Jay are RIGHT NEXT TO EACH OTHER. I was supposed to be there! I was supposed to help. Even if I couldn't *actually* help – guarding Isabella all night was kind of a joke – I was supposed to be there for moral support.

I flip through more photos. Even Amber was there. AMBER. How can I have done this?! I know exactly when Tomi's birthday is. I never forget it. I booked our tickets to *The Woman in Black* months ago – Tomi is a huge horror fan and somehow he's never seen it on stage. Only the bad film with Daniel Radcliffe.

Ughhhh. I've just been so consumed with everything happening in my own life. Aside from all the added work stress, my whole brain has been occupied with this stupid fiasco on top of spending time with Fliss, trying to muddle my way through. And I haven't even told Tomi about any of it.

Fliss's warning about making sure I carefully balance my time haunts me. I thought she was exaggerating, but I can't believe I let his happen.

'What's wrong? You look like you've seen a ghost,' Will comments.

'I wasn't at Tomi's birthday party,' I rasp. My throat's gone dry. 'I was doing something else.' I don't even bother to tiptoe around the meaning of that sentence . . . The 'something else' being another man. Will asked for this, after all, why *should* I keep shying away from the subject so that he doesn't feel uncomfortable? 'Oh my God. I can't believe it. I'm mortified. What am I going to do?'

Will shrugs. 'Calm down. It will be OK.'

Then he goes back to reading. But it's not OK. For the first time, I realise how his constantly telling me that things are OK doesn't actually make them OK. I used to think he was just encouraging me to be positive, but I'm starting to realise how often he makes me feel like I'm being overly emotional, ironically without letting me express my emotions at all.

But right now everything else seems very insignificant. I just need to make this up to Tomi, and I have no idea how.

'I'm going to Tomi's house,' I say.

Will looks up. 'What?' he says. 'You're going out *again*? You've only just got home.'

'Yep,' I say.

He keeps looking at me, expecting me to say more. But ten seconds ago when I wanted to talk about Tomi and he didn't, he didn't make the effort, did he? Why should I be expansive when he wants me to be?

'I need to,' I add before heading to our bedroom. I root around in my drawer for Tomi's present. Then with a jolt I realise he's going on holiday today. *Crap.* He's probably already at the airport.

I lie down on our bed and start writing out my apology text immediately.

Will follows me in. 'Why are you sulking on the bed?' he asks.

'I'm not sulking,' I reply. I just need a minute to think.

'You're the one going out again when we were supposed to be spending the evening together, and you're in a mood.' Will blows air through his lips. 'Madness.'

I prop myself up on my elbows and look at him. In my frustration with Will and my disbelief about forgetting Tomi's birthday, any inherent instincts I have to let things go to keep the peace have fallen by the wayside. 'We didn't actually agree to spend the evening together,' I defend, for once not trying to keep my tone of voice level or caring if I do sound 'moody'. 'Actually what happened was that you, once again, have assumed I'll plan around you.'

Will shakes his head. 'I don't know what's got into you,' he says, and leaves the room. Once he's gone, I realise that I'm shaking.

CHAPTER TWENTY:
IT HAS TO BE MUTUAL

FLISS

When Holly shows up at my door on Friday evening, I can tell she knows something's wrong. I've spent the week low-key avoiding Rowan by working from home and turning down all his invites and, even though I can see the sense in it, I feel glum.

'Hey.' She looks at me inquisitively and hugs me on the doorstep.

'Hey.' I hug her back and gesture inside.

'Oh wow, your place is gorgeous.' She steps inside and takes off her coat. She's wearing black jeans, white Converse and a white oversized shirt. She looks great. 'Thank you for inviting me over.'

'No, thank you for coming,' I say.

'Is everything OK?'

I lead her to the sofa and she sits down. Ash isn't here yet and Jenny and Henry are still upstairs so we have a bit of time to talk. 'I just . . . well. Rowan wanted to go out tonight and I lied and said I was seeing you. Then Ash overheard me and got all excited to meet you, because I've been talking about you loads. Plus I didn't want him to know I was lying to Rowan. That would seem weird.'

Now that I say it out loud, it sounds pathetic.

'It *is* weird.' Holly raises an eyebrow. 'Fliss, putting down boundaries with Rowan doesn't mean *pretending you're busy* when he asks you to go out. He's asking for a huge amount of time from you and you're allowed to say no.'

I know what she's saying is true. I've never had a problem drawing lines before. Maybe the problem is that I don't actually want to say no to Rowan, I'm forcing myself to, I think remorsefully.

'You've made it clear you're in an exclusive relationship with Ash now, and he should respect that,' Holly goes on. 'Yours and Rowan's relationship can't be exactly the same as it was before. You're in a different place now.'

The way Holly says it, it sounds so straightforward. In theory. But in reality, changing my relationship with Rowan doesn't feel simple at all. We have so much history. It's difficult for me to just hit a reset button on all of that.

'Right.' I settle into the armchair opposite Holly.

I must look unconvinced because she says, 'If he's making life this hard for you, I say cut Rowan out altogether.'

Cut Rowan out? *Totally?*

'Like . . . stop seeing him . . . at all?'

Holly crosses her arms. 'He obviously sees you trying to make it work with Ash and is making it his life's mission to get in the way.'

I feel like that's a huge exaggeration. Or is it? There's still a bit of a question mark over why he's here at all . . . Was it for me?! That thought feels a little narcissistic, although it would fit with what Holly's saying.

Either way, the thought of erasing him from my life entirely makes me feel hollow.

'It wouldn't have to be permanent,' Holly reassures me. 'But what good is he doing you right now? As far as I can see, he's just confusing you when you're trying to give this new setup with Ash a proper chance.'

'Maybe.' Deep down I can see there's logic in her guidance, even though what she's suggesting feels impossible. Suddenly I notice how boiling it is in here. It's like a million degrees because Jenny thrives in hot, arid conditions. Wow, I really prefer giving advice to hearing it. 'So what's going on with you?' I divert the conversation.

'Well, let's see.' She starts taking off her shoes and crosses her legs on the couch like a child. 'I had sex with another man. Then I accidentally invited him to my big work party. Then I had a fight with Will. And *then* I forgot my best friend's birthday party.'

'OK. That's . . . a lot. Let's go from the beginning. You had sex with Liam.'

'Yes.' Holly sounds stressed, but the corner of her mouth twitches into a little smile.

'It was GOOD!' I point at her. I'm creepily delighted by this. Damn, this must be what monogamous people feel like all the time; living for vicarious kicks.

'It was good,' she concedes, colour rising in her cheeks. 'But then I accidentally invited him to my big work party. Agh, this is a nightmare!'

'How did you *accidentally* invite him?'

'Well, he found the invitation in my bag. And then he got so excited about it. I felt mean saying no and a part of me wants him to come.'

'Isn't Will going to be there?' I ask.

'No.' Holly looks away and plays with her hands. 'No, he has a stag do.'

I sense I've hit a nerve. She sounds bitter. 'Well, is it so bad if Liam comes?'

'*Yes!*' Holly cries. 'He's going to talk to all my colleagues! What if someone asks who he is?! What's he going to say? My colleagues don't know anything!'

I shrug. 'Well, Liam knows to be discreet, right? I mean, he knows the deal.'

Holly bites her lip. 'Errr . . . yep,' she says. 'But I just have a bad feeling. It's too close!'

'Do you want me to come?' I ask. 'I mean, I could stand next to Liam and intervene if anything gets too revealing.' I wouldn't usually interfere in other people's personal lives, but Holly and I are *way* past that. Not only have we become proper friends, but I feel involved in her situation now. Plus, I want to see her killing it at her big work thing.

Holly's eyes light up. 'Oh, WOULD you?!' She puts her hand on her chest dramatically. 'That would make me feel SO much better, thank you, Fliss!'

Before I know what's happening she's launched herself across the room and flung her arms around me. As a non-hugger I feel instinctively uncomfortable but then I relax into it. I have to admit, it's nice.

'That was what I was supposed to do for Tomi,' she mumbles into my shoulder.

'Who?' I ask.

'Tomi.' She pulls away and sits back on the sofa. 'I was supposed to help keep his ex away from his partner and I put it in the wrong date. I don't know. I've just been so taken up with everything that's been going on for me. And Tomi's not the kind of person to keep reminding you or bugging you about stuff.'

I nod. I can see that she's really beating herself up about it and I don't know what to say to make her feel better. It's difficult to avoid this when you start open dating. You're trying to cram another time-consuming thing into an existing life that's hard enough to balance as it is. Inevitably, something like this is always going to happen before you get used to it. I didn't have it quite as bad because most of my close friends are in different countries, but it was still an adjustment.

'And then Will acted like it was nothing,' she carries on. 'He was only interested in whether I was spending enough time with *him* . . .'

Interesting. That's the first time I've heard her say something negative about Will. It's also the first time I've heard her describe them having any sort of argument. I wonder if things are OK between them. She sounds . . . not angry, exactly – I can't imagine Holly being angry – but . . . exasperated.

'Oh, sorry, Holly. Did Will mind about tonight?' I ask, suddenly realising I've stolen yet another night of Holly's time from him. 'He could have come?'

'*Eh.*' Holly shrugs. 'I didn't even want to do this. And now he doesn't like it that I'm not always available. Well, too bad,' she says bitterly.

As soon as she says it, she claps her hands over her mouth, realising what she's admitted.

'You what . . . ?' I repeat. 'You *didn't* want to do this?!'

She looks caught. I wait for her to deny it, but she just shrugs in defeat. Even if she denied it now, I'd see the truth in her face. All the little moments of doubt, over the past couple of months, start clicking into place. I knew she was apprehensive but I thought that was just jitters; ultimately I thought this was something she wanted. But she never wanted an open relationship at all. Oh Christ . . . And I've been *helping* her!

'Holly!' I exclaim. 'You shouldn't be in an open relation-ship unless both people want to be in it. For it to work it *has* to be mutual! Otherwise it's doomed from the start!'

'I'm sorry,' she squeaks.

'I can't believe you lied to me!' I try to level out my tone, but I feel betrayed. 'Why wouldn't you tell me that?!'

'Because I knew you wouldn't help me,' she says softly, looking down at her hands again. 'And . . . I really needed your help. You were so supportive.'

She looks so sad it's near impossible to stay mad at her. I feel my indignation cooling. It's true; I would never have helped her.

'I'm sorry, Fliss,' she goes on. 'When it started I didn't want to do it. I was just doing it because it was something Will wanted and I wanted to let him and then forget about it so we could move on and settle down.'

I cringe. Christ. That doesn't sound like they were going into this on equal footing at *all*.

'But that's not how I feel now.' Her voice wobbles. 'Now . . . well. Now I don't really know how I'm feeling.'

I sigh and resist the temptation to say *I told you so*. I've *definitely* impressed on her many times that if you go into this confused, you'll come out of it confused. But what would be the point? She already knows she messed up; she doesn't need me to scold her. And she could equally bring up all the good advice that she's given me and I've ignored.

I don't give out voluntary hugs often, but she looks so sad I move over to her on the sofa and put my arms around her again. 'It will be all right. You'll figure it out,' I reassure her.

'Thanks. So will you.' She sniffles into my shoulder.

We sit there for a moment. Once again I think how odd it is that two months ago I'd never met her and now here she is having a breakdown in my living room. I'm not sure exactly when it happened, but I genuinely don't know what I'd do without her anymore and I know she feels the same about me.

At that moment, Jenny walks in. 'Oh, hi . . .' she says awkwardly. I suppose we are sitting on the sofa in silence hugging intensely. We break apart.

'Jenny, this is Holly. Holly, this is Jenny,' I introduce.

'Hi!' Holly says, wiping the corner of her eye on her sleeve. 'It's so nice to meet you!'

Jenny sits opposite us and Holly pulls herself together. Within seconds, they're chatting animatedly about *Married at First Sight Australia*. I have no idea what they're talking about but apparently they were very put out by the behaviour of some woman called Ines a few seasons ago.

I go to make teas, laughing about how Jenny has made another instant bezzie through the shared bonding that is discussing the scandalous behaviour of people one has never actually met.

When I come back into the room Henry has joined them as well and they're still talking about an old season of *Married at First Sight*. Jenny is on peak form. It strikes me that she doesn't go out much, but brings people back to her lair and she's some sort of indoor-only social butterfly. Human beings are strange, delicious cocktails of contradiction.

'I was backing Cyrell and Nic,' says Henry.

There's a murmur of agreement.

'I really wanted it to work out for Heidi and Mike,' says Holly.

There's a collective 'noooo'. Jenny shakes her head, like Holly should be ashamed of herself. Who are Heidi and Mike?

Then Ash arrives. When he walks in Jenny and Henry greet him warmly and Holly lingers behind, waiting for an introduction.

'Ash, Holly, Holly, Ash.'

'Hi! I've heard so much about you.' Ash goes straight in for a hug and Holly makes an *aww* face at me over his shoulder. Ash is so genuine that people always fall in love with him within about three seconds, I swear. No wonder he gets so many dates.

'Did you watch *MAFS Australia*, Ash?' Holly asks. 'Any opinions?'

'I didn't.' Ash sits on the sofa next to Holly and takes off his shoes. 'My colleague told me to watch *Love Is Blind* Season 3, though. What a roller-coaster.'

This is one of the things I love about Ash. He doesn't especially love reality TV – he's more of a reading and classical music sort of guy – but Jenny, Henry and Holly do and he's interested in things because other people are. Whereas I find so many people mostly want to hang around people who share their own interests and echo their own beliefs, Ash legitimately appreciates other people's perspectives. I've never once seen him get defensive when people disagree with him.

'Oh my God! Don't mention the cuties!' Jenny shouts.

The three of them descend into moaning about 'the cuties', which I assume was some sort of controversial scene.

'Zanab, get it together, girl,' concludes Jenny.

'Aw, well, I hate to imagine my worst moments being broadcast on TV.' Ash cringes. Another thing I love about him; he's so accepting. Probably why he's not super into reality TV where part of the fun is being catty about the people on it.

They all start deciding what film to watch and what food to order. Holly sends me a sneaky text across the room, saying:

He's SO nice. He's exactly how I thought he'd be! X

I read it and smile. He is. But even though part of me is glad I'm here tonight, with Ash and all my friends, I can't pretend another part of me isn't thinking about how I'm not out with Rowan.

We have a lovely evening but after everyone's gone and Ash and I are reading on the sofa, I keep thinking about what

Holly said. Cut Rowan out entirely. He doesn't usually work with me. At some point I assume he'll go back to the States. We see each other rarely. He's barely in my life at all. Would it be such a big deal to stop speaking to him?

Except, OK, he's not around all the time . . . but he's *significant*. He helped me through a bad time in my early twenties. I have memories of him in so many corners of the planet. I wouldn't call him one of my closest friends, exactly, but definitely one of my oldest. I didn't realise becoming monogamous would involve cutting out so much.

My phone bleeps. It's Rowan sending me a stupid meme. We had been texting back and forth pretty constantly, until this week when I purposely slowed my responses down.

I look at the message and automatically go to reply. Then I remember what Holly said and put my phone back on the table. I'll ignore it. *Easy.*

Except . . . it's not easy. I might not be texting him, but I'm not concentrating on the book either. I'm physically here but I may as well not be. My mind is running over all the witty replies I might have sent but didn't. Thinking about what I'd be doing if I was out with him instead and how I might never be able to go out with him again. I try to focus on the pages in front of me and be present, in the room, with Ash. But if anything, by the time I go to bed, Rowan is even more on my mind than he was before. *Why* is it so difficult to stop thinking about him? Do other people have this much trouble getting people they fancy, who aren't their partners, out of their heads? They mustn't . . . or all monogamous people would be driven utterly bonkers.

Later, Ash and I settle into bed.

'Holly seems nice,' he says.

'Mm,' I agree.

'She and Jenny seemed to get on like a house on fire,' he comments.

'Yeah.' I smile. I can't imagine Holly not getting on with anybody. She's a sweet person.

'Are you OK, Fliss?' Ash asks.

I do a coward move and turn out the light before saying, 'Uh huh.'

'You seem distracted,' he whispers into the dark.

'Yeah, I guess I am a bit. Just work,' I whisper back. 'Thinking about everything I've got to do this week.'

It's still unbelievably odd, not being able to speak to Ash. Normally I'd tell him everything. He's the person I come to with my problems. Our relationship wasn't just open in the sexual sense. Having that sort of freedom meant I felt like I could be transparent about everything else. Now I have this huge problem and he's the person I want to talk to the most, but he's become the one person I feel like I'm not allowed to talk about it with. The last time I shared similar feelings in a monogamous relationship, it didn't exactly go well. I was left abandoned and heartbroken.

'Don't think about it now.' Ash strokes my hair. 'There's nothing you can do until the morning. Now all you can do is sleep.'

'Yeah, you're right,' I reply. That would be good advice if I was actually stressed about work.

'Night, Fliss.' Ash kisses my forehead.

'Night.'

Ash and I cuddle for a while, until I need to roll over

because I can't sleep without personal space. But I can't sleep anyway. I lie awake thinking about how unhappy I've become. It occurs to me that not only am I cutting out huge parts of my life to make this work, I feel like I'm having to change myself as a person. Something I swore years ago that I'd never do. Something that Rowan said when we were twenty-two keeps replaying in my head. *Not everyone is built for relationships.*

Maybe I was an idiot to think I was. Maybe some fundamental part of me that makes a 'normal' relationship work is missing. I'd convinced myself there was no 'normal' relationship and that the idea was a construct. That what I had to give Ash was enough. But maybe it isn't. Maybe all this time, I've just been cheating the system and now the system's found me out.

I never knew the meaning of the phrase 'lightbulb moment' until now, but it's suddenly clear to me I can't do this. Of course I can't. All I've been doing since we became exclusive is obsess over everything I'm giving up. That's hardly a healthy relationship, is it? That's not what Ash wants from me. He wants me to be content with those sacrifices and the truth is I'm miserable.

I've tried, but I find monogamy too difficult and stifling, and I shouldn't be doing this purely because Ash wants it. I can't change myself in the way Ash wants me to and I shouldn't have to. Relationships shouldn't be based on this much self-betrayal. I deserve to be free if that's what I want and he deserves to go and find a normal relationship with someone else who genuinely wants it, too.

All the shame and guilt I felt after my break-up with

James a decade ago come crashing back, except this time the consequences of my mistake are a thousand times worse.

I listen to Ash breathing in and out beside me. Sweet, intelligent, wonderful Ash. Thinking about him not being in my life anymore is unimaginable. He's my best friend. The idea of leaving him is devastating. But at this point, what choice do I have? Committing myself solely to him shouldn't be this hard, should it?

I feel like the worst kind of human being for having accidentally strung him along for this long, but I didn't do this on purpose. I thought I loved Ash, I really did. I *do* love him. But if he alone can't be enough for me, then I can't love him like I'm supposed to, can I?

It's embarrassing to have thought the last three years were a genuine lifestyle choice, that we'd found a version of love that worked for us, and screw everyone else. I was clearly misguided to think Ash and I were in an open relationship because that's genuinely the kind of relationship we both found satisfying. But I'm relieved, too. I've been struggling so much with this and now I finally have an answer. The hard, sad, awful truth is that something about me is lacking and I had it right in my twenties; I should stay away from relationships altogether.

At least I can stop fighting everybody now. I'm so tired of the stupid jokes, the raised eyebrows, my parents' disapproval. And I can stop fighting myself; I can't do what everyone else does, I can't be like everyone else. So I should just be by myself.

Ash rolls over in his sleep. I rub his back gently and plant a soft kiss on the top of his head. It causes me actual physical pain to think about Ash not being in my life, but it's better that we break up now than continue this charade, because it's only going to get harder the longer we keep pretending. I creep out of bed to the sofa next door.

CHAPTER TWENTY-ONE:
LISTEN TO YOUR MOTHER

FLISS

I don't sleep well, but better than I have been recently. I close my eyes knowing that even though ending this is going to be traumatic, I finally have clarity.

When Ash gets up in the morning, he's confused to find me tucked up in the living room.

He pads in, his hair ruffled, in his adorable, stupid Totoro onesie that I'm never going to see again. He crumples his face and runs his hands through his hair, squinting as his eyes adjust to the sunlight. 'Fliss? What are you doing in here?'

I hardly ever cry, but I feel myself start to well up. 'I'm sorry, Ash.' My voice quivers. 'This isn't working for me.'

Ash sits down on the edge of the couch and rests a hand on my leg. 'I know,' he says kindly. 'I know you've been finding the change in our relationship difficult. But it's just a transition period. It's only been a month. We just need to give it more time.'

'No.' I shake my head. 'No, it's not that. I think this whole thing has made me realise . . . I just . . .' Wow, this is hard. I see why people lie their way out of break-ups to soften the blow. Breaking someone's heart is a terrible feeling. I never want to do it ever again. 'I just don't think I should be in a relationship at all,' I finish. This is without a doubt the most difficult thing I've ever had to do, but I've just got to rip the plaster off. It's better for both of us.

I expect Ash to look more hurt but the words don't seem to land. He just looks at me lovingly and rubs my leg. I can tell that he's not taking in what I'm saying.

'Look, let's talk about how it's going to work. I was an idiot thinking we could go from something that was so rigid and structured, to something with no lines at all. I've been too much; I know I have. It's just I could feel you becoming distant so I overcompensated. I handled it badly, I'm sorry. But if you need more space we can make new rules. And more nights with our friends, or alone?'

That probably would have been a good idea, but still, I don't think that's going to be enough to fix this. Before I can respond he keeps talking.

'I pushed you,' he garbles. 'I'm sorry. I've been wanting to bring it up but I didn't think there was anything useful to say until we'd given it more of a chance. But let's talk about this now, OK? We can work this out. I know we can. It's *us*.'

I can feel my heart physically disintegrating. This is the worst moment of my life. My tears start spilling over and I press my lips together. 'I'm sorry. I don't think there's anything left to say.'

Ash laughs. 'Come on, Fliss. What, are you saying that's

just *it*? It's tough for one month and then goodbye? It was always going to be hard. We've done things one way for so long, now we're trying another. It's normal to find it difficult, Fliss. You can't just . . . *bolt*.'

I don't say anything else. I don't know what to say. He's hurt now, but he'll be better off in the long run.

'We can go back to being open,' he says. 'If this isn't working, if it's too soon, we can go back.'

There's so much hope in his eyes. I want to go back, too. I want to pretend the past month never happened. I was blissfully ignorant before. I thought I was happy, which is basically the same as being happy, isn't it? But ultimately Ash wants us to be exclusive. If we go back to being open he'll just be waiting for the day I say I'm ready to move on and that day isn't coming.

'I'm sorry, I just don't think I love you like I'm supposed to.' My voice has gone beyond wobbling. Now I'm full-on sobbing. Tears are rolling down my cheeks and I try hastily to wipe them away. 'Otherwise, I wouldn't be finding it this difficult, would I? If we were supposed to be together, it would be easier than this, wouldn't it?'

Ash looks away and stares at the floor. I think he's starting to believe me because he's only seen me cry twice since we got together, once when my nephew took his first steps and once in the Werner Herzog documentary where the penguin wanders off into the mountains.

I sit there crying for a bit longer. I'm desperate to fold myself into his onesie for a hug and tell him I didn't mean it. But I can't. 'I'm sorry, Ash.' I take a big breath through my mouth because my nose has blocked. 'It's over.'

For a moment, he keeps his hand on my leg. Then he gets up and swears loudly.

'I'm sorry,' I repeat.

He's quiet for a moment. He runs his hand through his hair and stands aimlessly, like he doesn't know what to do with himself.

After what feels like the longest silence in history, he says, 'If that's the way you feel, there's nothing to be sorry about. You haven't done anything wrong.'

I'm cracking into a million pieces. His reaction makes it worse. He's just so *nice*. I hate the word nice. It's generic and uninspiring. Something you'd say about a loaf of bread. But sometimes there's no other word for it. Ash is just really, really fucking nice.

Watching Ash leave the flat is surreal. I can't help but observe every little mannerism – like his throwing his stuff in his bag and running his hands through his hair – and think it might be the last time I'm ever going to see it. After he's gone I sit staring at the wall for a long time. There's no other way to put this; I feel like shit.

I keep telling myself I've made the right decision and ending any relationship is always hard, and it's only going to get better from here. I just need to get through for a while. Maybe I'll actually join Jenny and Henry on the sofa for some *Too Hot to Handle*.

I go for a long walk to clear my head. When I'm nearly back home, I get an alarming text from Henry.

Go to Ash's if you can . . .

Huh?

Mum and Dad are here.

I stop dead in the middle of the street. WHAT?! Mum and Dad have never dropped in on me unannounced before, they know better than that ... They'd *never* have done this before Henry arrived. And to state the obvious, I can't go to Ash's. It's too early to go to a coffee shop. I literally have nowhere to turn. Ugh! This is the LAST thing I need! And it's all Henry's fault!

This is all YOUR fault!

I take full responsibility. I'll try to get rid of them.

I'm nearly home.

Oh God. Sorry. Then we'll go down together. See you soon.

I walk as slowly as possible and think about waiting it out in the hopes they leave, but it's cold and rainy and I have no umbrella. My jeans are getting soaked. Unannounced parental visit? Mild physical discomfort? Unannounced parental visit? Mild physical discomfort? Ugh, what a choice to be stuck with. Eventually I go inside because wet denim makes me gag.

I let myself in and smell Mum's perfume in the air. It triggers some sort of animalistic defensiveness in me. My emotional cat fur is standing on end as I enter the room. I'm vulnerable, too, after everything with Ash. If she raises the eyebrow at me I might throw myself out the window.

'Fliss.' Mum rises from her chair. She's dressed very *Mum* in a gaudy, purple high-necked geometric-print midi-dress. Monsoon should really give her a cut of their profits for all the free advertising she gives them. I don't think she's bought a single item of clothing from another shop in at least a decade. 'It's so good to see you. Come here, my baby.'

I believe her, as well. I do think Mum and Dad are always genuinely pleased to see me. They just can't help themselves when it comes to sharing their uncompromising judgements about my life, and those judgements always end up getting in the way of us actually enjoying each other's company.

'Hello, Felicity.' Dad stands up too. He's wearing a classic dark-green dad jumper and badly fitting trousers. I hug them both in turn. I'm so upset that, babyishly, I find I am actually comforted by their presence. Even if they didn't like Ash.

'So.' I sit down on the leather armchair to the left of the sofa. Henry perches in the armchair on the other side. Mum and Dad sit in the centre of the room, smiling. It always starts with smiles. 'What are you doing here?'

'Oh, well, we hadn't seen either of you in such a *long* time.' Mum emphasises 'long' dramatically. We saw them at Christmas. It's February. I suppose, given how often they call in on Henry, Laura and Sam and how long Henry has been here, this is a long time to them. 'And we thought we'd come to London to do a bit of shopping and we thought, well, we might as well pop in and see our babies, here under one roof.' Mum looks around the room. Her eye lands on the dusty fireplace and dirty mugs left out on the side. Jenny and I don't live like students but we're not up to Mum's standards.

'Your mum's not been to Monsoon in a while,' Dad adds. 'Got to keep her happy.'

They grin at each other. Even though they're the suffocating kind of always-together couple who won't even drive a car without trying to hold hands, there are moments where I recognise that they're quite sweet. I thought I'd found my own version of happiness and I would smile sickeningly at Ash in my old age, but I'm sure I can find some other version of happiness where I'm totally alone. Maybe I'll smile that way at a pet iguana.

'We were just asking Henry when he's planning to come back to . . . Kent.' Mum tactfully avoids saying 'Laura'. I guess Henry hasn't told them yet that he's not coming back until he's bought a new place.

'Yes and I was just telling Mum this work thing's going to be a while yet.' *Work thing.* Henry's voice sounds strained. Mum and Dad aren't idiots. They know Henry's not here because of work. But they won't keep pressing it, for now at least. 'So Fliss, how's your weekend?'

Henry looks at me like a drowning man looks at a rubber ring. I can't even be annoyed at him.

Mum and Dad both turn their heads to me. 'Er, I . . . Well, we had my friend Holly over last night.'

'Holly? Which one's Holly?' Dad asks.

'You haven't met her.'

'Show us a picture.' Mum beckons eagerly for my phone. She loves to have a visual aid when discussing people she hasn't met. I show her Holly's icon on my messages.

'Oh, she looks like . . . What's her name, Mark? In that film, *Promising Young Women*?'

'*Promising Young Woman*,' Henry corrects.

'Carey Mulligan,' Dad supplies.

'Yes!' Mum slaps her thigh. 'Carey Mulligan! Except with different hair, obviously.'

I won't lie, I'm kind of surprised Mum and Dad have seen *Promising Young Woman*.

'Well, anyway, she came over for dinner. And then Ash and I were going to have a chill one tonight . . .'

'Oh?' Mum's voice takes on a crisp tone. 'No dinner plans?'

Whatever Ash does is criticised. If he doesn't take me out he's not making an effort. If he took me out for dinner he'd be accused of spending money he doesn't have on a social worker's salary and not planning for the future. He's never been able to do anything right when the real problem is that he has sex with other people. Not that it makes a difference now.

'Not this weekend,' I say.

No one says anything. Well, that conversation died faster than our class hamster in year six.

'How is he, then, er . . .' Dad dutifully revives the chat but typically avoids saying Ash's name. 'Work OK?'

I go to make up some bullshit or talk about Ash's case with the triplets or whatever, but as soon as I take a breath I realise I don't have the energy to talk about him like we're fine.

'Ash and I broke up,' I say. I've not been so forthright with Mum and Dad in years, but the truth drops out easily when I know it's something they're going to love to hear.

Dad keeps a relatively good poker face, but Mum's eyes

light up. 'Oh?' she gasps breathily, but she can barely disguise the glee in her voice or stop a triumphant smile from breaking out. 'Oh gosh, what happened?'

'Just didn't work out,' I say. I don't feel like going into detail with them.

Henry's eyes widen in horror. 'Fliss, what the hell?! Are you OK?'

'I'm fine,' I assert. I don't feel fine, but I will be.

'Oh, darling. Well, as long as you're all right.' Mum shuffles along the sofa and puts her hand on mine.

'Yes, we want you to be happy,' Dad adds.

They're not unkind. I really do believe they want me to be happy. It's just that their version of 'happy' can't look like anything except what they have. And they've been willing to make me miserable to help me to achieve that. It's mad logic, when you think about it. But maybe they were on to something. Maybe I should have been listening to them all along.

'We never thought he was right for you,' Mum can't resist throwing in.

In one way I am deeply livid that she was right about me and Ash and overcome with a childish urge to rebel against her, but there's also a part of me that's overjoyed to have gained her acceptance. A big part of me. I can't help myself warming as they speak.

'You always deserved better,' Dad agrees.

Again, it's sweet in one way that they want the best for me. They couldn't see an open relationship as anything other than cheating, and I realise a cheating boyfriend is not what anyone would want for their daughter. It's a shame they never got to know Ash. They'll never know his wonderful qualities and never understand how well he treated me, contrary to their belief, but there's no need now. None of it matters.

'So . . . anyone else on the horizon?' Mum claps her hands.

'*Mum*,' Henry chides. He still looks stricken. Unlike Mum and Dad there's only sadness and sympathy in his expression as he looks at me. 'Could you wait until their relationship is at least cold in its grave? For God's sake.'

'Well, I'm only asking.' Mum adjusts her blouse. 'There's no need to snap, dear.'

'I'm sure Fliss isn't even thinking about . . .'

'I, er.' I cough. 'Well, Rowan's back in town. We, yeah, we've been . . . spending a lot of time together.'

I'm not quite sure why I say it. It's not like Rowan and I ever are going to be boyfriend and girlfriend. But I know they'll like it. The irony that I was in a proper relationship with Ash, and Rowan and I have always essentially been friends who bang, but that they're so much more supportive of that relationship is not lost on me. I'm just so enjoying pleasing them for once.

Henry stares at me open-mouthed.

'Oh, Rowan, I knew it!' Mum claps again, towards me this time, like she's literally applauding me. 'I always wondered how you could let such a smart, good-looking boy go? He looks just like that actor . . . What's his name, Mark? The one in *Get Out*?'

'Daniel Kaluuya.'

'Daniel Kaluuya!'

What is with my parents watching all these woke films? I didn't realise they knew there was a world outside of *Strictly Come Dancing* and *The Apprentice*.

'And such good taste in wine. Remember the wine he brought round that Christmas?'

'Was that when Lizzie dropped all the pigs in blankets on the floor?' Dad wrinkles his nose. Of course that's what Dad remembers from that day; that he had to wait an extra half an hour before being fed.

'I did see that he was in London. Is he moving here permanently?' Mum continues.

'Well, he was head of marketing at a branding agency in New York . . .'

Mum and Dad look at each other smugly. I can see the dollar signs in their eyes.

'He's taking a break for a while, working out his next steps,' I continue. 'He's doing some freelance translation work with me at the moment.'

'Oh, well, that sounds sensible,' Dad comments.

I can't help but think if Ash had done the same thing they'd call it reckless.

'Lovely,' Mum crows.

Mum and Dad sit beaming at me.

'*Lovely*,' Henry adds caustically.

Neither of them pay him any mind. It feels bizarre to be the centre of their attention for once. Usually it's Henry this, Sam that, Laura this, move on from talking about Fliss's life as soon as humanly possible. I don't like myself for it and I'd always thought I was stronger than this but . . . it feels *good*.

'You always said Rowan was a good egg.' Dad pats Mum on the shoulder and sits back and crosses one leg over the other. 'Listen to your mother, Fliss, she'll see you right.'

Mum smiles and reaches for Dad's hand.

'Right, I'll go and put the kettle on, shall I.' Henry stands up and makes a bid for the door. He disappears into the kitchen and I suspect these teas are going to be the longest teas anyone has ever made.

Mum and Dad keep asking me questions about Rowan and, even though I'm still devastated about Ash and I feel bad for Henry, I can't help but bask in the glow of their approval. I can't help but relish that they're actually happy for me, for once, even if I am thoroughly miserable.

CHAPTER TWENTY-TWO:
STAY INSIDE ON VALENTINE'S DAY

HOLLY

By the time Valentine's Day rolls around, I am *not* in a romantic mood. It would be the one year Will actually decides to book a restaurant. He usually rolls his eyes at Valentine's Day and refuses to engage in 'another tacky money-making scheme'. Thankfully, Liam texted me to say he had a friend's thirtieth birthday and his friend always complains about people ditching it for Valentine's, so he'd be having Ladentine's.

I want to be excited about tonight but Will making an effort isn't stirring anything except apathy. The last time he booked a restaurant he asked me if he could see other people. I suspect he's only making an effort now because he feels guilty or maybe, like Fliss says, jealous. Plus, I've been thinking too much about Tomi all week to care. I've sent a lot of pleading messages but today is the first time I'll see him in person since he left for his holiday.

I'm just so disappointed in myself. I've never, ever made a mistake like that. I'm usually so organised. And I don't take my friends for granted, that's not who I am. Tomi *knows* that's not who I am. If he knew everything that was going on with me I think he'd understand.

When I think about confessing everything to him I still feel so full of shame and confusion that it feels like fully explaining myself isn't an option, but I think I have to. There's no other way.

On the way in to work, I hold on to the tube railings like a zombie. I barely slept last night. All I could think about was Tomi and what I'll say when I see him. I'd usually curl into Will's side for comfort but when I tried it, all I could think about was how frustrated I am that he hasn't even asked whether Tomi and I have made up.

Maybe he's right that I'm making too big a deal out of it. On this occasion I really want to believe he's right. I couldn't help wondering what Liam would say about it.

When I get into the office, I head straight for Tomi's desk but I can't see him.

'He's probably still hungover,' calls Claire from the other side of the room with a hearty cackle. 'Thirty now. The hangovers last for weeks!'

Ugh, even Claire was there. Claire hardly gets invited to anything because she always ends up drinking too much and complaining about how she and her husband don't have sex anymore. Way to kick me when I'm down, Claire.

I lurk by his desk for ten minutes. Then I hear his laugh echoing from the kitchen and pace over.

When he sees me he smiles, but it doesn't reach his eyes.

The person he's talking to, some woman from the fourth floor, senses the shift in atmosphere and hurries off with her morning bagel.

'Tomi.' I approach him. 'I am SO sorry.'

He nods. 'I know, you said.'

I grimace, thinking of the many, *many* apology texts.

I bring out the *Woman in Black* tickets from my pocket. 'Look, I got you these. Happy birthday,' I say weakly.

Tomi looks at the tickets and smiles. 'I've been dreaming of getting scared by that creepy rocking chair for the longest time,' he says.

'I know, weirdo,' I say.

For a moment everything feels normal. But it disappears again.

'Thanks for these, Holly, and for the apologies, but you didn't really say what happened,' he challenges gently.

'I . . .' I've been racking my brains for excuses all night and could come up with literally nothing good enough. Even my *actual* excuse isn't good enough, let alone a fake one. I'm resolved to tell him the truth. 'I . . .'

I was planning to tell him. I *want* to tell him. But it still all feels so overwhelming. Where do I even begin?

'Is everything OK, Holly?' Tomi's voice softens, even though he still looks upset. 'You've been a bit distant recently.'

No, everything is *not* OK. I wanted to marry my boyfriend of nearly ten years and he wanted to sleep with other people. I agreed to it because I desperately wanted to keep him and now I have no idea what I want. I'm not the same person that I was at the beginning of the year. I feel hurt and humiliated but also liberated and alive.

I'm so afraid that Tomi isn't going to understand. As soon as I tell him, he's going to have thoughts. Opinions. Judgements. And I'm just not ready to hear them.

'I'm OK.' I clear my throat. My voice is wobbling. 'I'm just *really* sorry.'

Tomi nods, not unkindly, but he looks disappointed. 'I know you're sorry, Holly,' he says. 'This isn't like you at all. Look, I just hope everything's all right.'

He walks away and I feel worse than I did before.

The rest of the day passes in a horrible blur. Tomi and I talk a little, but there's a huge elephant sitting in between us. I could not be less in the mood to go out with Will for a Valentine's outing if I tried. I'm too upset about Tomi and confused by everything that's happening to want to dress up and go out for dinner, but Will insisted. I know if I tried explaining to Will he'd take it personally and accuse me of blowing the situation out of proportion. I find myself reaching for my phone to text Liam.

> Hi. I'm having a shit day. I messed up big time and let down a friend and I can't believe it. I've never done anything like that before x

He starts typing immediately.

> Oh no! I'm sorry ☹ It feels like shit but don't worry, we all make mistakes. I don't know what you did but I know if you explain your friend will understand and forgive you, because you're ace ☺ Here to talk more if you want x

His words lift a weight off my chest. *This* was the reaction I needed. The way Liam speaks about things – acknowledging that it's OK for me to be upset – made me uncomfortable at first but now, when we're chatting, I feel like a very thirsty person drinking a huge glass of water.

I don't know . . . I used to think Will would downplay things so that I wouldn't feel so bad about them. I used to believe I really *was* overreacting to everything. But recently I can't help but feel that maybe my feelings are fine, he's just not interested in them.

By the time I arrive at the restaurant to meet Will, I'm in an awful mood. Apparently, so is Will. He barely says a word as he sits down opposite me at the table and starts perusing the menu. Why did he even want to come out if he's only going to punish me for the other night?

'This place was supposed to be good.' He casts his eye across the menu in a way that I assume means he's already determined that it *won't* be good. I feel my mood sink even lower.

When I first met Will, I used to love the fact that he had such discerning tastes and strong opinions. I realise that, tonight, I'm internally sighing. I never registered how exhausting it is to be with someone who is so easily displeased and to not ever know why. I always want him to be happy, but it's hard when he has such exacting standards that are difficult to pin down.

I look around at the rustic wooden tables and steal a glance at someone else's food. 'It seems nice,' I say in a half-hearted effort to cheer him up.

He makes an indistinguishable noise. I'm not sure whether I've helped or not. For once, I don't care.

'How are you?' I ask. 'How was your day?'

'Good.' Will nods. 'We finally got the website approved for that new gallery.'

'Oh!' I exclaim. 'Amazing!'

Even though things are tense between us, I'm delighted for him about this. Will was energised by this project when it first came in, but they've been incredibly unspecific yet picky about what it is they want. There are two guys running it who have quite different opinions and approve something without checking with the other, only to go back on it later when the other one sees what's been approved and disagrees. Will and his co-worker, Sal, have been tearing their hair out about it for what feels like forever.

'That's so great!' I continue. 'How long has it been now?'

'We started working on it in July. So . . . seven months.'

I remember when that job first came in. Will and I were on a trip in Lisbon. We both find it hard to stay off our work emails and we often flick on and off them when we're on holiday.

Was that trip really only seven months ago? That's nothing in the context of our nine-year relationship, but it feels like a lifetime ago. I remember having a good time, even though I was panicked about Will being too hot and not liking the food and I had terrible blisters that hurt with every step but I didn't want to cause a fuss because there was a lot that Will wanted to see. I'd have preferred to sit in cafés and read, but Will finds that boring. Looking back, I wonder whether that trip *was* as fun as I thought it was.

'Well, congratulations,' I say, raising my empty glass in a mock-toast. 'You must be thrilled. How does it feel to be free of them?'

'Yeah, I'm pleased with where we got to in the end,' Will

answers. 'It's not where I'd have taken it, but given what we had to work with, it looks all right.'

I find myself frustrated with his answer. I wasn't asking about the work itself, I was asking how he was feeling about it. It's not that I don't like talking about work with Will. I *love* talking about it. But recently, I feel like this gulf has appeared between us, and I'm not actually sure that I know what's going on in his head at all. Or was the gulf always there and I just never noticed it?

'Show me,' I say.

Will excitedly brings out his phone and takes me through the website. His energy changes completely. He comes alive as he explains the thought processes behind the final tweaks on the designs and the compromises made to achieve both the owners' visions and how the branding is going to carry over into other parts of the company. I *love* Will's passion for what he does, and I enjoy listening to him talk about it, but I still can't help this wave of disappointment that I still don't know if he's relieved, or elated, or lost, now that the project is complete.

'And are you happy?' I try again, once Will's done showing it to me. 'That it's over?'

Will shrugs. 'I'm glad to see the back of them.'

Is that it? Is that all I'm getting?

'I'm so nervous about the showcase,' I offer, longing to connect.

'Oh yeah, show me the final design one more time. You work so far in advance I can't remember what it looks like anymore.' Will gestures eagerly for my phone.

Again, I'm aggravated. I used to think Will was so nurturing because he was attentive to my work, but I'm starting to wonder if he's really that supportive of *me*, or if it's just that he happens to be interested in what I'm doing. I want him to reassure me by telling me I'm going to smash it, or that if I don't, it doesn't matter. Talking about the minutiae of my creations isn't what I need right now.

If I'm honest with myself . . . this date is a dud. If this was someone I met on an app I'd be bailing to go and have cocktails with Fliss. I'm starting to think the evening couldn't get any worse, when I see something that fills me with dread. The restaurant door opens and a familiar face walks in. I blink multiple times. This *cannot be happening*. Not here, in London, where you never run into *anyone*. That is the *one* good thing about this grey, polluted bewilderment of a city. One time I ran into Amber on the tube and hid behind my copy of the *Metro*, but never in five whole years of living here has it happened again, and now the universe is seriously having me bump into Liam? While I'm on a date with Will.

On VALENTINE'S DAY.

Really?!

This absolutely cannot be happening.

Giant, anonymous London, how you have betrayed me!

Oh God. Oh my God. Oh my God oh my God. Crap. Crap. Crap. Crap. Liam is talking to the waitress at the front of the restaurant. It will only be seconds before he turns around and spots me. What am I going to do? Do I hide? Can I shield myself with a menu? That won't work. Run to the bathroom? But that will only buy me minutes. I'll have to come out and face the music eventually. Unless there's a window in the bathroom I can crawl out of?!

Nope. It's too late. Liam has seen me. And he's smiling

and heading over because he's cherubic and has no idea what horrors lie in wait for him over at this table. It's not an exaggeration to say that my entire body has frozen solid. Liam is the *Titanic* and I am the iceberg and a huge crash is coming for him, he just doesn't know it yet.

How can I get out of this? Maybe it will be OK. Maybe nothing will happen. Maybe we'll just say hello and Liam will sit at another table and wait for his friends and Will and I can eat very quickly and leave and no one has to find out who anybody is.

'Holly?' Liam approaches.

Oh God. Oh God oh God oh God.

'Hi!' I try to be breezy but sound like I'm being held at gunpoint. 'What are you doing here?'

In this specific restaurant? Why why why?!

'My mate raves about this place.' As Liam is speaking, he's casting his eyes over Will, and Will is leaning back in his chair, assessing Liam.

From the look on Will's face, he obviously suspects how I know Liam. It doesn't take a genius to work it out. *Please, please don't say anything*, I pray.

'Oh, nice,' I garble. 'Well, hope your friend has a great birthday.'

Please go. Please go.

He doesn't go. 'What about you?' he asks. 'What are you up to?' He looks directly at Will.

I'm trying to figure out how to answer this, when Will leans forward with his hand outstretched. 'Hi,' he says. 'I'm Will. Holly's boyfriend.'

CHAPTER TWENTY-THREE:
KNOW WHAT THE RULES ARE

HOLLY

My heart sinks down, and down, and down into my shoes, and I don't think it will ever come back up. I try to find words but none are forthcoming.

Liam shakes Will's hand. He's obviously taken aback but he's keeping his cool. 'Is that so?' He's looking between Will and me, speaking very slowly and deliberately. 'Didn't know Holly had a boyfriend. So how long have you two been seeing each other?'

'We've been together nine years.' Will pointedly rejects Liam's choice of the phrase 'seeing each other'.

Liam whistles and rubs his temples. He's not bothering to hide his reaction anymore. 'Nine years.' He kicks the floor. 'Nine *years*?' He's stopped looking at Will now, and is staring incredulously at me instead.

Well, this is uncomfortable.

I don't say 'fuck' a lot. Not even in my head. But right now that one word is playing on repeat through my mind like a blaring siren. This is a Challenger-level disaster. I've been doing this barely two months and I'm already sitting amongst the blazing wreckage of my open relationship, and the only thing I can do is sit back and watch it burn.

Will is acting unbothered by keeping his facial expression neutral, but he's got his arms crossed high up over his chest like he does at a family party if one of his brothers contradicts him.

Suddenly, I want to laugh at how wildly ludicrous this all is. Not just that we ran into Liam in one of the biggest cities in the world, on VALENTINE'S DAY, but that I'm even in this situation in the first place. Dating two men and having neglected to inform one of them of that fact. Awkward, pained, inappropriate, hysterical giggles bubble up, but I sense laughing now would be the absolute worst thing I could do, so I bite my cheeks.

No one has spoken in at least five seconds. Which doesn't sound that long, but it feels like about a year of silence has passed.

'I didn't have you pegged as a cheater, Holly,' Liam says eventually.

'I'm not!' I give a strangled little cry. 'We're in an . . . *open relationship*.' Saying it out loud now, it feels utterly ridiculous that I wouldn't have told Liam that. I have no idea how I convinced myself it was OK not to.

'And you didn't think to tell me that?!' Liam carries on.

'I said I wasn't looking for anything serious . . .' My words are quiet, because I'm aware of how lame it sounds, but it's the only defence I have.

'*Really* not the same.' Liam whistles again. 'I thought you'd just come out of a bad relationship or something. You seemed a bit sad and guarded.'

When he says that, I can't help but think he was half-right, except I'm not out of the bad relationship, I'm still in it. Then I try to stuff the thought back down. Will and I have got ourselves into a mess, but we don't have a *bad* relationship. It's only been bad since Will had this wild idea. It's the open relationship that's made everything bad . . . right? But even as I try to convince myself of that, I can't. Recently I've become aware of so many problems I never realised we had, and they aren't new. They're embedded into the fabric of us.

'I liked you, Holly.' Liam shrugs. He looks so dejected.

'I'm really sorry,' I say. 'I'm really, really sorry. I've handled this so badly.' I want to say *I like you too*, but I feel like I can't, with Will sitting there.

Will scoffs. 'You're sorry?' he chimes in. 'You're sorry to *this guy*?'

The intonation in Will's voice is clear. He obviously thinks I've done something terrible to him, too, but I'm not sure what it is.

'I'm sorry,' I say automatically to Will, even though I don't think I have anything to apologise for from his perspective. I want to add *I love you*, but I feel like I can't with Liam standing there.

This is a nightmare.

'Look, Holly, I'm gonna go.' Liam leaves. Will and I both watch him go. He bumps into one of his friends on the street outside and starts talking and gesturing at the building, clearly explaining why they're going to have to relocate their celebrations.

Will and I sit in silence.

'Well.' Will turns to me. He shakes his head, like I'm a naughty child. 'I hardly know what to say.'

Me neither, so I don't say anything.

'A "Mr Blue Sky" tattoo, Holly, really?' Will says scornfully. 'And that shirt.' He laughs.

It's pitiful how he's looking for a way to bring Liam down. Will reducing Liam to a tattoo and a shirt in that way makes me feel small and livid at the same time. I've always cared about what Will thought. I've always looked to his judgements on everything. But Liam is a caring, fun, kind person and yes, sometimes it looks like he got dressed in the dark, but who cares? I feel protective over him and I want to shield him from Will's snobbery.

'I should've known this wouldn't work,' Will goes on. 'I should've known you'd get too emotional about it.'

'What does that mean?' I ask.

'You've *clearly* been getting romantically involved,' Will scolds. 'We were just supposed to be sleeping with other people, Holly, you weren't supposed to be having another relationship.'

On hearing his words, that little voice that says I'm too sensitive and always ruining things starts whispering. Perhaps this all could have been so simple and somehow I've managed to make an unnecessary mess of it.

Part of me knows that's true. I should have been up front with Liam and I wasn't. But another, louder voice in me starts taking over; one that says, clear as anything, that this *isn't* all my fault. I remember Fliss's advice right at the start of this – to agree on clear parameters between us and to know what the rules were – and we never did. That isn't just on me.

'How was I supposed to know that?' I ask. Defending myself is starting to come more easily to me. 'We never said that. We didn't say *anything*, really, except agree what nights we . . . *you* . . . would be out of the house.'

Will splutters. He obviously wasn't expecting me to argue. Which, to be fair, why would he? Will and I don't argue. I always thought that was a *good* thing about us . . . I've always felt proud of the fact we never shout, or scream, or bicker. We never so much as disagree on what we're going to watch on TV or order for takeaway. But now I wonder if never arguing necessarily means you're in sync. Maybe it can mean one person blindly accepting everything another person says.

'It's *obvious*,' Will states.

'It's not obvious,' I return. Tears are bubbling up and for once I don't try and stop them. I'll cry if I want to cry. Sometimes there's a reason to. 'Nothing about this was obvious to me,' I carry on, my voice getting louder. 'To be honest, I still don't know exactly why you wanted to do it in the first place. I don't know what you've been doing, or how you've been thinking about it, or what you wanted to get out of it.'

'You wanted it, too,' Will says.

'No, I didn't! You know I didn't! I just knew that you wanted it and that was enough for me to go along with it.' If Will has convinced himself that I actively wanted this, he's deluding himself.

'You agreed to it,' Will defends.

'Yes, and I shouldn't have done,' I assert, my voice getting louder. 'Everything was on your terms and I was just expected to follow.'

'Holly, please.' Will shoots a furtive look over his shoulder. 'We're in public.'

At this point, I couldn't care less whether the people at the next table hear our conversation. I just want to have it. 'Let's go home, then,' I offer. 'We can talk about it there.'

'I don't think there's anything left to say,' Will states. 'An open relationship clearly can't work for you. Let's just close this chapter, OK? Let's just go back to normal.'

Let's go back to normal.

I let the phrase hang in the air. Those are the words I've been wanting to hear since we started this. But somehow, they don't bring me any relief. What is normal now? How can we go back?

Do I even *want* to go back?

I don't think I do. At what point did I stop? Was it when I had sex with Liam? Or kissed him? Was it the first time he pressed me to talk about my feelings and actually listened? Was it thinking of Will going on a date with another woman? Was it as soon as Will even suggested this? At what point could he have said *hey, wait, let's stop this madness*, and we'd have been the same Holly and Will?

'I can't, not without discussing this properly,' I push on. 'Why did you *really* want to do this? I know you said it was so we'd be stronger having had all the experiences you wanted. But what experiences, exactly? Was it just sex? Was it just to . . . sow your oats . . . before settling down? Were you just curious?' And then, I voice my deepest insecurity; the question I've been avoiding asking this whole time. 'Do you think on some level you were waiting to meet someone better?'

Will splutters. 'That's *preposterous*.' His cheeks are flushed and he keeps surreptitiously glancing over his shoulder to check if anyone's listening to us. Probably the whole restaurant is.

Once I've started asking questions, I find I can't stop. 'Have you got what you wanted out of this? Who have you been meeting? Have you had fun? Has it made you feel ready to marry me?'

Will is going increasingly red. He looks like a tomato now. 'It's been *shit*, OK,' he spits. 'Dating is shit. I've had a terrible time. I've had a few awful dates. Stilted conversation with brain-dead idiots. I haven't even slept with anyone.'

It all starts making sense now. The breakfasts . . . The lattes . . . The Valentine's booking. He didn't meet anyone else and he was trying to win back my attention. Fliss was right . . . He *was* jealous.

'Is that what you wanted to hear?'

It is and it isn't, all at the same time. While I hate the thought of Will going off and having an incredible time with beautiful women, I can't help but suspect he might only want this to be over now because he had a crap time and I didn't.

Will reaches across the table for my hand. 'If we had a bit longer I still think I'd enjoy it . . . but it's clearly not working for you. We should never have started this. It's OK, Holly. Look, we tried it, it didn't work out. C'est la vie.' He rubs his thumb across my palm.

I don't like how he's putting this all on me. He's making out like he wants to end the open relationship because I can't handle it, but if he'd gone out and had a wonderful time, would he still want to end it? Something in my gut tells me he wouldn't.

'The reason it hasn't worked isn't because *I've* fucked it up,' I say through my tears.

Will drops my hand. 'What are you saying, Holly? You start a full-on relationship with someone else and I'm willing to forget it, and I'm somehow the bad guy?'

That's not accurate. And not what I'm saying. I've done things wrong, I know I have, and I feel terrible. But I'm not the one who wanted to do this. Neither of us communicated and neither of us set any boundaries. He can't make me feel bad for having developed some feelings towards Liam. Isn't that normal? I'm just a human being. Was I supposed to meet other people and spend time around them like a robot? I try to formulate this into a coherent sentence but I'm still not totally used to standing up to Will and I can't articulate myself properly. Before I can say anything else, Will keeps speaking.

'So, I'm sorry, what am I hearing? What's the bottom line here? Do you *not* want to stop dating other people? Because of Mr Hawaiian shirt?'

'That's not . . .' I start. 'Honestly, I don't know what I want now. Why am I being called upon to give a straightforward yes or no answer as soon as you click your fingers?! You started this! There's so much to talk about and sort through. It's not black and white, Will.'

Will sighs. 'I don't know who you are anymore, Holly.'

'That makes two of us,' I retort.

Will flinches, still not used to me speaking to him in

this way. He looks away from me and at the floor. 'Let's go home,' he says. 'I'm not hungry.'

We leave the restaurant and get on the tube without saying another word. When we finally get home, Will takes the spare blanket out of the cupboard, goes to the living room and closes the door.

I sit upright in bed, hugging my knees under the covers. I think about Liam, probably still out with his mates, being distracted by their banter but occasionally letting his mind wander to that duplicitous girl he was just starting to like. I think about Will next door sleeping on the sofa and wonder what's going through his mind. But for the first time, I'm more concerned with what's going on in mine.

I still love Will, but there are so many problems in our relationship that I never even knew we had. There are lots of things I need that I didn't realise I needed. I don't know if we can find a way out of this mess or not. So much has happened and things would need to change.

I pick up my phone and reach out to the one person I can talk to. Right now, I need her more than ever.

Fliss, everything's gone to shit. I never told Liam about Will and he just found out about us in the most awful way. I'm sorry to ask at this hour, especially when I ignored your advice in the first place, but can you talk? Xx

Ten minutes pass. I decide she must have gone to bed, when a reply appears.

It's late, Holly, and I'm too tired to be your relationship

tutor. I'm sorry. You'll have to figure this one out on your own. x

Ouch. The words sting. I put my hurt feelings at the comment to one side, because something is obviously wrong.

Are you OK, Fliss? Did something happen with you and Ash?

I don't need you to be my relationship tutor, either.

Something's clearly happened and she needs to be left alone right now. I put my phone down on the bedside table and roll onto my back. The irony that a few weeks ago I was struggling to juggle Will, Liam, Tomi, Fliss . . . Now I have no one. I lie staring at the ceiling, thinking about the mess I've made and how I'm going to have to fix it all by myself.

CHAPTER TWENTY-FOUR:
YOU DON'T HAVE TO BE YOUR PARENTS

FLISS

I feel a twinge of guilt as I tuck my phone away, but I'm exhausted. I don't have the mental energy to sort out Holly's mess right now. Plus, I really don't want to hear what she'll have to say about me breaking up with Ash. I already *know* what she'd say. 'That's a bit sudden, Fliss. Are you sure?' 'But you love Ash! And Ash loves you!' 'Have you given it enough time? It's going to take work to take your relationship into a new phase . . . This feels a bit impulsive.'

I don't want to listen to any of that. I just want to stop thinking about everything and go to the pub. I thought I'd be feeling more free, more immediately back to myself, but at the moment I just feel numb. It hasn't really sunk in yet.

I look towards the bar, where Rowan is currently queuing up to buy us another round. See, this is why I like Rowan. He doesn't follow any rules, like not drinking to excess on a Monday night. Anything can happen in his company. You never quite know what he's going to say or what he's going to do next. He's free and happy not having serious relationships, like I should be. We understand one another. I'm not supposed to be heading down the aisle to Ash; I'm supposed to be sitting next to Rowan on a bar stool.

I haven't told him yet that Ash and I have broken up, but we're out together on Valentine's Day and he's no fool.

Rowan sits back down next to me with two pints.

'Mama Henderson messaged me today.' He sets the glasses down on the table, equidistant from each other. 'Wants to know when I'm free for that dinner.'

'Of course she did. Am I invited or will I be too much of a third wheel?' I joke.

'I guess it would be OK if you tagged along.' He gets out his phone and forwards me the dates. I'm still traumatised by the break-up with Ash, but Rowan has always had a way of helping me disconnect from everything else happening in my life.

'By the way.' I've been waiting to do this for weeks. I pull a harmonica out of my bag – the one I secretly ordered a fortnight ago – and play a perfect set of notes that I've been practising every evening like a maniac.

Rowan cackles. 'Knew you could do it. Now we just need a name for our folk band. So . . . no plans with lover boy today?' he finally ventures.

I was hoping my newfound musical ability would distract him, but he's obviously been wanting to ask about it all evening. I'm not massively in the mood to talk about it but I'm not going to actively lie about it.

'We broke up,' I announce.

'Oh?' Rowan doesn't look even slightly surprised. There's a glimmer of smugness in his expression. 'What happened?'

I roll my eyes. 'Look at you. You can barely contain yourself.'

'Excuse me?' He puts on a mock-innocent face. 'What significance could this news *possibly* have for me?'

I roll my eyes harder.

'Look, no, I'm sorry. Selfishness aside, are you OK?' He takes my hand.

'It was pretty rough. But I'm OK.'

At some point, between his sitting down and my sharing the news of my break-up, Rowan has reduced the distance between us. He's sitting noticeably closer to me in our booth. His face is right next to mine.

He holds eye contact and I know that he's about to kiss me. My heart rate quickens. I've been thinking about this moment for weeks and now that it's happening it doesn't feel real. Usually kissing Rowan wouldn't be a big deal, or any sort of deal. It would be something I'd do without a second thought. But the last month of not being *allowed* to do it has made it into a Thing.

I hate that. I hate that I've been obsessing over it. Rowan and I are usually straight to the point. We definitely don't *pine*. But I have been, like a silly little school girl, and he knows it.

Monogamy really fucked me over.

He leans in and presses his lips against mine. It's satisfying, it's thrilling, it tastes like gaining my freedom back.

He puts one hand around the nape of my neck and the

other around my waist, pulling me closer. In one way it's familiar, like coming home – we've been down this road before – but it's alien and strange, too. Something's different and I can't pin down what it is.

It's probably just the fact that it's been forbidden for so long. The guilty, dutiful sense that I shouldn't be doing it. I tell myself I'll quickly readjust.

Then Ash pops into my mind. Ugh, I can't catch a break! When I was kissing Ash I couldn't stop thinking about Rowan and now I'm kissing Rowan I can't stop thinking about Ash. One month of monogamy has brought my sex life to its knees.

I remind myself that I broke up with Ash. Even though our break-up is fresh, what difference does it make if I sleep with Rowan tonight, or next week, or the week after? We aren't together anymore. And for the majority of our relationship we weren't monogamous anyway.

But as we keep kissing, Ash sticks in my mind and this just feels wrong somehow.

'Rowan,' I mumble into his mouth. 'I can't.'

He pulls away and fixes his gaze on me. 'I hear it's like riding a bike.'

I laugh, despite myself.

'You'll be OK, Fliss,' he adds. 'It was never going to work out for you with Ash. People like you and I are better off on our own.'

His words are intended to comfort me, I know that; but I can't help feeling a stab of something deeply unsatisfying. Monogamy or being alone appear to be the only two options on offer to me, so I guess he's right. I kiss him again, reminding myself this is where I belong.

I hear Holly telling me I'm moving too quickly. How I shouldn't jump straight from one thing into another. Asking me if I'm sure I can't make exclusivity work with Ash. I hear Henry's voice telling me that I'm drunk and I should go home. Take some time to think. But I'm desperate to feel better, desperate to feel less miserable, and I turn their voices down.

I'm still feeling terrible about Ash, about the train wreck of the last month and the denial I've been living in for the last three years, but it will pass. This is the right thing for me, and therefore for Ash, too. He wouldn't want me to keep moving forward when I have so many doubts. He wants to be in an exclusive relationship with someone who actually wants to be in an exclusive relationship with him. And as Rowan says, I'm probably better off on my own.

'I have been waiting so long to do that,' Rowan murmurs in my ear.

'Me too,' I reply.

'Hey, now you're allowed to be fun again.' Rowan nudges me with his shoulder. 'You know what we should do? Inter-railing. I've always wanted to do it. It's so quaintly European that you can actually make it around an entire continent by train.'

'Inter-railing?' I repeat.

'Yeah. It will be just like when we did that road trip across Connecticut. Except . . . safe.'

'Because you won't be driving?'

'Exactly.'

My head is slightly spinning, but that sounds fun. Way more appealing than staying in London surrounded by reminders of Ash, anyway.

'Fuck it, let's do it,' I say.

'YES.' He slaps the table. 'Sick. Let's start planning it. Do you want to come back to mine?'

Half of me wants to go back with him; the half that's desperate to do all the strictly prohibited things I've not been able to stop thinking about. But the other half just wants to go home. I feel a bit like I did as a teenager stepping out of my last A Level exam. Months of being chained to revision and trapped inside a dark hall on hot summer days, then when you finally get out it's anticlimactic and you feel directionless and overwhelmed.

'I should get home,' I say. I know I do want to sleep with Rowan, but not right now.

'All right.' Rowan gets up and offers me a hand. 'Woah there,' he says as I wobble. Suddenly I realise how drunk I am. I wish my response to strong emotions wasn't always to drink until I can barely remember my own name, but I *am* British. 'Someone's had a few too many.'

'Whose fault is that?' I return.

He holds his hands in the air. 'I take full responsibility. Come on, let's get you home.'

We say goodbye at the tube station and I start the journey back to north London. I think how strange it is that only a month ago, I would have said that I felt confident I'd be with Ash forever. I hadn't thought about Rowan in months. Now I'll probably never see Ash again and I'll be spending the foreseeable making my way across Europe on a train with Rowan in the next seat. But I think this is always how it was meant to be.

When I get home, Henry is still up reading. Maoam

wrappers are strewn across the floor. As I enter he starts clearing up his sugary detritus.

'Henry.' I sit myself down across from him on the floor. 'I have news.'

Henry raises one eyebrow, puts a bookmark between the pages of his book and rests it beside him on the floor. 'Oh?' he says. 'More news?'

I take a deep breath. 'I'm going travelling with Rowan,' I declare.

For a moment he says nothing, and then, 'You're . . . going travelling? With Rowan?'

'Yes.'

'What about your job?'

'I can keep working from anywhere. They're pretty flexible.'

'What about Ash?'

'Well, we broke up.'

'Yes, I know you broke up. But I mean . . . What about Ash?'

He keeps looking at me disbelievingly. He obviously has An Opinion.

'You've let me stay here with minimal guilt trips, and I've seriously appreciated you not prying about me and Laura, so, look, I'll just say have fun,' he concludes.

He clearly wants to share his thoughts and even though he's being cynical, I do find myself wanting to hear them. Maybe because the person I've been telling everything to recently wouldn't understand at all. Holly is Team Ash all the way and she has no context or understanding of me and Rowan. But Henry's been there for every stage of my life.

He knows both of them. He knows me. I think I can make him get it.

'I couldn't make a normal relationship work with Ash,' I explain. 'I tried.'

'A *normal* relationship?' Henry questions. 'I've never heard you say that before. What is a normal relationship, Fliss?'

True, there was a time when I hated people using the word 'normal' to describe relationships, and when people would talk about me and Ash as if we were 'abnormal' in some way. But since learning that the whole time even Ash secretly thought that as well, I know when I'm beat.

'You know what I mean,' I say. 'A monogamous relationship.'

Henry looks like he's just sat in something wet. 'So, let me get this right. You tried monogamy with Ash for one month and it didn't work, so you decide the whole three-year relationship was wrong. You think the answer is being alone forever and pretending to be Jack Kerouac?'

I wish I'd never said anything.

'Well, that's an incredibly reductive way to put it, but . . . yes,' I answer.

'That's stupid.' Henry shakes his head. 'If you're really breaking up with Ash, please, I beg you, don't immediately disappear off with Rowan to sleep on hostel floors. You're not twenty-two anymore.'

'It's not like that,' I retort. 'We understand each other.'

Henry frowns. 'Because you have good sex once a year on a trip down memory lane? Fliss, this man knows twenty-two-year-old you, not grown-up you.'

Wow. I see that Henry is being his best condescending self.

Sometimes, Henry has a tendency to speak to the rest of the world like they must be stupid, because he got everything together so young. I'd figured that his current predicament would make him less Yoda-like, but I guess not.

'Sorry, I forgot you know everything there is to know about relationships,' I snap.

Henry laughs. He gestures around him. 'Hardly. Look at me.' His face softens. 'I spent Valentine's Day eating sugary snacks on my baby sister's bedroom floor. I'm sorry, Fliss. All I'm saying is that you seem to be making this into a choice between monogamy and being a hermit. It looks to me like the solution is finding a different kind of relationship.'

I shake my head. 'I thought so too. But look what happened.'

'OK, so, you'll meet someone else. Ash isn't the only man out there who'd be interested in an open relationship.'

I can't even *imagine* getting into a relationship with anyone else and doing this all over again. The thought is like standing at the bottom of a very huge, freezing-cold mountain, staring up at it and knowing once you've climbed your way to the top there's a good chance someone might just push you down the other side. Everyone else seems to be aiming for monogamy in the end, and I'm too afraid anything new would end the same way.

'I was happy keeping it casual for many years,' I say.

'That was so long ago!' Henry exclaims. 'You were a baby! You still wore cardigans and carried that tiny handbag everywhere. You've changed so much since then. You've got to know yourself. You're a different person.'

I feel my frustration rising. Henry *always* thinks he knows better. I had it all worked out and now he's muddling me again. But he's wrong. 'It's not monogamy that's the problem, OK, it's me. I don't want to talk about this anymore.'

'I don't think it is.' Henry ignores me. 'But I can't understand why you're thinking so black and white all of a sudden.'

'Of course you don't understand!' I cry. 'You're the golden child! You got married when you were twenty-six to your high school sweetheart! You wear a suit to work and own a house in Tunbridge Wells. Your angelic son already knows how to use a hoover!'

I *hate* that I sound jealous, but I suppose . . . maybe I am. Not because I want any of those things, but because it would be nice to want them and to be praised for my choices instead of judged.

Henry looks a little shocked, as if he'd never considered this view of himself before, or that I might be envious of him. He snorts. 'Yeah, and look where it got me.'

'Oh, you'll marry another woman.' I wave a dismissive hand. 'You'll buy another house in Tunbridge Wells and spawn another cherub.'

'I won't,' Henry says decisively. 'I won't marry another woman.'

The way Henry emphasises the word 'woman' causes the penny to drop. We hold eye contact and I know what he's telling me. It dawns on me that I've been very blind.

'I'm gay, Fliss,' Henry continues. 'And maybe if I *hadn't* been so desperate to fit the mould, and to please Mum and Dad, I wouldn't be in this position now.'

I hate that I'm surprised, but Henry has played a fixed role in my family since the beginning of time. I'd not properly considered the possibility he might be gay. I guess, neither had he. It's ridiculous, because Ash even suggested it to me and I dismissed it. It was one of the things I naturally asked when Holly said she was going into an open relationship. I know tons of people who discover their sexuality later in life. But Henry is so set in my mind – so part of 'Henry and Laura' to me for so long – that I didn't properly entertain it as an option. In my head, the idea I had of my brother was unquestionable.

'How long have you known?' I ask.

'I'm not sure, exactly,' Henry answers. 'On some level, for a long time. Consciously, the last couple of years.'

'Does Laura know?'

Henry nods. 'She's been supportive. But obviously, it's hard. It almost would have been better if I *was* straight and I'd cheated on her or something. We thought we could stay in the same house at least, for Sam, and be friends, but recently it's become obvious it's just too difficult. Neither of us can really get on with our new lives when we still live together. We've been living in limbo.'

I can see why they tried that; it makes sense. But I can also understand that it's not going to work. I hope that they can find a way forward that works for Sam.

'Anyway, the good news is I've finally found a flat nearby, so Sam can stay with me half the week and Laura the other half, and see us both whenever he wants,' Henry says. 'The people living there want to get the ball rolling quickly, so I should be able to move in soon.'

I nod. 'Have you told Mum and Dad?'

'Christ, no.' Henry sighs. 'Let them process the divorce

first. Mum can only handle so much at once. Hey, do you feel like marrying Rowan to distract them? I'll tell them at the wedding.'

I give a feeble laugh. We sit in silence for a moment. Henry's really been going through it, and I feel awful for having no idea.

'You know, whenever you choose to tell them about it, I'm there for you, yeah? Just say the word. Whatever you need.'

'I know. Thanks.'

'I'm glad you're figuring stuff out.'

'Me too.'

'Love you, Hen,' I say.

'Love you too, sis,' he says.

Both of us seem to reach an instinctive understanding that the time for conversation is over for the night. We hug and start getting ready for bed. It's been a long, long day.

CHAPTER TWENTY-FIVE:
DON'T RUSH TO FIX THINGS

HOLLY

The next morning, I wake up to an empty flat and a note from Will on the kitchen counter.

> *Gone to my parents'. Design comments on top of your folder. Out of milk.*

It's a brutal attack on all three fronts. Firstly that he's abandoned me to go to his parents' house without any warning or discussion is infuriating. That is *so* Will. He's a classic youngest child and his mum will make a huge fuss of her darling baby and – whatever he chooses to share with her about what's happened – will probably tell him he's completely in the right. Then the fact that he's remembered to leave the notes on my designs that I asked for makes me want to cry, because even when things are totally shit he still wants to help, albeit in his way. Then the practical reminder tacked on the end knocks me backwards with the sheer contrast of simple domesticity against how complicated everything has become.

Who knew fourteen words could give rise to so many different feelings.

I can't believe he's just . . . gone. If he really needed some space then I would understand, but he should say that, rather than disappearing to Devon with barely a word. It feels more like he's having a strop and that I'm being punished. As if everything that's happened is my fault.

Peculiar heat bubbles up in my stomach. I think I am experiencing . . . anger? It's not something I'm familiar with; I can be upset, and anxious, but never angry. I'd always thought of that as a good thing, especially in the context of my relationship. Except, I'm starting to wonder whether an absence of this is really just code for having no expectations of how I should be treated. It's not OK that Will's just disappeared like this. Why shouldn't I get angry?

I glance at my phone. No messages. I was hoping Fliss would wake up in a better mood and send me an apology. But no.

I put the kettle on and sit down at the dining table. I open up my message thread with Will. The last thing in it, from yesterday, is 'where shall I meet you?' I start typing something about how I wish we'd been able to talk before he vanished, but I don't want to get into an argument over text. Then I start thanking him for remembering the feedback on my designs, but I don't feel like thanking him for anything right now. So all I'm left with is 'I'll pick up some more milk.' I don't send anything.

I open my thread with Liam instead. The last messages in there are his reassurances about Tomi. I start typing out a bunch of things, but where do I even begin? I set off on a very long-winded explanation of how we got here but anything I say sounds cringe-inducing, like I'm just trying to excuse myself of my *major* fuck-up. I write, delete, write, delete, write, delete, until I end up with 'I'm sorry'. I don't send that either.

The morning passes in this way, until I realise it's nearly time to go to work. With the amount that Amber's been heaping on me, I know I'm not going to have time to think about my personal life today, but I'm not going to be able to concentrate properly if I've not said anything to either of them, which means I have ten minutes to try and salvage things.

There's only one thing for it. I pick up the phone. Will answers after one ring.

'Holly.' He always addresses me on a call like that. No 'hello'. Just my name spoken in a short and monotone greeting. I used to find Will's unwavering assertiveness attractive. I'm not so sure anymore.

'Will.' My voice is breathless from nerves. Or maybe rage. I sound like I've been on a treadmill. 'You left,' I say lamely.

'I need some time to clear my head.'

'Are you already there?' I ask.

'No. I'm at Waterloo.'

'Come home,' I find myself saying. 'Please. Let's talk about this.' I'm furious that he just ditched and it's hard to see the wood for the trees in the ever-growing forest of our issues, but maybe if we could just have a proper conversation, we might be able to resolve this.

'Are you ready to give up on this preposterous situation?' he asks.

The way he's characterising it now is like this was my idea in the first place. Like I'm the one driving this. Like he's a victim. But surely all I did was go on a few dates with a man because Will asked me to and then end up liking him. Was what I did so wrong? How was I supposed to stop myself liking him when that is surely the very purpose of a date? I still don't quite understand what I'm supposed to have done differently. Maybe I *would* understand if I could actually hear more about Will's perspective.

'Can we just *talk*?' I try again in desperation. Exactly like last night, he doesn't want to hear how I feel or what I'm thinking, and he's not really offering me any insights into his own mind either. He just wants me to do exactly what he wants to do with no questions asked.

Will grunts. 'If you're not willing to give up Hawaiian Shirt for me, we have nothing to talk about.'

He hangs up the phone. That is *so* unfair. We started this whole thing because he wanted to and now he wants me to end it exactly when he wants to. Now I'm even angrier. Five minutes left until I have to leave for work. Before I can think about it too much, I call Liam.

'Hello?' he says. I'm relieved that he answered, but now have no idea what I'm actually planning to say.

'Liam . . . hi.' Always a good opener. Not sure where to

go next. 'I'm so sorry about last night,' I try. 'Well, I'm sorry about all of it.'

'It was a surprise, to say the least, Holly,' he says. 'What were you thinking?'

'I meant to tell you,' I explain. 'And then I just . . . didn't. Because it was hard. And I thought people would judge me. And I wasn't sure how *I* was feeling about it, so trying to describe it to someone else . . .'

'How long have you been in an open relationship?' he asks.

'Not long. Since the beginning of January. It wasn't my idea,' I say. I'm not sure why I add that last part. Maybe because it shows I wasn't planning this. This was all a result of being lost and out of my depth, it wasn't callous or manipulative. 'I sort of convinced myself that telling you I wasn't looking for anything serious was the same as telling you the truth.'

'It isn't.'

'I see that now,' I say. God, this is mortifying.

'I'd never have got involved in something so complicated. Not wanting anything serious is one thing, but not being free at all is another. When I date someone, I like to know there's at least potential for things to go . . . *somewhere*.'

I'm not sure what to say to that. I go with, 'I'm sorry,' again.

There's a pause. 'So you didn't *want* to be in an open relationship?'

'No.'

'And . . . God. This is a bit early to be having this conversation. But what was I, then? I mean, where did you see this situation heading?'

I'm glad Liam can't see me right now, because I am turning bright red and pulling nervously at my dress. 'Honestly . . . I hadn't thought that far ahead. But I really like you, and I wasn't expecting to, and I'm sorry.'

'So, are you just calling to apologise? Or do you want to keep seeing me? Are you and Will breaking up? Still together? What's your end game here?'

The honest answer is I'm not sure. Half-truths haven't worked for me so far, so I just say what I'm actually feeling. 'I don't know.'

Liam sighs. 'This is a lot, Holly. I need a bit of time to think, and obviously so do you. Bye.'

He hangs up. Great. I just made things ten times worse with both of them. 10/10 work, Holly. This time last week I had two men and I had the *audacity* to complain about it. Now I have zero men. God, I hate last-week-Holly. What did she have to moan about?!

I throw on my clothes in a rush and hurry to the office. For the rest of the day, I bury myself in work. Even Amber's constant 'have you done this yet?' questions about tasks she only gave me an hour ago are a welcome distraction from the horror of just how spectacularly everything has imploded around me.

I really, really want to talk to Tomi, but things are still strained between us. I wish I'd told him everything earlier, instead of some woman in a ladies' loo who I'll probably never hear from again. Maybe now I wouldn't feel so isolated. But at the time, that was Fliss's appeal. Complete detachment from my actual life. I was foolish to believe we'd actually become friends.

At seven-thirty I'm still in the office, and it's becoming increasingly evident to me how little I want to go home to our empty flat. It's just a big, taunting reminder of how things were and where we are now. Only a few months ago I was ready to marry this man and now, apparently, we can't even be in the same room. I can't imagine sitting at home right now, trying to do regular things like watch TV or, God forbid, sleep, when things are as far from normal as they could be.

I would usually have asked to stay at Tomi's or – up until a few days ago – Fliss's, but it looks like I'm rapidly running out of friends in this city.

The possibility has been at the back of my mind all day but, the later it gets and the less I want to go home, the more tangible it starts to become. I know the number by heart even though I don't call very often.

The phone rings, and rings. At first I think she's not going to pick up and then I hear her familiar voice.

'Hello?'

'Mum?' My voice cracks. I clear my throat. 'Mum, it's me. Can I come to stay?'

I hear the tapping of a spoon against a tea cup. A game show is on in the background. I can see her sitting in our living room, wrapped in a giant cardigan on the small, beige sofa in front of faded green wallpaper.

'This weekend?'

'Tonight.' I still have time to dash to the flat to pick up some things and make it back into Central for a train.

'Tonight? It's a bit late.' She sounds perturbed.

'I know, but I really want to come home,' I beg. Even if

home isn't perfect, it's still home, isn't it? And anything is better than trying to sleep in Will's and my bed.

The tapping resumes. 'Well, it's a bit late, but OK,' she says. 'What time will you arrive in?'

CHAPTER TWENTY-SIX:
DISTRACTION DOESN'T WORK

FLISS

By the time the weekend hits, I'm halfway through planning my trip with Rowan. We've identified the passes we want and looked up accommodation – a mixture of hostels and hotels – and I'm lying on his sofa, daydreaming about Italian cheese.

We haven't exactly defined what we are to each other now. I'm not sure if there is such a definition. Two lone wolves running parallel to each other instead of striking out totally alone? We don't *need* a definition, which is sort of the whole point of why we understand each other so well.

We both worked from his flat today. It was nice in one way to have a change of scene from the office, or the loud shrieks from Jenny and Henry playing Mario Kart when they're supposed to be working, but if Rowan is distracting in the office, he's a nightmare working from home. I didn't go five minutes without him asking me something like, 'if you could be insanely rich but walk at a snail's pace forever or have no money but be able to fly, what would you choose?'

I've had forty minutes of peace because he went to have a nap. I've mostly spent it nosing around the living room at his strange collection of possessions. His harmonica rests on a shelf next to a bird that he's in the middle of whittling and a tea towel that he's started cross-stitching. Everything is meticulously organised. His books are in alphabetical order – given he only just moved here and most of his stuff is still in New York, he only has six, which makes ordering them even weirder – and his clothes are arranged by colour. Earlier I moved a grey-blue T-shirt into the middle of the blues, rather than in between the greys and blues to see if he'd notice, and he immediately moved it back.

I hear him shuffling around in the next room. He must be awake.

'How do we get to Brixton from here?' he asks as he enters the room. He settles down next to me.

'Why?'

'I booked a table at this jazz bar.' He closes my laptop, signalling that I'm done for the day. As soon as it hits five-thirty – or, some days, before that – he makes it impossible to do any more work. I'm so behind on translating the French novel that I'm going to have to ask for an extension on the deadline, but I won't get paid any more for it. To Rowan, a job is something you *have* to do – usually for as much money and as minimal work as humanly possible – it's not something you *enjoy*. It's strange because he's interested in lots of random things, but it's almost like the concept of job satisfaction doesn't even register for him.

I think of Ash and how moving I found it that sometimes

he'd be up all night stressing about whether the families he was working with were OK. Then I remind myself that yes, Ash had amazing qualities, but it's irrelevant. Rowan and I are the ones with the similar outlook on what we want out of life, which is what matters.

Still, I imagine putting on make-up now and going out to a jazz bar and am tired at the thought. I don't want to be boring, but honestly I'd rather do my laundry. We started the week getting drunk on Monday and since then I've not had a chance to properly recover, so I've basically been running on a weeklong hangover. There's always something, somewhere in the city that Rowan wants to be doing. Tuesday was an independent film screening, Thursday was bowling. The one night we stayed at home he sat sewing on the sofa like a demon, as if his life depended on embroidering a tea towel at record speed.

Rowan's continuous energy is a trait that I like, so I haven't wanted to put a dampener on anything, but tonight I'm knackered. All I want to do is get into some – freshly laundered – pyjamas and lie still in a dark room.

'Oh, sounds *cool*.' I'm careful to inject enthusiasm into my weary grandma voice. 'I wondered about a movie marathon tonight, though? All eleven *Fast & Furious* films? Pretty ambitious, but I reckon we can do it.'

We'll never make it through all eleven: a) it's literally impossible and b) I'll probably fall asleep during the first one. But I need to tempt Rowan to stay indoors somehow and he likes a challenge.

'We can do that tomorrow,' he says. 'Come on, I already booked it. We've got a table right by the band!'

His eyes are all shiny with zest for life. It makes saying no to him very hard. Plus, when I'm out I'm too distracted to dwell on Ash. So I nod and start to get changed, making a mental note to pick up an energy drink on the way to the station and convincing myself he's improving my work/life boundaries and pushing me to do new and interesting things.

We do end up having a *fantastic* evening. The band is amazing, the atmosphere is buzzing, the cocktails are delicious. Ash crosses my mind occasionally, but every time he does I reach for another cocktail and manage to push him out of my mind. This is for the best. After this initial rough patch we'll both be happier going our separate ways.

A few times, I wonder what Holly would say about how much things have changed in a week and then I remember we've not messaged since Monday. I feel briefly guilty for what I said to her and then I remind myself that I don't need her judgement on my life, and she doesn't need mine.

Still, I think to myself, maybe she'd be pleased I finally have clarity . . . But my gut tells me she wouldn't think that. She'd probably tell me thinking about Ash all the time means I'm still in love with him. She'd have doubts about Rowan and going away with him and she'd support Ash. Like Henry, except unfortunately I can't hide from Henry because he's my blood relation and squatting in my bedroom. Well, they're *both* wrong.

Henry's not said anything else this week about Rowan, rightly sensing the conversation was closed. Every time I've said I was going out with him he's plastered on a fake smile or popped a jelly baby in his mouth.

Later, we head back to Rowan's flat. With Henry still at

mine, it's a little crowded. Plus, Jenny was so heartbroken when I told her Ash wouldn't ever be coming back that she baked three cakes in one evening and wouldn't let me have a piece. She hasn't spoken to me since.

As soon as we get to Rowan's the true force of how tired I am hits me like a tidal wave. Exhaustion from the week's activities and emotional upheaval weighs down every limb and all I want to do is be carried upstairs to bed. But as soon as I've taken off my shoes, Rowan pushes me against the wall and starts kissing down my neck.

I still haven't quite got rid of the feelings of wrongness, of delinquency, which makes the sex kind of hot and forbidden. When his tongue slips between my lips I'm breaking the rules; as his hand slides under my dress I'm doing something I shouldn't.

When we're busy, and when we're banging on the floor in the middle of his flat, I find it easier to stop thinking about Ash. But in the moments before I go to sleep, or when I look around at Rowan's flat and notice there aren't any houseplants, I can't help but wonder how he is, what he's doing. But that's to be expected, isn't it? I have a fleeting desire to ask Holly that question.

Finally, when we're eventually falling asleep, and I have just managed to get Ash out of my mind, my phone lights up. I fumble for it in the darkness. It's Ash.

Hi, I just wanted to say I hope you're OK. Thinking about you. Miss you x

The sense of wrongness that we're not together nearly over-powers me. Tears fill my eyes. I turn off my phone and shove it under my pillow. Despite being as shattered as I am, I know that text has ruined any chance I had of sleeping. I try to reassure myself that there's no alternative, because I can't give him what he needs. I can't give anyone what they need. And I shouldn't have to change myself so fundamentally to be with someone. He will miss me for a while but then he'll meet someone else and he'll be happy.

I tell myself this pain is normal and temporary, but I miss him so, so much and it's only been a week. I eventually turn my phone back on and reply:

I miss you too. But even the right decisions hurt. X

CHAPTER TWENTY-SEVEN:
WORK OUT WHAT
YOU WANT

HOLLY

I forgot how slowly time moves at my mum's house.

Or maybe that's because I have no friends or boyfriend(s) to speak of. My phone hasn't pinged once since I got here on Tuesday.

Amber was irritable when I said I'd be working from home for the rest of the week because I was having some personal issues. 'The showcase is *next week*, Holly,' she sneered, as if I didn't know that. At the beginning of the year I'd have caved instantly and probably felt terrible, as if the success of the whole event rested on my being present in the building. But I can't commute every day from our little village in Norfolk. And I can't face staying in the empty flat. Why should my mental health come below Amber's irrational desire to have me physically by her side just so she can dump even more work on me at the last minute?

Even though I'm busy, the hours seem to drag out here. I used to like that. Right now I'm not so sure; I have way too much space for my thoughts. Then again, it's still preferable to being surrounded by all of Will's things.

I'm in my old bedroom, sitting at my desk, positioned against a window overlooking some fields and a chicken farm. I'm wearing a pair of my teenage pyjamas. My stuffed bear is still out on the bed, where I left it, even though I only visit a couple of times a year.

I would visit more, but Mum hardly calls me and when I call her she doesn't stay on the phone for long. When I come home, it's hard to tell whether she's pleased or not. She leads a strange life. She goes to work, gardens and attends the occasional poker night, but apart from that she doesn't go out much. She mainly stays in this house, which is not very homely. I wouldn't use the word 'unhappy' exactly, more that she seems to have decided happiness is not a concern to her.

When I was a kid, there were phases when she was quite dependent on me. I would clean up, I would bring her food, I would make sure she remembered things. She was very emotionally reactive and I was often afraid of saying the wrong thing and upsetting her. There were better phases, too, but some days she wouldn't get out of bed. By the time I was an older teenager she didn't need me to do any of that anymore. She found a routine, she found a way to control what she was going through, and we never spoke about the bad times.

I think it's only just beginning to dawn on me that they *were* that bad. I was a kid and it was all I knew, so it was normal to me. We've never addressed any of it and I haven't spoken much about my childhood to anybody. Over the years I've sometimes wondered how she felt back then, whether she's lonely now, and I've been intrigued about my father who she's given minimal details about – he was a photographer and he abandoned us three months before I was born, that's about it – but she's so shut off that I've never dared press her. And I've never dwelt on any of it. I'm only just beginning to burn with curiosity about it all.

Mum knocks on the door, holding a cup of tea.

'How's it going in here?' she asks. 'I brought you a cuppa.'

'Thank you.' I watch her as she sets the mug down next to me. She looks the same as ever. Mum is about sixty and she's looked sixty since I can remember. 'It's OK, thank you. I'm making my way through everything. How's your day?'

'Oh, same old, same old.' She waves a hand, already exiting the room. That's usually Mum's style. Drink tea, say little.

It's been three days and she hasn't even asked me why I came. I doubt that she will. She must know that something is wrong, but she won't go near it. I wonder what I'd have to do to get her to ask me what was wrong. I could probably sit down for dinner dressed in a purple sequinned jumpsuit covered in lightning bolts and announce I was quitting my job to train for the *WWE SmackDown* and she wouldn't comment.

Normally I'm OK with it. I mean, normally it wouldn't have occurred to me not to be OK with it. But since I got here, I can't help but be deflated by the superficiality of our conversation.

Still, I remind myself, there were times when I'd have been grateful that she'd done something so simple as make me a tea or even got dressed. I wrap my hands around the warm mug as I listen to Mum's footsteps retreat down the hallway.

My phone buzzes. I've forgotten what an incoming message sounds like, so for a second I think a fly has got trapped and is banging against the window. It's Tomi.

> Are you OK? I assumed you were sick but then Amber said you're at your mum's . . . ?

HE'S CONTACTING ME VOLUNTARILY. He's noticed my whereabouts! Maybe I haven't totally screwed up this friendship. Without hesitation, I tap out a reply:

> Thank you for checking. I'm OK. I just needed a break from the city. X

But then I delete it. Have I learnt nothing? If I'd just been up front with Tomi in the first place, instead of hoarding all my problems away like some sort of secretive shame squirrel, maybe none of this would have happened. Instead, I write:

> Thank you for checking. Not really. Will and I had a fight and I didn't want to be at home. There's too much to explain over text so I'll tell you everything when I'm back? X

He replies instantly.

> I'm sorry Holly. Yes please. Here if you need anything. Look after yourself X

A KISS. HE DOESN'T HATE ME.

I finally resolve to tell Tomi everything and *actually* follow through with it this time. It's funny that a month ago I was desperate to not talk about what was going on and now I'm yearning to share it. My heart tugs thinking about Liam. He's *so* great to talk to.

Should I be only thinking about Will right now? I sigh. What's the use of thinking 'should' all the time? All my life, I've thought about what I *should* do. I should look after my mother. I should stay insane hours at work to make sure other people's shit is done. I should do everything that Will wants to make him happy.

The fact is that I *am* thinking about Liam. And for once, I'm not going to make myself feel bad about it. I'm going to do exactly what Fliss told me to do in the first instance. I'm going to think about what I actually want.

Firstly, what I want is for Amber not to detonate and for the showcase to go as smoothly as possible, so I stop staring out the window at the chickens roaming the yard and focus on my emails. Secondly, what I want is for my designs to be as good as they possibly can. Usually when someone is fully credited with an item in a trade showcase, and if that item is ordered by enough stores, they start to be invited to share more ideas and I *have* to be ready.

I get out my folder and sift through Will's comments that he left scribbled on my sketches. My insides melt slightly thinking of him writing them for me, casting his eyes over my work to help make it shine, gripping the pen in his large hand, furrowing his brow in concentration. I love – or I loved

– watching Will poring over designs; mine or his. But then, he's supposed to be my boyfriend. Not my work colleague. A shared interest in designing isn't enough to carry a relationship.

But his comments are spot on, as usual, and I add the finishing touches to everything. Then I turn my thoughts to something much more complicated. My love life.

It's 7 p.m. and I have aaaall evening. The chickens are clucking. The trees are swaying. The house is still. My wild Friday night will consist of Mum making macaroni cheese and us making small talk for half an hour across the dinner table, but apart from that I'm going to sit and Work. This. Out.

I stare into space for a few minutes before pulling out a pen and paper. I write 'Will' and 'Liam' as if just writing their names out will strike me with some sort of divine intervention. It doesn't.

That scene where Ross makes a pro/con list between Rachel and Julie springs to mind. What happens in that episode? He adds 'she's not Rachel' to Julie's con column. Well, it's not like I have any better ideas.

WILL

PROS	CONS
Shared interests (both designers)	Pretentious
Shared history (so much history!)	*Too* much history? Are we stuck?
Makes delicious food	Always dictates restaurant choices

Assertive in his opinions	Defensive about his opinions
Takes care of me	Talks over me
Decisive	Doesn't listen

LIAM

PROS	CONS
Unpretentious	Poor dress sense
FUN	Bad tattoos
Perceptive about people	There's nowhere to hide
Talks about feelings	Not tons in common
Kind	Not as smart as Will (or . . . different smart?!)

I gaze at the page, waiting for my 'she's not Rachel' moment to hit me, but it doesn't come. My head doesn't feel much clearer. My mind drifts to Fliss. She'd definitely make fun of my list. And I know she'd tell me this is not really about choosing between Will and Liam.

If only this were as simple as a choice between two people. Since going out with Liam and noticing how deficient areas of my relationship with Will are by contrast, it's becoming obvious to me that I've never worked out what it is that I actually need from somebody. How am I supposed to know who's right for me if I don't know that?

I move towards my huge collection of magazines, which I started spending my pocket money on when I was nine or ten. I remember discovering a whole new vibrant world in these pages, based around pure joy, indulgence and celebration

296

of identity, and feeling that I so badly wanted to live in it. I remember starting to pay attention to what I was wearing and expressing myself in every little detail, every item, every shade. I think back to Liam asking me why I like fashion, and how I couldn't answer. Since being back, I'm piecing together why it was so appealing to me. I spent so much time thinking about Mum, there wasn't much room for fun or thinking about myself. I wasn't brought up to be great with words, but clothes can say whatever you want to say without using any. It suddenly seems so obvious.

And it makes sense that I've spent my entire adult life caring for Will. Thinking about what he wants. Bending over backwards to make him happy.

'Holly,' Mum calls from downstairs. 'Are you ready for dinner?'

I crumple the list up and throw it in the bin, before heading downstairs.

As I suspected, Mum has served up classic macaroni cheese. She's wrapped in a big cardigan, sitting with two plates set out at the dark wooden dining table.

I can't help but think about her here, the rest of the year, all alone. There's barely anything on the walls, no trinkets, no rugs. There's a school picture of me on my first day on the old-fashioned cabinet, but that's about it.

'How's your work going, dear?' she asks as we start eating.

'OK,' I say. 'Busy. We had a few disasters. A shipment of fabric ended up in the wrong place and we lost some models but we found them wandering around Bond Street.'

'Oh, gosh.' She chuckles.

'How was your day?' I return.

'Oh, you know,' Mum says. But I don't. Not really.

'How are you, Mum?' I ask. I put dramatic emphasis on the word 'are'.

'Oh, you know,' she repeats. She doesn't ask me how I am.

Normally I'd carry on eating. Maybe chat to her about *Coronation Street*. But do I have to wait for her to ask how I am if I want to tell her? Do I always have to be led by everybody else?

I decide to volunteer it. My heart starts thundering in my chest. 'I've not been doing so great, Mum,' I admit. 'I'm feeling pretty lost.'

Mum fixes her gaze on her food. Her fork scrapes against her plate as she pushes pasta around. She looks cornered. Painful seconds pass as I wait for her response.

'You'll work it out, dear,' she says brightly.

End of discussion. It's frighteningly like trying to talk to Will; he dismisses my feelings in exactly the same way and I've never joined those dots before.

I'm not sure what else I was expecting, after all these years. She's not suddenly going to start behaving like we're twelve-year-old girls at a slumber party.

I don't blame my mother. She's not a bad person, she's just coping as best she knows how and, despite the distance between us, I love her so, so much. She'd never label it as such – she'd never have the self-awareness or the understanding and if she did, she'd never want to admit it or seek professional help – but I'm beginning to understand that she was suffering with mental health problems for most of my childhood, and that she found a way to muddle through by shutting off. It's sad, but she doesn't know any other way. It's her method of surviving.

I came home hoping for some sort of comfort and connection. In this moment I'm struck with clarity about what I might never get from her, but what I could get from somebody else.

We carry on eating. When we're finished, Mum starts clearing the plates away and invites me to watch some new Agatha Christie adaptation with her. We sit on the sofa together and it's not exactly what I wanted, but it's nice. Eventually I head upstairs.

I lie back on my bed, cuddling my bear. I might not have worked out *everything* that I want from a partner, but I know that I can't carry on feeling unheard, unseen, like I'm some sort of overly sentimental wreck who has too many feelings that I need to play down. I don't want to always come second to someone else's needs and putting them before mine; I want to be equals. My feelings are not strange, or a burden, or something to hide – they matter and I need somebody who's going to acknowledge them.

CHAPTER TWENTY-EIGHT:
DON'T READ THEIR MESSAGES

FLISS

For maybe the first time in my adult life, I'm looking forward to hanging out with my parents. I am slightly exhausted from another week of Rowan's fast-paced lifestyle – he wanted to go axe-throwing on a Monday?! – but it's been so much fun, and I've been looking forward to bringing him out with Mum and Dad. Ash is still on my mind a lot – the other day someone flicked on Classic FM in the office and I had to get up and switch it to Magic – but that's probably normal. You don't just stop thinking about someone after that many years.

'Urgh, they're here,' Henry groans as he watches their car pulling up outside the window.

'You didn't have to come,' I say, pulling on my chunky black boots. 'Although, I'm glad you did.'

'It's fine, I owe you,' Henry concedes.

I asked Henry to come because I want him to get to know

Rowan again and understand the choices I'm making. I know that he'll see that this is the right path for me if he spends a bit more time around us.

After Mum and Dad have parked their car, Henry and I get the tube with them into Central – Mum doesn't like navigating the underground without a guide as she says it makes 'her brain feel like soup' – and make our way to the restaurant. Mum's wearing a bright lime-green trouser suit and her chatter is loud and high-pitched; it's like walking a giant Monsoon parakeet. But it's so nice that she's actually excited about seeing the person that I'm with.

Sort of with, anyway. From Mum's perspective we're together so that's kind of all that counts for this evening. Again, the irony is not lost on me that she's happier about my indefinable relationship with a chronic loner, because he's loaded and went to Harvard, than she was about my committed relationship with Ash just because we were open, but I'm just happy that she's happy for once.

She's talking about the lost art of pen pals.

'Did *you* ever have a pen pal, Henry, I can't remember?'

'No.' Henry pushes open the door to the curry place.

'It's just such a shame. They should really reinstate it. It helps children to see a completely different perspective. And helps them practise their reading and writing, too, of course.'

We hang our coats on the pegs by the door and the waiter shows us to our table. Mum's still talking as we sit down.

'Everything is about instant gratification these days, so I suppose that's why it's fallen out of fashion with the schools. But you can't beat the excitement of a real-life letter coming in the post . . . Oh, the anticipation of waiting for our letters to arrive! I used to write to mine once a week. Josephine, her name was.'

'That's lovely.' Henry passes out the menus. 'Are you still in touch?'

'God, no – dreadful girl.'

As Mum peruses the menu Henry and I glance at each other and try not to laugh.

'So when's this Rowan getting here?' Dad asks. He's obviously hungry.

'He should be here now.' I look at the time on my phone and text him.

Hey, you nearly here?

Yeah sorry just got caught up. On my way

By 'caught up' do you mean finishing the tea towel?

You got me. I'm so close Fliss! I couldn't leave the sheep without an eye!

He is annoying and charming in equal measure.

'He'll be here soon,' I add.

We order some papadums as we wait. I can sense Dad getting increasingly irritable so after ten minutes I text Rowan asking him what he wants and we order. He arrives seconds later.

Mum and Dad stand as he approaches our table. When he reaches us he bends down to kiss my cheek and whispers, 'You look hot,' in my ear.

'Rowan!' Mum pulls him into a close, heartfelt hug as though she's greeting a long-lost relative. 'It's been too long!'

After Mum's done squeezing him, Dad shakes his hand and slaps him on the back. Henry nods and says, 'All right.'

'Yeah, hi, it's been ages,' Rowan returns. 'Good to see you. Sorry I'm a bit late.'

'Oh, please, you're a busy man!' Mum says as we all sit down.

I can't help but think – with a protective stab – that Ash wouldn't have had such a warm reception if he was fifteen minutes late. Then I banish Ash from my mind.

'So, Rowan, how are you liking London?' Mum quizzes, settling back into her seat. 'Are you missing New York?'

'Oh no. Incredibly similar pigeon population density, so I find myself right at home.'

Mum hoots like this is the funniest thing anyone has ever said.

'And now tell us more about what you were doing over there?'

'I was brand director at a marketing agency.'

'And what does that mean, exactly?' Dad's finished all the papadums and his eyes glance over to the kitchen.

'So I was managing marketing campaigns across print, broadcast and online platforms to help build the credibility of brands.'

'Oh, well! That sounds interesting,' Mum coos.

'Not really.' Rowan laughs. 'But it was sociable. And varied because we were working with so many different companies. And I got to travel.'

'How impressive. Do all your other Harvard friends have such prominent careers?'

'Please, Mum, let's not make his ego any bigger than it already is,' I interject. I don't want to give Rowan an excuse to start talking about his GPA, or how many student organisations he ran, or how he was the first Black student at his fancy high school to win the coveted Languages Prize. All incredible achievements, but I have heard about them at least fifty million times.

'And do you think you'll go back into marketing?' Mum continues.

'Mum.' Henry rolls his eyes. 'I'm sure Rowan didn't expect to turn up to a job interview.'

Henry's on the receiving end of one of Mum's glares when the food arrives. Despite Henry's comment, Mum and Dad keep grilling Rowan.

'So, Rowan.' Mum cuts a small piece of chicken into four smaller pieces. 'Do you think you'll stay in the UK?'

'As long as they'll have me.'

This does not satisfy Mum. She keeps dissecting Rowan like the chicken.

'But how long would you like to stay? You know, visas permitting?'

Henry groans.

'Rowan, why don't we get this out of the way now and we'll all have a much more pleasant evening.' He counts on his fingers. 'Are you thinking about settling here? Do you want to get married? Are you interested in children and if so, how many?'

I stifle a laugh. Mum goes bright red. 'Henry, what's got into you? Don't be so intrusive.'

Rowan smiles. 'Honestly, it's fine, Mrs Henderson. I could

see myself living here if I found the right job. Marriage and kids one day, sure.'

Mum smirks and smugly pops a tiny piece of chicken in her mouth. I can't deny that I'm pleased that *they're* pleased – for once – and thankfully Rowan doesn't seem to have melted into a pool of mortification on the spot. But marriage and kids . . . please. I know for a fact Rowan doesn't want those things. He's good with parents and he's just saying it to sate them. I can't help but think how ironic it is that Ash *actually* wanted those things with me but that was meaningless to them.

'Great, shall we talk about something else? Mum and Dad, how was the pottery class?'

Dad grunts. Mum's perpetually dragging Dad to some sort of class that he doesn't want to attend. The man just wants to eat and watch snooker. But for some reason she won't just go by herself; she has to have Dad there. It used to drive me up the wall as a teenager. I think it's one of the reasons I'm so insistent about doing things by myself.

'Well, the other day I attempted to make a pot in the shape of a cherry, but I confess it came out more like a bottom.'

'We should have booked you into erottery.' Dad guffaws.

'Cheeky.' Mum flips a serviette at him.

Henry looks like he's about to die. 'Rightiho then. And Fliss – how's your Japanese going?' He turns to me.

'Oh, er, fine,' I answer quickly. Truthfully, I haven't been able to look at it since the break-up.

We make it through the rest of the meal with a mercifully low level of awkwardness. My parents ask gleefully about plans for our trip – again, I can't help but think if

I'd planned it with Ash, they'd deem it 'irresponsible' – and Rowan is natural and charismatic and my parents obviously adore him. Ash was just as easy to love, if they'd given him a chance. Not that it matters now. Everything's working out as it should be.

At the end of the night, Henry offers to guide Mum and Dad back to ours so they can pick up their car and drive home and I can go back to Rowan's. On the way to the station Rowan walks ahead with our parents and I grab Henry's arm to slow him down, so that we're a few paces behind. I know Henry had some reservations and I'm desperate for his validation.

'Well?' I prod. 'What do you think?'

Henry does his I'm-being-kind-and-patient face. The one that he gives Sam when he won't stop chewing on shoes. 'Yeah. He's a charming guy.'

I elbow Henry. 'I know when you're being diplomatic.'

Henry sighs. 'Fine. Yeah, he's agreeable. He knows all the right things to say. He came, he held up well under fire, so points for that. But . . . I don't know. I just . . . What are you actually doing with this man, Fliss? Beyond going on an extended holiday? I mean . . . are you together now, or what?'

'Not exactly,' I hedge. 'We're . . .' I fumble around for the right words. 'We belong together in not being together, if that makes sense.'

Henry shakes his head. 'No? Sorry.'

'Neither of us can be in a relationship. We're the same.'

Henry snorts. 'You're *not* the same. Fliss, this guy can't sit still for more than an hour. I'm not surprised he can't make a commitment to somebody. That's not you.'

I knew Henry wasn't Rowan's biggest fan, but I didn't realise he was this unenthused. 'OK, I get it, you loved Ash and you don't like Rowan. Forget what works for me.'

'Oh, please, I like Rowan fine. He's fine. This isn't about *me* not liking Rowan and loving Ash. *You* love Ash.'

Argh, I was an idiot to think I could make Henry understand. He's always been stubborn and impossible to argue with.

'Yes, I love Ash. But I can't love him in the way the world wants me to love him.'

'I just . . . You never cared what the world thought before.'

'I didn't when it was me and Ash against the world. Now it's just . . . me.'

I sound so pathetic when I say this and Henry looks so full of pity that for a moment I think I've got through to him.

'I get it, but I still don't think boarding some sort of eternal party boat with Rowan is the answer. What do you want me to say, Fliss?' he goes on. 'That I agree with the decisions you're making, when I don't?'

'I want you to understand. But you don't, so fine.'

'You asked!' Henry gestures in frustration and I run to catch up with Mum, Dad and Rowan.

The rest of the walk is childishly tense. Every time Henry and I draw level I take a few extra steps to move away from him. Still, Mum is still so ecstatic that she appears not to notice and Dad and Rowan are distracted by their conversation about different kinds of beehives.

We say goodbye to my family at the station – I avoid eye contact with Henry – and Rowan and I get an Uber to his flat. When we get back I'm quiet and go straight to bed.

Thankfully, Rowan's too engrossed in finally finishing the tea towel to notice.

The next morning, I'm sitting at the island in Rowan's kitchen, sipping coffee and waiting for him to get dressed. As I'm playing with my phone, I notice Rowan's phone light up on the counter.

I've never *once* looked through someone's phone. I've never felt particularly paranoid. I suppose to be paranoid, I'd have to care that they might be sleeping with other people, which never bothered me. Apart from James back in the day, I've always assumed anyone I was seeing *was* probably sleeping with other people and so was I. And when Ash and I were open, I was never tempted to look through his messages. Yes, I knew he was seeing other people, but we'd established ground rules and we trusted each other. Did I want to actually *see* it? No. What would be the point? Whatever kind of relationship you're in, going through someone's phone – unless you have valid suspicions of a betrayal of trust that you need to prove, which is different – seems like crossing a boundary but also a bizarre form of self-torture.

So I am not looking at Rowan's phone on purpose but, given that it happens to be right in front of me, I can't help but notice the message that flashes up is from a girl called Ella.

What are you up to this week? I love you x

I sit back and stare at the message for a couple of seconds as I try to make sense of it. Rowan has never mentioned anyone called Ella to me.

I've never been a jealous person. I've always firmly believed people's feelings about someone else don't impact how they feel about me. So what I feel looking at this message is not jealousy, especially as we aren't even together. I think it's more like humiliation. Because whatever we are to one another, I thought we were straight with each other, and whoever Ella is, he's obviously not been honest with me . . . And *that* I can't stand.

Rowan walks into the kitchen.

'Rowan, who's Ella?'

He stumbles back in mock-shock, hands in front of his chest as if I've shot him. 'Woah! Where did that come from?'

I point at his phone. He moves forward and puts it in his pocket. 'Have you been going through my messages?'

I roll my eyes. 'Please. It was right in front of me.'

'She's a friend from New York.' Rowan shrugs me off. He obviously hasn't glanced at the message she sent.

'Oh, a friend?' I do quotation marks with my fingers.

'What's with the interrogation, Fliss? What happened to you? Are you one of *those* women now?' His voice takes on a defensive quality.

Wow. He'll have to try harder than that to turn this around on me. 'Oh, spare me the *all-women-are-crazy* act. I'm not interrogating you, Rowan, I'm asking a reasonable question.'

Rowan gets his phone out and looks down at the message. Panic briefly flashes in his eyes, seeing what I saw. He knows he's trapped. What 'friend' writes that kind of message? I can see the cogs turning as he recalibrates his story, working out what to tell me.

'She's my ex-girlfriend,' he admits. 'We broke up just before I left New York.'

So she was a 'friend', now she's an 'ex'. Something is not adding up here. But at least I'm starting to fill in the picture of his sudden departure from the States. 'Is that why you left?' I ask.

'I told you why I left.' He shrugs.

A change of scene. Vague enough to not be a lie. And *because we hadn't seen each other in ages*. Obviously he left out the bit about wanting to escape his ex. Or not-quite-ex, judging by the way she's talking to him.

'She doesn't sound like an ex, Rowan. That's not how I speak to my exes.'

'We're on a break,' Rowan says.

'Does she know that?' I ask. 'Because your story keeps changing.'

I can tell from the look on Rowan's face that she doesn't. At worst there's a woman out there, somewhere, who thinks she's in a committed, exclusive relationship with Rowan while he's been here, doing whatever he's been doing with me. At best, there's a woman who's unsure of where she stands.

'It's complicated,' he says.

'How?' I ask.

'She wants to move in together and I don't.'

The puzzle pieces start fitting together. This must be the first time Rowan's ever been so involved with anybody. I've never heard of him getting so far with anyone as to be saying 'I love you' or even describing them as a girlfriend before. He obviously panicked and instead of either moving in with her or calling time on the relationship properly, he fled the country. To hide with me . . . The exact opposite of everything he's running from.

I would feel used. Except I've been using him in the same way.

'Do you love her?' I ask.

He doesn't say anything but I can see in his face that he does. In that moment he looks like a child.

Any excitement I was feeling about our plan to cross Europe together deflates like a sad little balloon. We're not carefree, globe-trotting adventurers, too liberated to be tethered by the anchor of loving relationships. Rowan is just a coward running away from the person who cares about him and I'm just a sad girl coming out of a break-up and avoiding having to feel it.

Ugh. Henry was right. How is Henry always right?

'Do you think dodging her and cheating on her is the right way to go, here?' I suggest.

'Oh, are you really one to talk about cheating, Fliss?' Rowan gestures emphatically towards me. 'When have you ever stayed faithful to anyone?!'

What the hell? Is that really how he sees me? As a cheater?

I am *not* a cheater. Cheating is a breach of trust, and successful open relationships rely on trust more than anything else. I was more unfaithful to Ash when we were in an exclusive relationship and I was being technically 'faithful' than I ever was when we were open.

'Being in an open relationship and being a cheater are *not* the same thing.'

'Potato, potahto.' Rowan waves a hand dismissively.

I'm utterly baffled. I can't believe he's acting like I'd understand his logic. I've never been so insulted. But on some level, he must know that's not true, otherwise why wouldn't he have told me about Ella? We're usually straight with each other. He just didn't want his actions to be called into question. And now they have, he's lashing out and being defensive, and it's infuriating.

'Come on, Fliss.' The tone of Rowan's voice softens. He sits down next to me at the kitchen counter. 'You and I both know we're the same. Let's just forget about this and have fun. What do you want to do today? I found this immersive experience where you can pretend to be in a zombie apocalypse. Apparently you can tick a box if you want them to actually bite you.'

Part of me would love to just forget about this and keep burying myself in the sand and having fun. But another part of me knows I've outgrown this. I think of Henry saying *you're not the same* and I know he's right. This conversation has exposed the monumental distance that's widened between us over the years without me noticing. I have developed and changed, and Rowan hasn't. Just because I don't want monogamy, it doesn't mean I never want to get close to anyone or have meaningful, respectful relationships.

'Not tonight, Rowan,' I say. 'Maybe we can get bitten by zombies another time.'

CHAPTER TWENTY-NINE:
DON'T BRING TWO DATES TO THE SAME EVENT

HOLLY

By the time I leave Mum's the following week, I feel a little more clear-headed than I did when I arrived, and comforted in that childlike way that you can only feel after spending a week at your parents' house, even if you don't have the easiest relationship.

When I return to the office, it's bustling with showcase prep and buzzing with energy. Amber looks like she's been electrocuted.

'Holly.' She does what can only be described as a lunge towards me. 'There you are.' She grips my forearm like a vice. 'I need you to . . .'

And she starts reeling off a million things that aren't my job that need to be done today. Usually I would be listening intently, making a mental list and worrying I might miss something, but today her words fly straight over my head.

When she gets to the end of the list I realise I've missed half of it.

'Could you send me all that via email?' I ask. I didn't think before I said it – it just came out – and it takes us both by surprise. I've never asked anything of Amber before.

Amber stands up straight, her mouth hanging open in disbelief.

'It's just easier to work from a list than try to hold everything in my head as soon as I walk in the door,' I add quickly. 'And um, while we're on the subject, in the future, please can you give me proper deadlines? It's hard to plan out my time efficiently when things keep dropping on me at the last minute.' I don't intend this to sound rude, I'm just trying to explain my point of view, but Amber lets go of my arm like I've stung her.

'I don't know what's got into you recently, Holly,' she says, and starts walking off muttering to herself. 'As if I don't have enough to do . . .'

But, incredibly, half an hour later there is an actual *list* that Amber has written out, in my inbox. I still have to do all her shit, so it's a small win but a significant one. The world feels just a little bit more conquerable. Maybe in future she'll give me advance warning like I asked. Or maybe – do I dare to dream – stop getting me to do absolutely everything for her.

'What did you do to Amber?' Tomi appears behind my desk. 'She's livid. I heard her slagging you off to Claire.'

She must be fuming if she's seeking solace from Claire.

'I asked her to put everything she wanted me to do this morning in one email,' I reply.

'Outrageous!' Tomi booms.

We both burst out laughing. This tiny glimpse of normality makes me feel just how much I've been missing him.

'You were right. I have been doing everything for her,' I say. 'I'm kind of only just realising that it's unreasonable and that, horror of horrors, I can actually push back.'

'Are you feeling all right? Have you been taken over by an alien imposter?' Tomi takes a step back.

I shrug. 'Honestly, I don't know. I have SO much to tell you.'

Before I can think too much, I start dragging him to the third floor. There's a toilet just off the hallway that hardly anyone uses.

'Holly? Where are we going?' Tomi asks as he follows behind me.

Once we're inside I lock the door.

'Scandalous. They're going to think we're doing something untoward in here.' Tomi looks around.

'That would be a great rumour for me,' I say. 'But I'd massively bring down your average.' Tomi has historically had relationships with *very* sexy people. Isabella looked like Penelope Cruz. And then there was the man in the Burberry ad who looked like Tom Hardy. Oh and the *actual* fireman who didn't look like any celebrities but was so fit that one time when he saved a woman from a burning building she tried to go back in just so he'd pick her up again. (Tomi might have exaggerated that story over time, but he was very fit.)

Tomi smirks at the compliment. 'Nah, you'd drag it up.' He sits down on the closed loo seat. 'So, this is unlike you. Don't you have a billion things to do for Amber before the big show?'

I *do* have a billion things to do, but for once I don't care. I've done everything *I* have to do, officially. Now I'm literally just doing things that are supposed to be Amber's responsibility. What would she do if I wasn't here? She'd have to do them herself. I know she's exhibiting one of my designs and actually crediting me, and for that I am still grateful and *wildly* excited, but I've probably repaid her for that a million times over by now in blood and sweat.

'What is it, Holly?' Tomi goes on. We've had such carefree interactions about my sassing Amber I almost could have fooled myself we were back to normal. But the look he gives me when he asks me that question tells me there's still a lot of fixing to do.

I take a deep breath and start from the beginning. With me believing Will was going to propose, right up to Liam walking into the restaurant we were in. Saying each bit of the story out loud is nearly as mortifying as actually living it all. At least Tomi is a satisfying person to tell stories to. He always gasps and says 'no?!' and 'what!!!' at exactly the right moments.

When I'm done, he sits back and shakes his head over and over. 'Holly.' He begins to massage his temples. 'That's *wild*.'

I lean my head back against the door. I'm sitting on the floor by this point.

'You are such a dark horse,' he jokes.

I laugh. 'Hardly,' I say. 'I was just . . . embarrassed.'

Tomi leans towards me and rests his head in his hands. 'Why?!' he asks. 'Remember when I sang "Wuthering Heights" at karaoke night because I was convinced I could hit all the high notes? *That* was embarrassing.'

I laugh. I'm not sure why I was so reluctant to tell Tomi, now that I have. Deep down I think I knew he wouldn't judge me; I was judging myself. Really, I think I just didn't want him to point out how unhealthy the whole setup was. 'Honestly, I was hoping it would just be some stupid thing that Will would come to his senses about and then we would never mention again. To anyone.'

Tomi nods. 'I can see that. Well.' He shrugs. 'It sounds like he has come to his senses now?'

'Yeah,' I agree weakly. 'Yeah, he has.'

He has, but I can't muster the same enthusiasm for that as I would have done earlier this year.

'I'm really sorry, Tomi,' I apologise. 'For not telling you about any of it, but mostly for being a shit friend. I'm so sorry I missed your birthday. I put it in the wrong date but if I'd not been so wrapped up in this, it never would have happened. I've been completely self-absorbed for the past couple of months.'

Tomi sighs. 'Holly, it's OK. I knew there was something wrong. You don't have a great poker face. And look, you do a lot for other people, including me. Everyone's entitled to be self-absorbed and fuck up now and again.'

I'm so incredibly relieved to have my best friend back. I launch myself at him and we hug for about thirty seconds, before Tomi says, 'Holly, this is lovely and everything, but it *is* our busiest day of the year. Do you think we should, you know, do our jobs?'

I laugh. 'Yeah, I guess.'

But we keep hugging anyway.

Eventually, we let ourselves out of the toilet. Why do all

the most intense conversations always happen in toilets? I think of Fliss and hope that she's OK.

Downstairs it's a flurry of last-minute organising and putting out fires, but eventually, later that afternoon we're in a taxi to the site. Now that everything's taken care of and the day has finally arrived, my heart is pounding at the thought of something I designed actually being on display.

Half an hour later, we arrive at the hall where the trade show is being held. Brands from all over the world are already bustling to set up their stalls and the atmosphere is electric. At least, it is to me, because for the first time I'm a real part of it. Everyone who loves fashion and understands what I do every day is in this room, looking to be inspired. It's easy to forget that I love what I do, when I'm at my desk sorting out shipping invoices, but every so often – at moments like this – I'm reminded that I'm exactly where I want to be.

We get to our booth and unpack the clothes. Looking at the autumn collection together, it looks exactly as we'd wanted it to. Our brand is not quirky and outrageous; it's more classic and sophisticated, but fresh. That's always why I liked it. It's beautiful, but down to earth. I take extra loving care hanging up my item, which fits in perfectly but also – I like to think – stands out. It's a burnt-orange cord workwear dress. A large, buttoned pocket is stitched on the right side and more buttons decorate the collar and sleeves. It's hard to see your own work clearly, but I think I did a good job.

Once everything is set up, I stand back. *We made it*, I think. *There's nothing else to do now but enjoy it*.

Except my heart is beating a million times a minute. The buyers from some of the biggest stores up and down the country are going to be let in soon. What if everyone hates what I created? What if every other item in the collection gets a bunch of orders and mine gets a big ol' zero? What if I ruin the whole showcase for everyone by dragging down our average orders? I remind myself to breathe and that the design wouldn't have been approved if everyone hated it.

The buyers are let in. There's no going back. Tomi squeezes my hand.

'Holly, your dress looks phenomenal!' he whispers. 'You're going to smash it!'

'Am I?'

'Be confident!'

'I'm not confident.'

'Well . . . fake it 'til you make it.'

'Isn't that how you end up like Elizabeth Holmes?'

After Tomi heads back to the menswear stand, I allow myself a moment to put anxiety and stress to one side and feel proud of myself, even if my outfit ends up bombing. Whatever is going on in my life, my work is the one place where – when I'm not running around after Amber – I can feel good about myself and everything else is irrelevant. And I've come so far. When I was a teenager spending all my money on magazines, I could only dream that I'd one day work in this industry. Even when I started this job four years ago, seeing my own designs – in a category that wasn't jersey – felt like it would never happen. The fact that it *is* happening is surreal.

I try to distract myself by wandering around looking at other brands' booths, but it's hard to focus when I'm holding my breath wondering how my design's going down. I circle back around our booth a million times, low-key peering over buyers' shoulders as they scribble notes. Hopefully they're not writing 'the ugliest dress in the entire room'.

After about an hour – although it feels like five because I'm so tense – Tomi finds me and starts jumping up and down. 'Holly!!' He grabs my hands.

'What?!' I wonder if something exciting has happened over on the menswear booth.

'Priya just heard some early numbers from Lara Pearse.' So it's about womenswear. I want to vomit I'm so nervous. It must be good news, though, if Tomi's happy? 'Your dress is the second most popular on the stall so far today.'

Oh my God. I did it. I designed a thing and people didn't hate it and I can stop worrying and feel pleased with myself. Maybe everything's not going to be terrible. Maybe I'm actually good at this.

The rest of the show is an adrenaline blur. *Second most popular today.* When we get into our taxis for the after-party, which is being held in a separate venue, I'm momentarily sad that no one will be coming to celebrate with me – no Will, no Liam, no Fliss – but I know that's for the best right now. Given everything that's going on, I wouldn't be able to focus on my work. And I have Tomi.

The party is in a private room in a big, beautiful museum with fancy artwork and lofty ceilings. When we arrive, snacks and drinks are already floating around on circulating trays. I immediately grab a glass of champagne. I see Lara Pearse – head of womenswear – and Janine Bello – the MD of the entire company – standing chatting, and I down a big gulp.

And then, as I'm scanning the room, I see an unexpected familiar face.

What is Will doing here?!

For a moment, my heart soars. *He came. He came after all. He does care about me.* But then it drops. There's so much going on between us right now and I just want to be in the moment and feel proud of myself. I don't have the capacity for this.

He sees me and waves, and starts making his way over to me through the crowd. How did he get in? He must still be on the guest list from when I originally put him on there.

'Holly, I thought I just saw *Will*?' Tomi appears by my shoulder. 'I thought he was in Devon?'

I don't have time to answer him before Will reaches us. 'Holly.' There's that short, authoritative greeting that used to make my knees feel like they were liquefying. 'Tomi.'

'Hi, Will,' Tomi says in a falsely bright voice. I say nothing.

There's an awkward silence. 'OK then.' Tomi claps his hands. He mumbles something about 'seeing to the photographers' before sloping off to a corner to stare at us.

'What are you doing here?' I ask.

'To support you, obviously.' Defensiveness creeps into Will's voice. 'I wanted to see you in action. I *was* invited?'

Yes, he was invited. But he said he had a friend's stag do. Plus he pulled a disappearing act over a week ago and we haven't spoken since. Films always present people turning up out of the blue, after a big argument, like it's some passionate, romantic act. But actually I just feel blindsided and overwhelmed. Will's presence right now doesn't feel romantic, it feels selfish; like he has no regard for giving me more things to worry about.

And then, I can hardly believe my eyes, but I see Liam

talking to the woman at the entrance. I do a comic double-take.

ARE YOU KIDDING ME?!

Is the universe not finished having a laugh at my expense?

I can feel my blood pressure rising. The familiar pressure in my chest starts building, like a very heavy man is sitting on my shoulders, and I know I am inches away from a panic attack. What is he doing here?! I know I said I'd put him on the guest list, but again, we have not spoken in over a week. I'd entirely written him off as a no-show.

What is happening?

The woman he's talking to is searching the list for his name. I pray for some clerical error that he's not on there, but she finds it and crosses it out with her pen. I try not to look in Liam's direction. I desperately don't want him to see that I've seen him, or for Will to see him. Hopefully he'll notice that Will is here with me and go home. *I haven't seen him. I haven't seen him.*

Unfortunately, Will must notice me looking like I'm about to puke because he turns around and looks behind him. I see the glowering look of recognition cross his face as he catches sight of Liam.

'*Oh.* Now I see why you don't want me here,' he says scathingly. 'You double booked.'

'I did not *double book*,' I protest. 'I—'

'Save it, Holly. It doesn't matter.' Will is watching Liam. Liam has just thanked the woman at the door and scanned the room. His eyes meet mine, and then Will's.

Oh, this is not good. This is really not good.

Liam walks up to us. The twenty seconds it takes him to

cross the room are the longest of my life. For a millisecond, I think how nice it is that he's come. Unlike Will, who I sense is here to make a point, I know that Liam will have turned up genuinely in the spirit of supporting me. I think how reassuring his presence would be, if Will wasn't also here.

'I didn't think you'd be here,' he says to Will when he reaches us. 'I'm not trying to cause trouble. I just wanted to be here for Holly on her big night.'

'You didn't think I'd be here?' Will coughs. 'I'm her boy-friend.'

I'm about to point out he, in fact, *wasn't* planning to attend. Otherwise I never would have invited Liam. At this moment I happen to glance over at Tomi, who is still watching us. He mouths *OH MY GOD* at me and points at Liam, mouthing, *IS THAT LIAM?*

He's quite distracting.

'Look, I'll go.' I snap back to the moment. Liam puts his hands in his pockets. He's made an effort because he's at a fashion event, bless him, and his jacket almost goes with his shirt. He looks at me and, with a flutter in my stomach, I remember how kind his eyes are. 'Congratulations, Holly.'

Thank God. He's going. But just when I think everything's about to be OK, he puts his hand on my shoulder. Will, who has had his arms crossed high up on his chest up until this point, lunges forward and punches him in the face.

CHAPTER THIRTY:
MAKE YOUR OWN DECISIONS

FLISS

It's Friday morning and I'm sitting in the kitchen twiddling my thumbs. I can't concentrate on work because my brain's too busy attempting to process everything that's happened over the past month. I'm disorientated and unanchored and haunting the house like some sort of joy-sucking spectre. When I walked into the living room earlier I swear Jenny shivered.

I thought I knew myself so well. And I was so *smug* about it. It's always been important to me that, despite how my life might look to other people on paper, I always knew myself and what I wanted and how I wanted to live. No fear stopping me from taking chances or letting comfortable habits trick me into believing they're the same as happiness and no meaning-less societal norms dictating how my life looks. I knew *me*. I knew what was important to *me*. And I would go after it.

Somehow that's all become muddled. I don't know what I want anymore.

I find myself desperately wishing I could message Holly. When I snapped at her I felt like I'd been giving her so much advice and I didn't feel strong enough to give any more when I was in such a bad place of my own. And – mostly – I didn't want to hear advice on my life, because I knew she wouldn't say what I wanted to hear . . . But now I could really use it. I want to tell her everything, but she definitely won't want to hear from me after what I said. I can't exactly crawl back with my tail between my legs just because everything's gone to shit. I guess I really *did* need her to be my relationship tutor after all.

I hope she's OK.

Henry comes downstairs and starts pouring himself an orange juice.

'No Rowan today?' he asks carefully.

I know he knows there's something wrong, because I came home yesterday in a foul mood. He and Jenny were watching *Bridgerton* and I tried watching it with them for five minutes but all the longing looks and sexual frustration was too much for me. I muttered, 'Just BANG, for Christ's sake,' and stomped upstairs. Neither of them has approached me since.

'No,' I say.

There's silence as he puts bread in the toaster.

'Trouble in paradise?' he says finally. Henry could never resist the opportunity to say *I told you so* for very long.

'I'm not going away with Rowan,' I mutter.

Henry puts one hand to his heart and doubles over,

gripping the counter with his other hand. 'Oh thank the LORD,' he cries.

'All right, we get it, you're gay,' I say. 'No need to be dramatic.'

Henry smirks. 'Seriously, Fliss, you're properly done? Can I speak freely?'

'You already did,' I remark.

'That was *not* me speaking freely.' Henry leans against the counter. He's got that 'teacher' look on his face. I always thought if Henry wasn't so good at being Indistinguishable Moderately Well-Paid Business Man In Suit, he'd make an excellent teacher.

I prepare myself. 'Go on then.'

'Rowan is part of your history.' He folds his arms. 'And that's where he belongs.'

'Is that it?' I scoff. 'Your big pearl of wisdom? I sort of worked that one out for myself, thanks.'

Henry's eyes narrow comically. 'I know Mum *adores* him, but honestly, Fliss, based on what? It is hi-*larious* to me that Mum treats Rowan like he's some model man we should all aspire to be like, just because he went to Harvard and he bought her fancy dessert wine when he came to visit and he's in an impressive job. And by *impressive* I mean boring and well paid.' Henry does quotation marks with his fingers when he says the word 'impressive'. 'What do those things even mean? And yeah, so Rowan doesn't have open relationships, but he's about as loyal as Georgia Steel.'

'Who?'

'*Love Island* 2018? "Loyal, babe"?'

I shrug. Despite myself, I laugh. I can't help but also feel sad, as I listen to Henry talk, that he's partially talking about himself. Mum and Dad were always so thrilled with him because of his job – which his own sister can't even properly remember because it's so vague – and his house, and getting married at the 'right' age, and having a kid . . . Like his happiness was some sort of tick-box exercise. There's nothing wrong with that life, if it's the one someone actually wants. Up until now, I'd always thought Henry was happy with that life, too. But it's so easy to think you want things when everyone keeps telling you that you should and rewarding you when you do.

'Ash is *actually* loyal,' Henry goes on. 'Ash loves you. Ash is *good*. You've had three incredible years. You two are made for each other.'

My throat closes up. I shake my head. 'No. You're right about Rowan, but you're wrong about that. Maybe pissing about with Rowan isn't the right path for me, but neither is being with Ash.'

Beautiful, kind, funny Ash, who only ever loved me and treated me like I was the most special person in the world. He deserves to find someone who can return that.

'Argh, Fliss.' Henry pulls at his scalp, as if he is literally going to tear his hair out. 'Anyone who has seen you and Ash together knows it's something real. That doesn't come around every day.'

My eyes start to water. 'I know, but I can't give him what he deserves. Everyone else was right. I was kidding myself. You can't live the way that we were forever. Even Ash said it.' I swallow the lump in my throat and say what I know I've been fearing ever since Ash asked us to go exclusive. 'I can't give anyone real love. But I don't want to be alone either. I'm stuck, Henry.'

Henry stops pulling at his hair and fixes his gaze on me. He tilts his head to one side, like you would look at an unsuspecting snail that got crushed on the pavement. 'Fliss,' he says softly. 'Real love? What is *real love*?! Ash really messed with your head.'

I blink back my tears. 'What do you mean? Ash didn't do anything wrong.'

'No, I know,' Henry says gently. 'But you've always been so headstrong and it's sad to see you doubting everything you believe, because Ash decided an open relationship couldn't be permanent. The one person you trust most in the world suddenly undermining your entire belief system is obviously going to have an impact. It's a huge knock. It gave all those little brainworms of Mum and Dad's a chance to finally crawl their way in.' He wiggles his fingers like insects. 'I know them well. You've been resisting them for a long time. They were bound to get you at some point.'

'That's not . . .' I start.

'Banish them, Fliss!' Henry whisks his arms around like some sort of deranged witch and wiggles his fingers on my shoulders. 'Banish the brainworms!'

'What are you talking about?!' I brush his creepy fingers away.

'Relationships can look all sorts of ways. You already figured that out ages ago. If Ash doesn't want the same things as you anymore, then that's sad, but it happens. It doesn't mean there's something wrong with you. It doesn't mean that no one else will want what you want.'

I suppose he *could* be right. Ash, the only person I've ever felt truly on the same page with, suddenly started echoing my parents. I tried to give him what he wanted, blindly, and because it didn't instantly work I reverted to feeling like the only choice for me was being in a relationship where I don't feel free or being alone.

Somehow I've officially broken my own biggest rule. Don't let other people decide what you want, decide it for yourself. Holly pops into my head again and I laugh. Everything I've been supposedly coaching her on I wasn't living by. I've somehow become the world's biggest hypocrite.

Even after this freeing realisation, my exaltation doesn't last long. I don't *want* to meet someone else who wants the same things I want.

I want *Ash*.

'You don't look convinced,' Henry comments.

'No, I think you're probably right,' I say.

'Excuse me? Could you repeat that, please?' Henry puts his hand behind his ear. 'Don't think I heard you.'

'Oh, shut up. You're *always* right. I just . . . Either way, I still have to get over Ash.'

Henry frowns. 'This might sound crazy, but did you try *talking* to Ash about this?'

I think back to when he first asked me to be exclusive. The memories are all so foggy with panic that I can barely remember. 'Yes?' I reply hesitantly.

'Hmm, convincing.' Henry's getting more sarcastic by the minute. I should never have admitted he was right to his face. 'No offence, Fliss, but talking has never been one of your strong points.'

'It wasn't one of yours until you got a divorce, apparently,' I mutter.

'Marriage counselling will do that to a person.' Henry shudders. 'What was his reason for wanting this?'

I cast my mind back. 'That he wanted us to be with each other more.'

'OK, well, you can do that without being monogamous. Anything else?'

'That . . . it was just inevitable. That we couldn't go on like this.'

My insides go cold thinking about Ash telling me we couldn't go on like this forever, as if that was obvious. As if it didn't contradict everything we'd ever spoken about. As if it wouldn't throw me for a loop.

'Nothing else?' Henry prods. 'He gave you *no* other explanation?'

I shake my head.

'Well, that's a shit reason. That doesn't sound to me like a man who's really thought this through, either,' Henry concludes.

I nod. He's right. Now he's pointed it out, the reasoning *is* flimsy, and incredibly unlike Ash. Or at least, the Ash that I know. Ash is usually much better at thinking things through than that. What sort of reason is 'we can't go on like this forever', anyway? He owed me more than that. I was just too irrational to see Ash's irrationality.

Hope blooms in my chest. Perhaps there is a way we can work this out. I just need to do what I should have done right at the beginning . . . Actually talk to Ash, properly. For the first time in weeks, I start seeing light at the end of the tunnel.

'But look, Fliss, do me a favour, will you?' Henry's toast pops and he starts buttering it.

'What?'

'Just . . .' He sits down across from me at the table and starts shoving breakfast in his mouth. 'Give yourself a moment. You've been flitting around like a white-throated needletail.'

'A what?' I nick Henry's toast out of his hand.

'A very fast bird.' Henry snatches it back before I can take a bite. 'Fuck off.'

'You've been watching too many nature documentaries with Jenny,' I say.

'Just . . . slow down. I think you're so used to knowing exactly what you want that you freaked out as soon as you didn't. It's OK to not know sometimes. Just chill out. Give yourself some space. I wish someone had told me that.'

I nod. *Space*. That sounds good.

'I'll make you breakfast too if you want,' Henry offers. 'We can finish *Planet Earth*?'

I smile, suddenly wildly grateful that my idiot big brother invaded my home. 'That would be nice, thanks.'

I tell Traduire I'm sick – I don't have any looming deadlines, anyway – and spend the day under a blanket with Henry, watching TV and eating his sweets. It's like we're kids again, if you don't count the extortionate rent and failed relationships.

At about five-thirty, I go to my room for a hot-water bottle, when I see the glossy, gold invitation for Holly's work party sitting on my shelf. The embossed date reads 'Friday, 28th February'. It's tonight. I burn with curiosity to know how her trade show went; she was so nervous about it.

Before I can think too much, I jump in the shower, throw

on some lipstick and a dress and am heading out the door half an hour later.

'Where are you going?' Henry's still in the same position under the blanket. 'Movement bad.'

'I forgot I have somewhere I need to be!' I call breathlessly, heading out the door.

On the way, I pick up a bunch of flowers and a novelty card with a picture of a melon that reads 'You're one in a melon' that I think Holly will like.

When I arrive, I'm instantly reminded of Holly and her chunky, glossy magazines. The party is being held in a beautiful old building with high ceilings and marble floors. Glamorous, well-dressed people are milling around drinking champagne. I just hope I've made it in time to congratulate Holly.

And then I see her through the crowd. She's talking to two men and she looks . . . *highly* uncomfortable. At first I wonder what's going on, and then one of those men punches the other in the face.

Oh my God.

There's a collective gasp amongst the crowd. People start backing away and a circle forms around them as they begin rolling around on the floor tugging at each other. I'm guessing that's Will and Liam. Which one is which? Who am I rooting for? I can't help but think fights really don't look like they do in the movies at all. In reality they look very, very silly.

CHAPTER THIRTY-ONE:
FIGHTS JUST LOOK SILLY

HOLLY

When Will first hits Liam, there's a moment where it's like neither of them can quite believe it happened. Liam looks shellshocked, almost like he might laugh. Will looks frightened, even though he's the one who threw the punch. I can tell he's taken himself by surprise and already regrets doing it, but he's too proud to apologise immediately so he's half-heartedly posturing and standing by his lame punch, trying to look like getting in a fight is no big deal to him and something he does all the time.

I can also tell that Liam doesn't know how to react. His dignity won't let him do nothing, but equally he can't quite bring himself to respond by hitting back because he doesn't want to.

Seconds pass. There's a moment where they're both just staring at each other, frozen in fear and completely trapped by their own male egos.

Then Liam appears to decide he needs to make *some* sort

of response to this challenge. He gives Will a half-hearted shove to the shoulder.

For a moment, Will looks at the spot where Liam touched him, also deciding how to respond. He can't let this retaliation go, and gives Liam a weak shove to the shoulder in return.

It quickly devolves into a farcical cycle of lightly shoving each other's shoulders, to the point where it almost looks as if they're petting one another. By this point, people around us have started to notice the tussle. One lady's champagne gets spilt over her arm as Will's elbow bashes into her and Liam stops to apologise.

'I'm sorry, I'm so sorry,' he placates.

Will seems to take this as an affront, like he should be the one apologising to the woman. 'No, *I'm* sorry,' he declares, and lunges at Liam with fresh resolve.

They both land on the floor. There's a collective gasp and a ripple of whispers, and everyone in their immediate vicinity stands back. The whole room seems to fall silent and peer in our direction.

It becomes apparent that Will didn't have much of a plan for what he was going to do once he'd brought Liam to the floor, so he starts sort of tugging at Liam's shirt. Liam tugs back at Will's shirt and then they almost begin . . . rolling around? If it wasn't so embarrassing, it would be comical.

Then someone taps me on the shoulder. A familiar voice says, 'Can't leave you alone for a second!'

I'm so relieved to see Fliss I want to cry.

'Fliss!' I exclaim. 'HELP?'

'I think we're a bit past that now, my love,' she says,

giving me a hug, watching Will and Liam continue to grunt and wriggle.

I barely have time to be happy to see her before the security guards emerge at the doors and start making their way over.

In the movies, security guards always have to work hard to pull two men away from each other. But in reality, by the time they show up, Will and Liam are sitting opposite each other on the floor, looking bereft and confused, and seem only too glad to be forced to end their ridiculous display. Will is red-faced and wheezing. Liam is panting and adjusting his tie.

The security guards look at them on the floor, shake their heads and lead them out like naughty schoolchildren.

I can't believe those are the men I've been stressing about for weeks.

'Oh my God, Holly.' Tomi rushes over to me. 'Are you OK?' He rubs my shoulder. Fliss rubs the other.

'Holly, *what* has been going on?' Fliss asks.

I'm in too much shock to explain. I can barely process what just happened. Now it's over, I feel unspeakably angry.

'Are you all right?' Fliss squeezes my hand.

She and Tomi continue to stare at me.

'I think so,' I say finally.

'OK, well, now we've established you're OK, can I just say, that was *spectacular*. Will Smith hitting Chris Rock at the Oscars-type drama. Remember when we thought Claire spilling jam down her dress and having nothing to change into was the pinnacle of Christmas party excitement? Something *huge* is going to have to happen at our next event to top that. I mean, they were *literally* fighting over you. You're Bridget Jones. Incredible.' Tomi bows.

Despite how mortifying this is, I can't help but laugh.

'Oh my God. Did Lara see? Did *Janine* see?' I ask Tomi. Janine is our MD. She's glamorous, important and truly terrifying.

Tomi grimaces. 'Errr . . . *everyone* saw.'

'Do they know they were with me?!' I ask.

'I mean . . . they will,' Tomi says cautiously. 'They're pretty tight on the guest list.'

I shudder at the thought of having to explain my love life to our head of womenswear and our managing director. I'm so bitter. This night was supposed to be about *me*. Ostensibly they came here to support me and the evening has somehow ended up being all about them.

'Excuse me,' I say to the group. 'I'll be back in ten minutes.'

I squeeze my way past the throngs of people, all still gossiping about the 'crazy fight' – they clearly didn't have a good view – and make my way into the hallway where Will and Liam are sitting on a bench, side by side, like they're in a time out. When I approach, they both stand up.

'I need to speak with both of you,' I say. '*Separately.*'

I lead Will into the cloakroom. Not where I imagined having this conversation, standing amongst rows of coats, but nothing about our present situation is remotely close to my vision of where we'd end up.

'Will, I love you,' I say.

He looks relieved for a second. He's about to reply when I cut him off.

'But things can't go on like this. I need things to change.' My palms are sweating and I already need a drink of water. Will and I only had our first serious confrontation in the restaurant the other week and I'm still not well practised at standing up for myself. But I'm determined to stick to my guns. My voice might be quiet but I'm finally using it.

An almost bemused frown crosses his face. 'What do you mean? Is this about *that guy*?' He jabs a finger to the hallway.

'It's not about anyone else,' I explain. 'It's about us. You don't listen to me, and you can be selfish.'

'I'm selfish?' His voice has taken on a slightly condescending, what-nonsense-is-this-woman-speaking sort of tone that alights a flicker of doubt. *Am* I talking rubbish? Blowing things out of proportion? But . . . *no*. I'm not. What I'm saying is valid. I remind myself he only came here tonight – to one of the most important nights of my career – because he was jealous. Then he caused a scene.

'Yes, and if you can't hear what I'm saying then I can't be with you.' I stand firm.

'You're being hysterical,' Will replies.

'Agh, Will, you never hear me!'

'I hear you. You're being incredibly loud. We'll talk about this again when you've calmed down.'

'I don't want to calm down!' I shout. 'I don't feel calm! I'm done being measured, and polite, and obliging. You know what, Will . . . *fuck you*.'

I swore. I swore loudly. In public. For a moment I wonder if anyone else heard me and then I think, why do I care?

Will's eyes are bugging out of his head. He looks like he's about to say something else, but then he storms out of the cloakroom, muttering to himself under his breath. I watch him leave with crushing disappointment. There was still a tiny part of me that hoped he'd listen. That he'd hold his hands up and say perhaps there was some fault on his side and things could change. But deep in my gut, I knew that wouldn't happen, and he just confirmed it. If we weren't definitely broken up ten minutes ago, we are now.

I step outside and find Liam, who's still sitting on the bench looking like the textbook definition of having one's tail between one's legs.

'Holly.' He grabs my hand. 'I'm *so* sorry. I came here to support you, not cause a scene on your big night.'

I know that's true. He didn't know Will would be here, or that Will would punch him in the face. I can't blame him too harshly for fighting back in the moment. We all make mistakes. I don't want to say it's OK but I don't want to make him feel terrible, either.

'Thank you for saying that,' I reply. 'Look, Liam, thank you for coming here and for being a generally lovely person. I've had the best time with you. But . . .'

'But you love your boyfriend. I get it. You're unavailable.' Liam shakes his head. 'I don't know why I came tonight, I'm sorry. I don't want to get involved in anything complicated and I don't want to get in the middle of whatever you two have going on. I wasn't thinking much except I wanted to see you and cheer you on.'

I smile. It's really nice that he's interested in what I'm doing, because *I'm* doing it, despite having no interest in fashion whatsoever. And it's nice that he always considers how I feel and genuinely wants to hear about it. But, I think to myself sadly, it's very obvious to me now that I like this man purely because he represents everything I've not been getting from Will. All along I've been comparing him to Will rather than assessing him on his own terms. I have no idea how much we actually have in common.

It's not the best foundation for starting a relationship.

'Actually,' I say, 'I'm breaking up with Will. We have too many problems. I never even wanted to be in an open relationship.'

'Yeah.' The corner of Liam's mouth curls in a half-grimace, half-smile. 'It doesn't seem very you, from what I've got to know about you.'

'It's not.' I shake my head. 'I'm sorry you got dragged into this. I should never have agreed to get into something I didn't want to do and I definitely shouldn't have lied about it. I was in over my head and I didn't know what I was doing and the more I liked you the harder it got to say something . . .'

Liam smiles at my admission that I like him.

'But I don't think I'm ready to date anyone else now either,' I add. 'I like what I know about you so far, but . . .'

'But it's not a good time,' Liam finishes for me.

I nod. It would be too confusing to keep seeing Liam right now.

'I completely get it, Holly,' Liam says.

We both sit in silence for a minute.

'Look, if you feel differently in a few months, you have my number.' He grins. 'Who knows where I'll be then, but maybe our paths will cross again. Maybe not. But it was good to meet you. I think you're great.'

The people-pleasing part of me feels utterly relieved that he's taken that so well. But I remind myself that I don't owe him anything. I don't owe everyone all the time.

'You're great, too, Liam.' I give him a hug.

He gets up and I watch him exit the building.

I take a few moments to collect myself, sitting quietly in the coat room and taking deep breaths, before putting all of that to one side and going back inside. I want to make sure that I don't let anyone else ruin the moment I've been working so hard for. Pretty soon the head of our department will be making a speech thanking everyone and reading out the names of all the designers, and for the first time my name is going to be on that list.

Once that happens, I'll be able to make my case for a promotion and start officially designing, rather than just constantly contributing ideas I never get any credit for and spending ninety per cent of my life doing CADs. Maybe we could even get a new assistant who would have to help with *my* admin. What a wild thought.

When I get back to the party, Fliss is right by my side. 'Are you OK?' she asks.

I don't have time to answer, because there's a tapping of a glass.

'Ladies and gentlemen, please may I have your attention,' calls Lara Pearse. 'Putting together a showcase like tonight's is no easy feat, but I think we can all agree that we came together to make this year's autumn showcase the best yet . . .' She starts on her speech about the current trends and the year the company has had. I find it hard to concentrate; I'm rushing with pure jubilation that my name is finally going to be mentioned.

'Whether you're a designer, a model, a member of human resources or marketing, we'd like to thank you from the bottom of our hearts for making the last ten years such a success. And in fact, we had confirmation this evening that this year's autumn showcase broke company records for most orders received.'

There's a huge round of applause. That's brilliant news. I know the last two showcases, especially, were slightly down on orders.

'With personal thanks to our womenswear design team, responsible for the loving creation of each and every piece; Julie Carson, Lucia deMarco and Amber Lyall.'

I wait for my name to be reeled off, but she stops at Amber. Everyone starts clapping and whistling, before she moves on to personally thank other departments. Blood rushes to my ears. I feel like I can't hear or see anything.

I've worked . . . *so* hard. So unbelievably hard. And . . . *nothing*?! Amber promised me this would be the year I finally get recognition. That after this, I'd be able to share some of my ideas and finally be allowed into design meetings. What happened? Was there some sort of mistake?

I scan the crowd for Amber. My eyes meet Tomi's and he is mouthing *WHAT?!* at me.

'What about you?!' Fliss whispers in my ear. 'I thought you did some of the designs?'

'I did,' I whisper back, my blood boiling.

I locate Amber, near the front, sipping on a glass of champagne and tapping her fingers against one hand.

I start making my way towards her. Fliss follows me through the crowd.

'*Amber*,' I whisper once we reach her.

Amber looks simultaneously like a startled rabbit and like I'm a bad smell that's appeared under her nose. 'Holly.'

She looks at me like I'm deranged. Maybe I am. 'This isn't a good time.'

'Well when can . . .'

'And now, to speak on behalf of our beloved Julie, who is still on maternity leave, please welcome the very talented Amber Lyall.'

Lara steps to one side to allow Amber the microphone. Amber has the audacity to hand me her glass as she steps forward.

Standing there, holding her glass as she receives applause and limelight for all of my hard work, I've never felt so small and insignificant.

I am *so* done feeling small and insignificant.

'Team, what a year it's been . . .' Amber drivels on, but I'm barely listening. I'm only listening for my name, to see if she will mention me at all. But no, she keeps talking and talking about the inspiration behind the collection. She mentions Lucia and Julie again. But there is no mention of me whatsoever.

And then, it's like my limbs starts behaving outside of my control. One second I am standing there watching Amber speaking, and the next I am passing her glass to Fliss and stepping forward.

I am genuinely having an out-of-body experience. I watch myself walk up to Amber. I watch myself grab the microphone from out of her hand. She doesn't offer any resistance; probably too taken aback. I watch myself start speaking.

'Hi, everyone,' I start. My voice shakes. So does my hand. 'I'm Holly. You probably don't know me, because, well, why would you? But I've worked at this company for four years.

I was in fact solely responsible for Item no. 7 and mostly responsible for *all* of Amber's pieces, because she's a lazy hag and I do all of her work.'

The room dissolves into titters. Someone at the back whoops. Tomi tries to start a slow clap, although stops when no one else joins in.

'That's all I have to say really. Thanks . . .' I finish, and pass the mic back to Amber, who looks like she wants to beat me to death with it.

I return to Fliss, who is staring at me in awe.

'Probably just got fired,' I say loudly. 'Shall we go get drunk?'

She nods slowly and takes my arm gently, looking quite afraid of me but also proud. We make our way through the crowd, who are all still staring at me. I try not to look anyone directly in the eye because if I do I might throw up. Tomi runs out after us and we head to the exit.

On the street outside, Tomi's hands are glued to his face. 'Holly . . . That was . . . phenomenal. Stunning. ICONIC.'

Fliss is still lost for words. 'It was . . . really something.'

'People are going to be talking about this evening for years.' Tomi opens his arms out wide. His eyes are starry. 'You've made history.'

'Right then . . . er, where to, folks?' Fliss looks around.

Tomi puts his arm around me.

'I have absolutely no idea,' I answer. 'Anywhere.'

'I know a place,' Tomi says. 'Let's go.'

After my out-of-body experience, the reality of what I've done starts settling in. I briefly wonder if it's OK to leave right in the middle of the party. Am I making the situation worse? Should I hang around to apologise? Will I definitely get fired now? But I try to hang on to that feeling of pure rage. Maybe I will get fired, but at least I'm done being a doormat and letting people take me for granted. I link arms with Fliss and start following Tomi down the street.

CHAPTER THIRTY-TWO:
LET THE RULES EVOLVE

FLISS

For the next couple of weeks, I focus on myself. I read books, I chill out with Jenny and Henry, I carry on with my Japanese, I go for drinks with Holly. After the disastrous – but unforgettable – evening at her work, she forgives me for our argument straightaway.

Immediately after our disagreement, Rowan tries to tempt me back into our shared bubble of avoidance where everything is fun and light and easy. But after a few weeks, when it becomes clear that isn't going to happen, and maybe when he's had a chance to reflect on his behaviour, he tells me that he's going back to the States. He actually apologises for lying to me – which I admit, I wasn't expecting – and says he's going to tell Ella everything. I hope he means that.

In the end, our goodbye isn't too horrendously awkward or begrudging and I drop him off at the airport, which I figure is only fair given how many times he's taken me to JFK. I wonder what's going to happen with Ella when he gets back – God help her, imagine being in *love* with Rowan – and whether she's going to forgive him and whether he's actually going to start behaving any differently.

As I watch him wheel his case away from the car – wearing a badly knitted hat from when he started to learn how to knit last week – I think about whether there's still a place for Rowan in my life. Shared history alone isn't enough to keep someone around; it depends whether he actually grows up or not. I definitely don't want to be friends with someone who purposefully deceives the people who love him in that way. I guess we'll see.

Having given myself the time to reflect on the past few months, it's painfully obvious to me that I still love Ash, but the fact remains that he wants something from me that I'm not sure I'm able to give anybody.

I think if I'd just been able to tell him that, things wouldn't have imploded in the way they did, but I was so used to us wanting exactly the same things and understanding each other. I felt like if we were on different pages, I couldn't talk to him anymore. I felt like he was over there with everybody else and I was sitting far away, on my own little island, being a problem.

I'm not a problem. I love Ash, but if he's really looking for something different, I can't give him what he wants. But I need to at least understand why he wants it, and why now, and what changed, and get answers to all the questions I didn't ask before.

I loiter on the steps outside Ash's flat. Right now, in this moment, I still don't know how Ash is going to react. The day is still possibly the day that Ash and I work things out and he takes me back. It's also possibly the day that he tells me to get lost, but I can live with that being a *possibility*. If it happens in reality I don't know how I'll cope. So I keep loitering.

I can't believe I broke up with Ash. Did that really happen? Oh my God. If he tells me to get lost, I would deserve it.

Except . . . Ash would never say that. He'd tell me that I've essentially ruined my chances with him forever respectfully and sensitively, which makes it even worse.

Then the door opens and Ash's middle-aged neighbour – Arlene, I think it is, the one who is always having loud sex and baking post-coital lasagnes; you go, Arlene, just please close the window and chuck us some lasagne – steps out. 'Oh, hi, Fliss,' she says. 'Did you lock yourself out? Hang on, I think I have my spare key . . .'

'Oh, errr, no, I just needed some fresh air, thanks, Arlene.' I stand up.

She looks at me like I'm unhinged because it's a cold and drizzly Tuesday evening and I'm dripping wet, but she doesn't question me further.

'All right then,' she says, holding the door open for me. 'Take care.'

I walk past her into the hallway. Can I continue to loiter in the hallway? It feels less poetic than doing it on the steps.

I take a breath and knock on Ash's door.

I hear slow footsteps and I'm seized with fear. This could be the very last time I'm in this hallway, in his flat. This could be the very last time I see him.

When he opens the door I'm surprised by his appearance. Ash normally takes good care of himself, but he looks . . .

well, awful. He has dark circles under his normally bright, shiny vegan eyes and his hair is all greasy and he's wearing a tracksuit that has a questionable stain on it.

'Hi?' His voice cracks like he hasn't used it for days. He looks like he wants to cry at the sight of me and I try not to analyse whether that's good or bad.

'*Ash.*' I'm filled with the urge to hug him and never let go. This whole thing seems absurd. I just want to look after him. But I know that being on the same page about what we both want is important, no matter how much we love each other, so I resist the urge to fling myself at him. 'Can I come in?'

He steps aside to let me through. We enter the living room and, while it's never impeccably clean, it's a lot messier than usual. There's a pile of takeaway boxes on Ash's cream fluffy rug. Ash is a tasteful man, minus his unusual fondness for giant, fluffy rugs and onesies. It's because they remind him of his sister. I remember making that connection upon noticing Sara's own hideous rug and thinking that no matter how long I'd known Ash, I was always finding new things to love in him.

'How are you?' I ask politely, as if I haven't noticed the takeaway boxes.

In reply Ash glances at the half-eaten noodles and, even though it's not at all funny, we both start laughing.

'Well, I've been better.' He starts clearing plates and mugs from the coffee table.

'Did you . . . eat chicken?!' I notice meat in one of the boxes.

'No. But I thought about it.'

He takes all his rubbish through to the kitchen and I perch on the sofa waiting for him. I'm *nervous*. I don't often get

348

nervous. Usually if there's something I want, I think, well, if I don't get it, there are about a million other paths I could take. One shut door only means ten other open ones. And I genuinely do believe in that, but I really, *really* don't want Ash to shut his door. Our door. I'm not interested in any other paths except this one.

He comes back in and sits down, leaving a big gap between us. It feels odd to be sitting next to Ash on this sofa, where we've cuddled together a million times, so far away from each other.

'What is it, Fliss?' he asks. 'Are you OK?'

I shake my head. 'No.' My voice wobbles uncharacteristically. 'I . . . I fucked up, Ash. We should have talked about things more. I love you. I'm sorry.'

He puts his head in his hands. Is that a . . . good head-in-the-hands? Head-in-the-hands is never good, is it? I decide to carry on talking before he can kick me out.

'I was struggling with the new relationship,' I explain. 'I felt so alone because this completely blindsided me. I'd always felt like we were a team and understood each other and then to think you'd not really believed in our relationship, as it was, the entire time . . . It threw me. I started thinking there was something wrong with me because I was finding it so hard. . .'

Ash listens to me patiently. I can't read his expression at all so I just keep going. I tell him everything. Even if it still doesn't work out, at least I've laid everything out on the table.

'I think was easier for me to revert to thinking I should just be alone forever, but that was stupid,' I finish.

I want to laugh at how ludicrous that seems now.

'I didn't know myself at twenty. I know myself now. I know that I want *you*, but . . .'

This is probably the most difficult bit to say, but this is only going to work if we revive the transparency that was our foundation before.

'I don't want to be exclusive. I'm sorry. And not in a "not now, but one day" sort of way. I don't know if that's going to be what I want ever. Maybe, but maybe not. And I don't want it hanging over us like some sort of looming promise I may not be able to fulfil. I'm so sorry, and I want more than anything to get back together with you, but . . . not exclusively. I love you *so* much. I just . . . I need complete freedom. I love meeting new people and having different experiences and knowing I'm not duty bound to a person in any way is a huge part of me being able to love them properly. I can't see that changing, I'm sorry.'

Ash has been deathly silent the whole time and his expression is still impassive. He takes a breath and I have no idea what he's going to say. I savour the last moment of not knowing before he potentially says goodbye forever and crushes me like a bug.

'Fliss,' he says. My heart is pounding. 'I'm sorry too.'

What's he sorry about? Sorry that this is all over?! Sorry that we can't repair the damage? Sorry that I can't give him what he needs?

'I went about this all wrong,' he says. 'I knew you were finding it difficult and I should have tried harder to talk to you about it instead of crowding you and sending you stupid gifts. I just . . . I don't know. Being in a monogamous relationship really makes you feel like you can't talk about stuff, doesn't it? I suddenly felt like because we were Doing Monogamy that it meant if we admitted we still wanted to date other people or were finding it hard, it would be like admitting defeat.'

When he says that, it feels like air is being pumped into the room.

'And my reasoning for wanting it was so shaky, I'm sorry. But I think it was weak because . . . I'm not sure *I* want monogamy either. I think it's something, to be brutally honest, that I *have* always looked at as temporary, even though I pretended I didn't. I had, on some level, always kind of assumed we'd be monogamous at some point. I think that's just because that's what everyone else has always assumed about us – including my parents and my sister – and maybe I'm more easily influenced than I thought I was.

'So many of my friends started getting engaged this year, and I'm constantly around Sara and Ava's wedding planning, and Mum and Dad keep dropping hints about when it's my time because I'm older than her and asking when we were ready to give up dating other people . . . They kept talking about marriage and kids like they were things I could only have if we were monogamous. And I wanted us to move forward but I kept thinking this was the only way we could do it. Which is stupid; we don't need to become monogamous to move forward. I think now I properly understand the meaning of the quarter-life crisis.'

I laugh.

'But I'm not sorry any of this happened. I think it took you leaving for me to have clarity. I don't want to be monogamous and you don't want to be monogamous and I'm not my sister or my friends. I still want to move forward, but we'll just have to figure out our own way. I love you, Fliss. I think what we have is really special.'

I beam. I'm so overwhelmingly happy he's saying these words.

'What are you saying?' I ask. 'You want to get back together?'

Ash returns my smile. 'Yeah, I want to get back together. Felicity Henderson, will you move in with me?'

His words take a second to land. I was not expecting him to say that. *Move in together.* That's a huge step. A million questions start filling my head. Are we ready for that? How are we going to navigate seeing other people when we live in the same house? What's that going to look like? Is it going to be harder to compartmentalise those separate parts of our lives in the way we need to if we're in a shared space? Would we bring people back to ours? While I don't mind knowing Ash sees other people in theory, could I handle being closer to that? What if I run into one of his other partners in the hallway and they're super attractive and I'm in my shapeless pyjamas?

But all those questions fade into background noise. Unlike when he asked me to be exclusive, I'm not panicking or afraid, even though it's terrifying and there are so many unknowns. I could live with Ash, and one day marry him, have his babies, without freaking out as long as I felt like we were doing things our way and that I was free to be myself and keep having all the new experiences I wanted. Of course I want to live with Ash.

'Yes, I will,' I reply.

Ash launches himself at me across the sofa and we hug

tightly. I want to laugh with joy and at the sheer ridiculousness of the last couple of months. I can't believe we came so close to losing each other over something we both never wanted. Friends, family and the rest of the world can really get in your head.

Yes, there are lots of things to think about – the rules are going to have to evolve – but I know we'll work it out. I know we'll work it out together.

CHAPTER THIRTY-THREE:
HIDE THEIR POSSESSIONS

HOLLY

I look around our bedroom – the bedroom, my bedroom? – minus Will's things. Even a few weeks ago I couldn't stand being in this flat without him, but I'm getting used to it.

The first couple of nights after I asked him to leave, I continued living amongst his things, but that felt like sitting in a car right after you've crashed it into a tree. Then I packed all his stuff up in boxes – it was particularly satisfying to get rid of all the kitchen paraphernalia, like the herb scissors with the little herb brush that secretly drove me nuts because why can't you just chop herbs with a knife like a normal person? – but the gaping holes in the bookshelves, the empty cupboards, the space where the record player used to be, didn't feel much better.

Then I shuffled some things around to fill the gaps. I turned some of my favourite books face out. I put out candles. I spread out my tops and dresses, organising them into categories instead of having them all in one big pile.

I can't say that I've been loving living here – I swear I can still hear the whisper of Will chopping things vigorously at 8 a.m. – and I'll definitely look for a new place, but for now I've managed to make it my own and start to remember how to exist without Will.

One thing I am definitely loving is watching what I want, whenever I want. It's not like I ever deliberately decided to stop watching things because Will didn't like them, but it's strange what can happen slowly over time, when one person's will is that much stronger than another's. A little cough of judgement, or a snort, or someone plays on their phone to entertain themselves, and suddenly you can't enjoy it as much anymore because the other person is bored. So you offer to watch what they like and you don't snort, or judge, or play with your phone, because you don't mind doing what they want to do. Doing what they want to do makes them happy, which makes you happy. You'll watch the show you wanted to watch another time.

It happens again, and again, and again, and not just with what you watch but with everything, until the pieces of you that were once free to like what they like get smaller and smaller until you barely notice they're still there.

This weekend, all I've done is light candles, have obscenely long baths with no one asking me what I'm doing in there, flip through five different chunky magazines with no one judging how much money I spent on them, watched the shows I want to watch until the TV asks me if I'm still there, and gone to bed ridiculously early, and I've loved every minute.

Come Monday morning, it's a bit harder to feel Zen. My meeting with Lara Pearse and Janine Bello is at eleven. The day following the party they asked if they could 'book in some time' with me. They also suggested that it might be best if I work from home until then, so – even though I almost feel like I've been there from chatting with Tomi every day – this is my first time coming into the office.

I wake up at 6 a.m. and lie in bed for two hours, staring at the ceiling, trying not to run over in my mind what might happen a million times. I have that feeling like it's a momentous day that I'll remember forever. Being awake this early is not ideal, but I don't feel like I'm about to have a panic attack, so that's something.

When I'm on my way in, Tomi texts me.

The office is abuzz with news of your arrival. It's like Cher's coming into the office honestly. Tx

Urghhhhh

Please will you enter like Meryl Streep in DWP?

Huh?

You know, when she comes out the elevator and takes off the sunglasses!!

No. I will not.

You're no fun at all. Seriously though, good luck, hope it goes ok! x

Thankfully Janine's office is on a different floor, so when I arrive I don't have to walk past anybody I know or risk bumping into Amber.

Through the glass doors I can see that Janine and Lara are already inside. I enter, trembling but poised. Internally channelling Meryl Streep without wearing sunglasses indoors.

Janine stands to shake my hand and Lara, still sitting, nods and gestures to a chair opposite her.

'Ms Harper.' Janine takes her seat beside Lara.

'Hi.' I sit down. It feels like what I imagine being in the headmaster's office would feel like. I wouldn't know, obviously, because I've never been in trouble before.

'Well. That was quite the scene at our anniversary party.' Janine smooths her black bun and looks me dead in the eye. We're diving straight in, then.

I don't know what I'm supposed to say to that, so I don't say anything.

'I'll cut to the chase, Ms Harper. Ms Pearse and I have launched an internal investigation into the allegations levelled at Ms Lyall in your little toast, and we have found everything you said to be true. It appears there has been an unreasonable imbalance of work and, relating to the showcase, credit was not given where credit was due.'

I'm so happy, I could cry.

'But,' Lara takes over from Janine, leaning over the desk. 'I'm afraid to say, Holly, that we can't be seen to condone that sort of disruptive behaviour. It was entirely unprofessional. A complaint should have been raised and we could have dealt with it in the proper way.'

I clear my throat. 'Yes, I know. I'm sorry . . .'

'Ms Lyall has been put on a disciplinary, so rest assured that we take everything you said very seriously. But in this instance, given everything that's happened, I'm afraid there isn't a position as a junior designer here for you at this company.'

Oh my God. I'm losing my job. I'm *actually* losing my job. I can't feel my toes. Can I ever feel my toes?

'We're really sorry to be losing you, Ms Harper,' she adds. 'You're obviously very talented.'

She and Janine share a look. They do seem legitimately regretful to be losing me . . . But that doesn't change anything, does it? I'm still out on my ass and Amber still has her job – albeit on a disciplinary – how is that fair?

'That being the case.' Lara takes her hands off the desk and clasps them together. She glances at Janine. 'Despite not being able to keep you on here, we have put in a few calls. There's a junior designer position open at Bergman.'

Bergman is a lot like our brand, except a touch more expensive. I adore their clothes. Is she really saying what I think she's saying . . . ?

'You have come highly recommended to their MD, Poppy Symmonds, from myself and Janine personally. Let's just say I don't think you'll find the interview process too gruelling.'

'Poppy's an old friend,' Janine adds.

Oh my God. Oh my God. I might have another job. By the sounds of it, I basically have it. An actual junior designer position. At Bergman.

Janine smiles at me. I try to smile back, although I'm not sure what my face is doing because I'm too stunned. If I was just a tiny bit cooler, we'd be like debonair spies conspiring together.

Janine stands up and reaches to shake my hand again. 'Very best of luck with everything, Ms Harper. Thank you for everything you've done for the company.'

Lara stands too and walks me to the door. 'Yes, thank you, Holly. No doubt our paths will cross in the future.'

'Thank you, both.' I'm still too astonished to speak. 'Thank you so much!'

As soon as I'm out I immediately message Tomi. I swear I can hear his screams from three floors away.

Omg stay there! We're going for a celebratory lunch RIGHT NOW! Tx

It's 11.30?

Don't care!! x

I'm given a notice period and various tasks to finish up until they find my replacement, so for the rest of the week, I bury myself in work, daydream about being an actual designer at Bergman, and try not to think about Will coming over to collect his things at the weekend.

By the time Saturday arrives, I'm apprehensive to see him again – we've not seen each other since the night of my work party, more than two weeks ago – but I'm calm and resolved. The doorbell rings and my heart skips a beat, even though I know it's only Tomi arriving for moral support.

'Heyyyy.' He brandishes a bottle of champagne. 'This is for when Will's officially gone. You OK?' He hugs me.

'I feel better now you're here,' I say.

'It will be hard but it will be over soon,' he affirms. 'Remember, you're doing the right thing.'

He goes to put the champagne in the fridge, then helps me pull out Will's boxes from under the bed – I stored them there because I didn't want to look at constant reminders of him. We drag them out into the hallway for when Will arrives.

By the time we've moved all the boxes out there's still half an hour left until Will arrives. We sit on them, drinking the champagne because we're too impatient. I'm half-listening to Tomi sweetly trying to distract me by talking about Taylor Swift's new album, and half-thinking about when we moved into this place four years ago. We piled the boxes up in the exact same place and I stood looking at them and thinking about how we were unpacking our future. Now there's only my future and his future.

I hear the sound of keys clanging against each other. Then Will thinks better of it, removes them from the keyhole and knocks. Tomi jumps up and runs to hide in the kitchen. 'Good luck godspeed!' he stage-whispers, swigging straight from the bottle of champagne. 'I'm through there if you need me! Remember, you're everything, he's just Ken!' He gives me one final reassuring thumbs-up and disappears.

I open the door.

'Hey . . .' Will stops speaking when he sees the boxes. I think part of him didn't think I was serious.

'Come through.' I wave him in almost like I'm hosting a dinner party. God, this is so awkward.

Will walks past me and stands in front of his things.

'So, you meant it, then,' he says softly.

Will and I have spoken a few times on the phone and I'd

said I wanted to move out properly, and that I would be giving notice to the landlord. He told me not to make any hasty decisions and that I wasn't thinking clearly, but I think this is the first time in nearly a decade I've felt so sure about anything.

'Let's sit down.' I go into the living room and Will follows. We sit on opposite ends of the sofa where we used to curl up every evening.

'I meant it,' I continue. 'I don't think we can make it work.'

I know we can't make it work, because every conversation I've had with Will since the party, he still doesn't seem to understand me at all.

'I just . . . I don't . . . what do you *mean*, we can't make it work?' Will splutters. 'We've been working for almost a decade. Of course we work.'

I think at this point, in his desperation – he's starting to accept he's not in control anymore and that I am resolute about ending it – he is genuinely trying to understand me. But that sort of makes it even sadder. This man cares more about himself and how I accommodate him than he ever has about me, to the point where he's so embedded in his own point of view he can't even see mine if he tries.

'We worked,' I affirm. 'But only because I put up with everything being about you. What you want, what you need . . . and everything I need is silly or insignificant.'

'That's a preposterous thing to say,' Will replies, ironically demonstrating my point.

'It's how I feel.'

'Well, it's ludicrous.' Will shakes his head. 'What about everything I do for you with your work? The hours I spend looking through your designs!'

'Yes,' I concede. 'And I really appreciate that. But, honestly . . . I think you enjoy doing that. You like designing and feeling like you've helped me with mine. You don't do it *for* me.'

'So I enjoy helping you with work? We have stuff in common, so shoot me? Is that a bad thing?!' Will runs his hands through his hair.

'No, it's just . . . What if I was a writer? Or a dancer? Or an . . . events manager? Would you be so interested in my work then?'

'But you're not a writer. You're not a dancer!' Will laughs in exasperation.

Once again, he is sort of attempting to listen but just . . . not getting it at all. I used to think Will was one of the brightest men I'd ever met – because of his bold opinions at dinner parties or the way he can look at one of my designs that's not quite working and know instantly how to bring it together – but I'm starting to see there are all kinds of other ways a person can be lacking in intelligence.

'No, but what if I was?! As soon as it's something *you* don't value, it's meaningless to you. We eat where you want to eat. We watch what you want to watch. We go on holiday where you want to go. You never want to hear how I'm feeling about anything. I don't think you're doing it on purpose, I don't think you even realise you're doing it.'

That's part of the problem. If Will ever admitted to doing anything wrong – if he could grasp what I was saying – then maybe we could fix this and work on it. But he can't.

'*I* didn't even realise it until now,' I carry on. 'But now I've seen it, I can't live like this anymore.'

'You can't live like what? Not being a dancer?'

I don't bother replying, because if I haven't got through to him by now, I'm not going to. Now he's just being facetious. We're only going to keep arguing. The one final wispy remaining straw of hope I was clutching at dissolves in my hand.

Will's eyes rove over my face, like he's looking for the person he's been with for the last decade who isn't there anymore. And he's right. To be together now, we'd have to carve out something entirely new, which he's not willing or able to do. Eventually, he stands up.

'Well, fine, I'm not going to beg. But I seriously think you're having some kind of breakdown, Holly, and you're going to regret this.'

Again, I don't reply; let him have the last word. He huffs as he goes to move a box, but it's a heavy one and he teeters sideways and it kind of ruins the haughty vibe he was going for. He storms outside to the van.

I reach into one of the kitchen boxes and pocket the little brush that goes with the herb scissors. What are herb scissors without a herb brush? I watch him loading the box into the back of his car and think about how annoyed he's going to be when he eventually unpacks at his mum's and can't find it.

Will comes back up the garden path and catches me smiling faintly. 'What?' he snaps.

'Nothing,' I reply, and help him move the rest of the boxes.

Ten minutes later, he's properly gone. I'll probably never see him again. Tomi re-emerges from the kitchen. I feel like crying, but not in a bad way – I'm not regretting my choice or worrying if I'm making a mistake – it's just necessary mourning over a thing that had to happen.

We don't say anything for a moment. Tomi puts his arm around me and I lean into him.

'He really left,' I say.

'I know.' Tomi squeezes my shoulder. We're silent again. And then Tomi says, 'But that should be the least of your concerns. I'm afraid I drank all the champagne. I'm sorry.'

I burst out laughing.

'Shall we go out and get some more?' he suggests.

'Yes, please,' I say, and we go out in search of mimosas.

THREE MONTHS LATER

FLISS

Every time the doorbell goes, fresh fear strikes my heart that it's going to be my parents. I wish they'd just get here and criticise my new furniture already so we can all move on.

It goes again. I watch as Ash answers the door and lets in one of his friends from work.

'Relax. They'll love the flat.' Henry puts a reassuring arm on my shoulder and I return the gesture.

I can tell he's a bit nervous about them coming, too. I broke up with their golden boy and got back together with Ash, and Henry has invited a man to be his date this evening, so neither of us is exactly having the lives they pictured for us.

It's funny how you can not care what most people on the planet think about you but still be desperate for your parents to approve of everything down to your new cutlery. They're just *people*, aren't they? But people who made you and named you and once packed you off to school with little sandwiches in a novelty-shaped box.

I look around again. The flat looks beautiful, if I do say so myself. It's a split-level, two bed in West Croydon. The bedrooms are downstairs and the open kitchen/diner is upstairs where you walk in. It's not huge and it's so far out of the city we're barely in London anymore, and there's a bit of mould in one corner, which I'm hoping Mum won't point out, and Ash and I will probably be paying off this mortgage until we die, but we both agreed that we weren't ready to totally abandon London yet, and it's *ours*.

'Couldn't even spring for dip, Fliss? Poor show.' Henry points at the crisps I put in a bowl on the table in a lame attempt at playing hostess. Ash should never have left me in charge of the snacks.

'Oh, there's booze.' I wave my hand at him like I'm swatting a fly. 'What more do you want?'

The doorbell rings again.

'Chenny! YES!' I hear Ash holler and whistle.

I was apprehensive to tell Jenny I was leaving. We've lived together for three years and, despite our differences, there's a weird kind of reluctant, familial affection that's grown between us. When I decided to move out I realised I would actually miss her and her terrible TV. But, as fate would have it, we were able to find her a new housemate, who I think she's definitely going to prefer living with.

'Hey.' Jenny walks in and surveys the space. Her hair is extra shiny today. 'Nice digs. Where's the TV?!'

'Oh, we don't have one,' I say.

Jenny's mouth drops open in horror.

'I mean, we're not in a lot, and Ash reads a lot, and I don't mind watching stuff on my laptop . . .'

Still she stares. The doorbell sounds again and I see

a familiar well-dressed, short-haired outline through the glass panel.

'Jenny,' I say as I open the door. 'I think that's your new flatmate.'

Holly steps inside, looking incredible as usual.

'Oh wow! It's so nice!'

She looks around and I reach forward to hug her. She seems to be doing so much better since she broke up with Will and got her new job. Her manner is still soft but with an inner steeliness and self-confidence; she's not constantly people-pleasing – I noticed because she told me in no uncertain terms would she come to a pole-dancing class with me – and she's not looking to anyone else for answers about her relationships.

Before this whole thing, I have to admit I'd kind of low-key assumed that everyone in monogamous relationships was lying to themselves on some level. I used to think Ash and I were two of the few people in the world actually living their truth. But after months of speaking with Holly and hearing more about her perspective on it, I do genuinely believe that she wasn't shutting anything down or denying herself to be solely with Will for the best part of a decade. At least, not in that sense. Obviously, she was ignoring things about him and herself that meant he wasn't the right person for her, but I think she really could be the sort of person to be entirely happy in a monogamous setup.

Anyway, I'm off my high horse and no longer see monogamy as some kind of voluntary prison that the rest of society is going around choosing a cellmate for and locking themselves in with. It's not right for us – and I think probably some other monogamous people who haven't even thought to try another way – but I think many people really do get everything they want and need out of it.

I feel Ash's fingers lace through mine.

'Hey, come say hello to someone.' We leave Henry, Holly and Jenny to catch up. He pulls me in between various groups of friends to the other side of the living room and then down the stairs. Once we're in our new bedroom, he shuts the door.

'Oh my God!' I gasp, looking around. 'There's no one here. This was an elaborate ruse to get me alone!'

Ash kisses me deeply. 'Yeah, it was,' he mumbles into my mouth.

We kiss for a few minutes, until I forget we have guests upstairs. Then the doorbell sounds.

'We should probably get that.' I pull away.

Ash nods and grips my shoulders, turning me to face the other way. 'One second. Hey, look, this is *our* bedroom.' He slips his arms around my waist.

I smile. 'Hey, look, yeah it is.'

I look at the bed where Ash and I are going to sleep together, every night, and glow with warmth. For now, we've decided that this is only our space. We'll see other people on set nights outside of this flat. Maybe we'll adapt further down the line, but that's how we're starting and I'm excited to see where it takes us.

HOLLY

It's seven o'clock in the evening and it's still light. I love this time of year. As I walk up the steps to Fliss and Ash's new flat I can't help but think – and judge my own cheesiness as

I do – about how the longer days and blooming flowers seem to mirror my newfound sense of peace. At least, compared to my tumultuous sad-girl winter.

I ring the doorbell and breathe in the warm spring air. My phone flashes up with a work email and I remember to turn my Outlook notifications off for the evening. It's only been four weeks at Bergman – as an *actual* designer – and, so far, I've managed to leave by 6 p.m. most days. It's weird not working with Tomi anymore, but I'm loving the job so much, and Tomi gives me all the updates from the office. Apparently Amber is fuming that she's not allowed to use the new assistant and accused the company of 'contravening her human rights'.

I hear footsteps. Fliss answers and throws her arms around me.

'Holly!' She hugs me tightly. 'Come in!'

'Oh wow!' I say. 'It's so nice!'

As soon as I step in, my new soon-to-be-housemate Jenny appears by my shoulder.

'Hi Holly,' she says in one breath.

I adore this woman's intensity. I think we're going to have a lot of fun watching *Selling Sunset* together and analysing with great seriousness the dynamics between the various real estate agents. Although she did ask me in the interview about my feelings on 'volume control'. I reassured her that I was 'incredibly quiet'. Fliss later told me that was her way of asking whether I had loud sex.

'*One time* she heard me,' Fliss muttered. 'I swear to God. *One time.*'

I'd better keep it down.

The doorbell is going pretty frequently, so Fliss is in and out of our conversation. I quickly become embroiled in a long chat with Jenny about which new tumble dryer we're going to invest in.

'She definitely likes you better than me,' Fliss whispers as she walks past in between greeting guests.

'Most definitely,' I reply.

It's nice to see Fliss's brother, Henry, again and meet his date Paul, who seems fun. He instantly starts getting me drunk by refilling my glass basically as soon as I've had a sip. I can see why he and Henry would be a good fit.

'So you're moving in together?' Paul points between Jenny and me. 'When?'

'Next week!' I clap my hands together. I'm so happy my lease is finally up and I can leave. My stomach flips with the excitement of a new place and a fresh start, as well as the fear of change and the heartbreak of everything lost, all at the same time. It was a bizarre sensation seeing the flat that once contained all of our shared detritus and entangled lives stripped back and empty, ready for someone else's, but I try to focus on the exhilarating feeling of visiting flats and choosing a new place to contain all the memories I'm yet to have.

'So you're the one Fliss met in a toilet, right? And you happened to be in, like, weirdly parallel situations, right?' Paul asks me. 'Fascinating.'

'Yeah.' I smile. 'Fliss was giving me advice for open dating. She tried her best, bless her, but I was a hopeless case.'

I hear Jenny breathe an audible sigh of relief.

Henry laughs. 'It's not for everyone.'

We all seem to look over at Fliss and Ash at the same moment. Ash puts his arm around Fliss and they laugh at something and look at each other like if someone came along and melded their heads together they'd be fine with it.

I think how funny it is that the widely accepted idea of what love is supposed to look like nearly ruined that for them. And I'm ashamed to think that before meeting them, before everything that happened this year, I'm not sure *I* would have been convinced by their relationship either. They're so different to what I used to believe was a 'happy ending'.

I don't know if mine is the same as Fliss and Ash's . . . Dating multiple people at once did *not* suit me, although Will and I were going into it in so much the wrong way that it's hard to know for sure. I'm almost certain in any case it wouldn't work for me personally – I'm confident I'm more of a one-person-at-a-time sort of gal – but I'm not sorry that we did it. I'm sorry about *why* I did it, but I'm not sorry about what came out of it.

I was so blinkered about Will being perfect for me, when he wasn't, and now I would consider dating all sorts of people that I wouldn't have before. There were so many stupid reasons I previously would have dismissed people – like Liam – who I'd probably get on well with if I gave them half a chance. I've not gone out with anyone else yet because I don't think I'm ready, but I will be, and for now I'm just happy working and hanging out with Tomi and Fliss. And I sense there's going to be a lot of bingeing *Below Deck* with Jenny in my imminent future.

In any case, I know that my life is not with Will; a man who embodies lots of things I find attractive but won't hear or see me. I know that it's not Liam; a couple of months after the whole drama we met up again and went on one or two more dates and I'm glad, because we got to leave things on a friendlier note, but it hasn't gone any further. It may be simply that too much has happened between us and I just need more time on my own after everything, but I suspect we're not that compatible after all. He's so intense and – even though I'm grateful because he's definitely helped me to be more in touch with myself – his level of constant emotional interrogation is *a lot* for me. It was appealing when I met him because I'd been so starved of it, but over time I've started to wonder if he's more of a therapist to me than someone I have a genuine romantic spark with. Outside of him being a lovely man who was the total opposite of Will in all the ways I needed at that moment, I can't see us having a long-term relationship. But there's no bad blood. We may even end up being friends.

I don't think I have an idea of what my 'happy ending' looks like anymore. But, finally, I think I'm getting to know myself well enough that I'll know it when I find it.

Acknowledgements

Thank you to Katie and Asanté for being the best editors a gal could ask for, and I'm very grateful to Clare for being superwoman in Katie's absence. Thank you to Silé for all your support and great ideas. Thank you to Lauren for telling me to write it. So appreciative of Ginger Clark for getting my work across the pond and Tara for championing me in the scary world of film and TV.

Thank you Eldes Tran for doing a brilliant job on the copyedit. And huge shout out to Sarah Lundy, Claire Brett, Hanako Peace, Lucy Richardson, Angie Dobbs, Halema Begum, Stephanie Heathcote, Georgina Green, Brogan Furey, Sara Eusebi, Ange Thompson, Lauren Trabucchi and all of team HQ.

Every day I feel lucky to have Patrick in my life – I love you. Shout out to Edie for being fluffy.

Thank you to my mum for always making me believe I could do anything but equally not caring if I didn't. Thank you to Ellie, Dad, Tom and Fiona.

So much love to Nell for always being my biggest fan.

Big love to Hayley for holding my hand through the book

process as an unofficial agent and through non-fictional life as a friend. And thank you to Maddy, Giles, everyone at MM and all my wonderful authors for being so supportive of my double life.

I'm grateful to have so many lovely friends cheering me on: Sarah, Rachel, Catie, Rosa, Barla, Sophie, Sarah and Marcus, Katherine, Kate, David, Gabe and more I've definitely missed.

Lastly, sorry to Helen and the West Norwood bunch who lived with me during my hot girl summer and sad girl winter. And sorry to Nicola for all the moaning you had to put up with, even if you were being paid.

ONE PLACE. MANY STORIES

Bold, innovative and
empowering publishing.

FOLLOW US ON:

@HQStories